Chosen
Country

Chosen Country

John Dos Passos

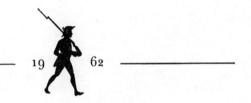

19 62

SENTRY EDITION

HOUGHTON MIFFLIN COMPANY BOSTON
The Riverside Press Cambridge

The Riverside Press
Cambridge · Massachusetts
Printed in the U.S.A.

TABLE OF CONTENTS

The cover design by Anita Bleecker makes
use of original drawings by Reginald Marsh.

Chosen
Country

Prolegomena

JAMES KNOX POLK PIGNATELLI

1 8 4 8 – 1 9 1 7

J IM PIGNATELLI was born in the year of victories. The recollection of his father he carried with him through his life, like the carnelian seal with the crest of a phoenix on it he wore on his watch chain, was mixed with the peppering of cinders and the smell of coalsmoke and steam on that journey east to Staten Island back in the early fifties when Jim was very little, and how he and his older brother Joe stuck their heads forward together jouncing with the jiggling of the car to try to hear. The lank black hair fell over their father's cheek as pushing his chin down into his black stock he leaned over them to explain. It was hard to hear what he was saying in his low foreign voice above the noise of wheels and the rumble and banging of the cars.

"The palms of my hands, understand, were bloody from rowing the heavy boat through the stormy night. Unaccustomed as I was to such work I kept letting the oars slip out from between the tholepins and the cloak over my shoulders was drenched from the waves breaking into the boat. Though I was a young man and vigorous I was fainting from fatigue when they dragged me aboard the tartane. My books and Mazzini's letter and the little bag of gold pieces that were all I had in the world were lost when the boat was crushed and sank. I had escaped from under the tyrant's heel. The sailors lifted me tenderly. I remember the peaceful slap of the waves as the tar-

1

tane heeled to the wind. They carried me into a low cabin
where under a swinging lantern sat my leader Garibaldi. His
face was like the face of Christ."

Jim Pignatelli never remembered whether it was in toscano
his father told the story or in his difficult English that sounded
like sentences in spencerian from a copybook. Jim had never
really learned Italian because his father was usually a silent
man and because his mother didn't like the men to speak
Italian or smoke cigars in the house. On that journey to Staten
Island they spent the first stormy night on a steamboat and Joe
was seasick but Jim wasn't, and Buffalo turned out to be a city
and not the shaggy bull he'd seen hanging in a butcher's stall
in the Cincinnati market; and he'd had to run so hard with a
stitch in his side in the hot summer morning to catch another
train of cars; and in Albany that night he dragged his feet and
cried for fear it would be stormy again, and had to be carried
on board the riverboat; but it was smooth and delicious (the
peaceful slap of the waves as the tartane heeled to the wind)
and a cool breeze in their faces and little lights of villages
slipping by on either side. On Staten Island it was hot and Jim
was so tired he kept stumbling on the cobblestones because
they had to ask the way so many times and Jim on one side and
Joe on the other were dragging on their father's arms when
they went into a green yard back of a white frame house like
Jim's mother's house and they were all Italians there, talking
toscano and waving their arms and playing boccie like Saturday
afternoons in Cincinnati in his mother's backyard; and, standing quiet in the center, looking down at him with kind blue
eyes, was a man with hair to his shoulders and a broad forehead and straight nose and bearded like the face of Christ and
Jim's father was saying, "I have brought you my two little
Americans," and the man lifted his arms slowly as if in pain
and put his hands on their heads and said maybe he was an
American too. Hadn't he been born on the Fourth of July?

Everybody talked so fast that that was all Jim could ever remember of his father or of Garibaldi because he'd never really learned Italian on account of his mother's being a New England woman and the daughter of Everett Luke Jones, the printer evangelist, and because his father died when Jim was eight, the year his little brother Luke was born, and after that everybody spoke English in the house except Joe who hung a print of Garbaldi over his bed and tried to get people to call him Giuseppe and went off after the war, working his way on the steamboat *Mississippi Belle* to New Orleans, to ship as a sailor to Genoa and his mother cried whenever she got a letter with a foreign stamp because she said they were full of unchristianlike bombast and she had so wanted her boys to grow up plainspoken Americans in the fear of God.

Jim Pignatelli grew up an American in the Queen City on the Ohio. His last name was foreign but his father had named him James Knox Polk because Polk was President when he was born and it was the year of victories. When Jim thought of his father he barely remembered what he looked like but tried to imagine him a man like Nicholas Longworth or Judge Thatcher. Judge Thatcher really was a father to him from the day the judge found that Jim who, while he was still studying at the Central School had got him a job in his law office across from the Burnet House running errands and sweeping up and even emptying the bespatten spittoons when the colored man got drunk, could write a good round hand and was a careful boy who could be trusted to copy briefs.

It was in Thatcher's brigade of volunteers Jim enlisted in '62 when the rebels were advancing on the Ohio and the state of siege was proclaimed. Days he lay with the squirrel hunters in the entrenchments across the bridge of boats and after the danger was over he was taken home sick and raving with typhoid and had all his hair shaved off and by the time he was well the volunteers were mustering out. He'd never shot his gun off except to shoot a crow. In the hard times after the war, since Joe never came back from helping Garibaldi recapture the two Sicilies, Jim was his mother's sole support and little Anne's schooling had to be paid for, and wages were low in Cincinnati; so he read law while he worked as office boy in General Thatcher's office and followed what law lectures they gave at the College and was eventually admitted as junior partner into the firm of Thatcher, Stockton and Bates.

Lucius Thatcher like Lincoln loved railroads. When, on account of his legal work on the organization of the Union Pacific, he found it necessary to move his office to Chicago Jim Pignatelli went with him. Jim was making enough now to buy his mother a house on the hill among the vineyards below the observatory and to send Anne to a fashionable seminary. In common with General Thatcher Jim had the love of railroads, of undiscovered blank places on maps of the western country and of reading the classics. He never stopped reading. He read every night in bed. He got up early in the morning to read before breakfast. When he wasn't reading law he was reading Plutarch or Caesar's *Commentaries*. General Thatcher used to declare that nothing rested his mind from the finaglings of the entrepreneurs like a good tough Latin gerundive. The Thatchers' big house on the Lake Shore Drive was Jim's home in Chicago. Jim developed a good singing voice. He was always ready to discuss a ciceronian phrase with the general or to sing a duet or to drive a lady home behind a pair of dark bays. It was there he met the general's niece Henrietta. As the general was retiring from practice to give all his time to his railroad holdings and his real estate interests, when Jim married Nettie, somewhat of an heiress in her own right since her mother's people were prominent hardware merchants in Indianapolis, he opened his own law office and began to make a name for himself as an attorney throughout the midwest.

The year his mother died when he was thirty-three Jim Pignatelli was the father of two small daughters, the owner of a castellated mansion on the North Side with a stable full of fine horses, senior partner of the firm of Pignatelli and Miller and listed in all the directories as one of the leading luminaries of the Illinois bar, but he wasn't exactly the plainspoken god-fearing bearded American his mother had hoped for. He was a scholarly man but a flashy dresser. Some of his friends called him the Dude. He boasted shamelessly of his successes. He wore his mustache with an insolent twirl. He was not even ashamed of his early poverty or of his father's foreign birth. He found money easy to make and easier still to spend. He lacked the reverence for money which, like church attendance, was the mark of the respectable man in those days. He was scornful of stupid people and what he called the worship of the Golden Calf. He liked horseracing and a polished tilbury and patent leather harness and Arabian stallions with arching manes. He had a taste for the theatre and could recite *Othello* by the scene, or read Dickens with so much expression that the whole room would get to sniffling. Better even than blooded horses he loved an audience of handsome women. When his mother died he took his sister Anita, who had not married because of a consumptive condition, home to Chicago. Nettie never really recovered her health after the birth of her second child, so Jim Pignatelli found himself master of a household of two proud sickly women who didn't get along any too well together. He had dreamed of establishing a family and buying a great plantation, but everything he did he had to do alone. He attended to the housekeeping and walked through the market stalls every morning on his way to the office followed by old Ben the butler carrying a large round hamper. He knew all the market people by name and the names of their children. His clerks adored him. He decorated his office with a mirror framed by gilt cupids and with bookcases full of editions of eighteenth century writers bound in calf and morocco and sat at a broad walnut desk empty of papers. His memory for the names and habits of the manipulators of railroad stocks was as good as his memory for Hamlet's soliloquies. He developed a connoisseur's taste for French wines and for the intrigues along the

rights of way of the crisscrossing railroads that were binding
the continent together with bands of steel. He had the knack
of insinuating under the scaly armor of selfinterest all sorts of
distracting independent notions so that before they knew it
contentious men sitting in Pignatelli's office found themselves
agreeing to concessions that redounded to their mutual advantage, and doubled the value of their holdings on the score-
boards in the exchanges.

He became known as an independent scholar of railroad law
and found himself called into conference on mergers on Wall
Street and in Philadelphia and Boston.

He was happiest when he was away from home. Among the
halfworlds of the stage and track and a few daring amazons of
the horsy set he found pleasures that Nettie's illhealth denied
him. Each erring nymph he made to feel that this was no
vulgar liaison; there was something special about her and her
alone that made this particular evening an exception to all
established rules.

The first time he went abroad, in pursuit of a defaulting
treasurer of a bankrupt railroad, he sailed from New York on
the *City of Charleston*. It was a rough voyage from the moment the narrow steamboat nosed out past Sandy Hook into
the scream of a northeast gale. Jim felt queasy and lay in his
lurching bunk for a day amid the creaking of the ship's timbers
and the sound of retching from the adjoining cabins; but the
second morning, to the amazement of Captain Elijah Jones of
New London whom he found sitting alone at the end of the
long table in the dining saloon, he turned out in a navyblue
peajacket to make a breakfast of beefsteak and eggs which he
washed down for his stomach's sake with a glass of champagne.
"You seem to have your sealegs sir," said Captain Jones. "Why
shouldn't I? My father came of a race of Genoese pirates," said
Jim. "Columbus after all was a Genoese."

"On that I have my own opinion . . . The Admiral of the
Ocean Sea," mused Captain Jones. "My great admiration."

He brought his fist down on the table. "Have you ever read his log?"

From then on Jim Pignatelli owned the ship. He spent his time on the bridge or in the chartroom back of the pilothouse. Captain Jones and his officers called him the Admiral. At the captain's dinner he sang "Larboard watch ahoy" in duet with the ship's doctor to great applause and for an encore recited the great speech from *Richard II*. When the pilot came aboard in the pale fog abreast of the Needles he brought a bundle of newspapers: Garibaldi was dead. "I knew him thirty years ago," Jim said to Captain Jones. That night instead of catching the first train to London he stayed over in Southampton to dine with Captain Jones and a group of skippers on the transatlantic service. There was even, in mufti to be sure, a waxenfaced captain of the Royal Navy who condescended to murmur a languid Hear Hear when Jim Pignatelli described being taken as a child to be blessed by the old seadog and warrior at his candlefactory on Staten Island. And his brother had worn the red shirt.

The month was June. Green England was in bloom. In London he stayed at the Langham and became fast friends with a circle of barristers. For the first time in his life (except for the early days in Lucius Thatcher's office in Cincinnati) he found himself among men who listened with respect, instead of with the boorish astonishment his associates affected in Chicage, to his paradoxical quips and his allusions to classical learning. "Of course a foreigner, an American, but an educated man . . . remarkable," he heard a learned judge whisper behind his hand to a member of Gladstone's cabinet the night he dined at the Inns of Court. Jim found himself a Bond Street tailor and a purveyor of rare books and etchings in a musty shop in Kensington. He went to the races, was invited to cold country houses and even stiffly to dine by a few of the more daring hostesses in Mayfair during that London season. When he sailed for home, after running his quarry to earth in a *pension* at Boulogne-sur-Mer and persuading him it was wiser to disgorge and to retire without scandal on a pension from the company, he had started to learn French and in English to use the broad "a." He brought home eight suits and ten waistcoats and cravats galore. He had spent exactly twice the amount of his fee. Education, he told himself, education never comes too high; despairingly he thought of Nettie and the girls. If he'd had a son he would have sent him to Eton.

When, the night he got home to Chicago, Jim described to General Thatcher and his old friend Walt McFarland the pleasures of London: the omnibuses in the fog, the theatres, the oratorios, the music of Haydn and Handel, the learning, the conversations that led further than smokingroom stories or tall tales of business deals, the two old men, in their broad easy chairs at the club, sat thoughtfully stroking their beards. "Can it be?" said General Thatcher, "that we butchered the red man and fought a fratricidal war only to establish a marketplace where our birthright is knocked down to the highest bidder?"

"We'll make our money here, I suppose," said Walt McFarland, "and spend it on the other side."

Chicago, rebuilding from the fire, with its dust and mud and rickety wooden sidewalks, and the striking workmen and the violence in the streets, and the Haymarket hangings and the stench of stockyards and the puffing of engines and slam of shunted freightcars and the lakeboats hooting at the wharves, seemed so rough and unpleasing after the lackeysmoothed silences of London's West End that Jim almost decided to try to practice abroad. Instead he opened an office in New York. It was a relief to be away from the big hollow house on the North Side where Nettie would talk only of her aches and pains and sweats in the night and of Dr. Jarvis' elaborate prescriptions. His dear Anita, whose evening chatter was the one thing that cheered him in his home, had married her physician and moved to Philadelphia. With Anita gone he employed a governess to take care of the children. The girls were cute; he loved buying their little dresses and pinafores and sashes and ribbons for their pretty hair, but nothing he ever said seemed to open their small closed minds.

The move to New York was largely at the behest of a minority group of investors he was representing who were in the process of being frozen out in a reorganization of the old Westchester Railroad. Fifth Avenue was far from being Rotten Row, but Gotham life had dash. Jim, mad for the sea after his first taste of salt water, acquired a small schooner yacht which he named the *Anita* and anchored off City Island and sailed weekends on the Sound.

For the yacht he bought a pair of firstrate marine binoculars. He happened to be trying them out from the open window of his office one warm spring day when he noticed a familiar figure in silk hat and burnsides alight from a cab on the street below and furtively enter the back door of the great bankers' offices that occupied the opposite block. Another arrived on foot. A third alighted from his carriage. "By George, Bill," he said to the new office boy, a tough pugnosed young customer he guessed would be faithful as a shepherd dog and whom he had hopes of bringing up to be his confidential secretary, "it's the directors of the New Haven road meeting the turncoats from the Westchester. The buzzards are gathered round the lion's kill." "Boss," said Bill Keezer, "look in that window opposite. The meeting's in the room across the street." Carefully they noted the names. He sent Bill down to loaf about the entrances and check on the departing magnates and went to work to write up a brief that named every name in the new ring. The big lion settled out of court. The minority stockholders were handsomely indemnified. When Jim Pignatelli totalled up his earnings for that year he discovered that he was a millionaire. He got some pleasure out of going to Tiffany's and buying Anita a brooch and himself a diamond stud, but that was the day in his life, he used to say, when he came nearest to blowing out his brains.

His clients kept him so busy, laughing he used to add, that he couldn't find the time. He worked every moment from dawn to midnight. Overwork would have killed him, he told his friends, if General Thatcher, now an embittered valetudinarian looking out from a bush of silkwhite whiskers with anxious monkey's eyes, hadn't engaged him to protect his interests in the sale of the Utah and Western to Pacific Trunk and taken him out to San Francisco on his private car. Young Jim, as his old mentor still called him, forgot the ache of his own homeless life in the circus he staged, mixing toddies, singing songs from Gilbert and Sullivan's new operettas, punning in hog latin and discussing Cicero's shortcomings as a politician, creating comic characters out of the conductor, the steward, the brakeman, the gandydancers along the track to joke the old man out of his hypochondria.

"Make your pile, Jim," General Thatcher wheezed sardonically at lunch one day at the Cliff House after a session with a consortorium of empirebuilders on whose faces greed glittered like grease in the sun. "Spoil the Egyptians, Jim. The American investor is like a field of alfalfa that can hardly be cropped too often . . . and then put a million in British consols and go abroad and live like a gentleman."

But there was something in the silver rivers and the enormous skies over the changeless horizon of the plains, and the tossing horns of cattle rounded up in corrals and in the faces of the leanwaisted men at the stanty stations, whiskery prospectors loading their burros at sidings to adventure into untracked mountains, in the smell of burning forests and the boasting of ranchers cropping the primeval silt of the valleys and the whoops of drunken loggers and the frenzy of the wheat pit and the intricate game of the exchanges; and money, money, money, tapped out in the Morse code over every telegraph, that sent him back east in love with the country again. After a few dreary days by the sickbed in Chicago and a trip to Philadelphia to take Anita, who loved seashells, a polished abalone from the

Golden Gate, he arrived in New York with the West still pounding in his blood.

He was full of it and talked, well he thought, of manifest destiny and of railroads girdling the world the night Alastair Barker invited him to dine with a few cronies who, he assured Jim, were interested in other things than money, at a new restaurant two hours brisk trot out of town on a hill that overlooked the North River and the lordly Palisades. The ladies were charming. One particularly, a Mrs. Randolph Isham, couldn't seem to keep her eyes off Jim's face when he told of the Colorado Canyon and the Salt Lake and the dreamlike waterfalls of the Yosemite. They were fine eyes, gray with a glint of green. Her carriage was queenly. When she laughed there was a confiding sweetness about her lips that made him feel taller and braver than he'd ever felt before.

"Who is the fair charmer?" he asked, taking Alastair's arm as they rose from the table. "Not for you, mon ami," whispered Alastair, "her virtue is impregnable. She's my distant cousin. She was a Miss Jay. My mother was a Jay. Her husband, from the first families of Kentucky, but alas a hopeless inebriate, had the grace to die some years ago but left only debts, so the dear creature makes her own living. A cruel world." As they waited for the carriages Jim put one more question. "What work would such a goddess deign to do?" "Quite honorable but tedious." Alastair yawned. "She's a librarian at the Society Library."

From that day on Jim found there were volumes on the shelves of the Society Library that were indispensable to the course of reading in international law he had recently embarked on. Instead of sending Bill Keezer for the books he fetched them or returned them himself on his way uptown from business to the Fifth Avenue Hotel where he had taken up his lodging. He would find the lovely Mrs. Isham with a sweet abstracted expression on her face toiling over catalogues in her small office. It filled him with tenderness to think of the long fingers of those graceful hands soiled by the dust as she smoothed the stale shreds of old bindings. He besieged Alastair, who loathed the outdoors, with invitations to sailing parties. He cultivated Alastair's female relations. He invited old Mrs. Barker and three fading aunts to lunch on his yacht and discoursed learnedly on ways of pushing the French spoliation claims they held against the government for loss of cargoes on prizes taken by the French during the period of the Directory. He would even tempt them out for a short sail if the afternoon were calm. On these excursions he could induce them sometimes to bring Mrs. Isham along. His carriage would pick her up at the door of the vinecovered house off Gramercy Park where she boarded. Then one Sunday he came for her in a phaeton he drove himself, full of excuses that his coachman was ill. It was a hot July day threatening thunder. She wore a navyblue basque and a little sailor hat he found irresistible. She was distressed but not too distressed when they arrived at the yacht to find a message from the Barker family that they feared the weather too inclement. "I should go home, I really should," she said, "but I love sailing so." "Bill Keezer shall be our chaperon." Besides Bill he explained there would be on board two Long Island lads who trimmed the sails and a colored cook and steward. It wasn't as if they were going out alone.

It was a day of squalls and reefing and shaking out reefs. The wind took them aback off Whitestone Landing and the topmast crashed to the deck. They scudded under jib and staysail. As the lightning flickered and the sheets of rain lashed about them, wetting them through the oilskins, they started reciting in unison verses from *Lucile*. The part about the storm they both knew by heart. The schooner labored and would not answer to the helm. Finally Jim had to bargain with the captain of a harbor tug to tow him back at vast expense to his anchorage.

Not for a moment did Mrs. Isham show any fear, only exhilaration in the storm. He learned that her name was Kathryn.

"Kate," he said, "I love the name of Kate." She loved to ride, he learned while Bill Keezer was rowing them ashore. Both of them were soaked to the skin. She was silent but smiling while he drove her home. "Oh Admiral, thank you. It has been a lovely day." What harm would it do if they rode occasionally early mornings in the park? "If I can possibly patch up my ancient riding habit, perhaps," she said.

Riding through the horizontal sunlight in the long shadows of the trees they exchanged life histories. As through plate glass each looked into the other's world. Could there be platonic friendship between the sexes? "To the pure," she said, "all things are pure." But every time their hands touched there was a burning spark. When their eyes met it was forked lightning. "It's terrible," she said, "to live on the edge of an abyss." It was only a question of time he explained before he could ask Henrietta to divorce him. Scandal, what did he care for scandal? But it was her health; it would be risking her life, and he had to consider her uncle, General Thatcher, to whom he owed so much. They were sitting over coffee at a pavilion in the park. Kate rose in great agitation. "James help me to mount," she said through bloodless lips and rode off at full gallop. He followed, standing in his stirrups to keep watch. At a crossing her mare shied at the glittering brass on the harness of a fourhorse dray. She was thrown. He jumped from the saddle and lifted her up in his arms. "I'm not hurt," she whispered. "I've been a silly fool. Now call a cab, and send me home."

It was months before she would see him. He wrote her daily. She answered his letters with little chatty notes that talked of the novels of Bulwer Lytton and George Eliot, of the incomprehensible poems of Browning and the beauties of *Sonnets from the Portuguese*. He had a messenger deliver every noon at her office a small bouquet. Malmaison roses, always Malmaison. That fall he sent her a basket of game every week: reedbirds, a brace of mallards or a dozen quail. When she fell ill with a bronchial affection he wired Dr. Meecham, Anita's husband, to come over from Philadelphia on the cars to see her. Dear Anita, who came along, arrived pale and wasted and coughing from a chill she had contracted on the drafty ferry, but she consented to call. There was nothing in the world she wouldn't do for brother Jim. When she came back to the hotel she burst out, "Jim she's the loveliest creature I ever met . . . Oh Jim be careful of her."

When Kathryn Isham recovered, she could hardly have the ill grace to refuse to lunch with Dr. Meecham and his charming wife who had been so kind. They met at the Astor House. She wore a palebrown tightfitting tailored suit trimmed with fur that matched her palebrown hair, at the neck a flash of green silk. He was resplendent in a pearlgray cutaway newly arrived from his Bond Street tailor. He wore a gray pearl in his ascot tie. "You came strutting like a rooster through those dull people in the lobby. Oh Jim you are a dandy," she said. And she laughed indulgently and had trouble composing her face to a polite smile to meet the Meechams. At lunch she was so gay he was a little frightened. A touch of the madcap, he thought. After that they were lovers. She forever after called him Dandy.

All of his life that was not work she filled. That summer he took his first vacation. They sailed to Block Island and Vineyard Haven, and lived ashore in a house he rented for two weeks on Nantucket. There he set seriously to work to collect his notes for a book on railroad law. News of Anita's illness brought them back from New Bedford on the cars. He arrived in time to sit beside the bed and hold her cold hand while choking in vomited blood she died. He couldn't have lived through, he told himself, if Kate had not been with him, saying so little, understanding so much, comforting poor Meecham, attending so gently to all the dread last offices.

Happily business with a group of French investors came up to take him abroad. They sailed on different boats. Thank

God the Atlantic was smooth that October. He was waiting on the quai when the *Bretagne* docked at Le Havre. "Eblouissante," he said aloud in French when he saw her with proud walk and head erect stepping down the gangplank. "From her walk I knew the goddess," he whispered in her ear. Financially the trip was a success. He scattered money like roseleaves in her path. In Europe there was no need for concealment. They had adjoining suites at the Continental and unlocked the door between. "It's fortunate we are old enough," he told her at breakfast before the french-windows thrown open to the balcony, as they looked out on the clopclop of traffic on the woodblocks of the Paris street. "A man under forty has no understanding of love."

When he was free from business complications they drove round the dovegray city in the dovegray mist under the russet trees. Every morning they rode in the Bois. Sundays they walked in the forest at Fontainebleau or fed the carp at Chantilly. They travelled to Rheims to see the cathedral. When they started home, she to sail on a French and he on an English liner, they paced in the rain the wharf at Le Havre. When she kissed him goodbye she whispered that she was enceinte.

"Nothing could make me more happy, Kate," he cried out. "It must make you happy. We cannot conduct our lives according to the dictates of ordinary mortals . . . We must live on Olympus"; and he gave her a great hug and she was gone.

All that crossing on the *Arabic* he was horribly anxious. The November sea was stormy. The ship pitched and shuddered in the westerly gales. He mistrusted the French sailors. Several nights he couldn't sleep and read in his berth till dawn. When they reached Sandy Hook and learned that the *Normandie* was safely anchored in the Narrows, he went down to his cabin and, a thing he hadn't done since he was a boy running around barefoot in the Cincinnati dust, fell down on his knees and thanked God.

For her lying-in they rented a little house at Cape May under the name of Mr. and Mrs. Isham Jay. Their only visitor was poor Meecham who neglected his practice to take care of her and haunted the house like a lonely dog. At last one sultry July night when the mosquitoes in swarms hummed on the screens, she was delivered of a boy. When Jim left, for a long overdue trip to Chicago, assured by Meecham and the nurse that everything was well, he was very happy. Sitting alone in his drawingroom on the all-pullman train he looked over the past and future of his life like a man looking east and west from the summit of Pikes Peak. He was still in his forties. He had made and spent a fortune. His position was unique in the New York and Chicago bar. His friends had been importuning him to enter politics but he was determined not. He would wear no man's collar. Freedom was what we Pignatellis came to America to find. If he lost his freedom of action and speech what would high office avail him? He must work harder at his writings he told himself. He had so much to say and no man knew how long he might live. He pulled out the yellow foolscap pad from his gladstone bag and in the small spencerian hand his mother had severely taught him back in Cincinnati in the days before the Civil War he began to note down the chapter headings for a work on corporations. The American Corporation: instrument of private greed or instrument of the democratic bent? As he wrote he found that he kept writing down a name among his notes and leaning back and studying it with a smile. Jay . . . Jay . . . Isham . . . crossed out. Let it go at that: Jay Pignatelli.

1

THE LITTLE RIVER RUBICON

EIGHTEEN YEARS OLD, Jay Pignatelli sat sprawled on the plush seat of the daycoach. Under the plush that clung to his pants broken springs quaked as the trucks rumbleclattered over the rails. Eighteen years old, he was telling himself and nothing done. Drowsy and sleepless he sat trying to read in the jiggling daycoach, breathing the sleepy smell of armpits and babies' diapers, old lunchboxes and orangepeels and cinders and coalsmoke and steam. The engine was right ahead. He could feel the urge of hot oilslick steel shuttling the connectingrods that turned the weighted wheels to grind down the miles. Eighteen years old, and nothing done . . . but a little reading maybe. His books jiggled beside him on the seat. He had Mallory open on his knees and read in snatches as the pages turned.

> And Sir Launcelot rode through many strange countries, over marshes and valleys . . .

Every line he read seemed to start him remembering some episode left behind on the track of his life like the north country stations on this long slow night's run, small grassy stations the locomotive entered with clanging bell, wheezing to a standstill and to sudden silence in which he could hear voices mumbling in the car behind him and shuffled feet and yawns and the stretch of cramped limbs and a child's quaver cutting the tension of the interminable wait; then at last would come the brakeman's shout and the engine's gruff puffing and couplings slambanging down the train and curling steam that blotted out the window and left only in his head, against the rumbling dark, memory of silhouetted figures, gesturing arms, a hatted head against an orange pane or a face pointed out by a finger of light. A waved lantern made the darkness darker as the train pulled out into the night that hid a country strange to him. *And Sir Launcelot rode . . .* The train bored into the night . . .

> *till by fortune he came to a fair castle and as he passed beyond the castle him thought he heard two bells ring and then was he ware of a falcon come flying over his head toward a high elm and long lunes about her feet . . .*

There was the time, Lord he must have been little, his eyes were on the blue shade over an orange melon of light and the little tassel like a little lady swinging swinging ". . . Oh qu'il a des beaux yeux," the lady said from the opposite seat. Petite Mère had whispered in English: "You must be polite Jay but you mustn't listen because flattery is bad for little boys. Flatterers are deceivers." And as the continental train went happily rumbledebump along he was looking at great red flares that rose and fell in the purple night outside — "Potteries," said Petite Mère — and there came all at once a shrieking and a clattering roar and the pressure of air through the glass. Shrieks he couldn't help burst answering out of him. Petite Mère was laughing: "What a silly boy that's just the engine whistling on the express train passing on the other track." He was staring with icy fear at the telescoped oblongs of light, punch and judy faces nodding in other compartments like the one they sat in, packed pink faces jiggling and then gone, and only Petite Mère's hand on his forehead smoothing his hair from the part and the cozy clatter clatter clatter of the other train going safely away through the night . . . Orange melon of light . . . It was sunlight and he'd been asleep and it was sunlight coming through the tall lace curtains onto the thick pink flowers of the tablecloth and the man was Monsieur Dandy and it was le petit déjeuner and Petite Mère was smiling sitting behind the coffeepot with long pink silk sleeves edged with lace and her pretty little curls all crisp across her forehead. Her arms flashed white in the sun under the long lace sleeves and she and Monsieur Dandy smiled together and Jay got the fidgets because they looked at him and smiled together. "What's that?" he cried and they both laughed and he felt all stiff and funny. The sweet warm spicy smell was the smell of the melon and there was Monsieur Dandy's smell of starched shirts and bay rum so strong. Jay wriggled away from the blue look of Monsieur Dandy's jowl glazed from shaving, when Monsieur Dandy leaned across the table and kissed him on the forehead and Petite Mère laughed and Monsieur Dandy laughed and Jay felt left out of it, but afterwards when he thought of Dandy there was the melon smell.

"The child hardly knows who you are," said Petite Mère.

"Yes I do," Jay squeaked, "it's Monsieur Dandy."

"Yankee Doodle went to town," Petite Mère was humming

> *Upon a pretty pony*
> *Yankee Doodle went to town*
> *For cakes and sugar candy*
> *Yankee Doodle went to town*
> *His name was Monsieur Dandy*
> *He stuck a feather in his cap*
> *And called it Pignatel-li."*

And they laughed again all happy and excited and everybody was en vacance and outside there were so many people all dressed in straw hats and blazers and bright ruffles going to la plage and awnings, all stripes, all shaking and flapping in the driven seasmell and la plage was so broad the people looked quite tiny out where the foamy waves began and there were tiny white houses on wheels all in a row and teams of big broad horses and whiskery bronze men with their trousers rolled up to their knees. Jay built a castle. You packed damp sand into the pail and turned it out to make a tower and Monsieur Dandy handed out wax matches for cannons and Petite Mère flashed a little American Stars and Stripes all silk and pretty out of her alligator bag. "We must never forget, Jay," said Petite Mère, "that we are Americans."

Jay pointed his finger at Monsieur Dandy though he had been told never to point. "He's Yankee Doodle Dandy," he shouted, and laughed so hard he fell right over on his back on the sand.

And after a while they all went out in a little white house on wheels and Petite Mère helped Jay pull on his bathing suit and he was scared to step down the ladder because each time a wave passed it splashed but Monsieur Dandy was there already dipping like a dickie bird and his mustache was wet. "Always wet your head first," he shouted. "Plunge in, Jay."

And the waves were trembly cold when Petite Mère lifted him down and made him follow Monsieur Dandy out to sea. "Come on," Monsieur Dandy was shouting and laughing, "out up to your neck. You've got to learn to swim." And Petite Mère was giggling-shivering dousing herself up and down in the blue and white ruffled bathing suit. Each time a wave passed it scared him when it slapped in his face; it was icecold and salt on his lips. "Jump Jay," Monsieur Dandy shouted. Underneath it was lovely smooth and all little silver ripples and bright gold shells.

Jay wanted to gather the valuable golden shells but Monsieur Dandy said he must learn to swim and grabbed him with strong hands and he felt the muscle of Monsieur Dandy's arms hard as rope and when his feet left the bottom he floundered and kicked and a wave slapped his face and he swallowed all the water. "Don't worry, I'll hold your chin up. You kick your legs like a frog," but it was too frightening and he was yelling and holding on to the hard arm. "Kick your legs. Don't hold on to me."

Monsieur Dandy was angry and Petite Mère was crying and

Jay was trembling so they had to take him up in the little house on wheels and dry him and a barelegged man brought a glass of hot milk and they made him drink. "It tastes funny," Jay whined. Petite Mère tasted it and made a little appraising noise with her tongue against her lips. "It's oilcake. In these countries they feed the cows on oilcake."

After that Jay and Petite Mère gathered shells while Monsieur Dandy ("Dandy don't frighten us," she pleaded) strode far out into the waves and swam out until they could only see his head, and then only a speck on the gray huge undulant ocean. "He's such a strong swimmer Jay and he wants you to be a strong swimmer too but I'm not, though I did swim a mile once. You've got to learn to keep up with him."

So Sir Launcelot rode many wide ways through marshes and many wild ways . . .

The train bored on through the night with a steady clatter of wheels on rails . . . And that time, Good Lord I must have been even littler. Those white bars must have been the bars of a crib. It was Easter morning and Petite Mère came with a fuzzy pink rabbit on a nest of chocolate eggs, and the nurse — was it Jeanne? — and I was rather proud because I'd done not only number one but number two in bed, oh but the rumpus and the scolding and screwed up disgustful faces and the pink rabbit taken away and the scrubbing and the shaking and the soap and slapping water . . . And that other time by the fire it was so delightful rubbing coal on your face from the coal-scuttle and piling it on the rug in front of the fire and you got all black like a charbonnier. Petite Mère was sitting in the drawingroom in a ring of ladies fluffly ruffly on gilt chairs with teacups tittering in their hands. "What will that child do next?" And he ran sobbing to Jeanne . . . I wanted to be a coal-heaver, they never had to wash. That was the Jeanne that used to take me into her bed at night and take my nightdress off and pull hers up to her neck and rub my poor little dingus up and down her bare belly, "faire les petits venventres," she called it and she was all furry around the place and when I asked her why it was wet there she said it was because she'd just washed it but it made me feel funny and I wouldn't do it with Jeanne any more because Petite Mère had said not to play with it, no never . . .

"I would keep that for my husband," shrieked the little lady from Louisville who was the wife of Monsieur le Consul des États- Unis. He was a colonel in the Civil War and he had two big gray silk mustaches and he walked very stiff and solemn. She laughed and laughed and Petite Mère laughed and Coco the parrot shrieked and fixed a gold eye on Jay while he walked on his perch upside down and began to croak like he always did. "Avez-vous déjeuné messieurs mesdames?" "I certainly wouldn't let any other man see me in the nude," said the little lady from Louisville and she and Petite Mère shrieked and laughed in their little high low funny furry sweet Kentucky voices (Petite Mère said they both had the Kentucky laugh) and tossed their frizzly curly heads under the potted palms in the gray glass conservatory at the consulate and Jay sat fidgeting on a green iron chair seeing the little lady from Louisville all undressed on a sort of a pink shell couch like a picture in a museum, so cute and pigeonbreasted, Petite Mère said, and the consul standing looking at her with his head cocked on one side and a comical expression under the big gray mustaches . . . "Jay you mustn't imitate the way he walks," Petite Mère had said, "because the poor man has a wooden leg. He was a very brave soldier. He lost a leg at Gettysburg." And outside through the tall window you looked out onto the gray boulevard in the gray afternoon and you could see the red and white stripes and the stars of the flag hanging from a pole above the portecochère and Kentucky was a state and all the states were stars and right here in the conservatory it was American soil like Kentucky, like one of the stars, and Kentucky was where the little naked lady lived.

Jay got up dizzy from his seat in the lurching car. He shook himself to loosen the drawers that were binding his crotch. Of course it would come back to that, he spoke to himself so clearly he most felt the other people in the car must hear his voice. It always comes back to that.

He dropped down in the seat that quaked and jiggled under him and picked up a Dumas in a torn bluepaper cover.

Le-22 Mars de l'an de grace 1718, jour de mi-carême, un jeune seigneur d'haute mine, age de vingtsix à vingthuit ans, monté sur un beau cheval d'Espagne, se tenait, vers les huit heurs du matin, à l'extrémité du Pont Neuf qui aboutit au quai de l'École.

He hardly had to read it he'd read so much Dumas between the dogeared bluepaper covers Monsieur Dandy had bought when he was learning French, nights in hotel rooms, up in the attic down in the country with a candle after everybody thought he'd gone to bed; he'd hardly read a page of the glib old storyteller's jaunty French before he was the Chevalier d'Harmental searching the faces of old soldiers who stumbled out of riverside dives and taverns until he found a broad forehead and broad shoulders he could trust and the penniless veteran of the Flanders war jumped up on the crupper behind him and they rode through awakening Paris to the Maillot Gate where the Chevalier had an appointment to fight a little duel with a young man he thought he'd heard make a slurring remark about a lady friend of his in an eatinghouse the night before. It was spring and everybody was young and handsome and welldressed and they were all expert swordsmen and fought merrily in a grassy glade sheltered by flowering trees from the prying of the watch and after several of the young gentlemen had been spitted neatly through their silk ruffles and their lacefrilled sleeves they called it off and sent for the wise old surgeon in the hackney cab and the rapiers had all been deflected by lockets or scraped ribs or had gone through the fleshy parts of arms so that nobody's wound was bad enough to keep him from attending the masked ball at the opera in the Palais Royale that night and they would all be fast friends forever afterwards; and the black eyes that flashed so bright behind the mask of the lady in the lilac domino belonged to the mysterious baroness who was the mistress of the reigning Duke and so the adventure began . . .

This was all kid stuff. Now Jay liked to dream Caesar sitting in his tent dictating three letters at once to the slow secretaries graving the clumsy latin capitals carefully in the flicker of the tiny flames of oliveoil lamps, to imagine the precise arranging mind that never forgot Spain or Bythnia or the hilltowns of the Apennines or the rivalries of centurions or the factions in the marble courtyards on the Palatine; while always there was the business of the moment: the sentries calling the hours round the square stockaded camp; Roman sense to be made of the babble of the barbarian scout who grovelled on his belly under the questions of the interpreter; the effort to anticipate the disorderly workings of the minds of hostile tribesmen who hallooed their warcries behind the forested hills; the prearranged sequence of the columns on the march, the plan for the trestled bridge, the topography of the battle to be kept in the head; the plot for a new forum on the old campsite; order to be imposed on the raw Gauls and Britons and the islands of the middle sea and the untruthful Greeks and the rotten Orient; measured with a compass, squared with a T square, the ordered layout for a reasoned world.

. . . "My people," Dandy had said that day they ate Lake Superior whitefish for lunch among dark panels and brass and jowly faces at the Lawyers' Club in the Loop near the courthouse, "my father's people and your people Jay were Genoese, the race of Columbus and Garibaldi, but my father's mother was from the Abruzzi, that last hidingplace of the old Roman blood, the blood of citybuilders and inscribers of laws. The English have poetry but no architecture. Your dear mother is all English, yeomen and gentry. There's none of the world's royalty you need be ashamed to meet face to face. You're as good as any of them. Never forget that."

Jay had sat there flushing and squirming in his chair. Maybe it was the English in him that felt that squirm of shame when Dandy boasted so. Dandy boasting in restaurants of the money he'd made, the railroads he'd reorganized, the stock issues he had helped launch on the market. It made Jay ashamed like that first time he'd felt ashamed; even now there was a kind of inner blush when he remembered Antwerp and the great spires and such a fine afternoon when they had gone to the Zoo with the nice lady and the little girl from the pension who had yellow doll's hair, and the animals were right in the middle of town and ladies and gentlemen and boys and girls with hoops and diavolo sets were sitting at marble tables of cafés all around; and there right at the café was the chimpanzee wearing red suspenders and eating a choux à la crème and smearing the cream over his big flapping lips; and the nice lady with yellow doll's hair had just ordered a plate of galettes Chantilly for the children; and there were other people there talking grownup talk above the tables in grave dull voices; and somebody said les Allemands and Jay piped up and shrilled "Je déteste les Allemands" and he'd hardly finished saying it when he saw the nice lady's lip quiver and the little girl cried and of course they were Allemands only nice Allemands and Jay felt so horrid he couldn't eat any more galettes, worse than he felt in the shop on the boulevard Anspach that had such smooth asphalt paving where the door had a little bell that made zing when Petite Mère opened it and Petite Mère said not to play with the little dog and Jay patted the little dog and snap the little dog bit him and he cried not so much because it hurt as because he was ashamed; and that was shame and made your cheeks go red in spite of themselves: the way he'd get so hot and fidgety and feel his legs were too long for his body when Dandy roared at him in Shakespearean actor style: "I charge thee Cromwell avoid dogmatism."

What a horrible childhood, he said to himself so nearly out loud that his lips moved. A hotel childhood. The little buttons, no he must have looked quite big to me, at the Lille et d'Albion — no it must have been the one under the arcade on the rue de Rivoli — who scared me so about the new Paris Métro. The trains never stopped, he said. You had to jump on and off while they were moving, or was that the moving platform at the Grande Exposition Universelle? And the Tour Eiffel and men in highbuttoned coats and bowler hats, just like the pictures in *Around the World in Eighty Days,* hourglass shaped ladies under big baskets of flowers and fruit moving slow sedately; and the Trocadero at night, les illuminations, colored water red white blue pink green flowing from all the fountains and the funny varnish rubbery smell in the real train of sleeping cars all shiny and new as toys in a toyshop window, and I felt like Phileas Fogg as the painted scenery went by; and, holding tight to Petite Mère's hand, had the uneasy feeling that the train was really truly moving . . . And the Hotel Dunstan where Dandy used to ask fat Pat the waiter how the Emperor William was today . . . But that was after St. John's Wood and being a double foreigner to all the little English boys wearing their schoolcaps and special neckties: A Man Without a Country. Lord I cried over that story and Ishmael the wanderer in deserts and Cain, that birthmark on the forehead the mark of the accursed like Cain, like all history's bastards . . . *Many wild ways through marches and many wild ways.*

Was it the bar sinister or the nearsighted eyes that made him always fumble the ball — what a terrible tennisplayer, no good at football or even at soccer — or the foreign speech or the lack of a home that made him so awkward, tonguetied, never saying the right word, never managing to do the accepted thing at the accepted time. He'd hated all those schools, all his life he'd hated everything but Petite Mère. At college he liked it better than at school. God he'd hated school. He had few friends even now, though like the Romans he believed in

friendship. Joe Newcomer was a prince, but even to Joe Jay
was the incomprehensible stranger who dropped in between
trains.

Caesar of course came from an old Roman family. The
patrician takes for granted that he always knows just the right
thing to say and do. Decision comes easy to him.

Jay squinted a little to read the fine print of Froude:

> To deal with this danger was the work marked out for Caesar.
> It is the fashion to say that he sought a military command that
> he might have an army behind him to overthrow the constitution.
> If this was his object ambition never chose a more dangerous or
> less promising route for him. Men of genius who accomplish
> great things in this world do not trouble themselves with remote
> and visionary aims. They encounter emergencies as they arise
> and leave the future to shape itself as it may.

There'd been times too when emergencies were fun. The
summer in Scotland when they rode in a carryall to see the
grouse and the gorse and the purple hills of heather and Dandy
bought them all Inverness cloaks blue outside and red inside
and Jay made them all laugh when he said it made him feel
like Roderick Dhu; and he and Dandy went out in a boat on
Loch Lomond to fish for salmon and the boat leaked and
Dandy rowed while the boatman bailed and the wind stung
their faces and the rain drove out of the mist that covered all
the hills and Dandy said, when wet and cold they reached the
pebbly shore, "By George the boy never let out a whimper.
The way he encountered that emergency proved he was his
father's son." And Jay, brave as the intrepid Passepartout,
threw open the cape to show the red the way Dandy did and
felt all Roderick Casabianca Julius Caesar Dhu, William Tell
too. Petite Mère had taken him to see at the opera in Paris
(les bals de l'opéra étaient alors dans toute leur furie) where
the painted canvas waves heaved up and down and the tinpan
thunder clattered and the electric lightning flashed and the
canvas waves stuck just at the moment the tall gentleman in

the François Premier béret was about to be shipwrecked and people tittered and the old ouvreuse was so waxy and hissed shush and the tall gentleman went on singing just the same and the orchestra clashing and braying dans toute leur furie; but the real waves were scarier and so wet and cold.

But Jay hadn't encountered the emergency the day they went coaching with the lady Petite Mère had met on the train and thought so charming that Dandy asked them all to go coaching and the first thing they heard was the horn and there were the gray horses and the brown horses, men in green baise aprons handing up a hamper to the coachman, and Jay got to sit up with the coachman tucked in a blanket that smelt of horses and off they went the day they went coaching like Mr. Pickwick going to Wardle's — Jay pretending all the while the coach was the elephant Kioni, ridden by the imperturbable Phileas Fogg when he saved the lovely Aouda from suttee at the hands of the Hindu fanatics — clippety clock and the harness jingled and the sun came out behind the little dovelike clouds and the footman blew the big brass horn and the sun stayed out and it didn't rain and it was such fun the day they went coaching on account of the coach being the elephant Kioni; until the pretty lady with the powdered face who always wore spangly hats like tippedup eastereggs pulled Jay behind the coach when everybody had gotten out to stretch their legs, and Dandy was pouring for the grownups into little silver glasses out of a flask. The powdered lady pulled Jay behind the yellow wheel of the coach and suddenly looked him in the face with a sharp quick prying spiteful look. "Is he your father?"

"He's my guardian," Jay said; that was what Petite Mère had told him to say.

"You'd better tell the truth, because I know more than you think," she'd said in little sharp mean pecks like a bird pecking at a worm and her spiteful cold claws clamped on his arm. He'd pulled away and she hadn't asked him anything more but all the rest of the day he'd felt cold and naked on account of those eyes picking into him like a beak and that clutching claw. What he'd meant to say was "My father was Phileas Fogg" but he hadn't had time (of course Dandy was his father but he had never dared call him that, not even now) "and my mother was the fair Aouda saved from suttee at the hands of Hindu fanatics, and I am the intrepid Passepartout."

The train was slowing down fast, the engine bell was clanging. The plush seat was pushing into the back of Jay's neck.

His fingers were turning the thin pages of Mallory, book XX chapter 1.

> *In May when every lusty heart flourisheth and bourgeoneth, for as the season is lusty to behold and comfortable, so man and woman rejoice and gladden of summer coming with her fresh flowers . . .*

The gray locusts drooped with wan white blooms in every hedgerow and the mockingbirds sang quaveringly and red against green the cardinals flew . . .

> *. . . So in this season, as in the month of May, it befell a great anger and unhap that stinted not till the flower of chivalry of all the world was destroyed and slain.*

Petite Mère was dead and Dandy was an old gray man taking her down to the country to be buried.

> *Alas, said the King, help me hence for I dread me I have tarried overlong. Then Sir Bedevere took the King upon his back and so went with him to the waterside. Even fast by the bank hoved a little barge with many fair ladies in it and one of them was a queen and all they had black hoods and all they wept and shrieked when they saw King Arthur. Now put me into the barge, said the King.*

So quietly they hauled the wet lines aboard and the streak of shining green water widened between the piling and the boat's white side and the engine churned astern, two little bells, then one and full speed ahead down the broad brown reaches of the river and the dank wind smelling of sedge in our faces whipped the fading flowers on the black box set on two sawhorses covered with black amidships and astern the half-mast ensign trailed.

Tiny cinders gritted on the page when Jay closed the book. What's the use of reading when all it does is set the memories off? Lord he looked lonely and I was just a tonguetied idiot with feet too big for me who had never found a way to speak. The train was gathering speed again.

Jay pulled out his watch. It was the watch they'd given him on his fifteenth birthday and Petite Mère remembered enough to tell him how Dandy came by it and showed him the toothmarks Jay had made as a baby teething on it . . . (11.28. Five hours and thirty minutes more. No emergencies to be encountered tonight. He wanted the long trainride, the solitude, the grinding hurtling darkness to go on forever. A train's the only place I feel at home he told himself.) That was the watch Petite Mère gave Dandy years before I was born. It was in Paris. They'd been riding in the Bois. She remembered something uncomfortable about her sidesaddle. It hurt her so. He'd ridden fast and hard "Come Kate, come Kate" and she'd kept her horse right up with his. Dandy was in a wild exhilarated mood he sometimes had, when he felt strong enough, Petite Mère said, to pick up the spinning globe and juggle with it. They stopped for lunch in the Bois, sitting out in the sun among the flowers at a restaurant beside a lake. He'd drunk so much champagne, too much perhaps, and talked about George Washington flinging a silver dollar across the Rappahannock River. He couldn't find a silver dollar. All he had in his purse were small goldpieces with a pretty little rooster on them, so he'd flung his watch across the lake. It landed on the other side but they never could find it again and so next day she'd bought him the little flat one on the rue Royale. Lawsie she was stiff the next morning and all black and blue where the horrid saddle gnawed her knee. "Jay I loved him so. You're not old enough to understand but you'll grow up some day and be a comfort to me . . . "

You see, Jay said, as if explaining it to an invisible companion inside his head, we never really had a home until it was too late for Petite Mère. It was at that hotel on Broadway where Pat the fat waiter was and Billy my 'possum got out of his cage and caused such a ruckus because they found him in a strange lady's bathroom all huddled up above the watertank under the ceiling and I brought him down by his tail and explained to everybody their tails were prehensile and it didn't hurt him; but he had to be got rid of anyway.

That Hotel Dunstan was where Jay learned first that Petite Mère was ill, the day she looked so pretty with her hair in little curls he loved so across her forehead and the black lace dress with pink under it and the legofmutton sleeves, and he was so proud of her waiting for Dandy in the lobby for dinner, who had phoned he'd been detained at the office, and when he came he had that tired look behind his eyeglasses but was full of pomp and boastfulness and Milton, and described in Miltonic terms a pandemonium council he'd attended with some financial men downtown. "Small men Jay. Not one of them worthy of lacing your mother's shoe," he'd said. "Too big for their boots though the newspapers call them captains of industry. Never forget Jay that the one place in the world where there's room is right up at the top."

That time was fun but mostly dining out with them took so long: the waiters, the fuss about the bill of fare, the chilling of wine, the waits between courses, interminable tedium. The tedium of childhood.

Suddenly in the middle of Dandy's proud talking Petite Mère looked so pale and she had walked off slowly, so straight with her head high in the black lace dress with pink under it that had legofmutton sleeves and a little train that dragged, to the lady's room and a woman had come and Dandy got anxiously to his feet and a doctor came and after that it was all doctors and nurses and sickness and nobody paid any attention to Jay until he went back to boardingschool.

And now I'm on my own, old enough to encounter the emergency. But how? Where to start? An Englishman in America and American in England and the only home I ever knew just grief's cramping tedium round Petite Mère's sickbed. No wonder I had no tears left when she died . . . And the old country hearse was dusty and the locust blossoms drooped in the hedgerows and the crows cawed overhead and the two old colored men had dug out the fresh red clay till it looked like a wound in the bleeding earth.

The engine had been puffing hard up a grade. Couplings clanked and steel shrieked as the train ground slow around a curve; then gathered speed again with clink and rattle of metal and roar of air past the windows as the engine tore into a straightaway.

> . . . *Finding that all the rest could be depended on he sent back over the Alps for two more legions to follow. He crossed the little river Rubicon which bounded his province and advanced to Rimini where he met the tribunes Antony, Cassius Longinus, and Curio who were coming to him from Rome . . .*

The Chicago River was Jay's Rubicon but would he ever dare to cross, doing everything so badly, "Frenchy," "Foureyes," couldn't even throw a baseball straight, only underhand like a girl and the cousins, Aunt Edie's children, always did everything so well, won cups in all the tennis tournaments. The one time he'd put it over them was canoeing that time they all spent the summer in Maine, up the Moose River. Aunt Edie was deathly afraid of the lake and wouldn't let the Robeson boys go out in a canoe though they won all the swimming matches . . . Petite Mère was such a good sport . . . She went along on a camping trip up the Moose River with guides to handle the rapids and to make flapjacks and fishing poles and balsam beds and it really was the Moose River because that

evening coming home they slid silently with the white sliding
crested current around a bend and there he stood, great snout
in the air, webbed antlers spread in the setting sun, kneedeep
in alders, and like smoke melted as they looked. "Oh Jay if
Dandy had only seen him," Petite Mère called from the other
canoe.

That was the last summer she was at all well or they had
fun walking the trails, cutting birchbark, collecting balsam
tips to make a pillow: For you I pine and sometimes balsam.

> *And he came to a black launde and there was a black haw-*
> *thorne and thereon hung a black banner and on the other side*
> *there hung a black shield and by it stood a black spear great*
> *and long and a great black horse covered with silk and a black*
> *stone fast by . . .*

It was quiet and dark in Dandy's library on Wharton Place.
No air came in through the dark curtains. The blacksnake was
asleep in his glass bowl. The books in their rubbed leather
bindings stood in protective ranks on all the walls. Jay sat trying to read in a red leather chair while Dandy's pen scratched.
How small and defenseless Dandy looked, like a pale old
whiskered worm inside the tight protective box of the stone
house and the oblong library, shuttered against the heat and
the city traffic. Jay got to his feet. And now I'm taller than
he is, Jay was thinking tenderly. Dandy turned and looked up
at him. Jay's eyes traced the blue so defenseless veins on the
temples, that throbbed as if Dandy's whole life were exposed
there, and the red marks the pincenez had left on his nose and
the withered skin round his eyes.

"Jay." His father inspected him with a critical aquiline
loving look and then put his glasses back on. "Never forget
that a man's work is what counts. Without my work I couldn't
have lived through these last years. Some day you'll learn what
it means when a man and a woman love each other." He
looked down at his writing again. "Our lives have to go on. I
haven't much time left to complete some accomplishments I'd

like to leave behind." He looked up again into Jay's eyes with a mischievous smile. "Suppose right now I give you a little money for a trip. You better spend it while I've still got it. Go up in the northwoods and stay with one of your college friends. You know some boys that aren't too stupid. You've got to freshen up before going back to college. You may have to do some telescoping. I don't know how long I can keep you in college."

Jay had felt the tears helplessly welling and had turned to the shelves for the refuge of a book. Dandy was leaning over his desk. His pen covered the long foolscap with fine even writing. There were things Jay wanted to say but he couldn't. He stared into a book without seeing the print on the page. He blurted out: "Dandy why don't you come too?"

Dandy laughed a fresh youthful laugh. "The place for me is the office. I'd like to hold on long enough to get you into the firm. Maybe if you get through lawschool real fast we'll take a trip. How would you like some salmon fishing in Alaska?"

That was only yesterday but it seemed as long ago as England or the Dunstan.

The train stopped! Jay felt suddenly terribly alone in the panting silence.

> *And then Launcelot said unto Guenever in hearing of the King and them all: Madam now I must depart from you and this joyous fellowship for ever so I beseech you to pray for me and say me well.*

Jay's eyes stung. He couldn't read any more. Minutes passed. The train stood still. He shoved his three books into the top of his suitcase and got to his feet and walked up and down the aisle. His whole body felt fagged and cramped. He walked out on the platform but he couldn't see anything, no light, no sound. There was only a little hissing in his ears, he didn't quite know whether it was in his head or in the engine. With the silence all his thoughts and recollections stopped. It was as if his life, that had been like the train in the night, pounding along out of the dimmest past leaving the remembered stations behind, now terrifyingly had stopped. He was alone.

He felt awkward walking up the aisle with one hand thrust selfconsciously into his trousers pocket. No one looked up at him. There were women and men limp with sleep, a prim little old lady knitting, a tired woman in a purple dress asleep with her mouth open, a stubblebearded man in overalls with his hat pulled over his eyes who looked like a tough customer, a pink baby laid out on a seat with eyes buttoned up tight sucking on a pacifier and opposite what must be the father and mother. Jay's eyes went all over them as he passed. They were going home with the baby. They didn't look much older than he was. The man had redblond hair sticking up straight from a narrow sunburned forehead. His neck was very burned. There was a V of brown on the white of his chest where the shirt was open. The girl's head was tucked into his shoulder and her blouse had come unbuttoned so that Jay's eyes could look down onto the soft swell of a breast. Probably she'd been feeding the baby. His eyes lingered enviously on them as he passed. He wished he were that man. When he sat down again beside his scuffed suitcase, an old one of Dandy's, the lonely feeling doubled. They were going home with their baby. He sat with his eyes closed imagining how they'd met, how they'd kissed, what it was like in bed together with the baby crying in its crib. He fell asleep imagining himself planting out rough-smelling sections of seed potatoes in a clearing back of a board shack someplace up in the north woods.

When the train started again he halfwoke and began, part dreaming part imagining, to dream the old dream that he was twins sailing in a boat down the Mississippi. If you were twins it wouldn't matter if you were tonguetied. Each could say what he liked to the other. Each would do what the other wanted. There wouldn't be that constraint that held him fast in a vice with other boys, with girls, with everybody. They'd use the motor most of the way down the river. On the wide reaches they'd learn to sail. They'd be skillful sailors by the time they reached New Orleans. Adventures would be easy because each would back the other up. He spent a lot of time carefully imagining the way the bunks would be, the acetylene lamp, the little details of the galley and the cockpit, what kind of odd jobs they would pick up in the old stagnant settlements like Sugar Creek Landing where they used to dock when they went to the plantation when Petite Mère was alive. On the long quiet days chugging downstream, when there was a favorable wind they'd save gasoline by spreading their big legofmutton sail. How they'd keep on studying law. No it would be better if one of them studied law and the other one studied mechanical engineering. That way the mechanical one could do repairs on the motor and make money as a mechanic wherever they went and the other one could practice admiralty law. They could go swimming every day and dry off in the sun so that they would be so sunburned when they crossed the Gulf of Mexico and sailed from port to port through the Caribbean people wouldn't know whether they were colored or white. Except when they were in port they would never have to wear any clothes. They wouldn't be afraid of touching each others' bodies. They would help each other get girls like the natives helped Melville in *Omoo* and *Typee*. In the South Seas it was easy to snuggle up to girls. Then he was dreaming. Awake and asleep, the explanatory dreamvoice said he'd had that dream before. It was the cook's daughter whom he taught to swim down at the beach that summer. The older people would be sitting under parasols on the shore and he'd say come on Annie I'll give you a swimming lesson. He was fourteen and she was fifteen and she wouldn't say anything but she'd come out almost to the raft where the water was quite deep up to their armpits and he would hold up her chin with his hand and she'd make frogmotions to learn the breaststroke and he'd hold

up her middle with the other hand and she must have liked it
because she never said anything when his hand slid up towards
her little breasts slippery with seawater or down past the belly-
button that's the same in girls as it is in boys till the skirt of her
bathing suit would wrap around his hand and she'd splutter
and grab on to his shoulders and they'd laugh and stand apart
a little and then he'd start another lesson. Already he knew
how the dream was coming out. It was really a dream now.
He'd try to stop it but he couldn't. It started with that time
he'd seen her naked in the bathroom when they came in from
swimming. She'd left the door open on purpose maybe while
she pulled off her wet bathing suit. From under the drawn
shade a hot bolt of sun caught her white legs and shone bright
on the goldred fur between them. The voice was saying that no
he hadn't gone in. He didn't dare. Somebody would come.
She'd have a baby. What could he do? What could he say to
Mary or Petite Mère? He didn't want to marry Mary O'Toole's
daughter. He'd rushed into his own room and dressed and run
downstairs to play the phonograph for Petite Mère. But in
the dream, he couldn't stop it now, he stepped in and locked
the door behind him and felt her body all over and pressed
her belly to his belly with his hand in the small of her back
and felt her arms with his arms, her legs with his legs.

He woke up all wet, saying to himself disgustedly; damn
and double damn there ought to be something a man could do
to help it. He stumbled forward towards the toilet hoping nobody would see the damp place on his pants. Natural, I know
it's natural, he told himself but why the hell does it have to be
so humiliating?

In the narrow toilet that stank of puke and was full of grit
and filthy papers underfoot, he scrubbed himself off with
scrunchedup paper. When he pulled the lever to flush the
toilet the wind of the train's speed blew the stale stench in his
face and the loose trucks slamming over the rails clattered loud
in his ears. His nose tight with disgust, he lurched back to his

seat. Gray sick tremulous waves of disgust were going through his veins as he settled back against the clinging plush and tried to find a rest for his neck on the worn rim of the back that was too low for him. He could taste the disgust like the bile in his throat. That was what that boy at school felt like when he jumped out of the tenth story window of a downtown hotel and everybody said it was on account of masturbation. Never dared cross the Rubicon, the trucks prattled on the rails. The teacher nobody liked they used to call Master Bates and the awful talks the Head used to give in chapel about selfabuse. It was the sin of Onan, not the one against the Holy Ghost; that was a relief and the Head's voice got quite jolly about nocturnal emissions, a boy couldn't help that sort of natural physiological safety valve. (Better cross the little river Rubicon.) But everybody must be sure to take plenty of outdoor exercise and guard against morbid thoughts and he hoped they would all marry the loveliest woman in the world and live happily ever afterwards.

Jay lay with his head back on the gritty plush seat trying to breathe evenly and deep while the wheels on the rails clattered fast: little river Rubicon, little river Rubicon, little river Rubicon and then he was asleep.

When he woke up the train had stopped. The young couple with the baby had gone. The passengers were all on their feet dragging at their bags and packages. Jay closed up his suitcase and tumbled out on the cinders of the track. The daycoach was well out of the station. The sun was high, so bright his eyes stung. In front of the mustardyellow station a colored porter in a white coat was helping welldressed ladies, girls in summer hats, nurses and children out of the pullman. Blinking Jay looked around at the lake ruffled to a dark slateblue by the sharp wind and the steep burnedover hills with their skeleton trees and the little brown shingled houses of the town. Like a piece of white layer cake under the brilliant blue the little steamboat from the Hiawatha House poked its nose past the firs of the point. Swinging his heavy suitcase Jay started to run down the weathered steps that led to the wharf. The ladies off the pullman in their bright summer dresses and the porter and the children came straggling after. Jay was first of any of them running and jumping down the steps. *He put the slughorn to his lips and blew.* (But this was no dark tower, this was Joyous Gard.) Puffing he stood beside his suitcase out on the wooden wharf hearing the slap of the small purple waves against the piles, the cry of gulls so far from the sea, and breathing in joyously the smell of birch bark and firtrees and moss. the evergreen smell, the northwoods smell.

The lakeboat came towards the wharf with a bone in her teeth. The engineroom bell sounded and she checked herself and began to back water. Gulls swooped. Jay felt the chill wind tugging at his necktie. There in the bow was Joe Newcomer holding onto his straw hat with that tall darkbrowed reserved look. He was making stiff little howdoyoudo motions with one hand. (Welcome to Joyous Gard.) Jay waved his arms spreadeagle and began to jump joyously up and down on the loose planks of the wharf until he noticed all the fluttering ladies off the pullman were looking his way and froze stiff in his tracks.

Prolegomena Continued

KATHRYN JAY

1862—1914

LITTLE KATHRYN never tired of the story and used to jog dear Mama's memory when she skipped the least detail. It was about how Mama and Papa were married a hot summer noon in '61 at Christ Church in Alexandria; "As our quaint custom was in those days," Mama used to say with a little comical creak in her voice, "the groomsmen and the bridesmaids and several friends made up the bridal party . . . We were ten carriages. There was a drouth that summer; the flies hung in clouds over the horses, and the dust," dear Mama used to say rolling up her eyes, "was a white pall." The ladies travelled heavily veiled: the gentlemen rode. Papa had been offered employment as an engineer in the construction of a new flour mill they were building in Richmond at the falls of the James. They were planning to settle in Richmond. The part that Kathryn liked best was about the arrival of the bridal party at their cousins the Barefords' plantation in Orange and how the darkies came trooping out to meet them with flambeaux and the quadrille they danced under the French chandelier glittering like ice in the high hall and the whippoorwills so loud outside you could hear them above the fiddlers under the portico and the tall young men, so slender and courtly, everyone in formal dress . . . "Within the year, my dear, the most of them were dead." They had gone on to Charlottesville and there they had learned of the action of the Richmond convention. "Your dear papa always said it was Mr. Lincoln forced Virginia into the war . . . He had to return to Washington City to settle some affairs. His prospects before the war were brilliant but he was a true patriot and made the decision, in which your poor Mama devoutly concurred, to follow his state; it was a terrible decision, to be arrived at only after meditation and prayer. He abhorred bloodshed and believed deeply in union . . . How different was our return to Alexandria. The city was full of rascally camp followers. We drove through the Northern lines right after our victory at Manassas. A most gentlemanly Northern officer, Colonel Bigelow was his name — he met a hero's death at Shiloh — that was a dreadful battle dear in the campaign for Vicksburg when my little Kathryn was a babe in arms. The colonel furnished us with a safe conduct, but it was so terrible to see the dead piled in oxcarts and the poor wounded calling for water in the dust along the roadside and the flies torturing them."

Kathryn sometimes fancied she herself could remember the young wounded men in bloodstained gray brought into their cave at Vicksburg during the siege, but she couldn't have, because even at Vicksburg she was but a babe in arms. It must have been dear Mama who told her how they stood in the mouth of the cave watching the flash of the guns from out of the dark shapes of the federal ironclads in the bend of the river and how the flaming *Cincinnati* lit up the houses on the bluff and how once a shell with fuse spluttering rolled right into the cave — their rathole they used to call it — and one of the darkies — dear Papa's body servant my dear — picked it up and threw it down the hillside and, "by the good Lord's mercy who watched over us and protected us," it rolled away without bursting; and how dreadful it was to leave dear Papa besieged in the hilled city; "but my dear I had to do what was best because I was expecting little Rob and you were a sickly child" . . . and the brave pale faces of the Confederate women as they crossed on the ferry to pass through the Yankee lines on the Louisiana side . . . "How I managed to reach St. Louis I never knew except for the Lord's guidance and there among strangers Robert was born. After his parole Papa managed, don't ask me how, to reach St. Louis and we took the steamboat, I think it was the Wild Wagoner, up to Louisville . . . The Gateway City, they called it in those days; to your poor Mama it seemed the gateway to peace and happiness, but alas!" There she would sigh and say no more.

In Louisville they lived in a little brick house under black-walnut trees where the wallpaper kept peeling off the walls on account of the damp even in the drawingroom and dear Papa had no money for repairs because, although his prospects had been brilliant before the war, and his services to the Confederate cause in the design and construction of fortifications was outstanding, his health had never recovered from the fevers he had contracted "and of course we lost everything, like so many others."

Papa in those days was a gaunt sanguine man with a small gray goatee who wore a broadbrimmed slouch hat and was always expecting to recoup his fortunes, by recovering the insurance on a warehouse full of cotton that burned in New York, or by investing in the canal company or in palatial new steamboats on the Ohio, or in the railroad that was to run direct to Richmond and link Louisville with a great seaport to be opened on Hampton Roads. His prospects, Mama would sigh, were brilliant; but the steamboats were already losing freight to the railroads and the Louisville and Nashville crowd blocked the projected Kentucky railroad at every turn. Kathryn always remembered how dear Mama who never cried broke down unexpectedly when she and Rob and little Edie who could barely toddle, playing in the weedy grass of the backyard, invented a new Red Indian game and smeared their faces with juice from the blackwalnut shells and got the stain all over their clothes; and sobbed: "My dears there is no money to buy you new clothes . . . The stain is indelible."

Papa's projects were brilliant but there never was any
money. Rob studied in the public schools and Kathryn, although they did manage to send her to Jefferson Academy for
a term or two, had to finish at the Female High School, and
poor little Edie was hardly educated at all. They had lost the
house by that time and were boarding at Mrs. Eberstadt's.
How Rob hated to have to tell his friends he lived in a boardinghouse. Rob grew up small and dark with the profile, so
the ladies said, of a Grecian god. He was a fearless horseman
and rode with a gay crowd of moneyed men.

Though Randy Isham was older, he was Rob's best friend.
Together they ran with a scapegrace crew, racing horses and
making wagers they couldn't afford and drinking more bourbon whisky than was good for them. Dear Papa, who never
touched a drop of spirituous liquor, looked on their escapades
with a bilious eye: "If Rob don't straighten up, by Gad I'll
disinherit him," he'd roar. Kathryn, who was growing up
quite the belle with a will of her own; and poor Mama, redeyed
from the fine sewing and the exquisite embroidery she sold at
the Gentlewomen's Exchange to help pay Mrs. Eberstadt their
board, were always begging him to give Rob just one more
chance. "When the boys have sown their wild oats . . ." Mama
would begin and Kathryn's eyes would fill with tears and Papa
would run his fingers helplessly through his steelgray hair. "I
never could stand to see a woman cry."

Even Papa was pleased when in Mrs. Eberstadt's seedy
parlor, beside the cabinet of dusty birds supposed to have been
stuffed by the famous Audubon's own hands, Randy Isham
dropped down on his knees one evening after supper and asked
for Kathryn's hand. Randy was an only son and old Colonel
Isham his father owned a thousand acres in Jefferson County,
and farms up the Green River and stables of trotting horses
and a stallion named Saladin, descended in direct line from
the Godolphin Arabian, who had finished third in the newly
instituted Derby. Kathryn was married in her mother's wed-

ding dress in the great parlor at Harmony Hall, the Ishams'
home plantation, and Robert was best man and Kathryn didn't
know who looked the handsomer, Randy with his reddish curls
or Rob whose hair swept black as a raven's wing across his
pale and narrow brow. After the ceremony while the guests
were gathering for the reception, Randy handed her about
the stables that smelled of clover hay and the paddocks with
their board fences white as curds and the sweetsmelling stalls
of his saddlehorses, and the kennels of his hunting dogs and
pointed out various colts and fillies grazing on the rolling pastures dark with bluegrass and whispered in her ear, "Dear, you
are the mistress of Harmony Hall. It is thine, all thine."

Randy had a sweet generous nature and was always the perfect gentleman but Kathryn began to notice with fear and apprehension a watery look in his eyes in the evening, a thick-
ness in his speech; there was always the smell of whiskey on his
breath. Before they had been married a year, when he left the
house she began to dread his return; it was so often that he was
not himself when he came home. Their baby died the day it
was born. They had not recovered from that grief before they
suffered another bereavement. Colonel Isham, hemmed in by
creditors on every side, went into Louisville one day to enter
a petition in bankruptcy and was driven home in the surrey
behind his two pacing bays. He walked straight into his
panelled study where an oil painting of George Rogers Clark
hung over the mantel, took the patent Colt revolver he'd used
in the war out of the desk drawer and shot himself through
the temple.

Randy never recovered from that blow. He tried to recoup
his losses at the gambling table. He bet great sums on horse-
races. He kept borrowing to pay interest to stave off his father's
creditors. He was unable to pay even his debts of honor. At
twentysix he was a hopeless inebriate. When they lost Harmony Hall Kathryn took him east on funds advanced by her
cousins the Barkers to consult a New York physician they rec-

ommended. The night of a blizzard he was found frozen to death in an alley.

The Barkers were kindness itself. They took Kathryn into their home and arranged for a small pension to be paid the elder Jays. All her anxiety now centered on her brother Rob. Instead of sobering him, the shock of the Ishams' ruin and the extinguishing of all his prospects in that direction plunged him deeper into dissipation. The day after Randy's funeral Kathryn took her last few articles of jewelry and a chest containing the Isham silver to a Fifth Avenue jeweller's and sold them to furnish the funds Rob needed to stake him on a prospecting trip out west. New scenes, the great outdoors the Barkers agreed . . . the West was his only hope. It was years before she saw him again.

Bronson Barker was a banker and a man of wealth but incurably afficted with a rheumatic condition that kept him bedridden; Evelyn Barker's spinster sisters lived with them in an oldfashioned house with a garden and stables off Washington Square. They were cousins of Papa's. Alastair, the son, Kathryn's second cousin once removed, had studied abroad and had learned at Heidelberg to indulge a taste for literature and art. Kathryn had always been a reader. She found her cousin in every way congenial. He didn't declare his love, but she began to find sonnets between the pages of books she was reading in the library. The situation became embarrassing. At last she wrote him a short note explaining that his importunities were driving her from her refuge. They met face to face one morning in the square, each one indulging his morgue on a solitary walk; she begged him to forgive her for troubling his peace of mind. It was her destiny to live alone she said; she never could be his. He behaved like a gentleman and a thoughtful friend, exclaimed that he understood how difficult for a woman of spirit her situation must be and offered to find her employment in an endowed library of which he was one of the trustees.

She moved to a boardinghouse and resigned herself to the widowed life of a gentlewoman in reduced circumstances. She only lived for a yearly visit to the old people in Louisville, which was all she could afford, and for an occasional scrawled note, sometimes hopeful, sometimes despairing from her brother Rob in California. Pretenders to her hand there were plenty among the literary journalists and bashful bookworms and students of divinity who frequented the Society Library. She had no trouble keeping them at arms length with whimsical gay chatter until the day when Mr. Pignatelli came in search of an edition of Grotius. The night before at dinner with Cousin Alastair he had interested but somewhat repelled her. Now she discovered that there was something about him that was not to be denied. Girlishly she still kept a journal. The day after her illness she lunched with him and with his sister at the Astor House, at the top of a blank page she wrote: I can't help it, I adore him.

It was the last entry that she ever made.

Instead of the untroubled gray of widowhood, her life was now all black and white: happiness with Dandy; misery when he was absent. The night before they were to sail for Europe, as usual on separate boats, when little Jay was a year old baby asleep in his crib, a hot summer evening at the Hotel Dunstan in the midst of open trunks and hatboxes, dresses piled on the bed for packing, there was a knock at the apartment door and before Dandy could slip his jacket and waistcoat on over his starched shirt, Robert was in the room, drunk, unshaven, ragged as a Bowery loafer. He pulled a pistol out of his pocket and walked straight up to Dandy. "Prepare to meet your God," he mumbled out of shaky lips. Dandy's eyes sharpened to bright points. Dandy's hands were very strong. He wrenched the pistol from Rob's hand. "Let us talk in the other room," he said in a quiet voice, "or we shall wake little Jay." When Rob took his hat off she saw his hair was gray. He stumbled after Dandy into the drawingroom of the hotel suite. What they said to each other she never knew but when Dandy came back he said, looking so gently and tenderly in her face that her heart melted: "Don't worry Kate. I've fixed him up with a room at the hotel. In the morning after a shave and a hot bath he'll feel better. I'll leave him with Bill Keezer. Bill understands these things. He comes of a family of drunkards."

"Oh my poor brother," Kathryn said. It was the first time she had admitted to herself that Rob too was a drunkard.

Dandy pulled her towards him with his strong veined hands. "If he's yours he's mine. Don't forget that," he said. For all her grief for Rob she couldn't help but feel proud of Dandy and a little proud of herself because she hadn't screamed.

Dandy was in funds that summer. He had business with some railroad men in Italy. To avoid the heat and the dangerous fevers, he chartered a steam yacht in Nice. A Bretonne woman, one of the sailors' wives, went along as nurse for Jay. They cruised for a month, never tiring of the blue and purple bays and the peaked towns on hills and the everchanging prospects up valleys into the mountains inland. Little Jay thrived on the sea air. At Rapallo Dandy unearthed another Pignatelli, an elderly mustachioed schoolmaster in bottle green whom the yacht's gig brought aboard daily for lunch, wearing yellow gloves and carrying in one hand a blue umbrella to ward off the sun and in the other a tight bouquet of roses for the signora. He talked a crabbed kind of French and could recite almost any passage you asked for from Il Dante or Virgilio. Afternoons while Kathryn rested in her breezy cabin that was always full of roses, Dandy took Italian lessons from il cugino. Dom Virgilio, as Dandy called him, went with them as far as Genoa, where he pointed out ancestral streets and was their learned cicerone to the breakneck stairways and the marble palaces and the cold proud churches of that hilly city.

"We should have lived then," Dandy cried out one day, "in the days of Lepanto and the war galleys. I would have had Titian paint your portrait. I know that Chicago and New

York will be the Venice and Genoa of the century to come,"
he would add, "but what I fear is that manhood will be
swamped in mediocrity. Kate we must teach Jay to avoid
mediocrity."

That winter, partly because she couldn't bear the thought
of meeting Rob again, and partly because Marie was such an
excellent nurse, Kathryn decided to stay abroad when Dandy
went home for the winter's grind in the courts. At first she
thought she would live in Florence; but one day when she and
Marie were walking little Jay under San Marco's sunny colon-
nade she caught sight, through the elegantly wrought iron-
work of an arched opening onto the street, of the Misses Jay,
lively and chirping as a cage of birds, bedecked with Baedekers
and lavender bonnets alighting from a cab. She hurried out
of sight into a confessional in the church while they trotted on
into the cloisters to visit the Fra Angelicos. She hustled little
Jay in his gocart and stout Marie, grumbling at the rapid walk,
back to the hotel. I'm such a coward without him, she thought.

After that Florence seemed a place accursed. She moved to
Brussels where Judy Cook, a girlhood friend with whom she
had been exchanging letters, had married the American consul;
and there she rented an apartment for the winter. The Vanderpools were warm and friendly people. Judy, who had lived long
abroad, had only recently heard of Randolph Isham's death,
so she took it for granted that Jay was poor mad Randy's son.
That spring, as Judy was childless and bitterly regretted it, she
was delighted to take in Jay and old Marie while Kathryn
went on a short trip, to meet friends in Paris she explained.

Dandy met her at the Continental. Her heart was wrenched
with shame when she caught herself thinking how easy travelling was without little Jay. Their trip to Italy, they used to
say afterwards, was a tornado. As the passes were open unusually
early that spring, they crossed the Saint Gothard in a landau
with two extra horses to pull them up the mountains. They
spent three days among the peachblossom marbles of Verona

before they took the train to Rome. In Rome Dandy discovered in the livery stable at the Hotel de Russie a pair of tolerable riding horses and a swarthy scarfaced fellow with shining white teeth named Pietro, who reeked villainously of garlic, to act as equerry. When Kathryn complained that he looked like a bandit Dandy laughed uproariously and said of course he was a bandit. "So am I," he added giving his mustache a twirl. "When in Rome do as the Romans do."

Every morning they rode out with Pietro as a guide. They pushed as far as was safe out along the Appian Way. "The people on the tombs look like any of my boards of directors," Dandy said. "I suppose we Anglo-Saxons are the Romans of the century to come . . . Kate you must think it odd that I class myself as an Anglo-Saxon when I'm only half a one, but I do it unconsciously. For all Dom Virgilio's learning, my mother's is the stronger strain."

They were sitting under a vinecovered arbor at a scrubbed oak table drinking the golden wine of the Roman castles and looking out over the pale campagna rising to the blueshadowed Alban Hills. "*At noon we'll sit beneath the arching vines,*" he quoted, "*And dream that love becomes immortal.*" They rode back slowly to their hotel, the horses' hoofs clattering on the cobblestones, through streets that smelt of oliveoil and heliotrope and drains. After lunch in the garden Dandy read aloud copiously from Gibbon until it was cool enough to walk for a while in the Forum. That night they risked the dread night air to hear the nightingales singing on the Pincian.

When they went on to Naples they exclaimed that it was like a painted backdrop for an opera. The night they arrived tired and dusty from the train at a hotel that fronted the bay of lapis lazuli Kathryn dreamed of Jay. She had picked him up from his crib but instead of Jay when she leaned to kiss him she held in her arms a broken china doll. Her scream woke her and after that she couldn't sleep. At breakfast Dandy sent a telegram and by night the Vanderpools had replied that all was well, but it meant that when she went back to Brussels Kathryn felt she had to explain why she'd gone from Paris all the way to Naples. One lie led to another until she felt her life was caught like a poor fly in a web of lies.

When Jay was five she moved to England. The next year she tried Rapallo but when Dandy went home in the fall she moved to St. John's Wood again. Little Jay was growing fast. There was the question of his schooling; he was beginning to ask why, since they were Americans, they couldn't live at home in one of the states that made the stars on the flag. Each year seemed to bring a heavier burden of evasions and untruths: how could she lie to Jay? When Dandy was with her his presence filled the days with light; from the moment she woke up until she fell asleep at night he kept her petted and amused with his tall tales and his playacting and his quotations from Shakespeare and the excursions he thought up, and the books he read aloud; but now little Jay had to be considered. He was beginning to develop a mind of his own. He asked continual questions and Kathryn began to fear that he was developing a resentment against his father. He whined and complained that he didn't have boys of his own age to play with.

Kathryn decided to try a winter in New York. She rented from an artist friend a big dark apartment on Sixty-Sixth Street west of the park, and for a while she was almost happy there. Jay went to a nearby dayschool and Dandy, who was dividing his time about equally between New York and Chicago, made a point of dining with her every night he was in town. It worried her how tired he looked, how the lines deepened and crinkled round his eyes. Dandy was working harder and harder. His fees were the largest he had ever made but in spite of everything he could do he ended every year in debt. His responsibilities, he would ruefully admit, kept growing. There were poor Nettie's doctor's bills and her trips to French Lick or White Sulphur and the girls' allowances and their débuts in Chicago society to be arranged and by God paid for;

his brother Luke had died without leaving a cent and little Luke had to be put through college and there had even appeared in recent years a widow of his older brother Giuseppe and her children and grandchildren all growing up penniless and clamoring from Bologna for remittances.

Brother Robert was a drain on him. Patiently Dandy had set him up to raise trotting horses, to operate a small track, to keep a crossroads store near Bowling Green, but each enterprise drowned after a year or so in whiskey. At last Robert had a serious accident. Drunk, presumably, he was thrown and dragged by his horse and spent many months in a hospital in Louisville recovering from broken bones and an injured kidney. In the hospital they wouldn't let him drink. For his convalescence Kathryn, though Dandy was against it, insisted on inviting him to stay with her and Jay on the farm Dandy had bought her in an abrupt green valley on the Kentucky side of the river about halfway between his old home in Cincinnati and her own home in Louisville.

Dandy, with his love of navigating on any kind of water, had found a small sternwheel riverboat rotting on a flat near Cincinnati and bought it and fixed it up for a houseboat. "They have dahabiehs on the Nile don't they?" he said to friends who teased him about becoming a steamboat captain so late in life. "Why not on la Belle Rivière? All those rich people in Chicago who don't know what to do with their money . . . I'll make steamboating fashionable and in a year every last one of them will be fitting himself up a sternwheeler."

Little Jay was back from his first year at boardingschool and the trip seemed to Kathryn, who had just been told by her New York doctor that she must be careful of her bloodpressure, a restful dream in green. The river was green and the great trees and the drowned scrub along the banks were green and the hills beyond were green. Dandy worked in his cabin all day and came out evenings to play her Gilbert and Sullivan on the gramophone, or to recite to her his favorite passage from *Othello* he'd quoted so often when he was courting her years ago:

> . . . *Wherein of antres vast and deserts idle,*
> *Rough quarries, rocks and hills whose heads touch heaven*
> *It was my hint to speak; such was the process;*
> *And of the cannibals that each other eat,*
> *The anthropophagi, the men whose heads*
> *Do grow beneath their shoulders. These things to hear*
> *Would Desdemona seriously incline:*
> *But still the house affairs would draw her hence;*
> *Which ever as she could with haste despatch,*
> *She'd come again and with a greedy ear*
> *Devour up my discourse . . .*

Of course he always declared that if he'd really been Othello, he would have wrung Iago's neck first thing; that is if Kate had been Desdemona.

The days were hot but in the evenings they would sit at a table set in front of the pilot house on the bow to catch the breeze that ruffled the still reaches of the river and Dandy would order up big beaded tumblers of an especially refreshing drink he had invented of limejuice and Saint Croix rum and seltzer. Every night they ate channel catfish cooked in a different way, and froglegs and snapping turtle, which Dandy claimed was every bit as good as terrapin. And old Tom made the best corn muffins. Dandy would lay his napkin down in the middle of dinner and put on his glasses and look around at the swifts skimming across the fading colors on the water and the mists rising in dainty tints over the glossy backwaters behind the massed greens of the everchanging points of the shoreline and cry: "Kate where would you rather be than here?" She would lean across the table and pat his hand. "Nowhere in the world," she would say.

What made her happiest was Jay's delight in the river. He'd read *Tom Sawyer* and was working through *Huckleberry Finn* and hardly knew whether he was living on the *Dahabieh*, as they'd named the boat, or in Mark Twain. He was always in the pilothouse listening to Eb Cole, Dandy's captain, who'd been a riverman all his life, tell tales of floods and icefloes and hunting bear up in the mountain counties. It was one of their happiest trips, but when they tied up against the plantation's old ramshackle landing at Sugar Creek they caught sight of a wizened little sourfaced man swinging his body painfully between his crutches as he made his way forward to meet them. Oh no, Kathryn thought, it couldn't be her handsome brother Rob. It wasn't his aging so much that wrung her heart as the change in the expression of his face. At least he was sober. His teeth were very bad. First thing he began to mumble accusingly, as if it were her fault, that he'd found Papa and Mama's graves all overgrown with weeds when he had gone to their graveyard, which he found in what was now the colored section of Louisville. "I don't know how you feel about it but it makes me see red to think of those damn niggers sprawling on my mother's grave."

Dandy tried to carry everything off as a joke. He announced that he thought the quiet and the country air would be perfect for Kate's health and that farming would be just the thing to put Robert on his feet after his accident. He found them a colored cook and butler and a yardman and a mulatto mechanic to drive the Ford touring car the local livery stable operator, who had just taken to selling automobiles on the side, would deliver when it came; and left them after a week at the plantation to hurry east on an important case.

The weather was hot, but the quiet green of the deep country was restful. For a while Rob seemed really to take hold. She could see he loved little Jay and fought temptation for his nephew's sake rather than his own or hers. He didn't love his sister any more, of that she was sure. He was out all day directing the ditching, interviewing tenants, overseeing the road they were building up to the hardwoods in the hills. Then one night after she'd gone exhausted to bed — for all she could do she could not throw off her fatigue or the feeling of a band tightening tightening round her temples — a noise downstairs woke her. She put on her dressinggown and walked in her slippers down the curving stair with the beautiful walnut rail, which was all they'd been able to salvage out of the old woodwork of the house when they had done it over, and found Rob with a bottle before him and a broken glass at his feet drunk and helpless in the diningroom.

She tried to help him up the stairs to bed but he drew away from her muttering that she had no cause to complain, what if he did take a drink now and then. He needed it on account of an upset stomach; what else could a man do but drink when his own sister had brought shame and disgrace on the family and the old people to a paupers' grave in niggertown, no she had no right to talk. She ran back up to her bedroom crying like a scolded child. Next day it was worse. When he drank up the liquor in the sideboard he insisted on her giving him money to buy more. She sent Dandy a desperate wire but he wasn't able to come on account of an impending conference and sent Bill Keezer who promptly loaded Rob, looselipped and shaking, into the buggy to drive the twenty miles to the railroad. Eventually he managed to entice him into a sanatorium. Kathryn was left too sick and helpless to stir from her room. Her only comfort was in little Jay, who though only ten was doing his best to take charge of the house, to order meals, to keep track of what was happening about the garden and the farm and to read to her and play records to her and to keep in his childish way a little circus going for her amusement the way his father did.

She was ill all winter in New York. In June, the day Jay came back from school, gangling and skinny, but sunburned and full of chatter, while he helped her hang sheets on the parlor chairs to get the apartment ready to be closed up for the summer, about the fun he'd had canoeing and how he'd learned to keep score for the baseball team and might run for manager, a cable came from Dandy. They must join him in

England. Important events would detain him there all summer. Stateroom engaged on Rotterdam Saturday . . . He would
meet them at Boulogne. Jay had to do most of the packing.
He and Bill Keezer between them got her trunks to the pier.
The trip, the quiet, the sea air, she kept telling herself; the
sea air always did her good. How young he looks, she thought
when she caught sight of Dandy in a straw hat and tweeds
perched jaunty as a sparrow on the top deck of the tug that
came to take off the passengers. For a moment when he looked
into her face before kissing her she saw the anxious look she
dreaded so form in the crinkled skin round his eyes but immediately it was swept away in boasting and bluster. It was
the Cape to Cairo this time, an international consortorium.
He was representing the American and some of the French
investors. He had been brilliantly received in London. He had
been asked to lecture at the Royal Institution. Next week he
was to be presented at Court. After he had sent Jay back to the
stateroom to fetch his mother's jewelcase which she had forgotten, he took her hand and said, "Kate we must watch your
health. After this I may retire . . . You'll have a farmer on your
hands" . . . He squeezed her arm. "We have great days ahead",
he said in a low grave voice. "While you and Jay were on the
high seas . . . poor Henrietta died."

The crossing on the channel boat was unusually tiring although the sea was calm. A large red automobile with a French
chauffeur met them at the quay in Dover. "Now we will really
enjoy the Kentish countryside," he said as he pulled the duster
over his light green tweed. Of course the thing broke down
and they had to spend the night at a Canterbury inn. If she
had only felt better, she would have enjoyed it so, the quaint
streets, the leaded casements, the chimney pots. After dressing
in the morning she had to lie down again on the unmade bed
while Jay and Dandy walked out to see the cathedral. By noon,
when they reached the Savoy, where a suite had been reserved
for her, she was complaining of shortness of breath. Dandy
sent a hansom cab to fetch a Harley Street specialist he knew.

The doctor gave her some drops in a glass of water and with his monocle and his boutonnière, lent the whole business a jaunty fashionable air; but after he had gone Dandy came back in the room with a face so woebegone she almost had to laugh . . . As usual he was staying at the Langham, but every moment he could spare he spent beside her bed. He found the son of a barrister friend, a haughty lad from Eton, to show Jay the Zoo and the Crystal Palace and Earls Court and the waxworks at Madame Tussaud's. Every time Jay came back from an excursion he would bring her flowers. It was as if she had two beaux. The day Dandy went, as he put it, to make his bow before Their Majesties, he appeared suddenly at her bedroom door in a barrister's court dress, knee breeches, silk stockings, his chest puffed out under the ruffled shirt, a rooster about to crow. She loved him for it. "Without orders or decorations I'll look bare as a plucked fowl among all those spangled birds," he said laughing with her, "but as an American perhaps it is more fitting so."

When the London season closed he planned to take them motoring in the Trossachs, but Kathryn was not well enough to go. That fall when they reached New York she gave up the apartment. Without the cares of housekeeping she would recover her health sooner, Dandy said. He engaged for her three rooms at the Dunstan. There the illness that had so long been threatening closed over her like a sudden squall. Nurses and the daily doctor moved in a painful blur through her bedroom. Occasionally Dandy's dear anxious face would loom as through a fog. She couldn't remember the Lord's Prayer. It was agony to try to search for words. Dandy, Kathryn, Jay. The words kept fading in her mind. For years whenever they were parted she and Dandy had written each other every day. He always wrote but now she would lie in bed staring uncomprehendingly at the beloved familiar handwriting that so neatly covered the sheets of lawyers' foolscap he liked to write on. When the nurse would want to read it to her, she would hold the paper tight in her hand and shake her head. No. No.

When little Jay comes . . . When I am better. Aphasia was a word she understood. She must be relaxed and worry about nothing and try to get well, the doctor and the nurses said. I must try to get well, she kept saying to herself and searched for words to pray to God: Our father which art . . . The days never seemed to end, waking was so near sleep. Days, weeks, months, sometimes she could make out the date on the morning paper. Later when the traffic was loud because the window was open she lay looking at an English sparrow on the sill in the sunlight. He made her laugh. He was preening his feathers. He cocked a sharp eye with a comical look that made her think of Dandy cocking his eye at her through his pincenez. He really made her laugh. Today she could remember scenes from the past. So clear. As clear as the sparrow she saw dear Mama's face against the stuffed birds in the parlor of Mrs. Eberstadt's boardinghouse, under the ruffle of lace she used to wear on her hair, and Dandy in his swimming suit about to dive — how bright the light used to be in those days, how high the sky — off the yacht's deck into the blue water at Rapallo, and little chubby Jay on the beach at Boulogne-sur-Mer so proud of a sand fort he'd moulded with his bucket pursing his lips and puffing hard as he stuck the American flag's little stick carefully into the center of the round tower and sat back to see the small flag flutter . . . Jay. It was so long since she'd written Jay. The nurse was trying to keep her from writing to her Jay at boardingschool. The paper was slippery. The pencil wasn't right. She must get new glasses. Trying to write cramped her fingers. At first it was only a scribble. The nurse must bring her more pillows. Such a scribble. These awful glasses. It was a shame to spoil so many sheets but she must try. She must try to get well. Words came up in French quite clear: *Petite Mere,* no matter about the accent . . . *Petite Mere taime taime taime* . . . "Please nurse," she mumbled weakly, when she could try no more because the room was getting dark, because outside the twilight was fading, "please send . . . to Jay."

2

NEW WORLD WIND NORTHWEST

Lulie was out on the back porch hulling strawberries. Now and then a berry squashed between her fingers and she set it aside on a cracked soupplate. The whole berries she dropped into a bowl for the shortcake. Her fingers were pink and smelt of strawberries when she raised the back of her hand to her face to brush the hair out of her eyes. There was strawberry juice on her cheek. Everything smelt of strawberries, stronger than the sweetclover smell that came in gusts of honey on the wind from the orchard back of the house. Her sharp pink fingers moved faster and faster. She had to get the strawberries hulled for the shortcake and be out of the house before Aunt Lyde woke up from her nap. When she thought of the long June afternoon stretching ahead of her and summer at the lake stretching ahead into so many long afternoons she took a deep happy breath and the fragrance of strawberries and sweetclover filled her little head and made her feel quite giddy.

A shotgun went bang under the brow of the hill and immediately she heard voices in the orchard. It was Doc Warner's voice: "Never mind the law Georgie shoot the birds." She recognized the squeaky complaining tones. The hesitant rumble was Georgie. It was the first time she'd noticed how much Georgie's voice had changed. Two more barrels went off. The Warners were coming up towards the house. She yanked at the stems of the last few berries in the bottom of the basket. They were all so clean she didn't need to wash them. "There you little bastards," she whispered as she rushed them, rolling merrily in their big white bowl, through the screen door into the kitchen. She blushed at the word she'd whispered. Those awful boys, she thought.

Already there was the creak of a step and the rustle of Aunt Lyde's dress on the front stairs. The girl dashed out through the screen door again just in time to see two figures, one gangling and the other bearded and stocky, emerge from out of the appletrees' tangled blur. Each wore a new green corduroy cap with earflaps tied at the peak; each carried his shotgun aslant in the crook of an arm. Georgie had one finger to his lips and was making mysterious signs with the fingers of the hand that held the shotgun. She let the screen door slam behind her as she ran towards them laughing.

"Lulie," Georgie whispered in a weighty whisper, "Come into the orchard."

My he's a lout, she was saying to herself as she followed him back among the trees taking in at a glance his unbrushed hair in black spikes on his forehead like an Indian's and the line of grime round the open neck of his blue shirt — but a sweet lout.

Doc Warner was out of breath. He bared his yellow teeth in an uneven grin. "We've been trapshooting," he panted. "I'm going to teach that boy to shoot if it's the last thing I do on this earth."

Georgie had dropped on his heels behind one of the bigger trees and rested his gun against the trunk. He began to pull handfuls of fluffy rosygray birds out of the pockets of his hunting jacket. "Doves," he whispered. "They're for you. I know Grandmother Waring'll like 'em . . . We dasn't take them home because mother'd raise a storm."

"Who'll clean them?" asked Lulie tittering.

"Ben home?"

"He and Zeke are someplace in the orchard spraying."

"I spotted their sprayer in the crotch of a tree." The nagging tone of Doc Warner's voice took the fun out of everything. "Off skygazing I guess."

"Probably Blondine's broken out and they are rounding her up," said Lulie protectively. She didn't like to hear people use that tone of voice when they talked of her brothers. "Blondine's a card," she added.

"You people will lose that cow . . . You ought to run a strand of barbed wire round your fence."

Georgie broke in on his father. "I'll clean 'em," he said putting on the stagy expression he wore when he felt he was being big about something.

"Do it in the woodshed, Georgie, and please don't make a mess . . . Remember that porcupine?" Lulie let out a shriek of laughter. "I thought I'd never hear the last of that porcupine."

"Honest I'm pretty good now . . . I've finished the course. I want to save a couple of skins to stuff."

"If everything else fails," Doc Warner said in his sarcastic voice, "I'll be able to tell the world that my son Georgie is a graduate taxidermist."

"But Doctor Warner," cried Lulie on the defensive again. "It's wonderful to be a good taxidermist."

Georgie gave her a grateful look out of eyes that had begun to fill with tears. Doc Warner had a knack of bringing tears to Georgie's eyes just by the tone of his voice. He seemed to enjoy doing it. Lulie stood, the wind blowing her hair, under the swaying appleboughs, with her mouth half open not quite knowing what to say next. She looked from the son's sullen brown countenance to the father's pallor where too red lips curled cruelly above a scraggly gray beard. Then she heard her own voice, in clear ringing tones that brooked no argument and reminded her of her Aunt Lyde's, saying:

"Georgie you take the birds in the woodshed and skin them . . . I'll finish my kitchen chores and see if Aunt Lyde won't let us go canoeing."

Georgie shambled off through the long grass mumbling that he wished people would stop calling him Georgie.

"All right. After this I'll call you George Elbert."

Lulie's laugh broke off sharp when she found herself alone with Doc Warner, facing that whiskery snarl. The expression on his face sent a chill up her spine like the feeling when somebody walks over your grave. "My children" — he was enunciating his words sharply and bitterly — "and their friends would rather do anything in the world than help me spend a pleasant afternoon." He spun round on the heel of his hunting boot and left her.

Immediately Lulie was enjoying herself again. She lingered a moment under the appletree watching the young leaves shiver in the wind against the blueblue sky. All about her under the weight of the warm sun bees bumbled on the tall white spikes of sweetclover. A tiny wren, tail tilted straight up, perched for a second on a branch above her head, gave her a beady look, and was gone among the leaves.

"Lulie!" Aunt Lyde's voice rang like a bell from the back porch. Lulie turned and ran back through the orchard, jumping high over tufts of new grass, pretending for an instant she was one of the king's deer and Doc Warner was a caitiff bowman trying to shoot her with his longbow. Out of breath with her hair all over her face she hung for a moment helpless on the handle of the screen door. When she slipped into the kitchen Aunt Lyde was shaking her neat head of wavy white hair: "Lulie aren't you ever going to grow up?"

"Oh Aunt Lyde, I hope not."

"Who was it?" Aunt Lyde had pinned up her gray silk dress and wore an apron over it. She adjusted her pincenez and gave Lulie one of her calm level looks.

"Just Doc Warner being mean to Georgie again. My he's horrid. I told Georgie we could go out in *Redwing* this afternoon."

"Isn't it too windy? I had hoped you would stay and help

your grandmother and me make the preserves."

Grandmother Waring's voice piped up dry as a cricket's from beside the range. "Let the child go Lydia. It's such a pretty day . . . Lawsee," her voice rose to a little shriek. "We almost let the shortcake burn." A hot whiff of baking cake filled the kitchen as she opened the oven door. Clucking like a pair of hens Aunt Lyde and Grandmother Waring pulled out the pans of brown cake and set them on the deal table. Grandmother Waring's little crinkled face was flushed as a winter apple from leaning over the range. She was a tiny little woman, smaller even than Lulie, almost lost in her ruffled apron. She wore a little triangle of lace on top of a tight coil of braided hair which was much less white than her daughter's.

"I never saw such a girl," went on Aunt Lyde in her even tones. "All she seems to think of is romping out of doors with the boys . . . When I was a little girl. . ."

"She's my favorite," interrupted Grandmother Waring shooting little twinkles into Lulie's face out of round eyes ringed with fine lines. "And so are you, pet." She gave her daughter's hand a quick brisk pat.

"The cake looks wonderful," said Lulie snatching with pink fingers a curl of brown crust off the edge of the pan, and popping it in her mouth. "I'll whip the cream right now," she added, seeing a chance to bargain for her liberty.

Aunt Lyde hesitated for a moment. "The child's going to the dance at the Hiawatha House tonight" — She talked to Grandmother Waring across Lulie's head. "I don't want her to get overtired."

"I never get tired out on the lake," said Lulie eagerly arguing her case. "I need some air before going into that stuffy old ballroom."

"Well if you get back in time to have a little liedown before supper."

"Oh goodie!" Lulie ran jumping up and down round the kitchen while she got together a bowl and some powdered sugar and the eggbeater to beat the cream up with.

"Set the bowl in icewater darlin'," said Grandmother Waring.

Lulie was already turning the handle of the eggbeater with cramped fingers. It seemed hours before the cream was stiff enough to satisfy Aunt Lyde.

When the whipped cream was ready to place in the icebox on the back porch Lulie noticed the cracked willow soupplate she'd left there full of mashed berries. "Those'll do for Georgie, he's always hungry," she whispered to herself. She snatched up a spoon and put a blob of whipped cream on top and started out the door.

"Don't forget your sweater," Aunt Lyde called after her.

"I'll be back. I'm just taking those berries to Georgie." She poised for a second on the wooden step.

"Where is Georgie?" Grandmother Waring was asking.

"Out in the woodshed skinning doves," called Lulie in a whoop of laughter as she ran along the railfence that divided the orchard from the lawn round the house.

The plate of strawberries held in front of her Lulie stood in the door of the woodshed blinking into the brown halflight. She could make out Georgie's broad back bent over a row of bloody little bare corpses on a plank laid across the sawhorses . . . "Goddamn that knife. Shit!" he was swearing to himself in a singsong mumble.

"Georgie, don't swear," said Lulie giggling. "There are ladies present."

"I'll swear as much as I damn please. . . The dadgasted knife slipped. Ben back?"

She shook her curls that the wind had blown every which way: "Blondine's leading them a lovely chase through the woods, I'll bet. That's the meanest old cow."

"I thought Ben and Zeke were playing baseball this afternoon."

"Aunt Lyde said they had to spray the orchard."

"Nobody ever lets anybody do anything they want to . . . I'm sick of this life," Georgie was grumbling as he worked.

"I'm going out in the woods with the Indians."

"They don't live in the woods. They live in smelly little shacks and sell baskets and don't ever bathe."

"They are dirty and no account just like me," said Georgie in his most sorryforhimself voice. "I'll get used to the fleas, and lice too probably. I'll have nits in my hair."

"Cheer up Georgie and eat some strawberries."

Lulie held the plate under his nose the way she would with a dog.

He snatched up the spoon and started to cram the creamy berries into his mouth. "You said you'd quit calling me Georgie," he said with his mouth full.

Lulie was laughing. "The only thing wrong with you George Elbert is you're hungry."

He turned his back and studied a row of tattered birdskins tacked on shingles along the studding. "Dad made me so mad I left the table and didn't get any dinner . . . Dad and Mother both."

"What's the trouble?"

"College," he talked fast with his mouth full of berries. "Dad can't afford to send me and my marks aren't good enough to get a scholarship. They could all right but they are too damn selfish."

He'd finished the strawberries and handed her the empty soupplate.

"Georgie don't you worry. We'll think up something. We've got all summer to think up something . . . How about going to work as bellhop at the hotel? They make oodles of money."

"And have all those high hat kids giving me the raspberry . . . They all hate me anyway. I'm going out in the woods with the Indians. Joe Sawbuck likes me."

"How can you tell? He never says anything." Lulie broke into giggles again.

"He's the best damn shortstop the Hiawatha team ever had."

"Well, we'd better go. You meet me down at the landing, Georgie. I mean George Elbert . . . I'm running back to get a sweater."

The wind was rattling a loose shingle on the roof of the woodshed. "It'll be rough out there," he said in a foreboding tone.

"We'll stay under the lee of the shore."

"I've got my rod down at the float." Georgie was beginning to cheer up. "You paddle in the stern and I'll do some casting and we'll see if I can't catch us a pickerel."

Lulie used a long chip of pine to tumble the little carcases off the plank into a pile on the soupplate and ran back to the house with them. "Grandmother, Georgie brought you some doves."

"Now isn't that elegant?" said Grandmother Waring, raising up two little withered hands. "I don't believe I've eaten doves since I was a girl down at Sandy Ford. My the game we used to eat in those days."

"They are against the law," said Aunt Lyde. "That boy'll come to no good. You mark my words."

"We used to believe," said Grandmother Waring, "that Almighty God in his infinite wisdom placed an abundance of game in the world to satisfy the needs of his children. I don't see what the law's got to do with it."

"Anyway the game warden is umpiring the ballgame so he'll never know," said Lulie. "He shoots duck himself at the head of the lake every morning of his life. He even shot a wood duck and that's wicked."

"If the law isn't within our hearts," said Grandmother Waring rinsing the doves off under the faucet at the sink, "it's no use giving it much mind. My, they are fat as butter. Elegant." She smacked her lips. "I know just how to cook them with a speck of onion in a covered pan and a shaving of fat bacon over the breast."

Already Lulie was galloping up to her room to snatch her

yellow sweater from among the books on the bed. She came back down the stairs two steps at a time and grabbed up the paddles that leaned against the coatrack in the hall and ran out through the front porch and down the path that zigzagged soft with moss and pineneedles between granite outcroppings, towards the shore. Ahead of her beyond a fringe of tamarack and fir the lake shimmered blue in bright dancing lights. As she ran she heard Aunt Lyde's distant voice, "Be sure to be back in time to milk and have a good time Lulie dear."

Georgie already had *Redwing* in the water. He was sitting on his heels at the end of the float holding the thwart of the canoe with one hand and a fishing rod and a box of tackle with the other.

He gave her one of his black looks. "I was willing to bet you'd forget the paddles."

"But I didn't."

Lulie stepped into the stern. It was *Redwing,* her own glossy red canoe, and she loved it more than anything. "Now George Elbert be careful . . . You know how tippy *Redwing* is."

"Don't worry, I don't want to lose my rod."

As soon as they had pushed her off from the float and she felt the silky glide through the darkgreen water of the cove and the canoe veering true to the twist of her paddle, she felt outrageously happy. All the anxious feelings she'd had through lunch and while she was hulling the strawberries for fear she wouldn't get out canoeing that sunny Saturday afternoon slipped away. *Redwing* slid happily up the lake past the point of birches beyond the Newcomers' boathouse and the two little gray shingled cottages beyond, up into a wider empty cove that was sedgy in spots. She could see the Alexanders' cows grazing in the meadow and, through the willows beyond, the sprawling white farmhouse where the Alexanders took in summer boarders. Behind the Alexanders' place the hills rose into piny ridges against a slatyblue sky full of billowing northwesterly clouds.

In the broad mouth of the big cove they bucked a sharp gust of wind. Lulie had to paddle hard to keep the canoe on its course.

"I wish Ben had come," Georgie was grumbling. "It's no fun going fishing with a girl."

Lulie laughed breathlessly: "When gentlefolk meet compliments pass, that's what Grandmother Waring says."

"Now Lulie you know I didn't mean anything personal." He was talking through his teeth as he paddled. "We don't count you as a girl . . . You're one of the Tribe. You passed the initiation and swam a hundred yards with your eyes closed and bit off the head of a live perch like all the braves do."

Lulie made a little whinnying sound. She was out of breath from keeping the canoe headed into the wind. Georgie paddled like a demon in the bow.

"Don't know how I managed it," she panted. "It was a mighty tiny little one."

Now and then Georgie caught a crab and the cold drops stung her face. In the gusts the lake water boiled past her paddle in dark ruffled waves.

"You'd like it better if Ben was along," Georgie asked after a while, "now wouldn't you?"

She gave a hoot. "Of course . . . I love Brother Ben and besides I wouldn't have to paddle."

Each time she raised her paddle the wind snatched sparkling drops off it. "Ouch," she shouted as she barked her knuckles against the side of the canoe.

"Shut up Lulie . . . We are near the spot." Georgie glowered back at her over his shoulder. "Indian squaw no make jabber jabber." He grinned to make up for his rudeness.

Once they were out of the wind and in the lee of the trees the still air warmed with the smell of dry evergreens. The canoe shot forward smoothly. She tried to dip her paddle in without a sound. The brown water was clear as glass under the shining surface. A school of minnows scattered flicking their tails past her paddle. Last fall's dead leaves made brown and gold spots among the bright green feathers of waterweeds on the bottom. Ahead were patches of sedge and an occasional ruddy new lilypad. Georgie had laid his paddle in the canoe behind him and held his rod tight between his knees while he fastened a leader on the line.

"Now watch me cast," he whispered in a strangled voice as he got to his feet. The reel sang as he pulled back his arms and shoulders in a slow swing to shoot the little artificial frog out into a slick of open water between the lilypads. The canoe gave a dangerous lurch. He balanced it cleverly with his hips and brought the frog slowly along the surface of the water in a series of tiny jerks. "We ought to have a real frog," he was muttering. "This damn thing's no good."

"Ladies present, Georgie," Lulie giggled softly. "I hate to see people fish with live frogs, it hurts them so." She kept the canoe moving gently along the shore of the cove.

"I keep forgetting you're only a girl, Lulie."

"But they have five fingers on their little hands just like people."

"Sh-h. I think I saw something. Pickerel are smart. We'll never catch a pickerel if we don't keep quiet." The reel gave a sharp hum as he cast again.

"Well, who's making all the noise?"

Trailing her paddle in the water, Lulie lay back in the stern looking up at the clouds above the hemlock branches. A great cloud overhead looked like a castle, Morgan le Fay's castle. She began to think of Launcelot and Guenever and Joyous Gard and the fine print of the volume of Mallory she was reading. Lost in the dream she went on paddling gently, trying to move her shoulders to catch the lurch of the canoe each time Georgie cast.

"Yay I got a strike," Georgie yelled. At the same moment Lulie was in the water. It was icecold and her feet were sinking into the soft ooze. She stood up and grabbed for the canoe to right it.

"What the hell happened?" Georgie was spluttering. He was standing waistdeep in water with the line wound around his neck.

She burst out laughing. "Is he still on?" she yelled.

With dripping faces and the cold weeds and water weighing down their clothes they waded through the mud, pushing the swamped canoe between them. "Wait, my box of lures," whined Georgie.

"Georgie, I can't wait. I'm cold." She felt the cold mud squushing through her toes as she trudged towards the shore with her wet sweater under one arm. On a strip of sand they turned *Redwing* over to empty the water out. Lulie's tennis shoes and stockings were full of black mud. "Poor *Redwing*," she was saying through chattering teeth, "I just finished varnishing her."

"Oh, it'll wash off." Georgie growled. "I lost two trout flies."

"I'm frozen. Let's make tracks."

"We could make a fire and dry our clothes."

"Got any dry matches?"

Georgie gave her one of his angry glares, and shook his head. His forehead was all knotted up with frowns. "That cures me of going fishing with girls."

Paddling home they had the wind behind them. Georgie paddled in the stern and kept catching crabs and cursing as the drops spattered into the canoe and stung icily on Lulie's wet back. Of course Ben and Zeke had to be down on the float to watch them come in, both looking tall and blond and clean in white pants and turtlenecked sweaters. "Come on in the water's fine." They jeered at them. "One of these days you men will learn how to handle a rod from a canoe," Zeke had to say in his priggish collegeboy voice.

"Brother Ben." Lulie put on a little tremulous pleading

tone as Ben helped her out of the canoe. He was younger than she was but my his arm was strong. "Do you suppose you could be a tried and true knight errant and milk Blondine to-night?"

"But Sister Lucy I just changed my pants."

"We've had enough of that cow for one day. We spent all afternoon chasing her through the woods," said Zeke who was standing well away from them on the float to keep his clean pants from getting splattered. "And the flies about ate us up . . . Anyway, we got the orchard sprayed."

"And I missed the ballgame," said Ben dejectedly.

Lulie's teeth had started to chatter again. "I'm a drowned rat," she said looking down at the sopping dress that clung to her legs over a pool of muddy water oozing from her shoes. "How am I ever going to get my hair dry before the dance?"

Ben's blue eyes suddenly looked so sorry she thought he was going to cry. "I'll do it, Lou. I'll pull on some overalls."

"What you'd better do," said Zeke, in his loftiest elder brother tone, "is go on up to the house and get Aunt Lyde to give you a hot drink and put you to bed."

"Ben, put *Redwing* in the boathouse like a good feller . . . I'll take the paddles."

She started dragging her dripping feet up the path through the woods. She turned at the first big firtree and called back in bell-like tones like her aunt's, "Ben, put Georgie into some dry clothes. I'll fix up so's he can stay to supper."

She ran shivering up the roundabout path through the woods that came out in the pasture. She tore her wet dress on a bramble as she scrambled across the stone wall between the pasture and the orchard and came to the kitchen porch by the back way. On the step she pulled off her stockings and her oozy shoes. It was just her luck that they were all in the kitchen: Aunt Lyde and Grandmother Waring and Mrs. Willard in a lavender lace gown. As Lulie opened the screen door she saw Uncle Purdy, who must have come in on the afternoon boat, standing in the pantry doorway. There was a big kettle of strawberry syrup boiling on the range and the sink was full of jellyglasses. The clatter stopped and all their eyes converged on Lulie as she stepped in through the screen door trying to look, she was telling herself, *nonchalante.*

"Well I declare," cried Aunt Lyde. "You went and tipped over."

"We did ship a little water," said Lulie laughing to hide her shivers.

"Shipped the whole lake, I guess," roared Uncle Purdy. "Haven't you got a kiss for a hardworking old uncle just arrived from the grime of the city?"

Lulie ran over to him and gave him a peck on his big jowl. Uncle Purdy had a stuffy cigarsmoky smell she'd never liked.

She started for the hall.

"I thought Georgie was such a woodsman," Aunt Lyde was saying. "Isn't that boy good for anything?"

"It wasn't his fault, honest, it wasn't."

"Well, you ought to have been here, Lulie," said Mrs. Willard in her deep contralto. "Your grandmother has been teaching us how to make strawberry preserves."

"Aunt Lyde, I said you'd ask him to stay to supper."

"Well, we can't let him go home all wet and catch his death of cold. But I don't know what you and Ben see in that boy."

"We've been havin' us a time," cackled Grandmother Waring. (My she's cute, thought Lulie.) Grandmother Waring's cheeks were all rosy and her eyes sparkled. "It's a recipe mother saved when the old house burned at Sandy Ford. You put the fresh berries in syrup and ripen them under a pane of glass in the sun . . . Now you hurry along and get on some dry things, child, and your grandmother'll fix you some hot lemonade with honey. That's the best thing to ward off a cold. Purdy, you be a good boy and squeeze me out the juice of a lemon . . . I hate to see menfolks standin' idle."

Lulie was already walking upstairs on cold bare feet. It was cozy to get into her own room and lock the door. Pulling up the portcullis, she called it to herself. She tore off her wet clothes and put them in the washbasin. She rubbed her wet hair with a towel and jumped into the pink wadded robe her uncle and aunt had given her for Christmas. She stopped for a second to look at herself in the mirror. "You've got the funniest little tiny face," she whispered to herself, "and you won't have a curl on your head for the dance and you look pale as a worm."

She took her brush and comb and the worn green *Morte d'Arthur* into the bathroom with her. While the water ran in the tub she combed the ratsnests out of her hair as fast as she could. Then she got into the half filled tub and soaped herself and started reading. She forgot everything in the slow lilt of the prose. A sharp knock on the door was certainly Aunt Lyde's.

Lulie jumped out of the tub and still wet pulled on her robe and opened the door a crack. "Why Lulie, I thought you'd gone to sleep in the tub. Grandmother Waring's lemonade is on your dresser. It is probably cold by this time, but you must drink it so that she won't feel badly. If you come into my room I'll help you do your hair."

"Aunt Lyde, it's all stringy. I'll be a sight. I don't think I'll go."

"Too late to change your mind now," said Aunt Lyde. "Joe Newcomer's already here. I asked him to supper and you can walk down to the hotel together afterwards."

"Decent Respectable here already? Oh lord," groaned Lulie. "It'll take me hours to dress."

"He certainly is. He's the nicest boy."

When Lulie came out of the bathroom she tried to hide her book under her arm but Aunt Lyde spotted it. "Reading! I thought so. When I was a girl your age I always thought of my appearance first. I always slept for an hour before going to a ball just to let the muscles of my face relax. A woman can't start too young to take care of her appearance. You come into my room as soon as you have your petticoat on. I'll curl your bangs for you."

Lulie submitted humbly to everything, sitting meek at the dressingtable, staring gloomily at her own little long pointed face in the mirror while Aunt Lyde heated the curling iron over the alcohol flame.

"I don't know what you children see in that Georgie," Aunt Lyde was saying in her cool severe voice. "He's so unbalanced. Lulie, there are some people in this world who never have had anything and never will have anything. A girl has to learn early to associate only with the right kind of men. To tell the truth most men are hogs rolling in the gutter with tobacco in their mouths." When Aunt Lyde said that, Lulie couldn't help thinking of Uncle Purdy and wondering if that's who she meant.

"Ouch," she cried, "that tickles."

"If you just wouldn't toss your head around," said Aunt Lyde.

Lulie was beginning to sniff the excitement of the dance to come in the smell of her own hair scorching a little under the curling iron. Her heart had started to beat fast.

"Of course I think the world of Decent Respectable," she tried to explain. "He's a college sophomore too, but he isn't half as stuck up as Zeke is. It's awful sweet of him to take a little girl like me to the dance instead of one of the willowy Willards."

"I declare, child, how you do go on. Esther Willard's one of my oldest friends."

"Of course I just love Hortense and Hildegarde but they have gotten awful willowy this summer . . . it's those new dresses they brought back from New York."

"I haven't the slightest idea what you mean."

"Grandmother Waring likes Georgie . . . She says he's the ugly duckling."

"Your grandmother, child, is a very tolerant person." Aunt Lyde gave Lulie's curls a last pat with a long cool hand. "Now you get into your pretty green dress as fast as you can and don't try to pull it over your head and get your hair all mussed up . . . I'll start them into supper because I know your Uncle Purdy is starved."

Lulie came down the stairs on tiptoe. She was dreadfully late; they'd be half through supper. They were eating at the long mission table out on the porch. She could hear their chattering and munching. She waited a second behind the flowered chintz portière in the diningroom for a chance to sneak into her seat without being noticed. Mrs. Alexander's Ella, a tall, bony pale girl who came up to help Aunt Lyde Saturday nights, blundered past through the french window clattering a tray of empty soupplates. "Better hurry. The chicken'll be all eaten," she hissed in Lulie's ear as she passed.

Still Lulie lingered behind the portière listening with a feeling of dread to Uncle Purdy holding forth about the income tax . . . "Once we allow the government to pry into every man's private business . . . the power to tax is the power to destroy . . ." and to the clink of knives and forks and the tense constricted silence of the young people trying to sit still in their chairs. She was wondering how she was ever going to abide sitting through supper. When she finally ducked past the curtain it had to be Zeke who caught sight of her and piped up, "The late Miss Harrington."

As she slipped into the empty chair beside him she grinned up at Decent Respectable who was gazing towards Uncle Purdy's end of the table with a politely attentive look on his face. He started to get to his feet but she stopped him with a yank on his arm. Good Lord, Decent Respectable had on a tuxedo. They all looked stiff as ramrods. Her brothers had on their white flannels and blue coats, and Georgie looked miserable stuffed into Ben's secondbest gray suit that was much too narrow for him. She took her napkin out of its birchbark ring and tried to look as if she'd been there all the time. Aunt Lyde addressed her in low, pained tones under the boom of Uncle Purdy's voice; Ella would bring a plate of soup if she wanted it; but Lulie was too excited to eat. She shook her head and made a little stabbing motion towards a chicken wing on the big platter in the middle of the table.

"Why Joe Newcomer. Aren't you the man of the world? . . . I surely am flattered," she got her courage up to whisper to Decent Respectable.

"Jay was wearing his, so I reckoned I'd better wear mine," he whispered back.

"Who's Jay?"

"Jay Pignatelli. He's a foreigner almost. He's my roommate. You'll meet him."

"Is he decent and respectable too?" Lulie stifled a laugh when she caught a quelling glance from Aunt Lyde. She took a gulp of iced tea that immediately made her stomach ache and settled back to listen to the grownups.

"We never paid the federal government much mind in my day," Grandmother Waring was saying. "Poor Benjamin, he was a rebel through and through. He always said the country would go to the demnition bowwows under the Republicans."

"In the opinion of some eminent jurists this process began with George Washington's first administration."

"But it never quite gets there," said Mrs. Willard letting loose her rolling contralto laugh. "Now does it Purdy?"

People took an endless time to eat the strawberry shortcake. Uncle Purdy kept sending his plate down for more. Lulie's face was beginning to stiffen with boredom. She didn't have enough spirit left to answer a whispered crack from Ben. She felt her eyes getting glazed. She had tried to make herself feel better by looking out over the lake where a sail flashed rosy yellow in the level sunset light. When at last Aunt Lyde began to push back her chair Lulie thought for a second she was too paralyzed to move but suddenly she had Decent Respectable out of the house and they were scampering down the grassy slope towards the road. She was jumping and hopping though it was awkward running in her silver dancing slippers.

"I often wonder," he was saying in his thoughtful tone, "if I'll be as fond of the sound of my own voice when I'm fat and fifty."

"Why, Decent Respectable, you'll be awful. You'll probably be a judge."

"What about you, Lou?"

"Not me," she shook her curls as she ran. "I'd hate to be grown up."

As they stepped over a fallen rail in the fence Lulie smelt a stale smell of smoky lamps and out from behind a bush stepped a snakeyeyed young man with straight black hair. He wasn't looking at her. "Where's the other feller?" he asked abruptly with his eyes on some point way off beyond.

"They'll be along in a minute."

The young man stepped back behind the bush.

"Who's that, Lou?"

"Why, don't you know our shortstop? That's Joe Sawbuck waiting for Georgie and Ben." She let out a hoot of laughter. "He follows them around all the time. I guess he's half Indian, but he never even says 'ugh.' "

She tucked her hand under Joe Newcomer's arm as they walked up the broad wooden steps of the hotel porch. It was a help to have Joe with her when they ran the gantlet of the eyes of the old hens in the rockingchairs she always thought of as the hostiles. Lulie's legs felt made of wood as they walked towards the central entrance into the lobby. The way they looked at her Lulie was sure her petticoat must be showing. Or maybe it was a run in her stocking. Fred Dukes, the clerk at the desk, smiled a sad damned smile at them as they passed. He wouldn't be going to the dance, he was on duty. In the teagarden beyond the lobby they found the friendly faces of the younger crowd all rosy under the Japanese lanterns. Hortense Willard, looking tall and smooth and selfpossessed in nile green, was already waltzing with a strange young man with a mustache. Zeke was just arriving at the other end of the room with a pale proud look on his face because he had Hildegarde on his arm. Lulie knew what he was thinking: his little sister was going to disgrace him by raising cain or something. She was the youngest girl there and she felt that her green tulle dress had a homemade look beside the grownup evening gowns the Willard girls wore. Zeke was probably ashamed of her and wished she hadn't come. No, she was telling herself, she wouldn't get the giggles and act like a hoyden. At the edge of the dancefloor she had just for a moment that feeling of being all elbows and knees, but as soon as they started to dance she began to enjoy herself. My, Joe's dancing had improved since last summer. He must have been taking dancing lessons all winter. She let herself go, as they glided around to a waltz from *The Chocolate Soldier,* into an affectionate quiet feeling she had about Joe, like she had about her brother Ben and about Zeke when he didn't make her mad by being so uppety. She let her head droop on one side and halfclosed her eyes as she danced the way the Willard girls did.

As she waltzed with Joe she watched the faces of the boys and girls she knew drifting blissfully past and the paper lanterns and the potted palms and the grim expressions of the hostiles looking on from the chairs along the wall. There was one pink and green lantern she liked particularly; she wished she had a dress with a pattern like that. Why there with his gray mustache bristling was Mr. Willard out on the floor with Mrs. Willard, and Aunt Lyde and Uncle Purdy. The musicians looked sweaty and earnest, the lame man who lugubriously stroked the cello and the little Italian from the South End of Chicago who sawed on the violin and doubled as night clerk and Miss Potter the dancing teacher moving plump arms over the keyboard of the piano with her blue sateen bottom sticking out over the piano stool. Occasionally she caught a glimpse of the new young man with the mustache and of a longnecked piefaced boy with glasses. She hoped the one with the mustache was Jay Pignatelli but she didn't quite like to ask Joe.

When the waltz stopped they were right next to the dais the musicians sat on. Lulie and Joe clapped and smiled and nodded Good Evening and Miss Potter gave them a reluctant sort of a wink as they walked past.

"Poor Miss Potter," giggled Lulie up towards Joe's ear, "she hates popular music. She'd be playing us the 'Moonlight Sonata' if she had her way."

"And making us dance to it in cheesecloth," said Joe.

They went out on the porch to look at the lake all shining orange and the forested hills purple in the last afterglow. Joe excused himself for a moment and left her looking out over the familiar conformation of the lake and the hills that suddenly looked strange and scary like a picture of some foreign place. Right away he was back with his roommate. Of course it wasn't the one with the mustache. It was the one with the glasses. He was nervous and his adam's apple stuck out and he spoke English with an accent. He asked her to dance and she couldn't say no because he was Decent Respectable's roommate.

"I dance pretty badly . . . I hope you don't mind."

"Well the worst we can do is to stumble over each other's feet," Lulie piped up cheerfully. "I'm really too young to be at a Saturday night dance anyway. I'm only here on suffrance."

"Me too," said Jay Pignatelli in a vague sort of way.

Miss Potter had started pounding out a twostep, the violin and cello chimed in in a hurry. Pignatelli made a false start but finally he got his long legs waggling haltingly in time to the music and Lulie was able to follow him around the floor. She didn't like the twostep much anyway. He was perspiring profusely.

"Joe says you like canoeing," he stammered. "Sorry."

"Yes. Don't you?"

"Gosh yes," he said eagerly. He went blundering on. "And you read the *Morte d'Arthur* and you don't like Tennyson?"

"Don't you?"

"Gosh yes . . . I m-m-mean the *M-m-morte d'Arthur* . . . Oh Lord," he added when the music finally stopped and he was following her out onto the porch. "Now I suppose I've got to learn to dance. There are so many things I've got to learn. I've got a waiting list."

"So have I," said Lulie.

The afterglow had almost faded. Stars were beginning to prick their pinpoints through the robinsegg blue sky.

"It's like . . . like being inside a gigantic easteregg," spluttered Pignatelli. "In Europe," he added pronouncing the word like a Frenchman, "they have eastereggs with little scenes inside."

"My father told me once about a religious sect that believes we live on the inside of the globe instead of on the outside." The idea made her feel quite crawly down the spine when she said it.

"Most ingenious," said Pignatelli. This time he sounded like an Englishman instead of a Frenchman.

She looked up at him with her mouth a little open to show her pretty pearly teeth. "Is that your religion?"

He looked quite uncomfortable at the question. He shuffled his feet. "Your father . . . Is he here?"

"No, he never comes." She brushed the subject aside. It was her turn to look uncomfortable. "When he retired he gave his library to the university and now he has to live there because he can't live without it."

"I tried to read a book of his and I couldn't understand a word of it, honestly not a single word. That's how good it was . . . I've got to learn some sociology but I never get time. I'm trying to get through college in three years."

"Why?"

"I got to get through lawschool."

"When I get to college I'm going to stay there for years and years."

"Lord, I wouldn't want to do that."

They couldn't seem to find anything more to say. They

stood there staring out over the darkening lake at a great nasturtiumcolored planet that blazed in the west. Lulie began
darting glances up and down the porch. It was about time
one of the boys turned up to ask her for the next dance, but
they were all in a swarm round the Willard girls down near the
main entrance.

"Do you suppose — er," Pignatelli began timidly, "you
could stand another dance?"

Miss Potter had run one of her preliminary trills. Then she
was off. It was *The Pink Lady* waltz. They were playing it too
fast. Lulie gave her head a cheerful little toss. "I can stand it
if you can," she gave one of her little hoots of laughter.

"The trouble is," whispered Pignatelli as he clumsily
grabbed her hand, "that all I know how to do is go round and
round."

Billy the colored bellboy, who, Lulie was explaining was
the only one of the help who wore a uniform, because most of
them were collegeboys who played on the ballteam, was shaking powdered wax on the floor out of a can. They followed
him whirling as they went. As they passed a window Lulie
caught sight of Georgie and Ben making jeering faces at her.
She and Pignatelli spun and spun. Next time they passed the
window Georgie and Ben were whirling too in exaggerated
solitaire waltzsteps. They clamped their fingers to their noses
in a clothespin gesture.

"What do we do," asked Lulie beginning to get the giggles
for fair, "when we get dizzy?"

"We reverse," gasped Pignatelli, "but I've forgotten how."

He went into reverse but too suddenly and they ran smack
into another couple. Fortunately it was Decent Respectable
who was dancing with that goodnatured Johnson girl. They
all laughed.

"Honest, I'm awfully sorry," stammered Pignatelli.

"Have a heart, Jay . . . Miss Johnson, meet my roommate,
Jay Pignatelli, the whirlwind wizard of the waltz."

They stood in a circle laughing, while the other dancers gave them a wide berth. Lulie had never seen Joe being funny before. She was proud of him. It was Pignatelli's cue to ask Sue Johnson to dance so that Lulie could go back to Joe Newcomer and do some real dancing but he just stood there giggling foolishly. Fortunately Aunt Lyde and the rest of them had gone off to the progressive euchre tournament in the reading-room. Lulie gave a hasty glance past the windows but Ben and Georgie had disappeared too. Lucky or she'd never have heard the end of it. She saw Mrs. Judkins the manageress looking disapprovingly at her from the lobby end of the tearoom. The hostiles glared from the chairs around the wall.

"Joe, let's go down to Pringle's and have some icecream," said Lulie.

"Oh yes, please come," said Pignatelli. Joe said he and Miss Johnson would be along when they finished the dance.

"I hope you weren't hurt. I'm so darned awkward," said Pignatelli, in a concerned tone.

"I'm small, but solidly built," said Lulie.

As they walked down the hill towards the soft drink parlor she caught sight of skulking figures disappearing around the corner of the post office. She waved but they didn't wave back and hurried out of sight. As they passed under the light hung over the asphalt path she caught a glimpse of Georgie's scowling face. Georgie was carrying his shotgun. "It's my young brother Ben and Georgie Warner and our local redskin. Those boys are up to something."

There wasn't anybody else at Pringle's. Mr. Pringle, his haggard face drooping in a series of little muddy pouches, sat drowsing behind his tiny counter under an unshaded electric light bulb round which pale millermoths ceaselessly danced. Lulie asked Mr. Pringle if he could make them banana splits and he mumbled something they couldn't understand. They sat there looking at the magazine covers with their garish lettering along the rack in front of the counter, listening to the zizzing of night insects outside the screen doors. Pignatelli seemed to have lost his tongue again. Lulie sat there working her toes inside her dancing shoes wishing she were back on the dance floor with Joe Newcomer or any boy who knew how to dance. If only people would just dance at dances. Hours seemed to go by and still Mr. Pringle didn't bring the icecream.

"Do you smoke?" she asked suddenly.

"No, do you?"

She gave a little hoot of laughter. "Aunt Lyde would be horrified even at the question. She doesn't like Uncle Purdy to smoke in the house. She says the smoke gets into the curtains. He claims it keeps out moths."

Mr. Pringle was standing over them with two plates of icecream. "No more bananas," he said in his hoarse dejected voice. They ate the icecream up like winking and started back up the hill towards the Hiawatha House. Right where the asphalt path branched off from the village street four figures with handkerchiefs tied over their noses and hats pulled down crowded out of the bushes round them. Georgie came down the middle of the path with his shotgun pointed at their feet. "The Tribe," Georgie's voice seemed to come from his boots, "doesn't allow its women to consort with foreigners."

"Georgie, don't point that gun at me."

"The elders have sat in council. The elders are very angry."

Lulie was beginning to get mad.

"Quit that, Georgie." She glanced up at Pignatelli's face to see how he was taking it. He had an odd aloof interested expression. "Georgie, take off that handkerchief and meet Jay Pignatelli, Decent Respectable's roommate."

They none of them answered.

"Dance," said Georgie pointing his shotgun down at Pignatelli's feet and jiggling his finger on the trigger.

"Shall we dance?" asked Pignatelli in his most English accent, bowing elaborately in Lulie's direction. He pulled her arm way out and spun her around in a couple of waltz steps.

Lulie yanked herself loose and ran up to Georgie and flicked the handkerchief off his face. She'd expected to find him laughing but his face was serious as a thundercloud.

Piggy Johnson was giggling under his handkerchief. "We've been shooting bats," he started to explain, "behind the Alexanders' barn. My, they are hard to hit. Georgie hit two."

"Foweign paleface all dwessed up better dance quick," said Georgie starting to fake an English accent and then dropping it. "Pick up your dogs or I'll shoot you in the foot."

"Miss Harrington, I'm a stranger here. What is the etiquette of this occasion?" asked Pignatelli.

Lulie was really mad now. She could feel the fire in her cheeks. She stepped up to Georgie. "Put up that shotgun and make sure it's on safety . . . If you don't put up that shotgun Georgie Warner, you're going to blow up and burst. You are beginning to swell up right now. You'll split at the seams and burst."

"No I'm not," said Georgie slipping the shotgun into the crook of his arm as he raised his free hand to feel his face. "I feel all right."

"It probably wasn't loaded anyway," said Pignatelli.

"Who's the damned foreigner who says it isn't loaded? I'll show you. Want me to shoot out that light?"

Georgie aimed at the bare bulb that hung out on an arm from the telephone pole overhead.

"Georgie, don't be silly."

He fired. A pink tongue of flame came out from the muzzle of the shotgun. The bulb popped and tinkled down in pieces onto the asphalt path.

They all stood staring at each other in the dark.

"And what's all this about, I'd like to know." The stocky figure hobbling down the path towards them on a cane was Pat McCarran, the hotel watchman. Lulie ran up to him. "Mr. McCarran, it's just one of the boys showing off. He tried to show us how he could hit a bat and shot out the light instead. We'll replace it Monday morning, honest we will."

"I've a great mind to call the sheriff. Mrs. Judkins don't allow no vandalism on the hotel grounds."

"Oh, Mr. McCarran, he's probably playing progressive

euchre up at the hotel. You know how Mr. Swazie loves his euchre. Honest, it won't happen again. Mr. McCarran, meet Mr. Pignatelli, Joe Newcomer's roommate at college. He was brought up in Europe. He was just asking about you. Somebody told him you had had some interesting experiences with the Sinn Fein."

"Did he now?"

Lulie gave a quick glance around. The boys had faded into the dark.

"Like every patriotic man in Ireland," said Pat McCarran walking between them as they started strolling up the path towards the hotel. "I'm an exile from her blessed shores. The bloody English . . ."

When at last they got away from Green Erin's wrongs and up on the porch again Miss Potter and her assistants were starting on *The Merry Widow*. Joe Newcomer met them in the entranceway.

"My, that was a long icecream," he said.

"Mr. Pringle's slow as cold molasses," chirped Lulie, "and he's run out of bananas."

"If you don't mind Jay, this is my waltz . . ." Joe took Lulie's hand. "Well, how did you make out with him? He's an odd fish, isn't he?" he asked as they slipped off in an easy glide over the wellwaxed floor.

"He's very much the gentleman. As Aunt Lyde would say, every evidence of wealth."

"He's a pretty good feller when you get to know him. The guys can't make him out. They think he's stuck up but he's one of the most modest fellows I ever met."

Lulie let out one of her little hoots of laughter. "I know who he is. He's Don Modesto."

"Who is?"

"He is. You know, Joe, there was Don Quixote and now there is Don Modesto."

The music had stopped. Lulie and Joe stood side by side clapping as hard as they could. All the couples around them were clapping for an encore. Behind them two boys were already arguing about who was having the next dance with Hortense Willard. Lulie let her eyes run round the flushed faces and the bright eyes under the Japanese lanterns. At the door of the teagarden she caught sight of Aunt Lyde's head of haughty white hair. For an instant Lulie tried to pretend she hadn't seen her, but Aunt Lyde had given her chin a little determined toss that could mean only one thing.

Lulie put her hand on Joe Newcomer's sleeve. "Decent Respectable," she said, "you were an angel to bring me but little Cinderella's got to go now."

"Can't I take you home, Lulie?"

"Don't be silly. You stay here and finish out the dance with the willowy Willards."

"But the proper thing," he said in his deep solemn voice, "is for me to take you home."

"Let's be improper." As the music struck up again she slipped away from him and slid through the dancing boys and girls toward the door. The euchre tournament must have been getting down to a few tables because the lobby was full of older people. Uncle Purdy was helping Aunt Lyde into her wrap. As Lulie ran past them she pointed up the hill with her hand. On the path through the firs her feet began to drag a little as the *Merry Widow* waltz faded into the silence and the lights of the hotel were blotted out behind the trees.

Ben was sitting in the living room with his feet drawn up under him in an overstuffed chair reading the *Saturday Evening Post*, with an expression of angelic innocence on his face.

"You'd better take your feet off that new chaircover before Aunt Lyde comes up and catches you."

"Lou," he began in a pleading voice without looking up from his magazine.

"And I never want to speak to you again as long as I live," Lulie said, and tried to make her petticoat rustle like Aunt Lyde's did as she swept up the stairs to her own room.

3

IMPUTATION OF LACHES

READING LAW in the rackety Cambridge roominghouse the men called Mooney's Pleasure Palace, in the attic room with sagging wallpaper stale and pitted as the trodden yellow snow in the Cambridge streets, or in the breathedout air of the library, or over sour coffee and cornflakes in the onearm lunch, Jay kept having the same attentive expectant almost apprehensive feeling he used to have waiting in the lobby of Dandy's lawoffice in the old Merchant's Building, where the electricity was always on in the brass chandelier to cast a dusty yellow light on the lawbooks in scuffed calf that crowded the walls to the ceiling and Jay would try not to look at the half-length oil painting of his father in a gray bowler hat with yellow gloves in his hand and a suggestion of horses and hunting fields in the distance that hung in a gold frame over the reception desk lighted by its own horizontal tinshaded bulb. The mustache was so truculently glossy, the eyes were so truculently bright that it embarrassed him to look at them. It was the wop look, guess he had it too, he told himself bitterly. His back to the portrait he would sit with tense muscles on the edge of a chair leafing through dogeared dictionaries of legal terms piled on the mahogany table in the center, lifting his eyes from time to time to look at the groundglass door blue with daylight in the opposite wall where the small gilt letters read: James Knox Polk Pignatelli.

Jay could forget himself in any page of print: as his eyes focused through the thick glasses on the letters hurrying in single file across the page to make up words and sentences the feeling that he wasn't doing as much as he ought to be doing would drain away. Voices inside his head would start to talk back at the things the book said. His solitude would be peopled . . . *Abstract . . . Animo Jurandi . . . Bastardy . . : Bastardus nullius est filius aut filius populi* (but I'm Dandy's son. You can legitimize a bastard. Bastardy's no bar in America). *Common Law* (that's what I have to soak up. Dandy says a young man's mind soaks up the law like a sponge) . . . *Confidence Game . . . Felonious intent . . . Felony . . . Laches: the rootmeaning of which is laxness, negligence, neglect . . . consists in not doing something which a party might do or be reasonably expected to do . . . It does not rise to the dignity of estoppel* (that's death) *while time is an element it moves independently of limitations . . . Ladder: in using it one stands erect or practically so facing the structure and takes hold of the rungs or cleats or side pieces in order to keep his balance and goes up hand over hand* (Dandy says there is always room at the top) *. . . Larceny . . . Misdemeanor . . . Riot . . .* That was the year "The Girl on the Saskatchewan" kept running through his head.

> *Flow river flow*
> *Down to the sea.*

. . . Out of a summer of pretty girls. Joe Newcomer's friend, the one with green in her eyes and a pretty pert quick toss like a bird with her curls, or the sullen redhead with such a pale skin on the steamboat through the Rideau Canal, or the blueeyed Irish one with big breasts and a tinily twisted smile at the party on the South Side where they all turned out to be gaely gaels and the Irish poet with ducktails over his ears strutted up and down the room playing the bagpipes; and she'd danced an Irish jig; and he'd taken her home in a taxicab and found he didn't have enough change to pay the fare; and she'd run off into the house laughing; and he'd had to ride the taxi to a drugstore to call Ed Dirks who always had money and run up seven dollars and fifty cents driving out to Oak Park to get bailed out . . . When the little steamboat pulled into the wharf at Ottawa after they spent all day together watching the kingfishers dart into the swaying reeds and the blue pickerel weed so much darker than the sky and the bobbing lilypads and turtles scrambling off logs in the steamboat's wash. At Ottawa it was all over; they heard the hawsers squeak as the steamboat was made fast and the jingle of the gangplank's winches. He'd tried to make a speech about how he wanted to know her always but she was already waving at her family on the wharf and they'd swept her off in a car before he had time to ask for her address. Lord and he'd made a fool of himself with Joe Newcomer's friend. She'd been so cute and crazy and he waltzed like an oaf and stepped on her pretty little silver slippers and been such an ass with those illmannered kids . . . He ought to have socked that big lout in the jaw . . . What is the etiquette of this occasion? *Laches: the omission of something which a party might do, or might reasonably be expected to do . . .* (convicted of Laches, suffering under the imputation of Laches, pleading Laches doesn't make sense). *Legal residence . . . His legal residence for the purposes already indicated may be ideal, but his actual residence must be substantial. He may not actually abide at his legal residence at all but his actual residence must be his abiding place.* (Mooney's Pleasure Palace on Linden Street in the Cambridge sleet is far from ideal for the purposes already indicated: Procedure, Contracts, Liability and Torts and the whimsical little man on Cases on Criminal Law) . . . *A want of activity or diligence in making a claim or moving for the enforcement of a right, particularly in equity, which will afford ground for presuming against it and for refusing relief . . .*

"Hard at it Jay?" Old blueeyed Bill Keezer with his wheezy

breathing and his mustache of a pipestained viking is standing over him. "Boss'll see you now. I bet he likes to see you study . . . None of the other Pignatellis ever did . . . A chip of the old block if you ask me."

Bill Keezer's stooping figure leads the way through the ground glass door.

Dandy's office is full of sharp steel light from three windows. Light gleams on Dandy's glasses and on the bulge of his bald head and on the silver inkwell and on the red white and blue stones of the ring that glistens on the veined hand across the papers on the walnut desk.

Jay roams uneasily around listening to the noise of traffic from the street and the little hiss of the air through the screen and the light scratching of his father's pen filling the margins of the typewritten brief with notes in blue ink in a fine slanting hand.

"Rest perturbed spirit. I know it's hard for you to sit still," Dandy says without looking up. Jay reaches for a pamphlet off the corner of the desk and lets himself drop into a chair, while his eyes greedily seek out the lines of print. It's the lawschool catalogue; he turns to first year: Procedure, Contracts, Liability and Torts. Now Dandy's looking at him across the desk with his pincenez in his hand. There's tired wrinkled skin under his eyes. The lines from the corners of his nose to the curve of his mustache have deepened. As if he knew Jay's thoughts he sets his glasses down before him and gives the points of his mustache an upward twirl against his thumbs.

"When I was a boy Jay, you didn't go to lawschool to get your head stuffed. Judge Thatcher paid me two dollars a week and I swept out the office and emptied the scrapbaskets and copied briefs and carried messages up and down Fourth Street. When I had a spare moment I read law. He was a good lawyer and a good man. It always seemed that when I hit something particularly difficult he was there looking over my shoulder ready to explain it. We were all for the treatise system in those days.

You'll study by cases which is more practical but you'll have to make up your own theory as you go along."

. . . Procedure, Contracts, Liability and Torts. Sitting solitary in Mooney's Pleasure Palace Jay's ears tingle with Dandy's voice three months ago.

There he is sitting in front of the walnut desk in the Merchant's Building, trying to keep down the fidgets.

"Bill Keezer says you always read while you wait. That's right Jay never go out without a book in your pocket. The secret of a wellstored mind is never to waste time. As you get older you'll find you have less and less time for things you want to do. As ambition, and I trust and hope you are ambitious, sets you harder and harder tasks you will find that you can spare money better than you can spare time . . . You are going to have to make your own money, Jay. You are fortunate to have been brought up in an expanding America in an age when a young man with ambition can carve himself any niche he wants. You are getting an easier start than I had. I hope you'll go further. I've made money, plenty of it. and I've spent it freely . . . too freely perhaps. Spending money well and cheerfully is one of the magnificent amusements but it's only one of them. I'd rank swimming and walking in the country and horseback riding and fishing higher. When I say not to waste time I don't mean not to get all the fun and pleasure you can out of life. A walk down country lanes, a good day's fishing gives you a chance to cogitate on what you've read. Money's a secondary thing. You'll find ways of making money as I have but I hope you won't spend it as fast as I have." Dandy's laugh sounds youthful and fresh, full of wop insolence like the portrait. "George Miller, who later was my lawpartner — my he had a fine baritone voice; we used to sing duets — he used to say to me, 'Jim, your fees are twice as big as mine and you have twice as many cases but every year's end finds you in the red and finds me in the black. I'll die a rich man and you'll die a poor man.' Poor old George was right; he died a right rich man and his widow and daughters frittered it away. Poor George he never had much fun. At least I'll die with a wellgarnished mind. Jay I have two or three important cases pending. If I carry them through to a successful conclusion I'll pay off my debts and make some careful investments and retire to devote my time to a treatise I am writing on a model corporation so organized that every man in it, from the janitor to the chairman of the board of directors, will receive a just reward for his work. There is too much inequality in this country. A man should be recompensed in proportion to the work he puts into an enterprise. Mutual ownership instead of fixed wages. Sharing the profits will put an end to the war between the working man and the managing man that is tearing our society apart. The American corporation Jay is a magnificent instrument for a democratic society but it's been wrongly used."

Jay's eyes were already following the flight of a swallow across the Chicago sky.

. . . In the room on Linden Street in the Cambridge sleet under the sagging wallpaper Jay's mind had wandered back to that winter's eternal argument about Caesar and Napoleon, with Fred Wallace who was a German scholar and knew Gothic and had a bust of Napoleon on his bookcase that Jay used to like to make paper hats for. "If Napoleon had succeeded Europe would have been spared this present war and civilization would have gone ahead . . . immeasurably," Fred had insisted in his dry dogmatic voice.

"But Caesar did succeed."

"What's any of that got to do with making a success of the law in America in 1914?" Lawrence Raisen would ask in his gentle wheedling way. He loves it though, Jay would be thinking; Larry loves the idea of being a member of a group of serious thinkers.

"America is a half baked country. We still think we can beat the game. We are incorrigible empiricists," Fred would say in that heavy German manner Jay to tease him used to say he'd picked up from the study of Gothic.

And all the time through Jay's head was pouring

Flow river flow
Down to the sea

and some times the girl on the Saskatchewan looked like the Irish girl and sometimes like the redhead on the boat and sometimes like Joe Newcomer's girl and sometimes like all of them put together . . . *Laches does not rise to the dignity of estoppel, while time is an element it moves independently of limitations.*

Cambridge voices were moving along the sidewalk under his window accompanied by the sound of feet slushing in arctics through the sludgy snow.

"If a dog had an idea of God would it be a greater dog?"

"That's metaphysics . . . practically man is dog's god."

Again Jay was remembering himself sitting there full of the fidgets in front of Dandy's walnut desk with the light streaming into his face from the bright windows in the Merchants' Building. The swallow had gone.

"Well Jay tomorrow you start for the lawschool. I'd hoped we might dine and spend a last evening together but I have been unable to obtain a postponement and shall have to work late tonight. People in this country have no deference for age Jay. They think of me as an old man when actually I feel younger than I did five years ago. You have to be able to mix it up with the youngsters in the same old rough and tumble." For the first time in his life Jay saw anxiety in the tired skin under Dandy's eyes. The insolent laugh belied it. It was the man of the portrait again, with the bowler hat and yellow gloves. "They haven't put me down yet Jay. Failure is a word I have never admitted to my vocabulary." (What could Jay say? How could Jay help?)

"Here you'll need some money." Dandy changes the subject abruptly. His blueveined hands are counting out the crisp new orangebacked hundred dollar bills. "You'll have to open a bank account when you get there. Be careful of your money Jay. Until I pay off my debts, remember that any money you get from me may be the last. When you start to make you can start to spend."

(And all the time Jay is trying to force his lips to say: Dandy suppose I stay? Suppose I go to work for you in the office? Would it help?)

Dandy had roared at him impatiently. "What are you waiting for Jay? I've got work to do and you'd look silly if you missed your train." His gray hawkeyes had swooped over the papers on the desk. Before Jay was out of the office the light scratching of the pen on the margins of the brief had begun again. All the way to Boston on the jouncing pullman he had kept thinking of things he should have said. . . .

Jay jumped to his feet. His head ached from close reading, his legs were cramped up from being coiled under the table; he was hungry. At the foot of the stairs on the cracked mirror on which someone had pasted a card advertising FELIX TONSORIAL ARTIST he found a familiar envelope with his name in Dandy's small confident hand staring off it like a snapshot. Munching an egg sandwich in the onearmed lunch he read the cadenced eighteenth century sentences:

> *In our last interview I noticed, or fancied I noticed a certain hesitancy and indecision of speech which might tend to give strangers a false impression of your character and abilities and which you will, I trust, strive to overcome . . .*

"As ambition sets you harder and harder tasks," he heard the ring of Dandy's voice clear in his ears as if he were sitting beside him, the voice of the glossy portrait with bowler hat and yellow gloves he hadn't dared look back at as he left the office in the Merchants' Building.

> *. . . You are reaching the time of life when you must start consciously to organize your powers. God grant I may be at your side for a few more years with the counsel necessary to launch you on a great career. Si jeunesse savait, si viellesse pouvait!*

Jay felt himself blushing when he read the postscript:

> *Speaking of jeunesse, and knowing you are your father's son, I had intended to warn you of the precautions you must take if you have to do with ladies of the evening and to express the fer-*

vent prayer that you will manage to avoid them. Social diseases
are said to be rather prevalent in Boston.

If he only knew the prevalence of laches, Jay was saying to himself; but already he was dreaming over the empty plate and the weak rank coffee of the redhaired Irish girl on the Saskatchewan with the cute way of cocking her head to one side and looking you straight in the eye to the tune of "Flow river flow." The summer of pretty girls already long ago made nugatory by the omission of something a party might do, or might reasonably be expected to do consciously to organize your powers . . . The classroom words, the indigestion of classroom words. The longago lost girl. He tried to remember what she looked like. Which? He couldn't even remember what Petite Mère looked like. He felt dizzy with the immenseness of the solitude about him. You go back to your room and work, he told himself sternly as he swallowed the last of the egg sandwich and got to his feet. The girl behind the cashregister was redheaded but pimply. As the quarter and dime warm from his pocket rode towards her on the punched check across the glass counter his nostrils noted a tired smell of armpits and stale clothing. Just for an instant a query rose to the surface of her eyes behind their glasses. You? But suppose he'd guessed wrong. He had thirty pages left to read. He looked away. "Thanks, good night," he said and blushing walked off home. As ambition sets you harder and harder tasks . . . Even Caesar fidgeted, while he waited to cross the shallow stream.

Jay had forgotten his overshoes. His toes squdged in icewater as he waded back through soft slush to his roominghouse.

Prolegomena Concluded

EZEKIEL HARRINGTON
1 8 5 0 — 1 9 1 9

Ezekiel Harrington came from a family of dissenting ministers established since the time of the Revolution in the Shenandoah Valley. His father, who was also named Ezekiel, had graduated from the theological seminary a Methodist and accepted a call to a church in Fredericksburg where he had married a relative of Bishop Madison's of William and Mary. Whether it was the broadening influence of the astronomer bishop's republican episcopalianism or the writings of William Ellery Channing or his own observation of the peculiar institution on his very doorstep, the Reverend Harrington became during the years of national debate that followed the Dred Scott decision not only an abolitionist but a fervent Unitarian. While young Ezekiel was still in dresses and the girls were tiny squalling things in cradles and cribs he moved from Fredericksburg, where he was finding himself more and more estranged from a large part of his congregation, to accept the pulpit of a small Unitarian church in Washington City. There during the years of dust and crowding and troops and muletrains, amid the alarms and anxieties of the irrepressible conflict, young Ezekiel went to grammar school.

As a boy of thirteen he bore arms for the first and only time in his life. The family homestead near Front Royal had been burned in a Northern raid and not many months after emancipation, one rainy summer night, his father received word that the family Negroes to the number of sixteen with their wives and children had come trooping hungry and penniless into the District to get help from the Harringtons. The Reverend Harrington had for sometime been planning to settle them on some land near Willow Springs in Ohio set apart for that purpose by Northern friends. The only way to get them to Ohio was by the B. and O. Railroad from Baltimore. Ezekiel begged his father to let him go along on the expedition. His father consented but with frowning face produced four pistols, showed the boy how to load them and placed one pair in the pockets of his great coat. "We'll fire only in the last extremity," he said. They reached Baltimore safely with their pathetic troop of trembling Negroes. At the depot the omnibus driver refused to take the Negroes, so that they were forced to walk the whole distance in the noonday heat carrying on their shoulders their old hair trunks and patched carpetbags and bundles of ragged shawls. Ezekiel never forgot the heat or the smell of the open sewers that ran down the middle of the cobbled streets. His father led the way and Ezekiel took up the rear. There was something about the frightened but jubilant faces of the Negroes that attracted the attention of passersby. They began to be trailed by a threatening gang of toughs and loafers. "These damned abolitionists brought on the war," Ezekiel heard one man mutter to another. When they reached the B. and O. Railroad they found they had three hours to wait for the train. The railroad officials refused to let the Negroes inside the station. The mob of rough white men around them became more and more threatening, boys began to pick up stones. Ezekiel's father climbed on a barrel and addressed the mob in his booming preacher's voice. "These are my family's servants," he said. "I am conducting them to a place of safety. Molest them at your peril." Ezekiel's father was a tall man with long white hair and a prophet's beard. It was either the determined yet benign expression of his face and the haughty carriage of his head or else the butts of the pistols protruding from his pockets that held the mob at bay until the ticket agent, to avoid a riot, let the Negroes board the cars. Even after the train had started they were not safe. Whenever the cars stopped through the endless afternoon and night, Ezekiel with his pistols loaded and cocked had to keep watch on one platform of the coach and his father on the other. At last at a siding in the mountains in the early dawn word went round among the Negroes huddled over their sleeping children that they had crossed the Maryland state line. They burst out in hymnsinging and hallelujahs.

His father rose from his seat, stretched and yawned and put away the pistols in a haversack. "We are safe now," he said. "We are in the free states . . . Son you behaved well under the ordeal. Had I known we should be in such danger I would not have brought you along." The lines round his eyes all at once crinkled with smiles. "I fear I was somewhat less than truthful with those sons of Belial," he drawled. "I said they were slaves, which was true; but had I told the whole truth, that they would soon go free, we might not have escaped with our lives . . . If it strains our faith in the brotherhood of man," he went on in his resounding preacher's vein, "we must not forget that in that terrible moment outside the depot something stayed their hand. Though their hearts be as black as these poor Negroes' skins, our Father's spirit stirred in them and allowed us to proceed to board the cars. In Ohio we will be safe and the Negroes will go free."

After Mr. Lincoln's assassination the atmosphere of Washington became distasteful to the Reverend Harrington and he was glad to move north when he was invited to a church in Roxbury near Boston. There he placed his son in the Latin School. By this time Ezekiel was a tall blond solitary youth, somewhat the romantic Southern rebel among the downright Massachusetts Yankees. His father was discovering that he had as little in common with the Northern Radicals of reconstruction days as with the faction in his old church back in Fredericksburg that had wanted him to prove by the Bible that slavery was ordained of God. Ezekiel was the only son. The other children were a swarm of girls. His father was immensely gratified by young Ezekiel's appetite for Latin and Greek and even Hebrew and for the fine showing he made at Andover Theological Seminary. His fellow students there nicknamed him the Prophet.

The day he graduated he went into his father's study and stood erect before his desk to tell him that he felt no call to the ministry. His father burst out laughing. "I've known that son for years. You are a born scholar. Ezekiel, in our Father's house there are many mansions . . . As theological school offers the best classical education to be had and, I might add the cheapest," he added with his mischievous smile, "you are certainly not the loser." Then he brought out of a side drawer a check on a Washington bank for two thousand dollars. "Ezekiel you were probably too young to remember our house on I Street. These are the proceeds from its sale, which I have destined to defray the cost of your education in Germany. Spend it carefully because there will be no more when that is gone. The education of the girls will prove a heavy burden."

For economy's sake Ezekiel's passage was arranged as supercargo on the brig *Centaur* owned by a vestryman of his father's church. The month was August. The wind was fair. The first landfall was in the Azores. Ezekiel was awakened by a cry and the patter of bare feet above his bunk. He pulled on his pantaloons and ran up on deck. The first thing he noticed was an indefinable smell of flowers borne on the light breeze. The brig slipped through the still waters with every sail set. The bellying canvas gleamed overhead in the light of a waning moon setting astern. Far off the starboard bow the dark peak of a mountain rose into a wreath of silvery clouds. "The islands of the blessed where Rhadamanthus ruled," Ezekiel whispered to himself, "or Venus rising from the sea."

There were rumors of cholera in their first port, Cadiz, so the captain refused to allow any man ashore, except the crew of the longboat that took him in to have his papers seen by the captain of the port. When the American consul came aboard to dine, his conversation, spiced with tales of smugglers and Spanish witches and bandits in the hills, sounded like a page from Washington Irving. The fishing boats they saw as they skirted the Spanish coast, with a seabreeze by day and a landbreeze by night, might well have been Phoenician. They passed between the Pillars of Hercules and entered the Mediterranean. As the towns drifted by, white as sugar in the folds of the tawny hills that rose to clouded snow, Ezekiel had a feeling that he was sailing back through history beyond the Roman and Grecian epochs into some remote Homeric past.

At Marseilles, with a lump in his throat that he hid behind tight lips, he left the gruff friendliness of the Yankee ship, the familiar food, and the nasal accents of home for the strange babel of foreign tongues in the turbulent streets of the Phocian port. Sitting under a planetree, after having intrusted his baggage to a mustachioed porter to take to the station, to wait at a sidewalk table until it was time to catch the train to Paris, he studied his phrasebook and conversed with the waiter. Already he was busy trying to improve the French "of Stratford-atte-Bowe" he had learned in Cambridge. German he found easier and it was not long before he was carrying on fluent discussions about the *Nibelungenlied* with the wife and daughters of Professor Schwartz with whom he boarded along with three other students from the States in a vinecovered house on a hill under the schloss in Heidelberg.

Europe like his own dear country was recovering from the ravages of war. Among the German students he detected the same coarsening of moral fiber which his father had pointed out as the aftermath of war in New England. He hated their bragging and licentiousness, their idiotic duels, their caps and sabercuts, their absurd national and sectional prejudices, but he could hardly find words in his letters home to his mother and sisters to express his admiration for the spirit of scholarship, of rigorous ratiocination, and even for the cult of hairsplitting inquiry he found in the lecture halls. He read Strauss' *Life of Christ* and embarked on the higher criticism. In the coy rationalism of Renan he suddenly saw the religions of men spread out before him in the rising light of history like an archipelago at dawn. Anthropology was another discovery. After a winter of hard reading and careful attention to lectures he was able to write on the flyleaf of his notebook with profound conviction: the chiefest study of mankind is man.

He decided to model his life on Goethe's, but he had no money with which to indulge the sensual side. He studied hard and lived abstemiously. Whenever he drank a glass of wine or chipped in with the other students on beer and sausages in the evening he felt he had cheated himself of an extra week's study for his doctorate. In walking through the country he discovered a recreation that cost nothing. He did an immense amount of walking, joining in every students' excursion through the Rhineland or the Bavarian lakes or across the mountains into Switzerland. In the fatigue and exhilaration of mountainclimbing he found a way to put behind him the too-bright images of the eternal feminine that teased his dreams. His studious life left him no time for women. As the custom was he toured the universities; Goëttigen, Leipzig, Frankfort, Dresden . . . At Munich in the cold marbles he felt the perfection of Attic form. Under the stultifying drumbeat of the Prussian drillmaster forming the new Reich he could still catch the diverse and civilized melodies of the old medieval German towns. In Bayreuth he attended an opera by Wagner.

It was in Berlin itself that he strayed into a lecture of Max Müller's on the Vedic Hymns and was immediately entranced. Max Müller spoke of building a bridge over which his students could cross from the nineteenth century A.D. to the nineteenth century B.C. There was none of the classroom dust about his ruddy face and sparkling eyes and erect aristocratic figure. There was no trace of cant about his evenly pitched voice. Hearing him explore the writings of earliest India was like reaching, footsore and full of sweat after a long climb, a pass in the Alps and seeing undreamed of snowmountains, waterfalls, valleys, glittering lakes unfolding in the sunshine beyond. Ezekiel was Saul he told himself on the road to Damascus. He came away giddy with new understanding of the richness of the mind of man and threw himself into the study of Sanscrit. At Bonn in a little room overlooking a small green stream with swans on it he put the finishing touches on his thesis. The two thousand dollars would not last forever.

On his way home he stopped for a few days in Paris. It was May; the horsechestnuts were in bloom. His father had sent him a letter to his old friend Moncure Conway, with whom, although he somewhat deplored the lengths to which he carried his freedom of thought, he still corresponded. From a chance word overheard at the consulate, Ezekiel learned that Mr. Conway was in Paris. He put on his only good suit and went to call. He found Mr. and Mrs. Conway about to leave their hotel. Treating him like an old friend they explained they were off to see the unveiling of a statue of Voltaire at the Château d'Eau. They had tickets. Come along. Hurry, they said, there was room in their carriage. The crowds that packed the great circus at the Centenary Festival, the bands, the tricolor banners, the speeches, the spontaneous outburst of the Marseillaise, the cries of Vive Voltaire, Vive la République that rose like rockets from the throng prepared him for the excitement of the oration by Victor Hugo that reverberated later in the day through the breathedout air of the Gaieté Theatre. Ezekiel was unable to procure a seat, but luckily he was a head taller than any of the frockcoated dignitaries who jammed the back of the orchestra, and could see, over their pomaded heads, the figure of the great Frenchman, his white hair spreading like a halo in the glow of the gaslamps on the stage, standing beside Houdon's bust of Voltaire. In the flamboyance of the old poet's French cascading in his ears he felt the elation of mankind's struggle from out of the slimepits of superstition and tyranny up into the sunny uplands of rational thought. He joined wholeheartedly in the frantic bravos of the audience. He left the theatre feeling that the ground of freedom was firm under his feet. That night walking through Lutetian streets full of mirth and bunting and flowers he seemed to find in the expression of every face a mirroring of his own exultation in the power of reason to triumph over violence.

His exalted mood, fed by the sanguine spirit of the circle of eminent men he had the good fortune to be introduced to, lasted through the summer month he spent in England. War with Russia had been averted. It was felt on every hand that an era of peace and rational progress was opening for the world. The Conways, who had invited him to Hamlet House, treated him like a son. After warning him that as an American he must be prepared for some sharp sarcasms, they took him to call on Carlyle. He met Froude in their drawingroom over crumpets and tea. They gave him letters to friends at Oxford. At Balliol he was received by the great Dr. Jowett. After one of the Hibbert Lectures in the Jerusalem Chamber at Westminster Abbey Mr. Conway introduced him to Max Müller himself who, in English almost without accent, was explaining gleefully to a group of friends that he had returned to England for the freedom he found there. Had he stayed in his dear German fatherland he would have ended in prison. "Here people abuse me but they cannot bite. Every man barks at his own door."

All through the fortnight's crossing home on the creaking bilgesmelling old City of Washington, Ezekiel busied himself preparing a paper in defense of Max Müller against the strictures of Professor Whitney of Yale. It was not until he was trundling in a fourwheeled cab, hemmed in by boxes of books on every side, through Manhattan streets to the railroad station, that he began to think seriously of his own career. The happy wanderyears were over. He must find himself an academic niche. He'd try Harvard. That was nearest home. That evening the brick streets of Roxbury had a grim mean air. When he arrived in the last afterglow even the elms looked parched. He had forgotten how small the house was. His father's face had begun to sag with age and weariness. There were stains on the lapel of his black coat. His mother complained constantly of her health. His sisters were growing up plain dispirited girls who sang in the choir and belonged to sewing circles and distributed baskets to the deserving poor. Feeling the energy draining out of him day by day, beset with uncertainties and hopes deferred, he dragged through a stale Boston August. It was too late to procure a situation at Harvard for that year. The professor at Yale to whom he wrote seemed appalled by his interest in the higher criticism. One of his father's friends had been trying to hold open for him an instructorship in Oriental Languages at the Andover Seminary, but the head of the department there shook his head over the new philology. Ezekiel's life seemed at a dead end in Roxbury when a letter from an old classmate, which had been accidentally misdirected, reached him at the breakfast table. He was offered an assistant professorship at a rural college in Ohio, which was just beginning to aspire to the rank of university. He folded the letter and slipped it in his pocket, said hum loudly to get his father's attention from the pamphlet he was perusing. "Pater do you remember our journey to Ohio?" he asked. "There is something about the name that is congenial to my ear."

Ten years he lived in the same faculty boardinghouse at Willow Springs until his books crammed all the walls and he was forced to rent an extra room for the overflow. He enjoyed his lectures, he sympathized with his students, he was on terms of cheerful though distant badinage with the other members of the faculty, but after Heidelberg and London, and those peopled days in Paris and at Oxford he felt that he was living in a desert. He began to understand why so many learned Americans preferred to live abroad. He became more and more a solitary, a man of solitary walks, of solitary studies. Among his colleagues he spoke few of his thoughts; for conversation he had to rely on correspondence with friends. As among the faculty, and the pleasant enough people of the town, he felt among the students a profound disinterest in the workings of the mind. There was no taste for learning for its own sake. The people about him only kindled to talk of worldly success or money or gossip and scandal. The professors seemed to think of the subjects they taught as sets of words arranged between the covers of books. Learning was a stairway to the attainment of degrees which would afford higher salaries. Few of the men about him felt their blood heated by a new discovery.

Life would have been insupportable without his studies. He arranged his hours on a rigid schedule: three hours for college work, twelve for reading and study and the rest for eating and sleep and a fast crosscountry walk. The farmers round Willow Springs became accustomed to the sight of his tall unbending figure skirting their fields. The students complained they had to rack their brains to follow his lectures. His articles in learned journals his colleagues found abstruse. In spite of the aloof sarcasm of his manner of writing and certain personal misunderstandings he gradually became famous among men competent in his field.

When he was offered the chair of Comparative Anthropology at the university in Washington City, then in the midst of one of its periodical revivals, he accepted, not so much for the increased salary or the hope of finding intellectual stimulus among the changing throngs of the national capital, as with the intention of finding himself a wife. He had developed an aversion for the academic females he encountered in his courses or in the library, with their flat heels and mannish dresses. He found himself yearning for the airs and graces he remembered from antebellum days among his mother's relatives and friends.

At first the men and women he met in Washington seemed strident and coarse, lacking the sober honesty he respected in his associates at Willow Springs, but then one New Year's Day at a reception at the home of a colleague connected with the Smithsonian, he met two lovely girls who were the daughters of a senator from Kentucky. Immediately he began to cultivate their acquaintance with the same unremitting energy he had applied to the study of Sanscrit in Berlin. He became a constant caller at Senator Waring's house. There was nothing hightoned about the Senator but he couldn't help but be flattered by the attentions of a learned professor. Mrs. Waring's mountaineer wit delighted Ezekiel. One of the girls was dark and the other blond. Both had blue eyes. Admirers swarmed about them, army officers, continental diplomats from the embassies, young men from the State Department. Ezekiel felt himself a boy again. He'd always had a good seat on a horse. He could play tennis with the best of them. In spite of his stiff manners, and the smell of the midnight lamp he feared hung about him, both girls seemed to like him. Lydia was the blond, a little cold and heartless perhaps. A French officer adored her. By spring it was clear that it was Lucy whom Ezekiel loved. Her interest in learning seemed more naïve and fresh than her sister's, she was an accomplished watercolorist. She had a little knack for languages and something of her mother's pithy tongue. When he made his proposal, as long-windedly it seemed to him as if he were explaining an Aryan root, she put both hands in his and threw back her head and laughed. "Of course dear Ezekiel. We have no choice. Who else would we marry?"

In Washington their first boy was born. Some years later the prospect of a larger salary, less classroom work and greater opportunities for research drew him to Chicago. After the drowsy treeshaded calm of the District they found the city noisy and raw, but they were there together. From out of their love they looked out on the Middle West with indulgent amusement like travellers looking out from the windows of a palanquin at the hubbub of a strange bazaar. Lucy decorated their house charmingly. They gave jolly dinnerparties. They found appreciative friends. Ezekiel began to indulge himself a little in a taste for Bohemian glass and Wedgwood. The children were a delight. Little Lulie was the charmer. He called her his gentian flower. Their summers they spent in their cabin on their primeval lake in the north woods. They were making plans for a sabbatical tour abroad when the children should be a little older. Lucy's beauty became more dazzling as each year passed. Five days after the third child's birth she died.

Lucy's death left Ezekiel Harrington bereft of everything in life outside of his study. He loved his children but he had no knack for caring for them. An apoplectic stroke had carried off the Senator and when Lydia lost her gay young husband in a hunting accident it seemed natural that dear Lucy's mother and sister should come to keep house for him and bring up the children, since Lydia had none of her own. In that fashion some years went by. He lived aloof from the household, going straight to his study when he came home from a lecture. Often for days on end he had his meals sent up and ate them off a tray at his desk. He was so little in touch with their daily lives that it came as a surprise to him when Lydia married again, this time to Purdy Rumford, a wholesale druggist whom Ezekiel had considered a cloddishminded fellow when he had put some searching questions to him meeting him one day in the entrance hall. While they were off on their honeymoon abroad, Ezekiel announced to Mrs. Waring that he was resigning his professorship and returning, as a student only, to his old rustic university, as he liked to call it, at Willow Springs. "People will say of you, Zeke," she said laughing her creaky laugh "you would rather be a big frog in a small puddle."

He returned to his old boardinghouse, a whiteheaded sharp-spoken old man with a white wisp of beard. He had begun to glory in his solitude. He could find no place to store his books where they would be accessible to him, so he gave them to the university library. There with renewed passion he set to work to indite, in rigorous and caustic prose, a work that he referred to as his novum *Novum Organum,* a compendious theory of knowledge in which the new sciences: anthropology, sociology, the comparative study of religions, stripped of all dubious quackery, should form the backbone of an enquiry ever renewed, ever tested on ascertainable facts, into the behavior of man in society. It would be a work of many volumes. In solitude he compiled his notes at the broad mahogany desk Lucy had bought him at an auction when they first moved to Chicago. Every hour he felt her loss. Even after years he could not see her picture without the tears blinding him. Instead of her picture he set into the silver frame a succession of snapshots of little Lulie: the chubby baby, the curlyhaired fouryear old, the hoydenish highschool girl trying to keep her face straight under a commencement hat. Something of Lucy lived on, he said to himself, in the child; but, before she would be old enough to share the thoughts that rose constantly to the surface of his mind like bubbles in a boiling spring, it would be too late.

4

LADY OF THE LAKE

Lulie never stopped laughing from the time she caught sight of the boys on the bow of the *Minnehaha* that loomed suddenly white with whistle throbbing out of the dazzle of mist over the lake. The boys had turned out at five o'clock to go down to Calumet Point to meet Georgie arriving with the new friend he'd talked so big about in his letters, and there they were posed in a group like the House of David ballteam dressed up in false whiskers and black straw hats round a tall figure covered with a sheet. "They are going to unveil him," squealed Lulie, laughing so hard tears came to her eyes. The Willard girls were in stitches. Hildegarde was laughing so she could hardly take the snapshot. The other two started clapping. The hotel people in blazers and fluffy summer clothes who had come down to the wharf to meet friends arriving with fishing rods and golf bags and leather suitcases must have thought they were all crazy. Some of them began to titter and a few even clapped a little too as the boys trooped down the gangplank pushing the sheeted figure ahead of them. Joe Newcomer holding on to his whiskers with one hand ran ahead into the express office to borrow a packing case and the figure in the sheet was stood up on it and Zeke made a speech with gestures beginning "Friends Romans and Fishermen, lend me your beards" which everybody thought was very funny indeed and Brother Ben presented the keys of the lake cut out

108

with a scrollsaw and they yanked off the sheet and there stood a tall curlyhaired boy with a lot of freckles on his face shaking hands with himself in different directions like the winner in a prizefight and getting redder in the face every second. He couldn't seem to find a word to say for himself. Georgie was beginning to sing his awful song about the mountaineers with shaggy ears when Lulie suggested they all go to Pringle's for some icecream. She was hopping back and forth shepherding the gang down the wharf when she noticed that an erect old man who was the last to leave the gangplank was smiling at her. He had closecropped white hair and a small white pointed beard. His eyes were the blue of the lake water. He was her father. She ran back and tried to snatch the familiar old gladstone bag out of his skinny blue and white hand.

"Why Father where on earth did you come from?"

"I was amused by the masquerade. I didn't want to interrupt it. How is my wild gentian flower?" Lulie found herself standing before him with embarrassed downcast eyes. "I was becoming anxious about your Aunt Lydia's health. I decided to see for myself."

"Father I really think Aunt Lyde is better. Doctor Warner thinks so."

"I have never known a physician in whom I had less confidence."

"The Warners are all peculiar but Uncle Purdy thinks he's a good doctor."

Professor Harrington didn't answer. He stood looking over her head across the lake. She turned to look where he was looking. A northerly breeze was catching the mist up into ragged white patches that gleamed against the wooded hills and tangled in the tall firs that were very dark in the shade and bright green where the sun hit them. The lake shone blue in the sun and was marbled with opal in the shadows. "A landscape in continual mutation," her father was saying. It seemed minutes before he spoke again; Lulie could feel her heart's impatient beating; out of the corner of her eye she could see the boys and girls milling around under the maples in front of Pringle's little whitewashed store.

"Father at least won't you let me carry your bag?"

He held it up out of her reach with a teasing smile. "No little gentian. I shall walk slowly up to the cottage enjoying the sweet odors of balsam and fir and thinking of the many metamorphoses in our destiny since your dear mother and I first started to spend sylvan summers on the blue arm of this boreal lake. That was before the hotel was built and the loggers came and ruined the forests. It will be hard not to be met by sturdy old Mrs. Waring . . . and now Lydia bedridden. She had none of your mother's effervescence but in the gestures and features I sometimes caught an intimation of those lost graces."

Lulie was thinking how slowly her father talked.

"Look at me child." She looked up at him smiling as if her face would split. "The boys don't lack brains but you are all I have of that loveliness. Perhaps you will grow up to be a beautiful and noble woman." He had taken a dollar bill out of his wallet while he was talking. "This will pay for a round of icecream. Here child run along now." Walking firmly but slower than she remembered he left her.

She stood with her back to the lake watching his erect figure move gradually along the road past the hotel. She was afraid it was tiring him to carry the bag. He looked so like a strange and solitary bird stalking among the resorters scattered along the shore that she felt like crying.

The feeling that she was free again swept over her and she scampered off down the gravelly road towards Pringle's. When she slipped in through the screen door nobody seemed to notice that she hadn't been there all along. They were all listening to Georgie who was holding forth on the plans for the fishing trip, waving an icecream cone about and looking into one face after another out of burning brown eyes. The Willard girls sat in a row on the bench with their wavy heads, one reddish, one blond and one dark, bent over their sundaes. The dark one, Hildegarde, who had become Lulie's best friend that summer, was holding the rolled geographic survey map open on the table with one hand while she ate with the other. She looked sullenly up at Lulie and said: "Don't you wish we could go?" Lulie shook her head.

"Only braves on warpath," said Georgie out of the corner of his mouth and went on addressing Zeke who was sitting with Joe Newcomer on the bench opposite the girls. "We'll camp on the north shore of Little Fly Lake. There's a cove with a circle of low cliffs behind it that will give us fine shelter. Joe Sawbuck says his grandfather told him the three brooks that run through these little hills here would always be full of fish." He was jabbing at the place on the map with the grimed nail of his long forefinger. "Nobody ever fishes them."

Brother Ben was strutting around doing whatever Georgie did. As soon as he could get a word in he piped up "No paleface squaws." Lulie wanted to slap him but she didn't. She was ready to burst with trying to think up some way she might get to go, but she wasn't going to give the boys the satisfaction of knowing it. She fixed her wide eyes on Georgie's curly-haired friend who was leaning over the end of the table measuring the distances off with a little folding rule. She liked his silent competent manner. When Joe Newcomer looked up he noticed that Lulie was standing. He got smiling to his feet and walked over to Mr. Pringle who was watching them out of sunken eyes in that long muddy birddog face from behind the counter.

"There's vanilla and strawberry sundae. Which will it be Lulie?"

"Always Sir Walter," she said giving him one of her gentle admiring looks as she slid into his seat next to Zeke. "Strawberry sundae please, if it's Mrs. Pringle's own strawberry sauce." Mr. Pringle didn't smile but a little of the droop came out of the corners of his mouth. "It sure is," he said. "It sours real quick this weather. Last night I had to throw a whole bucket of it into the swill for the hogs."

Lulie had turned to Zeke and was poking the dollar bill into his hand. "Father said to pay for a round with this," she whispered.

Zeke gave her a startled look.

"He came in on the boat."

"That's a help," said Zeke bitterly.

Lulie frowned at him. "He's worried about Aunt Lyde," she whispered, "and so am I."

Suddenly Georgie was poking his face into hers, so close that she noticed the slight cast that sometimes appeared in one of his eyes and the upsetting jiggle of the pupils. "Lulie you haven't said a word to Jasper Milliron the best flyfisherman in the Rocky Mountain States. I want you two men to know each other."

Lulie tossed her head with one of her little shrieks and said, "You were so busy with your old fishing trip you never introduced us."

"Jasper meet the whitest whitewoman in the northeastern section of the middle United States including parts of Canada and Newfoundland," shouted Georgie.

Jasper grabbed her hand across the map on the table gave it a hard grip that hurt and pulled his big brown paw away fast as if she'd burnt it.

"I bet your ears rang all the way across the continent," she said. "We've talked of nothing else for weeks." He smiled and showed a set of very even white teeth, but there seemed to be no way of getting him to say anything.

"Out in Montana last fall you ought to have seen him track elk. He taught me how to smell 'em. He not only got Dad an elk but he fixed it so that Mr. Allardyce, Dad's rich patient, Dad's only rich patient, shot an elk. I always said Jasper lassoed him and tied him to a tree. When Mr. Allardyce shot we all fell flat on our faces, but we had to get him an elk because he was paying for the trip."

Jasper started to mumble something in Georgie's ear. Georgie let out a hoot. "Jasper's trying to say it was Bob Sykes, the other guide, held him by his tail . . . The elk, that is, not Mr. Allardyce. And you ought to have seen the trout we caught. When we weren't tracking elk we were catching trout."

"I bet they were all that big," said Zeke making various measuring motions with his hands across the table.

"How big were they Georgie? Come clean," echoed Joe Newcomer.

Everybody was laughing at everything anybody said. When Lulie finished her sundae she slid off the bench. "Don't forget you are all eating lunch at the cottage," she called back as she went out through the screen door. Joe Newcomer nodded vigorously. The rest were already listening to Mr. Pringle who, addressing nobody in particular from behind his counter, was starting on one of his narrations. "Even in my time," he began, "there's many a man drowned in Little Fly Lake. There's aircurrents from them hills. Now there was that party from the Elks' Convention tipped over in a squall right out from the portage."

As Lulie ran up the little path through the birchtrees back of the hotel she forgot everything in the pleasure of the day. In a ferny clearing she turned to look back at the sweep of the lake and the pitch of the wooded hills in the sunlight. There were wild roses in bloom round the outcropping of granite under her feet. The sun had sucked up the mist over the water but everything still looked pearly round the edges. At the mysterious little stile where the path crossed an old stone wall and ducked into a tunnel through dense balsam and arbor-vitae the spiderwebs were spangled with tiny jewelled drops. She walked carefully doubling and ducking so as not to tear the starry webs nor to disturb the tweedy brown and white spiders that lurked round the edges. The air smelt of sweet-fern and birchbark. She walked slower and slower. In spite of herself she was beginning to imagine the family group on the porch: Aunt Lyde lying in her nilegreen negligée with the lace frills on the daybed with a tiny pout on her thin lips and Father and Uncle Purdy walking up and down talking at cross purposes the way they always did, and glowering at each other when Aunt Lyde wasn't looking. When Lulie's reluctant feet brought her to the cottage she slipped in the back door and stopped in the kitchen a moment to cheer up Ella. "Ella, don't be discouraged. There'll be more boys and girls here for lunch than you ever saw but the lake trout is all cooked. We'll eat it cold and I'll be right back to make the mayonnaise. We'll need plenty of iced tea and some whipped cream for the peach cobbler."

"But I made turnovers," said Ella in tearful tones.

"All right. Turnovers it is. All the better. They won't need whipped cream."

"Nobody ever got discouraged when old Mrs. Waring was alive," said Ella glumly pushing a string of hair off her forehead with a knobby red hand. "Even down at the farm we all miss her. Mommer says when she came it was just like a ray of sunshine . . . None of us ever seen an old lady like that."

Lulie slowly got the things together for the mayonnaise and put them into the icebox to get cold. She wished she could stay in the kitchen forever but she forced herself to tiptoe out through the dark diningroom. "Nugatory my friends, the results of that argument are nugatory." She could hear her father's sarcastic classroom voice and a kind of angry spluttering from Uncle Purdy. When she went out through the double doors onto the porch she noticed that Aunt Lyde had been crying and ran to her to fluff up her pillows. The three strained faces turned to hers with a kind of beseeching look. Right away she started to tell them about Mr. Pringle's mournful narration of the tragedies on Little Fly Lake and it wasn't long before she had them smiling. She ran off back to the kitchen.

The mayonnaise just wouldn't go right that day and she was beating it back into a fresh eggyolk when she heard the girls shrill voices and the heavy tramping of the boys' big feet on the porch steps. It wasn't long before Joe Newcomer stuck his head in the door and asked in that deep brotherly tone she liked so much: "Anything I can do Lulie?"

"You can take in the icetea and the icetea glasses and make Georgie do something."

"You try. He's on one of his talking jags."

"Joe, whatever happened to your friend Don Modesto?"

"What made you think of him?"

"I don't know. Maybe it was Georgie's Montana marvel."

Joe looked glum. "The foreign phenomenon?" He tried to kid.

"You know. The wizard of the waltz who came up to stay with you for that dance."

"I'm afraid he's swimming out of our ken. He managed somehow to double up on two years of college and get into Harvard Law School. He's working his head off."

"I thought he was a darling. I like a scholar."

"Darn it, I get pretty good marks myself," Joe blurted out. "I wish somebody would think about me sometimes." Then he stopped short as if amazed at what he found himself saying. Lulie started laughing. Joe was getting terribly red in the face.

"But Decent Respectable what's the need of thinking about you? You're right here." She laughed so that she got him laughing too. The mayonnaise had suddenly started to thicken. Beating and beating she didn't take her eyes out of the yellow bowl until Joe had gone.

When she went out to the porch with the mayonnaise and the big platter of lake trout in aspic she was relieved to find that broad competent Mrs. Willard had come and was getting everybody settled into their places at table. Aunt Lyde was always better when Mrs. Willard was there because she was her best friend. Lulie moved the little table up to the daybed so that she could reach it better and served her some fish and mayonnaise.

"The salad darling, where's the salad?" Aunt Lyde asked

with an impatient quaver in her voice.

"I'll fetch it, Aunt Lyde."

She stood on tiptoe in the dooorway for a second and let her eyes run round the faces at the table. They wouldn't be so cross when they got some lunch inside them, she was thinking. All their jaws moved. Uncle Purdy, like a dog returning contentedly to an old bone, was beginning his usual grumble about the Administration and to point out to Mrs. Willard who was always a good audience that the Democrats called the Republicans imperialists but that they were the ones who were getting us entangled in this European war as fast as they could. Professor Harrington was sitting silent at the other end of the table with his eyes cast up towards the ceiling and a mischievous expression that Lulie knew only too well on his mouth above the tilted beard. Oh Lord he's going to lecture and that'll spoil everything she whispered to herself as she ran out after the salad.

She found Ella cracking her knuckles in the middle of the kitchen with her fascinated eyes fixed on a little wisp of smoke curling out from a corner of the oven door. Ella was a girl who always gave up when anything got difficult. Lulie heard herself give a little shriek that reminded her of Grandmother Waring and ran over to snatch out the pans of apple turnovers. The smell of burning made her remember with a little pang a day long ago when everybody was so happy and Grandmother burned the shortcake. Those had been the happiest summers.

"Just in time," she shouted cheerfully. "Now Ella you lay these out on the blue Canton platter while I serve the salad."

"They're ruint for fair," Ella was muttering shaking her head over the charred edges of the piecrust.

On the way back to the diningroom Lulie heard her father's high teasing voice: "On the contrary, to my view, perhaps somewhat prejudiced by the predilection for this country's still imperfect institutions . . ."

Joe Newcomer jumped up as soon as she reached the table

and whispered in the voice of an usher talking under the sermon at church, "You eat Lulie, I'll pass the salad."

She settled down in her place and gave a few quick pecks with her fork at a piece of fish, just to see how it was. She was too excited to be hungry. Amused by Joe's deferential expression, as he passed the salad as if he were passing the collection plate, she sat listening apprehensively to what her father was saying. ". . . In spite of the brilliant corruscations of some of the younger critics of our society and the undisputably caustic comments of the new generation of the sons of Marx who erupt in various weeklies into periodical geysers of smart talk . . . smart talk by young men who are a little overimpressed by the faces they see in their own mirrors in the morning . . . in spite of these, somewhat premature, pallbearers of civilization it is my considered opinion that there is reason for a certain restrained optimism as we view the grandiose march of human affairs."

Lulie had taken a tray from the serving table and was quietly collecting the plates.

". . . It is hard for a dispassionate observer of the human scene not to be distracted by the purely meretricious aspects of the tumults and confusions that agitate the surface and testify to disturbances resulting from the explosive nature of the process of the liberation of the human mind for which the Enlightenment shall we say lit the fuse?"

When Lulie came back with the turnovers Uncle Purdy was exploding. "Where's the money coming from? That's what I want to know."

"An interesting question, Purdy, but one which demands a certain rigor of definition. If we examine the concept 'money' we shall I am afraid discover that although men have sweated and cheated and browbeaten and bludgeoned their fellows from earliest times with the sole and singular purpose of amassing coin of the realm, nobody has ever explained the essential nature of money."

"If you'd ever had to meet a payroll, Professor, you'd know, by golly you'd know."

Lulie caught a dangerous blue flash in her father's eye. "The argumentum ad hominem, Purdy, tends to generate more heat than light." Lulie felt the anger in his slow voice. "With your permission I shall complete my little homily which may perhaps intrigue some of our young friends who are reaching the age when one sometimes is capable of fresh observations unmarred by the distorting lenses of selfinterest. Money, I was about to say, has borne through history a dual aspect: on the one hand the coin of the realm is a symbolic token used to facilitate the exchange of commodities and on the other it is one of the more important instruments of sovereignty."

Lulie was flitting round the table asking people if they wanted afterdinner coffee. She noticed a trembling in Uncle Purdy's fleshy jowl as if he were about to explode. She plucked at his sleeve.

"Uncle Purdy," she asked. "What's the silly name of that disease people get when they can't make up their minds?"

"Abulia," said Uncle Purdy givng her a flattered grin and putting on his false fatherly expression she never really liked. "Why dear child?"

"That's what Ella's got," Lulie said mischievously. "She's so scared of Father she won't stir out of the kitchen."

When she got back with the coffeetray whatever the tension had been about it was over. "Well if we're going we'd better get a move on," Zeke was saying. The boys and girls were all standing round Aunt Lyde. Father was out on the porch steps looking across the lake. When she'd set the tray down in front of sweet Mrs. Willard who always had a smile ready for her, Lulie ran out and slipped her arm in her father's. The early afternoon sunlight had flattened the hills and broadened the lake, making it look like any old lake. "Father, Joe Newcomer has asked all us small fry to go sailing. You'll stay over till to-morrow won't you?"

"No indeed little gentian. At five o'clock I board the good

ship *Minnehaha* to return to Calumet. I shall spend the night there with my old friend Elliott Spingarn the geologist, an ingenious and learned man from whose conversation I imbibe both entertainment and instruction."

"Then I won't go sailing," Lulie said with a dry throat.

"Of course you'll go with your merry companions, little gentian," and he quoted a line of Greek. She looked up at him puzzled. "This is the season for sailing and for launching the hollow black ships . . . When you come to the University in the fall I'll try to find time to teach you some Greek."

She put her hands on his shoulders and jumped up to kiss the corner of his beard. "Father you won't be patient enough. I'm such a little stupid . . . Goodbye Father."

She ran off after the others who were already streaking down the rutted woodsroad that led to the Newcomers' boathouse. The boys were playing leapfrog as they went and the girls were skipping and whirling.

"My lord Lulie that was heavy weather," whispered Zeke in a breathless groan when she caught up with him.

"Damn good lunch though," said Georgie. "Lulie's a better cook than even her grandmother was. Mother's been reading a book about diet and we never get anything home any more but boiled vegetables standing in their own water."

"The turnovers tasted like more," said Ben, "but there weren't any more."

"There'd have been plenty if you hadn't been a pig and eaten six of them," said Zeke.

The Newcomers' little sloop *Waterfowl* looked neat as a duck with her polished mahogany and brass trimmings lying in the still green beside the float at the boathouse. Joe and Jasper went right to work to unlash the canvas cover on the mainsail. Zeke gave everybody orders and got ready to take the wheel. Georgie talked. "This is the first time Jasper's ever been on a sailboat and just look at him work. You'd think he'd been raised before the mast."

For Lulie the minutes dragged while they got the sheets

and hoists in order. She was waiting breathless for the moment to come when the wind would fill the sails and the boat would heel and she'd hear the bow crunching through the small waves. At last the boys pushed off from the wharf and the boom swung out with a rattle of tackle in the sudden swoop of wind that hit them when they got out from under the lee of the steep shore. Lulie had pulled her green tam o'shanter down over her hair so that it wouldn't blow. She stretched out in the sun on the slanting deck under the jib and fell happily asleep.

When she woke up she was under a red blanket and Joe was sitting crosslegged beside her. The *Waterfowl* was running up into the wind towards the wooded islets Lulie liked to call the Three Witches. One side of her face was warm from the sun, the other tingled a little from the draft under the jib.

"Good morning," Joe said grinning.

She laughed. "I'm like a cat . . . sometimes I need a little nap . . . After that family luncheon . . ."

"I'd say a kitten," said Joe, "the cutest little kitten in the world."

"Now is that nice? To call me a little cat?"

Joe got very red, and gulped.

"Father and Uncle Purdy never could stand each other," said Lulie.

"It's tough on you."

"The more I see of grown people," said Lulie, "the better I like us."

"But I'll be a senior next year," said Joe soberly. "I'll have to grow up fast. Dad wants me to go into his business."

"Look Joe, there's the little cove on the island where we all went on the picnic that fall and Grandmother Waring put feathers in her hair and we called her old Nokomis and Ben was just a little fat boy and fell off the log into the water when we were playing buried treasure and had to be dried out in front of the campfire. Brother Ben," she shouted aft, "that's the cove where you turned blue."

"Look," said Joe getting to his feet. "If we are going through the channel between the islands I'd better take the wheel. I don't think Zeke knows where the snags are."

Zeke was a little huffy about giving up the wheel but Lulie pointed out that even if he was the oldest, after all it was Joe's boat, so Zeke and Josephine, who was the Willard girl Zeke was going with that summer, took the blanket and sat up in the bow together with it wrapped around them and Georgie and Ben pointed and jibbered and carried on and had to be suppressed. Then Ben and Jasper crouched in the cockpit to go over the list that Jasper brought out of his pocket of things they needed for tomorrow's camping trip and Hildegarde and Hortense looked over their shoulders and teased Ben because he wanted more pancake flour and made silly suggestions till they all got the giggles. Joe steered and Lulie sat beside him looking out over the lake. "Oh I love just to look," she whispered in his ear. Georgie stood barefoot in the stern with his legs spread above the traveller trolling with a home-made spoon of his own invention. "Now Joe if you come about you give me plenty warning, do you hear?"

"Your life is in my hands Georgie," jeered Joe. "Just a flip of the wheel and you'll spill in the drink."

Lulie had lost herself looking at the slow parade of wooded headlands and snaggly points and at the cutover hills gently pirouetting behind them. She could barely hear Joe's grave pleasant voice telling her how his father wanted to retire and couldn't wait to have him get into the firm. He wasn't sure he was fitted for the leather business, sometimes he thought he'd like to teach . . . Lulie's eyes were travelling along the little pebbly beach where she and Hildegarde had gone in swimming without any clothes on and had such fun about being a pair of September Morns . . . It would be tough working into the firm, Joe's voice droned on, old employees didn't much like having the boss's son upgraded ahead of them . . . When the *Waterfowl* nosed out beyond the islands Lulie could see High Head, and the cove at its foot where she and Ben and

Georgie had landed when they decided last summer they ought
to do some rockclimbing. Georgie had lashed them together
with clothesline. She could remember the smell of the little
plants in the crevices and the way the warm rough rock tore
her fingers as she pulled herself up from ledge to ledge. At
the top she'd gotten dizzy and squeaked and squalled and
Georgie and Ben weak from laughing had had to boost her
bodily up a crevice in the last escarpment and she had lain
flat on her stomach in the sweetfern and blueberry bushes at
the top giving herself a good scare by looking down at the
canoe tiny on the beach of the cove below, and declaring that
she'd never get down, no never; she'd spend the rest of her life
up there and would be known as the hermit of High Head;
and it was nearly dark before Georgie, boasting terrifically
about his old topographical seventh sense, found a dry watercourse full of bushes that led them down slipping and sliding
and barking their shins on the pebbles, and brought them into
a glen dark with enormous hemlocks where they had to
straddle fallen mossy trunks that crumbled under their weight.
The boys had had to paddle like crazy to get home in time for
supper with Lulie lying back on the cushions in the waist of
the canoe barking at them like a coxswain and that night she'd
dreamed of being a hermit like the hermits in the tales of
chivalry who were always there to cure the knights of their
grievous wounds with herbs and simples, only not one with a
beard but an old lady hermit like Grandmother Waring and
since then she had played the hermit instead of Guenever in
her Arthurian reveries . . . Dad had a crackerjack organization,
Joe was saying. He'd start right in at the tannery as soon as he
graduated next spring because Dad thought a man who was going to tell other men what to do ought first to learn how to do
things himself . . . The *Waterfowl* had passed High Head and
was skimming up the long reach between steep slopes they all
called Warner's Deep because that was where Georgie had
caught the gigantic lake trout that his parents hadn't let him

get mounted because it would cost too much and Mrs. Warner had made him so mad by presenting it to the Ladies' Aid to serve at a church supper. Poor Georgie. It was to get even he'd taken his course in taxidermy . . . By rights, Joe was saying, he ought to have gone into the tannery this summer, a dirty smelly trade but he didn't care, he'd have to learn to get his hands stained, but Dad and Mom had said they wanted him to have one more real vacation at the lake before he took up the grind and then there was another reason. He might not be coming back to the lake for years except for an occasional weekend and there was something he wanted to settle with somebody . . . Something very personal . . . "Why Lulie you're not listening."

"Yes I am, Decent Respectable. I can look and listen too . . . mostly I was looking."

"Oh Lulie I love . . ." Joe started to mumble, but instead he shouted "Hard alee!" Ben jumped for the jibsheet. The boom swung over their heads with a crack. The jib fluttered a second and the *Waterfowl* settled into the other tack.

"I almost ran into a floating log," said Joe. "That comes of daydreaming."

"But Joe we've lost our taxidermist," wailed Lulie. They looked astern and saw Georgie's angry face bobbing up and down in the wake.

"Hold on to the log. It's just aback of us," shouted Jasper. "How good does he swim?" he asked Lulie, already peeling off his shirt.

"He swims all right."

"Jibing," shouted Joe and swung the *Waterfowl* round on a dime hauling in on the sheet with all his might. Jasper was already kicking off his shoes. Joe brought the sloop's bow into the wind and bore up slowly on the black bobbing head.

"Of all the lowdown Irish tricks," spluttered Georgie as Jasper leaned over the counter to pull him aboard. "You thought I'd lose my rod too, didn't you?" Lulie took the rod out of his upthrust hand. With Jasper tugging on the collar of his shirt he wriggled aboard dripping like a wet dog. The first thing they had to do was to disentangle the many hooks of the spoon from the seat of his pants.

"Well, that's the biggest fish you ever caught out of this lake," said Zeke.

They were all laughing except Joe. "Gosh Georgie I'm sorry . . . I don't know why I didn't see that log in time," he was saying. "My wits were woolgathering I guess."

"All's well that ends well," chanted Lulie. "That's what Grandmother Waring would have said."

"Tried to drown me," muttered Georgie scowling. "Now I'll catch my death of cold." His teeth were chattering from cold and rage. Jasper wasn't laughing either. He had his fists clenched as if he wanted to hit somebody.

Joe pulled off his sweater. "Here put on my sweater. Zeke, you take the wheel. I'll see if I can't rustle up some dry clothes." He dove into the cabin. "There's a pair of pants and a towel on the bunk." He tried to put his arm round Georgie's big shoulders. "Gosh I'm sorry old man." Georgie pulled away from him and jumped angrily down into the cabin. He slammed the little doors and they could see his tousled head bobbing under the boom and his bare arms waving as he rubbed himself off with the towel.

"You were wonderful, Jasper," said Lulie, looking up into his face with her wide eyes. "I never saw anybody get out of their clothes so fast." Jasper was sitting on the seat beside her glumly tying up his shoelaces. "Best guy ever," he muttered. "Couldn't see him drownded. Got the makin's of a good shot too."

"Georgie, you certainly showed yourself the fisherman," she called forward. "We ought to take a picture of you standing beside yourself. How much do you weigh?"

"A hundred and sixtyfive pounds," growled Georgie from the cabin; "stripped," he added bitterly.

"I bet that's the world record for freshwater fish," said Lulie.

"Maybe we'll get him mounted," said Ben.

"At least we know he's had one bath this summer," said Zeke. They all got to laughing. "Poor George Elbert," said Lulie. "He hates cold water." Georgie was still mad but he made a feeble effort to laugh too. They kidded him all the way home. It was already late; Lulie was thinking ruefully to herself how soon it always got late; if some day she could have one afternoon that didn't have the specter of family supper waiting for her at the end of it. The *Waterfowl* ran before the wind all the way to the point of birches opposite the New-comers' boathouse. "Look Georgie," she pointed teasingly into the sedgy cove that led into the Alexander's pasture. "That's where you had your other dunking two summers ago."

"Where? When?" said Georgie vaguely.

"Oh George Elbert, you must remember. You were just telling me how awful it was to have to go fishing with a girl and *Redwing* got mad and tipped us over."

"I bet he hasn't had a bath from that day to this," said Zeke, coarsely Lulie thought.

Georgie's dark brows blackened and the truculent look came back on Jasper's freckled face. "Jasper," said Lulie smiling into his eyes, "you mustn't mind us. We're like the Lord. Whom we loveth we chasteneth."

The mainsail flapped over their heads while they bobbed out from under. With jib flapping Zeke brought the sloop neatly in beside the boathouse. The boys had already set to work to furl the sail.

The girls clambered up onto the weathered boards of the shaky little landing and stood stretching their stiff legs, watching the boys lash the cover on the sail and coil the sheets and close up the cabin. It was chilly in the shade of the woods. Lulie was looking down through the bottlegreen water at a pair of tiny perch nibbling round the piling. "Joe we've got to run, Dad'll be waiting for his supper," called Hildegarde Willard. The others too chimed in, "We've had a wonderful time." "You were sweet to take us." "And Lulie what a lunch." The Willard girls were off. Lulie's eyes followed them running slender and fluttery round the path that followed the pebbly lakeshore just above highwaterlevel towards the hotel. She would be late too Lulie was thinking. A cloud covered the sun. If only people would give up this idea of getting home for supper. She shivered suddenly cold. She ought to start home.

"Lulie," Joe was asking her in a choked beseeching voice, "please help me paddle one of the canoes over."

"But it's suppertime."

"You can get to the cottage just as quickly as by the path. We want to take the duffle over to have it ready for a five o'clock start from your boathouse in the morning."

Lulie found herself paddling in the bow of one of the big Old Town canoes loaded with tents and camp equipment.

"That Jasper," she said as soon as they'd gotten out of ear- shot headed across the cove. "He'll be a jewel on a camping trip. George Elbert may be crazy but he certainly makes nice friends."

"Speaking of the present company?" asked Joe.

"Um hum," said Lulie paddling away.

"Jasper's the strong silent type that appeals to women."

"I'm not women," said Lulie suddenly angry.

"You are to me. You're all lovely women."

"Decent Respectable, you read that in a book," she answered paddling hard with her head down. Joe was letting his paddle drag. "And you are making me do all the work."

"You're the Lady of the Lake."

"That's better. All in white samite. The arm that catches Excalibur."

"Lulie you read that in a book."

Lulie couldn't help laughing.

"Lulie, let's not get to the raft too soon."

"Poor Aunt Lyde gets all upset if I'm late."

"But I've got to say something."

"Joe we've got all summer."

"I want to ask you something now. Oh, I don't know how to say it," he was whining. "Lulie let's get engaged."

"But Joe I've got to finish college and take care of Aunt Lyde and maybe Father too . . . I'm the hermit type."

"Lulie, you know all the boys are crazy about you."

"Why Decent Respectable that's a great big awful lie."

"You're thinking if you got engaged you wouldn't have any dates in college . . . We could have dates."

"At least you aren't going to cut me off without a single date," said Lulie tossing her head.

They were drawing up to the float. Lulie put away her paddle and started carefully to lift a canvas bag out of the canoe.

"Lulie please be sensible. It was because I was all upset about you I forgot about Georgie. If anything had happened to him I never could have forgiven myself. Maybe before we go back to school you'll let me give you a ring. Then I wouldn't have the awful feeling that somebody else'll carry you off."

"A fat chance."

They were both standing on the edge of the float leaning over to pull up the canoe.

"Please, Lulie."

"Joe let's wait till fall."

"Will you then?"

Suddenly Lulie burst out crying. "I just want to be one of the Tribe and have fun like we always have." The other canoes were coming alongside. Lulie ran snivelling off up the woods path to the cottage. As she ran she felt that she had spent her whole life running out of breath up that path late for supper, always late for supper. She stopped at the edge of the orchard to dry her eyes with the hem of her dress because she had lost her handkerchief.

She went into the house through the back door; that was easier. Ella was clattering the pans in the kitchen. "Oh Lord

I'm glad you've come Lulie," she whooped even before Lulie got in the door. "I'm alone in the house and your aunt's havin' a spell. Your uncle he's gone to play bridge at the Willards' . . . She's took real bad Lulie."

Lulie hurried through the house. Aunt Lyde lay rigid on the daybed with her eyes closed. Her thin white fingers were plucking at the blanket. How could Lulie be so thoughtless? Aunt Lyde's singsong started right away, that she wouldn't allow her to go out on the lake at all if she couldn't get home on time. "I'd think you would have more consideration than to leave me alone with that stupid girl. My dear, she's deficient. I don't know how we've put up with her all these years. I asked her to bring me the aromatic spirits of ammonia and she brought household ammonia. She could have poisoned me."

Lulie was fluffing up the pillow under her aunt's head. "Aunt Lyde, Ella's so worried about you she can't see straight." . . . "I love to have the young people. They always make me feel better." Aunt Lyde let her transparent eyelids drop over her eyes. Tears ran down her cheeks. "And you know how I love Esther Willard." She gave a sniff. "Your poor father is too brainy for me, child. He always did wear me out."

"Aunt Lyde let's climb the mountain high and I'll put a little headache cologne on a handkerchief," Lulie said putting her arm around her aunt's slender waist and walking with her up the stairs. Aunt Lyde tottered feebly to the washbasin in her room and patted cold water over her face with her hands. It made a lump rise in Lulie's throat to see her aunt's silky white hair which she always remembered puffed over her forehead in a perfect pompadour, tumbled every which way so that the rat showed and the hairpins. "Let me take all the pins out of your hair Aunt Lyde and brush it for the night."

Lulie poured headache cologne on a handkerchief out of one of the gilt bottles on the dresser and spread it out on her aunt's forehead. "Thank you darling, now go down and heat me a little bouillon. A little bouillon usually settles my stomach."

When Lulie came back with the supper tray prettily arranged she thought, with nasturtiums on it, her aunt was crying again. "You put too much cologne on the handkerchief," she whimpered. "It ran down into my eye and like to put it out. I had to get up and bathe it with boric acid. I know it's not good for me to wait on myself like that."

Lulie felt quite hurt that Aunt Lyde didn't notice the nasturtiums. "Aunt Lyde dear I'm awfully sorry," she said a little tartly. "This is one of the days when I can't seem to do anything right."

"And the boys aren't home. What can be keeping them?"

"Aunt Lyde, they are down at the boathouse getting the stores packed for their trip."

"If they had any consideration they wouldn't leave me in this condition."

"Now Aunt Lyde dear. They've been planning it for so long. This is the only time they can all go together."

Aunt Lyde had been sipping a little bouillon. "It does settle my stomach," she said in a complacent tone. She let her head fall back on the pillow and halfclosed her eyes. "Lulie read to me. It soothes me to be read to." Lulie took away the tray and started to read to her out of the redbacked novel she found on the table beside the bed.

When her aunt began to get drowsy she patted her pillows again and arranged the window so that the shutter wouldn't bang and lit a nightlight on the marbletop washstand and tiptoed out. She felt tired and hungry and discouraged. She let herself drop on the stairs halfway down and sat there gobbling up the supper her aunt hadn't eaten. She ate the roll and the chicken wing and drank the glass of buttermilk and the cold remains of the bouillon. When she carried the tray into the kitchen it was almost dark. All at once, feeling frighteningly alone she went out on the back porch. Ella had gone home. The afterglow was green and orange and salmon pink over the orchard. Overhead the immense pearly sphere of twilight swelled as if it were about to burst. The evening star glittered in the west.

It was a relief to hear the boys' wrangling voices and their thumping feet as they came up the front porch steps. She whispered to them to keep quiet because Aunt Lyde was asleep and laid out a platter of cold chicken in the diningroom and told them they had to rustle up their own suppers because she was going to bed. She left them all munching round the oval table under the big painted glass lamp that hung from the ceiling. From the stairs she looked back enviously at their smooth excited sunburned faces. Their eyes glittering like the first stars with anticipation of the trip.

Lord, she wished . . . She was imagining the plash and the strain on the shoulder when you pushed on the paddle to drive the canoe up through the hurrying water over the brown shallows in Runaway River, and the singing of the reel when you cast in the deep pools under the rocks, and the smell of pine chips and bacon sizzling in the open and of freshcut balsam twigs, and the feeling of little wild eyes looking out at you from the shadows in the shaggy woodland. Once in her own room she locked her door and scampered back and forth letting her clothes drop where they fell as she undressed. She pulled on a nightgown and jumped into bed with Mallory in her hand. It was two summers since she'd read any *Morte d'Arthur*. At first she was disappointed. It wasn't as enthralling as she remembered it. But then the cadenced narrative began to catch her up as it had when she was a very little girl and she read until she fell asleep.

In the morning she awoke at the sound of the boys' voices and Georgie grumbling about something and their heavy footfalls on the stairs. It was still dark. She whispered to herself spitefully that she bet they felt redeyed with sleep and turned over comfortably under the warm covers. When the sunlight finally woke her she was startled by the unnatural silence of the house. Downstairs she found Uncle Purdy reading the papers over his coffee on the front porch. "A little peace for a change," he said smiling. "Uneasymaking," she said. The day dragged on, reading *The Iron Woman* and playing double solitaire to entertain Aunt Lyde. By afternoon when Mrs. Willard and Hildegarde came Aunt Lyde seemed almost herself again and started gossiping with her old friend in such a normal way that Lulie and Hildegarde decided they could sneak out for a few minutes paddle in *Redwing*.

It was a still hazy day. There was no wind. Each little wave had a blurry dark shadow. Once they got out from shore there was no sound except for the suck of their paddles and the trickle of the bubbles along *Redwing's* sleek bottom. Each floating gull showed a misty reflection. On the shore the shadows under the trees were purple. The haze was reddish overhead. They paddled straight out into the lake without speaking.

"Oh dear," sighed Hildegarde after a while, "I'd like to have gone on that fishing trip."

"I can't do anything ever on account of Aunt Lyde."

"Mother never would have let me, not unless Dad or your uncle or somebody had gone along and that would have spoiled the trip for the boys."

"I say we get up a trip for girls one of these days."

"I bet they're having fun."

"They're just acting silly and talking big and using a lot of vulgar words. I'm just as glad they're out of the way for a while," said Lulie.

"Lulie are you going to get engaged to Joe Newcomer this summer?"

"Hildegarde, I declare that's the silliest thing I ever heard. I'm not going to get engaged to anybody till I get through college, and probably not then."

"Josephine and Zeke are mighty close to it."

"I'd love that. They make a wonderful pair. They are both

so tall and blond and uppety . . . But Zeke won't have the sense. He thinks no girl's good enough for him."

"I'll never get married," said Hildegarde.

"Why not? The boys just love you."

"No they don't. They are attracted at first like Zeke was, but then they lose interest. There's something about me that makes men lose interest." She pulled her paddle out of the water and laid it behind her in the canoe and put her hands over her face and sobbed.

Lulie changed the subject briskly: "Do you know what this is? It isn't mist, it's smoke."

"Oh I hope it's not a forestfire," said Hildegarde grabbing up her paddle with a gasp.

"That's just what it is. Look how red the sun's getting."

"Let's go home." Hildegarde started to paddle hard.

"Scaredcat . . . It may be a hundred miles away. My, it'll make it exciting for the boys on their camping trip."

"Suppose it's where they are."

"They've got all the lakes in the world up Runaway River. They can just move someplace else."

"It'll be getting towards suppertime," said Hildegarde primly.

"It's always suppertime," said Lulie in a bitter voice.

As they slipped in beside the float a killdeer flew wailing over their heads. A kingfisher chattered at them from a dead maple branch as they were lifting *Redwing* up on the float "The birds are worried," said Lulie. "They smell the smoke and they are worried."

The next morning the smoke was thicker. Everything had an amber look. At breakfast Uncle Purdy said he had been down talking to Mrs. Judkins the manageress at the hotel and that she had heard from Captain Jansen of the *Minnehaha* that the fire was on Ranger Lake to the westward. It had started on the railroad right of way. All the firewardens had gone off to fight it.

The rest of the week the days dragged glum and smudgy. Only swimming was fun off the float in the smouldering sunlight before lunch every day because the lakewater was like opal when you swam in it. Saturday afternoon everybody was edgy. The boys ought to be getting home. Aunt Lyde began to worry. Round five o'clock Lulie went out in the garden with her head tied up against the flies to pick a basket of sweetcorn. The air was muggy and brown overhead. She couldn't wait to hear their tall tales. They'd be starved when they got in. The table was all laid for supper. She had two big steaks in the icebox. All at once she saw Dr. Warner's bearded face squinting sideways at her through the cornstalks. "Where's your uncle?" he asked curtly.

"He and Aunt Lyde are on the porch."

"Ask him to step out here will you? It's no use worrying Lydia."

"Nothing's happened to the boys, Doctor Warner?" Lulie felt her voice strangling in her throat. In her head she saw the flames, figures running along a lake shore, the terrible crackle of burning trees, the hurrying smoke.

"They are safe enough," said Doc Warner giving his lip that sarcastic curl she hated so. She set down her basket and ran to the house. Zeke was sitting quietly on the front porch with Aunt Lyde and Uncle Purdy. He looked tanned and handsome but his face had a glum look. At his feet in their muddy moccasins was an open hamper full of rainbow trout. "Hello, Lulie. We had better get these on ice," he said in his offhand uppety way. "The ice melted paddling up the lake . . . Gee I'm tired." He stretched his long arms.

"Where's everybody else?"

"Joe's down at his house. The other canoe's still at Calumet. I guess they'll come in on the morning boat. If we'd had any sense we'd have waited too. That was a tough paddle in this heat."

"Everybody all right?" Lulie asked insistently.

Zeke looked at Aunt Lyde and nodded.

"Uncle Purdy, please help me with the fish," said Lulie. "They are too heavy for me."

"Why they're as light as a feather," grumbled Uncle Purdy as he followed her out to the kitchen. "There's hardly enough for one good mess. A fine set of fishermen."

"Doc Warner's out in the vegetable garden, Uncle Purdy. He's got something on his mind."

"Hum," said Uncle Purdy, "Zeke had something he didn't want to tell me." He strode off down the back steps. Lulie followed and hovered with her basket back of the rows of sweet-corn listening.

"What do you think those precious boys of ours have done now?" she heard Doc Warner's shrill angry voice. "Shot out the lights in Calumet City . . . Damn little fools." Then she heard Uncle Purdy's low grumble. "Turned Ben loose," Doc Warner went on shrilly. "He's over at the Spingarns. I talked to Professor Spingarn over the phone from the hotel. He says the sheriff has got Georgie and Jasper in jail with a lot of drunken Indians. He'll let 'em go but one of the parents has got to appear. He wants to make sure they get what's coming to them. We have to pay for the lights . . . What that damn boy's cost me!"

Lulie found herself crashing through the rows of corn with her basket on her arm.

"Uncle Purdy, let me go. Sheriff English is sweet. I know I can talk him around."

Doc Warner was looking straight at her without seeing her. Uncle Purdy's brow was furrowed. "What a mess. I wanted to spend a nice pleasant evening playing bridge down at the Newcomers'. This is my last weekend."

"Mrs. Judkins would lend us their truck," wheedled Lulie. "We could drive it over the logging road."

"Lulie you go back to the house and take care of your Aunt Lyde," said Uncle Purdy. "Doctor Warner and I will decide what to do."

When Lulie got back to the house she gave Aunt Lyde the corn to shuck. That was something she could do sitting in a chair on the porch. She caught Zeke in his bathrobe coming out from a hot bath and stood outside his door while he dressed. "Now Zeke don't be a meany. Tell me everything that happened," she whispered through the crack.

"It's just Georgie and his damn redskins," Zeke was saying. "We got in from the river about five o'clock yesterday afternoon. Lord, we came fast. You ought to have seen us shoot the rapids. That boy Jasper's a great hand with a paddle. Joe and I had one canoe and Georgie and Jasper had the other with Benjie for a passenger. Somebody ought to give that boy a good hiding. I've got half a mind to do it myself."

"May I come in now?" Lulie caught Zeke looking in the mirror and holding up a blue necktie in front of his shirt. "That matches your eyes very nicely," said Lulie giggling. Zeke flushed and gave her a sulky look.

"All right I won't go on with the story," he said.

"Now Zeke, please."

"I told Benjie not to go along with those roughnecks . . . "

"He has to do everything Georgie does. That's the phase he's in," said Lulie.

"Well we paddled over to the Spingarns' boathouse and they fixed up so we could sleep in the loft and asked us all to supper. But Georgie and Jasper — I thought at least he had better sense — had to go find Joe Sawbuck to see how the ballgame came out. Joe and I sat around making chitchat with the Spingarns. Suppertime came and they didn't turn up. After supper Joe and I took a turn around the town. No redskins, no Georgie, no Brother Ben. We were tired I tell you so we went back and hit the hay. Then in the middle of the night the sheriff drives up in his Model T and routs poor old Professor Spingarn out of bed and he routs us out and there's Benjie looking like a scared rabbit. Georgie and his redskins had been out in the woods drinking firewater or maybe in one of those houses across the tracks. Don't even ask where they've been. Those logging towns are rough places. The sheriff collared them shooting out the streetlights back of the depot. It was a good thing for them it was Sheriff English and not the railroad police. Anyway he locked 'em all up in the hoosegow to think it over except Benjie who looked too young. At least Ben had the sense to keep away from the rotgut. In the morning we tried to get him to come in our canoe but he wouldn't, not with his precious Georgie under lock and key."

"Why Zeke you might have been able to do something."

"I don't tangle with a lot of drunk halfbreed Indians, not for anybody."

Somebody was sounding the gong downstairs. Lulie ran off to her room. "I've got to change my dress," she wailed back over her shoulder. "Tell Aunt Lyde I'll be right down."

When Lulie crept down the stairs, late as usual, she found Mrs. Willard and Josephine and Hildegarde and Joe Newcomer sitting at the table. The girls were waiting on Aunt Lyde who looked quite perky propped up on the daybed with her white pompadour gleaming. "It's a pretty kettle of fish," she was saying, "when the guests have to cook their own supper." Mrs. Waring laughed cozily. "All I had to do was put on the corn." "Lulie had everything set out and ready." Hildegarde put in a word. "The steak's wonderful," cooed Josephine, with her eyes on Zeke.

As they ate they looked out into the threatening murk. The smoke was so thick they could hardly see the lakeshore. The sun smouldered an unhealthy red in the west. Nobody talked of anything but the forestfires. A notice had been posted in the hotel asking for volunteers to fight a new blaze on High Head. Mrs. Willard was saying that all the ablebodied men in Calumet City had been called out to go up the line in flatcars to Crawford's. The famous Indian ballteam, she added laughing, had all gotten spiflicated after winning a ten inning game and the sheriff turned the hose on them to sober them up and sent them out to fight the fire. "Thirtyeight consecutive days without rain," Mrs Willard exclaimed. "The whole country will burn up if we don't get a rain."

Aunt Lyde was so pleased with the company and having everybody waiting on her and the excitement about the forest-fires that she didn't seem a bit worried about Uncle Purdy and Ben. Lulie was wondering if she'd noticed they weren't at the suppertable. Joe helped Lulie carry out the dishes. He caught her alone in the kitchen while she was stacking the plates in the sink and ran over to her with a little white box in his hand. "It's the ring. I bought it down in Calumet," he said quite out of breath. She backed away from him. "Decent Respectable, I can't wear it . . . I'm not ready to, but I'll keep it and if you want it back you tell me . . . It'll be a kind of secret engagement." She dropped the little white box into the pocket of her apron. "Won't you even look at it?" She put her finger to her lips. Hildegarde and Josephine came clattering in with the coffeecups.

"You can see the fire," they said. "High Head's burning."

Lulie felt the tears coming to her eyes. "Oh it can't be," she cried running out of doors. "It's my hermit hill." She ran halfway down the path to the hotel and stood on a granite rock straining her eyes to make out the tiny distant tracery of flame like the fire on damp paper smouldering in a grate. The tears were running down her cheeks now. She looked up at the starless sky overhead. "Oh please somebody make it rain," she whimpered.

When she got back to the cottage the Willards were getting ready to go home. Joe Newcomer tried to hang around a while but Zeke carried him off down to the hotel to see what the news was. "If you'll excuse us for eating and running," Mrs Willard was saying. Lulie grabbed Hildegarde by the wrist and whispered fiercely in her ear: "Garde you've got to stay."

After Hildegarde had helped her make Aunt Lyde comfortable for the night they had just settled down to tell each other everything when there were footsteps on the porch and the

sound of Uncle Purdy's voice. Hildegarde ran off for home and
Lulie went out. Uncle Purdy hadn't had any supper and was
tired and hungry and peevish after the drive into Calumet
and back on that bumpy rutted road in the jouncing truck.
Ben who did look as if he'd had a fright was begging to be
allowed to go across the lake with the rest of them to help fight
the fire in the morning. "But Uncle Purdy what happened?"
Lulie was asking in the pleading voice.

"I'll tell you when I've had some supper," he answered.
"I've got to talk to this young hooligan first."

While Uncle Purdy went on giving Ben a piece of his mind,
Lulie went into the kitchen to reheat the leftover steak. It took
her a while to get the range going. She cut some cold corn off
the cob and fixed it with paprika and butter and heated up the
coffee. She was flushed and sweaty and the hair was over her
face when she got back to the diningroom carrying the
tray. Uncle Purdy was sitting hunched in the armchair at the
head of the table with his heavy jowls sunk over his collar.
He straightened up with a start when she set the tray down in
front of him. "Uncle Purdy you must be starved . . . Now
please tell me what happened." "It's not for a young girl's
ears," he said. He leaned back in the chair and looked at her
intently out of dark pouchy eyes. "Lulie you're getting dangerously pretty." He let out a little whistle she didn't like at
all. It was a lewd expression, she was telling herself. "The boys
are in for a bad time." He gave a short laugh then he started
eating ravenously.

If you love somebody, you like to see them eat, Lulie was
telling herself, remembering how she loved to see the boys
gobble up their meals. If you don't, it's disgusting.

"Don't go away," said Uncle Purdy, as he ate he talked.
"You know it hasn't been all cakes and ale trying to bring you
children up, and since Lydia's been sick life for me has been
frankly hell. I've worked hard all my life. The medical supplies business is a matter of endless detail. You have to be hail
fellow well met with all these damn doctors whether you like

them or not. You have to keep in touch with the latest developments. I've slaved my life away working to bring you children up decently . . . You weren't much trouble being a girl. Our troubles with you young lady are just beginning. But it hasn't been easy licking those two young cubs into shape and all the time way up above the clouds somewhere your father pursues his noble studies that people like me are too crass to understand."

"But Father's paid for our education," Lulie heard a strange cold voice so like her aunt's saying out of her mouth.

"Education's all he thinks of. He forgets the grocery bills. It's sound business principles that pay the grocery bills. And now just when my business has reached the point where I can look forward to all the things that poor Lydia and I used to talk about having when we got on easy street, this had to happen." He let his knife and fork drop on his plate and slumped down in the armchair again. "And my pretty niece won't do a thing for her old uncle."

"But Aunt Lyde's getting better," said Lulie earnestly. "Doc Warner thinks she's much better. The Chicago specialist he got in said a few months at the lake might produce a miracle."

"That's where I differ from all of you Harringtons." Uncle Purdy was looking up into her face with a sneering look in the dark eyes over the tired pouches. "Miracles don't happen."

"But they do," she wailed running up the stairs.

"All right," she heard him grumbling, "leave your poor old uncle alone."

She ran into her own room, doublelocked the door and threw herself face down on the bed.

Sunday morning was awful. The brown smokehaze hung over the lake. Aunt Lyde fretted because she kept losing count of the stitches in her knitting. Uncle Purdy sulked over the newspapers complaining that there was nothing to read anymore but warnews from Europe. Just to spite her, Lulie was thinking, he still wouldn't tell her what had happened about

Georgie and Jasper. Aunt Lyde had been saying she'd feel better if she could only start going to church again so they hired the Alexanders' surrey and drove down to the inter-denominational services in the tearoom at the hotel. It seemed to Lulie that the service would never end. When finally she was helping her aunt down the steps to the surrey again she noticed that the wind had changed. "Sure," said old Fred Alexander and clucked to his horses. "My geese are ·standing in water. It'll rain before sunup. An east wind never fails."

By nightfall a drizzle had started. Zeke and Ben got back soaked to the skin in time for supper. Even after changing their clothes they smelled of smoke. They were full of big talk about setting backfires and cutting firelanes and evergreens exploding into flames with a report like a cannon. After sup-per Joe Newcomer, looking very much the college senior, wear-ing white flannels and a green bow tie under his raincoat, came to call and Lulie had a little talk with him out in the delicious driving mist on the porch. This rain sure would fix the fires he assured her in his deep comfortable tone. He had heard all about Georgie and Jasper from Ed Edmonds the deck-hand on the *Minnehaha*. Georgie and Jasper had come back from Crawford the best buddies in the world with Sheriff Eng-lish. They'd organized that baseball team into the best firefight-ing squad you ever saw and the sheriff had sworn them in as deputies and sent them up to Crawford's and paid them two dollars a day. "They didn't pay us a cent," said Joe laughing. "All we did was stand around in the woods and get cussed out by the Alexander boys. We did cut a firelane that saved that great stand of timber back of High Head."

"You saved High Head . . . My hero," cried Lulie. Before she knew what she was doing she'd thrown her arms round Joe's neck and kissed him. When he tried to kiss her back she shook her head laughing and backed away. "Decent Respect-able, if I'm going to be a prisoner let me out on bail for a while . . . I'm almost as young as Brother Ben and the sheriff said he was too young to lock up."

"Is that a nice way of talking?" groaned Joe, but he couldn't help laughing too.

"The ring's darling," she said suddenly. "And so are you." She ran off into the livingroom and set to work vigorously winding the gramophone. "Let's have a dance," she shouted and she put on *The Pink Lady*.

It wasn't much of a dance because she was the only girl and nobody wanted to dance with her except Joe. Zeke and Ben had settled down sulkily to play chess. Joe looked awful happy when he said good night and walked off home through the driving rain. As Lulie went upstairs to her room to read she was saying to herself that maybe she could fall in love with Joe, once she got through college; she sure ought to love him, he was the nicest boy in the world.

Monday Lulie went about her housework in high spirits. She hardly admitted to herself that one of the reasons she felt so happy was that Uncle Purdy was leaving for the city on the afternoon boat. Georgie and Jasper would be back soon and the Tribe would have the lake to themselves except for the hostiles at the hotel. It would be like old times. She couldn't wait to hear Georgie's tales. Georgie could spin out a yarn better than anybody, particularly in the first person singular. It rained all day but she didn't mind. The rain was putting out the fires. That night the house was very quiet. Nobody was home but Lulie and Aunt Lyde. After supper she finished reading *The Iron Woman* and Aunt Lyde said with a contented yawn that it was a very strong book.

Next morning the sun came out after breakfast and the mists began to roll up over the wooded hills. Lulie was out in the kitchen with Ella cutting up green tomatoes for piccalilli, while Aunt Lyde looking neat and brisk superintended the operation from an armchair, when Lulie caught sight of a dark soiled figure sitting on its heels in the shade of a hydrangea on the lawn. She went out down the back steps and stood beside him pretending to pick some flowerheads for the house.

Joe Sawbuck sat on his heels looking across the lake through his narrow slits of eyes. "Other feller," he said after a while. He tipped his head towards the orchard and then slipped away through the shrubbery.

Lulie walked in among the trees and found Georgie and Jasper sprawled on the grass munching green apples.

"Excuse us if we don't rise," said Georgie in a formal tone, "but we're dead beat."

They smelled of smoke. Their faces were smudged. They had stubble on their chins. Their shirts were filthy and they looked as if they hadn't washed for a week.

"Well, you sure do look like a pair of firefighters," laughed Lulie as she dropped on the grass beside them. "I can't wait to hear the story."

"The only thing we got to tell is that we're pulling out," said Georgie giving careful emphasis to his words, as if he had rehearsed them many times. "I'm not going home and let them nag me to death. Mr. Allardyce has a camp over on Ranger Lake. There'll be a lot of work there because he pretty near got burned out in the fire. He offered Jasper a job any time he wanted one when we were out in the Rockies. Jasper thinks he can get me taken on too. Mr. Allardyce may be a millionaire but he's a damn fine person. If I go to work for him that'll square things with the family. They think he's God on earth. We've come to say goodbye."

"Oh Georgie," said Lulie. She was trying not to cry.

"Tell her George," said Jasper getting to his feet. His steely gray eyes were fixed on Lulie's face.

"When we've saved up a little dough at Allardyce's we're going up to Canada to enlist."

"Oh Georgie do you think you ought to? I hoped you'd go to college."

"The family doesn't think I'm worth sending to college and its no use trying to hang around here any more when my friends try to drown me."

"Georgie, I declare."

"Don't call me Georgie."

"Tell her, George. Go on tell her," said Jasper in his glum tense tone. She could feel his eyes still fixed on her face.

"You know"; Georgie cleared his throat. "Jasper and me . . . I mean Jasper and I . . . If we can't go to college we might as well see the world. Since the world's at war it's up to us to take a look at it."

"But Georgie there'll be plenty of time. This war'll go on till kingdom come."

"Tell me it may go bellyup any time," said Jasper showing his white teeth. "But go on George."

Georgie got to his feet and grabbed Lulie's hand in his big dirty mit. She could feel that his fingers were trembling. "The Canadian army takes plenty losses. War's no game of croquet. Maybe one of us'll come back, maybe neither of us, but if one of us does, unless we're too cut up to be fit to look at, will you marry him?"

"We don't look too good now," said Jasper hanging his head.

"But one of us might turn out to be a winner, see," said Georgie.

"I don't know what to say. It doesn't make sense. We'll all be so different. Georgie, you'll probably have a mustache."

"Just say yes. You're the only girl I'd ever want to marry."

"But suppose you both come back," said Lulie giving one of her cheerful shrieks.

"Most likely it'll be neither," said Georgie glowering glumly at the grass.

"Just say yes," said Jasper. When he smiled his teeth showed very white in his smudged face. "Or say yes maybe. Just something we can remember."

"Yes, maybe," said Lulie.

"Let's go," said Jasper with a jerk of his head. "We've got to hitch a ride on a truck down the logging road."

Lulie noticed how broad their shoulders were as they swung round to walk away. The two of them suddenly looked grownup as they moved off through the orchard.

Footnote on a Vanishing Culture

ELIOT STORY BRADFORD

1872 — 1918

Eliot Bradford learned that the Germans had violated Belgian neutrality from a weekold Athenian newspaper he picked up off the counter of Papadopoulos' greasy emporium in Umm-es-Salaam just to see if he could make out the modern Greek. He pulled in his breath, screwed the monocle tighter into his left eye and read out the word: polemos. The fat old shopkeeper who sagged in grimy shirtsleeves among his bags of lentils under the blood puddings dangling from the rafters scratched his cropped gray head and gave an enormous helpless shrug. Eliot felt suddenly stifled by the close smell of garlic and muttonfat and spices. He shook his head frowning and walked out into the moonlight.

He untied his horse's bridle from a ring in the clay wall, swung into the saddle and rode off up the pebbly bed of the watercourse. His nostrils fluttered with disgust as he passed through the reek of filth and smouldering charcoal that hung in streaks over the huts of the oasis. At the first summit, where the crumbly path climbed out of the wadi, he breathed deep of the sweet night air and looked out over the oblongs of the forum, clean and square and sharply defined in the moonlight, and the exedrae, and the curved steps and arches of the theatre, and the bases of the columns of the Temple of Fortune and Rome which he and Marmaduke Ames had worked so many months to bring to light. In the far corner of the temple under a pile of fractured marbles he had found the head.

144

Fortunately Achmet was waiting at the door of the tent to take the horse. The moonlight flashed on the even teeth in his dark face as he yawned. "Tutto quieto?" Eliot asked. "Quieto," answered the Arab. Inside the tent the acetylene lamp was spluttering. Eliot adjusted it. First he made sure that the head was still in its box beside his cot, then deciding not to wake Marmaduke who lay asleep with his mouth open under his mosquito net, he sat down at the table to write his wife:

> . . . *The Germans have forfeited any claim to civilization. Every nation will become embroiled sooner or later. Let's pray to God that the French with their magnificent army will stand firm. I suppose our own smug citadel of the full dinner pail will remain aloof and rake in the shekels. My work here will take a few weeks to wind up. In spite of all our troubles with the Arabs and my bouts of malaria and poor Villeneuve's death and Marmaduke's afflictions as yet unclassified by science, it has been a memorable experience. Fortunate is the excavator who has added to the world's store of beauty an object such as our head from the best period of Greek sculpture. I face with some misgivings the distribution of the opima spolia among the various institutions whose contributions made the work possible. I should suggest that you go begin preparations for a return home. Europe at war will be no place for bringing up children. Don't say anything she could oppose but if you could induce Mother to let the Villa . . .*

It was in his mother's villa on the lovely height in Asolo that Eliot Story Bradford was born fortyfour years before. Elizabeth Bradford insisted that it was because she had such a poor head for figures that her third son saw the light in Asolo instead of back home in Hingham, but Peabody, her husband, was of the opinion that it was part of a plot to baptize the infant in the Roman Church. When she arrived in Boston on a Cunarder with the new baby Peabody would not be mollified by her telling him that the Brownings had stood as godparents and insisted that the ceremony be performed over again by his own Congregational minister. He hadn't minded too much Elizabeth's spending so many months in Italy although it made him keep bachelor hall most of the year, but when she became a Catholic and made over a large part of her inheritance to endow a convent of nuns it did cause him pain. Of course it was hers, she had the right, he admitted. He met that reverse, like the other disappointments that came to him in his life, by going down to State Street and making a lot more money.

From boyhood he had been made to feel a low coarse fellow in a family of highminded Cambridge Brahmins because he knew more about mortgages on worsted mills and debentures at four per cent than he knew about Theocritus and Dante. Peabody's the practical man, the others would say. When pushed to the wall he would announce in raucous tones that he had tried both Craigie House and the Stock Exchange and that he'd chosen the Stock Exchange because he found it more rewarding. Winthrop and Standish among his own children had been on his side from the beginning but little Eliot had a curious and erratic mind that stemmed from his mother. Peabody tried to counteract the influence of Elizabeth's madonnas and incense and easterlilies by taking Eliot fishing in summer and on a good tough hunting trip every fall. Eliot didn't become a financier . . . "What's the use of my making money Dad?" he said one afternoon when they were both wading about in a Newfoundland river, swathed in netting against the black fly, and Eliot had just pulled in his sixth large salmon to his father's none; "It'll take me all my life to spend the money you've made . . ." but he did become an outdoor man. He was too light for football at Groton so he played on the tennis team. He was an excellent shot, tried to revive polo on the North Shore, and in spite of his short arms rowed for Harvard in a winning race against Yale.

In college he was very much the dandy. Since he belonged to an old Bay family he made the best clubs as a matter of course, but he barely escaped being considered a grind by his mates on account of the illconcealed passion with which he followed the lectures of his cousin Charles Eliot Norton. He read Ruskin out loud and as a sophomore started making his own translation, in prose modelled on Pater's, of Dante's *Vita Nuova*. He came out of Harvard College convinced that only good taste and a profound study of the Italian trecento could save the life of the spirit from moneygrubbers like his father and from the crude iconoclasm of the unlettered mob they had imported from the slums of Europe to sweat in their mills. His mother was delighted to see her youngest stand up against dear Peabody in behalf of the finer things, but it was a bitter cross to bear that he would not follow her on the path to Rome. The religious art he studied and collected would mean so much more to him if he believed, she would try to explain. One day soon after Eliot's graduation, in the little cottage at Nahant overlooking the harbor and the shipping which his father liked to escape to from their family mansion, so sunk in greenery at Hingham, and from the formal rooms of Elizabeth's house with lavender panes on Beacon Street, Eliot made them both furious at breakfast by announcing in the middle of an argument on religion that his gods were Athena and Apollo and the naked Aphrodite. "Be pagan if you will, but there's no need to be vulgar," his mother wailed. "Rot and rubbish," growled Peabody, getting very red in the face. Eliot excused himself and walked out of the room. The little tiff with their son brought Elizabeth and Peabody together more than anything that had happened in years.

Eliot rented himself rooms on Appian Way and went to work to study for a master's degree and a doctorate. His first publication was a monograph on headdresses on Florentine cassone. He followed it up by an article on snuffboxes at the court of the Dukes of Tuscany. Every summer he spent in Italy ransacking sacristies in the hilltowns for interesting primitives. At a function at the British Embassy in Rome he met Charity Wedgwood, a young lady from a great English family whose long auburn hair had recently been painted by Burne-Jones. When he returned to Boston, wearing a monocle and points on his waxed mustache, to explain his intentions to his mother, he confided in her that he feared Tattie would find America unbearably provincial. "Why not be married at Asolo with a high mass?" his mother suggested brightly. In the end they were married in a small church in Mayfair and went to Asolo to spend two weeks soon after, where to Eliot's great surprise, he found that his mother and his wife got along almost too well.

That summer the Bradfords went to America to visit the Jameses in Newport and spent a month at Bar Harbor while Eliot completed his paper on Attic fragments at Hadrian's Villa. Perhaps it was due to the spirit of contradiction that was such an important part of her nature that Tattie loved it so in America. In fact she made it plain that she never wanted to go back to Europe. With some difficulty he induced her to let him accept an appointment at the American School in Rome. She wouldn't even follow him in his moral revulsion against William Randolph Hearst's Spanish war. "No worse than the British fighting the poor Boers. Of course I was for Oom Paul all along," said Tattie. His disgust with his own country over what he considered a shabby aggression was so profound he could hardly bring himself to speak of it. "Eliot now just explain to me why it is that you are willing to spend your time, and so much money darling, to send that Mirandola frieze home if you are so disgusted with your Americans?" Tattie would ask him teasingly while they were drinking their early caffè con latte in the garden, during the summer months he remained in Rome conducting the negotiations that were eventually to bring part of the frieze safely into the Boston Museum. They'd sent the children to their grandmother's in Asolo for fear of the fevers, but Tattie wouldn't budge. She loved the heat, it reminded her of dear America, she said. "If they are the vulgarians you say they are Eliot what good will it do them to see the frieze?" She cried out once in her thin wailing voice. "I know I wouldn't waste my sustenance trying to send home a fragment of Praxiteles to the Midlands. They'd much rather look at a glass of pale ale."

"Well you've already got the Elgin marbles," Eliot grumpily replied.

The fact was he couldn't explain even to himself why he put such passion into the acquisition of the Mirandola frieze. Of course it was an incomparable fragment. The rhythm of the draperies of the dancing figures was in the finest Attic style. Earlier than Praxiteles, perhaps from the chisel of some dimly discerned master of Praxiteles. The business degenerated into a low intrigue and he loved it. Half of the frieze was immovable in the Vatican but somehow the other half, in three pieces, had come into the hands of a certain Count Barbareschi, who claimed to be the last descendant of Aldobrandinis. The count's representatives were the Grandi brothers, bankers. It was in a room off a little court in the rear of their counting house that Eliot was first allowed to examine the fragments. There was no doubt of their genuineness. Professor LaPerière of the Louvre agreed with him in that. Of course the Grandis demanded an impossible sum. The situation was complicated by the fact that they seemed to hold some sort of lien on the frieze. All sorts of dealers were after it, but nobody seemed able to get in touch with the count directly. There was a Professor Reinach who represented a German museum and had the personal backing, so it was rumored, of Kaiser Wilhelm. Then there was a mysterious Dr. Brandt who was buying for a Swedish munitions magnate, a representative of the Rothschilds and ubiquitous Professor Balbi of the Ministry of Fine Arts whose business it was to see that the masterpiece remained in Italy as part of the national patrimony. Through the stifling July days these various agents eyed each other, as they circled stifflegged among the potted plants in the Grandis' courtyard, like dogs about to pick a fight.

When the rumor got around that a Boston lady of great wealth had put an immense credit at Eliot's disposal with

Sebasti and Reali the rest of them began to look at him with glances that could kill; he half expected to find one of them trying to stick a stiletto into his back.

He was leaving the banking house late one afternoon after one of those oft repeated conversations with the younger Grandi, whose Tuscan was so polished it offered not a word of commitment to hold on to, when he was startled to hear his name pronounced behind him on the street. The voice sounded like a woman's. "Please Mr. Bradford." When he swung around he found himself being addressed by a youth in a shabby black velvet jacket, who had a little of the look of one of the models who waited for painters at the foot of the Spanish Stairs. The youth gave him a slippery Luini smile, whispered "Antico Caffè Greco" and set off down the street, rolling his hips as he walked. Thinking of the hermaphrodites of the Augustan period he had catalogued by the hundreds in an effort to isolate the Hellenistic prototype, and highly embarrassed by the thought of being seen following such an androgynous creature, Eliot stalked warily after him into a dark inner room of the cramped little café. He wished he had remembered to carry his sword cane.

"Capisce Italiano?" "Capisco," said Eliot tartly as they sat down. The creature said his name was Dino and launched into an account of his poverty, his artistic leanings, the illness of his mother, the sum of money he needed for his sister who wanted to become a nun. Oh he just wants money, Eliot thought with relief. His embarrassment left him. For a moment he thought Dino might be the count, but no the count was his amico. Quante lire signore would a personal introduction to his excellency be worth? Eliot explained at some length that the dilettanti americani he represented would naturally want to express their gratitude to His Excellency's friends once the purchase was completed and the fragments were safely on shipboard for New York or Boston. Dino narrowed his eyes and led the way to a cab. Sitting beside the sprawling youth made

Eliot, who sat bolt upright as far away as he could get on the seat, feel quite itchy. They drove past the Pantheon and through deep narrow streets to the Tiber and across a sunny bridge into a tangle of lanes in Trastevere that smelt of damp stucco and rancid olive oil. Eliot was beginning to fear he was being led into a trap when the cab stopped under an arch in the entrance to a courtyard full of flowers and sun. He gave Dino a couple of coins to pay the cabman and let him keep the change.

They walked up flight after flight of dirty marble stairs with a rail carved with putti and garlands in gray sandstone and were met at the top by the yapping of a black and tan. A strapping young woman in peasant dress ran out on the landing to hush the dog. Dino brushed past her and ushered Eliot out onto a terrace under vines where in a cheap wicker chaise longue lay Count Barbareschi. If Dino was the hermaphrodite the count was a laughing Bacchus. Eliot thought he had never seen a human figure that expressed such depravity. It was a delicate sensuous face in the style of Filippino Lippi that dissipation had begun to bloat into the coarse semblance of a Negro. Immediately the bargaining began. The count shrilled out in querulous falsetto that the Grandi had been keeping buyers away for their own purposes. The girl, evidently his mistress, whose name was Francesca and whose upper lip bore more than a touch of a mustache, joined in with shrill cries that the Grandi were ladroni. There appeared a barefoot friar with remarkably large and soiled great toes who joined in the discussion. Everybody shouted at once. The Grandi were hounding him to his death, cried the count. They were the architects of his ruin, he shrieked. Eliot tried to impress on him that perhaps if His Excellency would authorize him to deal with the Grandi, they could be induced to see reason. But he must be allowed to retire to consult with his dilettanti.

The friar padded after him down the stairs, explaining with garlicky breath that Francesca was his sorella and that any little gift the dilettanti americani intended for her would be safer if placed in his hands. As Eliot was leaving the palazzo an old man with a portfolio seized hold of both his lapels, asked if he were not il millionario americano and immediately launched into a complicated plan for getting the fragments out of the country through Naples in a box of Venetian mosaics. It must be Naples because his cousin was in the customhouse there and could expedite the authorization. He was the father of the lovely Francesca. She had a sister, he added rubbing his hands, while his face took on a most repulsive leer, who was a virgin. "No thank you," said Eliot.

When Eliot got back to the hotel he took a bath and changed his linen. At dinner he told a somewhat bowdlerized version of the story to Tattie and to her halfbrother Marmaduke Ames, a lanky young man with a long sandy mustache, on leave from one of those English regiments of horseguards where everybody had to be very tall. He murmured, "My word what a ripping adventure . . . Boccaccio, eh what?" and he said he had better go along as a bodyguard for the next interview. Marmaduke was a great help during the remaining course of the intrigue. He understood no word of Italian, but he stood behind Eliot and twirled his mustache and stared people in the face in a most disconcerting way.

They both carried swordcanes the night when after the Grandi had been paid off, a first installment was delivered to the count, and the fragment, in four packing cases, was placed in their hands for shipment to Naples. Eliot and Marmaduke, their faces muffled in cloaks against the miasmas of the campagna, kept watch all night on the cart until the freight office at the railroad station opened at sunrise amid the crowing of all the cocks and the squalling of the babies in the adjacent tenements. Taking full advantage of their license as mad English they rode clear to Naples in the baggage car, dazzling the brakeman with largesse and sending him out for wine at every station. At Naples the complications were endless. The customs officials, the captain of the port, the prefect of police and minor officials without number had to be bribed to assure the shipment on a British steamer bound for the port of Boston of this remarkable collection of modern mosaic. The stevedores seemed to sprout as many outstretched hands as Hindu divinities. Every palm had to be crossed. Even after the packing cases were deposited on board Eliot had to lift the lids for a last time, to make sure that there had been no sleight of hand, before making the final payment to the agents of the count. When at last they left the frieze safe under the protection of a Scotch supercargo and of the Union Jack, they drove in triumph to the station and climbed aboard the wagon-lit of the night express. Tattie met them at the station in Rome with the baggage. The three of them had a very jolly journey, though they felt some apprehension as to what action the Italian government might take if the departure of the masterpiece were discovered. When they crossed the border at Modane they drank a bottle of champagne and toasted the master of Praxiteles. They then proceeded to spend a week beside a cool Swiss lake before returning to Asolo to pick up the children.

After the successful conclusion of this adventure Marmaduke, who came to look on archaeology as a sport like pigsticking or the shooting of grouse, spent as many furloughs as he could wangle as Eliot's partner in excavations that took them to Cyprus, to the Fayum, to Cyrenaica. He became remarkably good at negotiating for permits with the Turks. Arabs respected him to a man. As British intelligence became more and more appreciative of Captain Ames' laconic reports he spent less and less time with his regiment. In the ruins of Palmyra, while Eliot was choking in the dust of his excavation in a corner of Zenobia's palace, Marmaduke hunted gazelles on the desert and managed to flush a brace of German engineers disguised as Druses, who were surveying an alternative route for the Baghdad-Bahn. At Umm-es-Salaam after the shooting affray, provoked undoubtedly by agents of a Central European power, in which poor Villeneuve met his death, he saved not only the lives of the rest of them but the magnificent fifth century head their researches had added to the world's store of beauty, by his coolness in keeping the excited bedouin at bay while Eliot mollified their sheikh by the present of a Winchester rifle. The news of Belgium's invasion and the declaration of war sent Marmaduke hurrying back to England. It was his death in one of the first holding engagements in a beetfield in Flanders that first brought the full pain of war home to the Bradfords.

They heard the news in their suite at the Crillon in Paris where they had reached their wit's end in daylong arguments with Eliot's mother, who insisted she was quite strong enough to serve as a trained nurse on the battlefield, while they tried to convince her that it was her duty — and a post of honor and danger at that — to escort her grandchildren and their nurse home to Hingham. When she finally consented to take passage on a Dutch boat she remarked that she would be back in the spring. "I'll make poor dear Peabody care for the children next summer." As soon as the family had been safely installed aboard the liner they returned to Paris. Tattie joined the British Red Cross and Eliot, with a reckless energy and an organizing skill he had been developing as he grew older in his archaeological projects, threw himself into creating a volunteer ambulance service for the French, whose plans for care of the wounded had advanced not a whit since the Franco-Prussian War. The first time he drove, in a converted Rolls Royce he had furnished himself, a load of muddy bandaged piouxpioux through the deep ruts of a shellpitted road from the lines to the quiet and the soothing smell of disinfectants of a field hospital, he felt a profound satisfaction both in the fact that he was not afraid of shellfire and in the fact that he was helping, while his own country in callous stupidity stood cravenly aloof, to defend civilization from the onslaught of a barbarian horde. He became so absorbed in the work that he hardly felt a pang when news came that the head of Athena from Umm-es-Salaam had been lost at sea in the torpedoing of the steamer *Coptic*. After Louvain and Rheims, and so many brave men dead, the wreck of another tiny fragment of the precarious beauty France and England were bleeding themselves to protect from the hammerblows of the Hun seemed sad but irrelevant. He would have exchanged the head gladly, he thought, as he went over the figures of expenses and donations at his desk in the Paris office, for half a dozen wellequipped motor ambulances.

5

THE CENTURY THAT I SHALL LIVE TO SEE

LURCHING with the green baize bookbag over his shoulder, out of the hateful Cambridge April day into Mooney's Pleasure Palace's close cabbageflavored vestibule, Jay Pignatelli saw in the grime of Mooney's mirror forever cracked his name reversed on a telegram. He never remembered tearing the yellow envelope; immediately the message spread across his hand YOUR FATHER PASSED PEACEFULLY AWAY AT 4.30 A.M. THIS MORNING YOUR PRESENCE URGENT IN CHICAGO . . . LUKE. He saw Cousin Luke's noseglasses with gold rims like Dandy's, the adamsapple fidgeting under the sallow skin between the turneddown points of the lustrous starched collar over the horseshoe pin that sparkled in the Bond Street necktie, the raised eyebrows topping a smooth hairless face that was a meager shaven snapshot of Dandy's face. Dandy was dead.

Dandy your father is dead, it said in Jay's head as he stuffed shirts into Dandy's passed on portmanteau. I lived in Dandy's world like in his old portmanteau. So much to say that now never can be said . . . Toothbrush. Socks. Coat. Hat. "So much unsaid," he said aloud as he hefted the portmanteau. He could barely lift it, it bulged so with books. All the way to Harvard Square, he had to lug the scuffed portmanteau, his coat flapping in the knucklechapping Cambridge wind, mashed brown hat pulled down over eyes that skimmed the sidewalk for fear of seeing some face that was familiar, before his hand could grasp the cold handle of a taxi door. He had no words to use for a familiar face. As the cab trundled him down the hackneyed street the words in his head were milling in confused crowds along the curb while the letters of the telegram like soldiers marching strode stiffbacked past YOUR FATHER which art in heaven PASSED PEACEFULLY . . .

. . . Peace is past; at every streetcorner headline over headline clamored war. HOUSE IS READY TO PASS WAR MEASURES . . . READY TO DIE FOR LIBERTY MAYOR DECLARES . . . And Dandy's voice in the library at Wharton Place while with a small smile on the big lips under his mustache he fed squares of raw steak to Diogenes the black snake in the bowl and Jay, a smaller skinny squirming Jay, listened, tonguetied, inattentive, constrained but listened. "If we can seize what we are beginning to call the psychological moment to unite the Englishspeaking peoples in a league for peace there need be no wars. Call it a league for war if you prefer that name, so long as it becomes a league of the likeminded. Any powerful league would make for peace. The great forces of international finance are already more than half convinced that peace is in their interest. But only the Englishspeaking peoples of common speech and the Common Law have enough political education to set up institutions to enforce the peace. To do that we must unify . . . Jay, if I said this outside my own library I should be crucified. We must meet the Britishers halfway. To a certain extent we must repeal the Declaration of Independence." (It was like the man without a country; it was like saying Damn the United States, Jay thought.) "You're shocked." Dandy laughed. "It even shocks Diogenes the old cynic living in his tub who I am sure is an upright patriotic snake. New ideas give people pain and must be whispered very carefully in the ears of snakes and small boys in the privacy of the library. The question is how to state the necessary new ideas so that people will give them consideration. If we could form an Englishspeaking league this century that you Jay, not I, will live to see, would be the greatest in human history."

The century that I shall live to see. Jay stretched his legs out in front of him as the cab poked into the packed traffic that churned the thin slick of mud in the cowpaths of the Boston streets under the flags, the curling stripes, the staring stars that so stirred his blood. Less danger of familiar faces in the Boston streets. Nobody to tell that Dandy was dead, that peace had drowned on the *Lusitania*, that the psychological moment had gone pop with the shots at Sarajevo, that Dandy's world PASSED PEACEFULLY AWAY AT 4.30 A.M. THIS MORNING. MY PRESENCE URGENT IN CHICAGO to discover the century that I shall live to see . . . What the devil would he find to say to Luke?

Once in the South Station he felt easier. It was the place he liked best in Boston. (A railroad station is your only home, thought Jay.) After he had paid the taxi and wired Luke he had just enough money left for an upper on the nocoach train. He had hours to wait. It made him feel good to sit expectantly in the waitingroom with two cents in his pocket watching people passing to and fro, with strange faces he didn't have to speak to, until suddenly grief, the grief he had felt for Petite Mère, welled up in him and like ink poured into water filled the bright world with black. Dead. Tears blinded his eyes. He had to clamp his lips tight with his teeth to hold the sobs. He pulled a volume of the old brown Gibbon out of his bag:

> *In the last days of Pope Eugenius the Fourth, two of his servants, the learned Poggius and a friend, ascended the Capitoline Hill, reposed themselves among the ruins of columns and temples, and viewed from that commanding spot the wide and various prospect of desolation. The place and the object gave ample scope for moralizing on the vicissitudes of fortune, which spares neither man nor the proudest of his works, which buries empires and cities in a common grave . . .*

Long before the time came for the train to be made up Jay found he was hungry. One cent he spent on an evening paper and the other on a slab of stale chocolate out of a slot machine and then swinging the bookbulging old portmanteau he walked through the gate into the foggy gusts off the Grand Banks that mingled with the choky coalsmoke of the trainshed and climbed aboard his sleeper, where the yawning pullman porter settled him into the plush and stuffy steamheat of his reservation. He sat with his hands in his empty pockets noting with aloof interest the proprietory air with which the other passengers occupied their seats. There were women with babies and roundfaced businessmen, a whitewhiskered old gentleman with polished luggage who looked like a Boston banker, matrons in furcoats, but nobody young enough to talk to. Jay had a couple of Gibbons, *Napoleon the Last Phase,* a yellowbacked Casanova and a blue Turgeniev piled on the seat beside him but he was so out of patience waiting for the train to leave that his eyes couldn't seem to stay on the rails of print. When the train started, breathlessly he was telling himself, he'd leave his useless old self standing on the Boston platform. A wiry new Jay, seasoned and tough, alert to lay hold on life, would go rumbling towards Chicago, towards the century that he would live to see.

As the train slid smoothly out of the station a small canvascovered trunk appeared swaying above Jay's head. Jay ducked and pulled in his feet as the occupant of the lower berth popped from behind the bulky Negro porter like a jack out of his box. He was an army captain, signal corps, a small alert ramrodstiff personage in a burberry with a camelshair overcoat over his arm and a number of polished leather cases of various sizes hung from his Sam Browne belt. He settled himself on the edge of the seat opposite Jay, bouncing up and down a little with the motion of the train as if he were made of springs inside. He wore steelrimmed spectacles and had his dark hair cropped like a shoebrush. His short mustache bristled dangerously at the tips. Not a man to trifle with it seemed to say.

Jay found a pair of black eyes probing him through the spectacles.

"Harvard?" asked a crisp voice.

"Lawschool," said Jay.

"So was I. College and lawschool . . . How do you come to be reading Gibbon?"

"I find him soothing in times of stress."

"When I went through lawschool they didn't leave you any time for extracurricular reading . . . I thought the law was a bloody bore."

"May I ask you a question sir?" drawled Jay in his smoothest tones. "I notice you are wearing glasses . . . I've been trying to get in the army. I've tried everything in Boston and Cambridge. They tell me I'm too myopic . . . They even told me I had flat feet which is a base libel. The only people who'd even put my name down were the ambulance service. That doesn't seem very . . . very active. How did you do it?"

"Plattsburgh?" asked the captain, picking up his inquisitorial manner again.

"To tell the truth I never had time. I've been trying to compress my education into the minimum."

"I understand," the captain said in a sarcastic tone, "that they are graduating men who join the service without examinations."

"It's not entirely that. I'm through this spring anyway."

"Law Review?"

"Not quite." Jay blushed. That failure stung. "Perhaps the question was out of order, sir."

"Not at all. Want to make the world safe for democracy, eh? Well, there's a little thing known as a waiver."

"May I ask how you go about getting a waiver?"

The captain didn't answer. The train had reached Trinity Place. He was looking intently out the window. "How lovely," he whispered dreamily. "What ankles . . . Damnation she's not taking the train."

The engine huffed and puffed. Vestibule floors banged as

the train began to pull out of the dark station. "We've got a novice engineer," grumbled the captain. "Unusual on this train."

He turned back to Jay and looked him up and down. "Since our fair one has deserted us perhaps you'll eat dinner with me. You'll tell me about lawschool and I'll tell you about the real significance of Gibbon, or Turgeniev if you had rather." He gave a short huffy laugh. "Within a month I expect to be dining at Turgeniev's table at the Café de Paris."

"On the avenue de l'Opèra where he used to have conversations with a certain countrygentleman from Normandy."

"You speak French? I took you for an Englishman but you pronounce French too well for an Englishman . . . Perhaps we had better introduce ourselves. Captain Bronson . . . F. Scott Bronson."

He thrust out a small knotty hand. Jay shook it. "Jay Pignatelli," he muttered indistinctly. "Glad to meet you Captain Bronson."

"I know that name. I used to know a Mrs. Pignatelli with two browneyed daughters in Indianapolis."

"She was not my mother," said Jay. The words seemed to cut his tongue as he said them.

"Hum," said Captain Bronson. He looked out of the window. Jay's eyes followed his and studied the rows of threedecker frame houses of the Boston suburbs. "Wouldn't be much of a life, would it?" said Captain Bronson. Then he turned back and looked Jay in the face. "You'll get a commission if you really want one," he said. "How's your memory?"

"Pretty fair."

"It's not too hard to memorize an eye chart."

"I speak a couple of languages that might be useful over there," said Jay hesitantly.

Captain Bronson stuck out his chest. "The language of command is the only language an officer needs."

"If we get to sending troops we'll need interpreters."

"There's no 'if' any more. We should have been in a year ago if it hadn't been for politics. The show would be over by now. If the people of this country hadn't lost all stamina . . . If you let people step on your toes it isn't long before they are kicking you in the face." Captain Bronson all at once looked at Jay so hard Jay began to blush. "You must be Jim Pignatelli's son . . . The famous Jim Pignatelli . . . I heard him in court several times before I went into the diplomatic service."

"He died this morning," said Jay.

"My my," said Captain Bronson in a surprisingly gentle tone. He began to busy himself with the bristle of his mustache. "Gibbon is good for that," he went on softly . . . "I have a theory about Gibbon . . . The sense of the grandeur of history, sentences like majestic colonnades . . . I used to have a whole lecture on Gibbon when I was on the Chautauqua circuit . . . Gad it used to be hot in those tents." He gave Jay a confiding smile. He's cheering me up, Jay said to himself and felt grateful.

"An added reason for going to the war. Nothing to hold me," Jay insisted.

"Just keep trying," said Captain Bronson. "In my experience interpreters are cringing miserable creatures. I have a theory that they invariably mislead you . . . You can do better than that. You get your waiver. Tell me how do you like his chapter on Justinian?"

They talked Gibbon and Roman law until the colored man in a white coat went through announcing first call for dinner. Jay held back when the captain told him to come along, getting very flushed until he finally confessed he didn't have a red cent in his pocket. The captain laughed. "Well that makes my presence providential . . . I like to feel providential."

All at once they were friends. The captain talked and Jay listened and ate his head off and drank half a bottle of wine and it wasn't until he climbed into his upper berth that he remembered the grief weighing like a stone in his chest.

Jay woke late. When he came back from shaving in the empty smokingroom the porter handed him a note from Captain Bronson who had left the train at Cleveland giving him a phone number to call in Chicago. As Jay didn't have any money for breakfast he sat looking sullenly out at the barns and the factories and the endless ranks of dry cornstalks marching across the level furrowed fields still scabbed with stale snow all too familiar in the haze of the April thaw. He fell to reading Turgeniev's *Smoke* and could hardly tear his eyes from the page when the porter came through with his whiskbroom. Jay didn't have a quarter to give him and was still debating with himself whether he ought to have taken his address to mail him one while he dragged the unwieldy portmanteau down the platform at the Chicage depot.

"What you got in there, gold bricks?" growled a voice in his ear as a hand snatched his bag away from him. Bill Keezer shuffling along beside him looked so old and hunched with the yellow mustache hanging in a limp frazzle over his mouth that Jay hardly recognized him. (It's not the dead, thought Jay, it's the living who suffer death.)

"Gosh Bill let me take it . . . It's books. You know I can't do without books, like a drug addict."

Bill Keezer clung resolutely to the portmanteau. An incomprehensible growl came out from under his mustache.

"Bill," said Jay, "loan me some money for breakfast. I just had enough for the ticket."

Bill's glum face pulled itself together into something like a grin. His back straightened. He rummaged in his wallet with his free hand and pulled out a ten dollar bill. "Take this Jay," he said. "You kin have more if you need it. Right up to the hilt . . . There's many a time the boss has dug into my savin's when he ran low, and he always paid it back with interest, with very liberal interest. I owe everything I have to him, Jay. He picked me outa the gutter, you know that. I always said you was a chip of the old block . . . But maybe we'd better just get a cup of coffee at the counter. Your Cousin Luke and Mr. Mortlake are waitin' for you."

"First," said Jay feeling the strength coming into him from every word Bill Keezer said, "I'm going to eat my breakfast . . . We've got a tough day ahead."

"The girls wired Mr. Mortlake their power of attorney from Pasadena. Him and Luke are waitin' to read the will . . . It seems there are pressin' matters. The boss's creditors were closin' in all these last weeks. 'Bill,' he says to me, 'if I get out of this I'll never borrow another dollar.' We were fightin' with our backs to the wall."

"All the more reason for a good breakfast."

"The boss did used to say Napoleon never expected his armies to fight on an empty stomach."

Jay led the way into the acreage of tables spread with starched tableclothes and shining silver of the station restaurant. Bill Keezer followed after humbly carrying the portmanteau.

"You better have something yourself, Bill," said Jay.

"I can't eat," said Bill. "I'll smoke my pipe."

Jay ordered up fruit and cereal and liver and bacon.

"The boss," said Bill Keezer in a critical growl, "never et a breakfast without two softboiled eggs."

"And two softboiled eggs," said Jay smiling up at the waiter's congenial black face.

Driving, his belly warm with breakfast, through slambanging streets past hurried sidewalks in a cold gray wind to the Merchants' Building, the words, "the learned Poggius urgent in Chicago," kept circling round inside Jay's head.

> *The place and the object gave ample scope for moralizing on the vicissitudes of fortune, which spares neither man nor the proudest of his works, which buries empires and cities in a common grave . . .*

Going up in the elevator Jay with dread remembered the portrait, the insolent gloss, the highlights in the eyes. He wouldn't look at it. Gibbon was good for that. When a glum-faced new elevator man, not the jolly one Jay knew, opened the door into the dark lobby of the offices of Pignatelli and Miller, the first thing Jay felt was the emptiness. There was no receptionist at the desk. The light over the portrait was out. Its outlines were dim. It was like Sunday.

His throat stiffened as he pushed his way without looking to the right or left through the groundglass door into the brightness of Dandy's private office. Empty, he thought. Then he noticed Joe Mortlake's tall dark longjawed countenance, topped by dark hair parted in the middle, rising up out of one of the brass studded leather armchairs. He looked the perfect undertaker. Pale as its own ghost Luke's face, eyebrows aloft, mooned over Dandy's desk.

"Your train must have been late indeed, Jay," Luke was saying in his prosecuting attorney's voice as he fluttered a white hand over the bluecovered documents that littered the desk. His solitaire diamond blinked in the sullen light that came in through the broad windows off hurrying April clouds. "Sit down Jay and give us your concentrated attention, if you can. Much of what you are about to hear will be unfamiliar to you."

The way Luke pronounced his words, the pauses between his sentences, his gestures, the cut of his clothes were a maddening parody of Dandy. (I could wring his neck, thought Jay.)

"To be brutally frank we have to go to work fast to avoid being pushed into bankruptcy. Your father's major asset was his partnership. He has as you will note left his interest in the firm, if it can ever be evaluated" — Luke threw in sarcastically — "to you and to your two halfsisters in equal parts. I'm sure it is no news to you that before he died he made Mortlake and me full partners. As executors of his estate he has appointed you and Mortlake and me. Between the estate and the firm we can, if we aren't careful, get into enough litigation to keep the courts busy for years and land us all in the poorhouse.

There are some rather complicated provisions by which you are supposed to take your father's place in the firm 'when your legal standing and ability shall justify this step,' " Luke quoted in a high jeering voice. As Luke reached to pick up another bluecoated document, Jay noticed that he'd already had a broad band of crape sewn on the sleeve of his green serge coat. Luke gave a short dry laugh. "I have taken the liberty of perusing the will." (You would, thought Jay.) "Your father my dear boy, like many a good lawyer before him, has I fear written a very bad will. We must set about to remedy its deficiencies."

As Luke cleared his throat respectfully his heavily starched cuffs shot out from his sleeves over his small hands.

"Know all men by these presents that I James Knox Polk Pignatelli," he began to read, *"being of sound mind and in robust health,"* (Boasting again, thought Jay.) . . . For the life of him he couldn't keep his mind on what he was listening to. . . *"That a state of war between the United States and the Imperial German government is formally declared . . ."* Urgent in Chicago the learned Poggius reclined among the broken columns of the Capitoline and looked over the ruins of Rome . . . "Rome," Dandy used to explain. "What we need most in this country is an understanding of history. Jay you must go to Rome before you can understand the greatness and the curse of empire." It was no longer Dandy's voice. It was his own he heard in his ears. And Caesar bent the world to his will. How did he go about it? Detail. A thousand daily actions, inflections of the voice, nods of the head, small decisions, notes scratched on tablets, the language of command established the Roman Empire for Gibbon to describe and it declined and fell until the learned Poggius found nothing but old stones propping up pigpens and rubbishpiles pasturing goats.

"Jay are you following me?" shrilled Luke giving Jay a contemptuous look as he let the document fall out of his hand. "Surely your studies at Harvard lawschool have given you some intimation of the traps and pitfalls with which such a document is filled. We shall need your signature on the petition to probate. Furthermore Mortlake and I have prepared a series of papers which I am sure you will consider it in your best interest to sign. Although the office is closed in token of mourning we have asked Miss O'Higgins, who, as you may remember, is a notary public, to stand by."

Mortlake suddenly chimed in with his heavy booming voice. "Your halfsisters have assented in principle."

"You will execute, my dear Jay," Luke's voice was flutily persuasive, "a power of attorney empowering good faithful old Bill Keezer to take any necessary steps to protect the interests of the firm, and yours of course. The instrument must be couched in the broadest terms."

"That's very foresighted of you Luke," said Jay, "to think of a power of attorney. I happen to be trying to get into the army in the worst way."

"We expected as much," said Mortlake heartily.

"No slackers in our family," said Luke.

Inside himself Jay felt all at once very bitterly amused. "Suppose I stayed on in Chicago?" he asked.

"The Selective Service Bill will surely pass," Luke tittered.

"It will be war without stint," intoned Mortlake. "I envy you, Jay. The young men of America have a rendezvous with destiny."

"It's going to take all the pull you two've got" said Jay and burst out laughing, "to get me into Uncle Sam's army."

Luke frowned. "It will be necessary for us to have your power of attorney," he said; "because among the real assets are some tolerably large blocks of stocks. The market fluctuates. There is the need for hairtrigger decisions. If we can stave off the creditors until the market reacts from the declaration of war and the taxation scare we may be able to sell to some advantage . . . But don't expect miracles. We are all going to have to work for our living."

"I'll need a waiver," said Jay, "to get in the war at all . . . on account of my eyesight."

"John Hines," boomed Mortlake eagerly, "I'll call him up."

"Joe Coates," chirruped Luke. "As soon as we have concluded our business I'll get him for lunch. He's just been promoted to the rank of Major General in the National Guard."

"In my opinion," went on Luke, letting the solitaire diamond flash in a ray of sunlight that had just broken through the clouds, "the next few days will see a phenomenal rise in values. A rise of ten points on the board in Consolidated Electric will be enough to enable us to wipe out a substantial part of our indebtedness." He pushed the cuffs back into his sleeves and reached for the pushbutton on the corner of the desk. "Your dear father, Jay, was a very poor bill collector. He would never allow Mortlake or me to dun his clients. There are thousands of dollars in outstanding accounts that we can collect if we have a little time . . . Come in, Miss O'Higgins." Luke's voice assumed a formal courtroom tone. "No matter how heavy our hearts in this sad moment we must proceed in the spirit of mutual confidence . . . As the English say we must carry on."

Miss O'Higgins gave a sniff as she tiptoed toward the corner of the desk. She was a dry little woman with gray hair tied in a knot behind. When Jay got to his feet she gave him a mournful bow. As he dropped back into his seat he happened to look at Bill Keezer. It seemed to Jay for a fraction of a second that Bill was shaking his head just a little from side to side as if to say don't.

Jay signed the first set of papers, and a second and a third as Luke laid them reverently before him blotting each signature with pursed lips as if he were going to kiss it. When he came to the power of attorney to Bill Keezer Jay paused with his pen in the air. Someone had come into the room behind him. He turned guiltily feeling suddenly ashamed of being caught in this group of men crouched like conspirators round the blue and white documents. A stocky dark stubblefaced man in blue denims stood in the door. He had a set of black belts looped round his waist. He carried a bucket. A smell of sweat and soapy water came from him.

"Where de boss? He no sick? Big boss no sick?"

"Don't you read the papers, Nick?" Luke asked without looking up.

"All day work. No read," said the stubblefaced man.

"Nick," said Mortlake, choosing his words carefully as if trying to explain something very difficult to a child, "the big boss is no more."

"Pneumonia. He passed peacefully away," intoned Luke, "at four thirty yesterday morning."

The stubblefaced man's face was contorted with the effort to understand.

"Dead," said Mortlake with a boom like a cannon shot.

The stubblefaced man dropped to his knees beside his bucket and made the sign of the cross with two thick fingers. When he got to his feet tears were running down his face.

"Boss my frien', my fader . . . I love him," he said, groping blindly for his bucket. "Every Sat'day tirty years I washa de window."

"There there," said Mortlake. "We are all very much shaken. Better let the windows go until next week."

Miss O'Higgins took Nick gingerly by the sleeve of his shirt and led him towards the door.

"If there's anything I hate," said Luke, "It's a vulgar display of emotion. . . By the way, you'll have to let us sell Wharton Place."

"The girls have already consented," Mortlake rumbled.

(If there's anything I hate, thought Jay, it's Luke's damn

supercilious face.) He laid the pen down beside the inkwell.

"I don't really need to sign the power of attorney, Luke," he said in his pleasantest voice, "until I actually leave Chicago. Now do I, Mr. Mortlake? Since I'll be right here to execute any instrument that is needed."

"Of course if you assent in principle," said Luke huffily.

As Miss O'Higgins filled in the notary's forms and slipped each paper into her shiny stamp Bill Keezer, making a little humming noise in his throat was stacking them in even piles on the desk.

"That's all, Miss O'Higgins," said Luke yawning behind his hand when she had finished. "Thank you," said Mortlake. "Bill will you close up."

Miss O'Higgins drew in her breath suddenly looking very pale. "When," she asked in a choking voice, "will the funeral be?"

"Tuesday at Wharton Place at eleven, and no flowers please," said Luke still yawning. "Lord I need some sleep."

Miss O'Higgins hurried out sobbing into her handkerchief.

"Now Joe," said Luke briskly. "Let's see what we can do to further the patriotic designs of our budding hero." He reached for the phone.

Jay had begun to walk up and down in front of the windows. He had to get out of this office. He had to get out of Chicago. If he didn't get out of this office he'd break down and cry, he'd haul off and sock Luke in the jaw, he'd make a vulgar display of emotion.

"All right Jay," said Luke coming up behind him as if he'd read his mind. "We are off. General Coates is bringing a man down to the club who is recruiting for the Judge Advocate's corps . . . The time will come Jay," said Luke severely as he pulled on his gray suede gloves, "when you will realize that we have your best interests at heart."

"By the way," said Jay. "I've got to have some dough, Luke, just to tide me over. My Cambridge bank account is darn dry. How can we arrange that?"

"Right at present," said Luke in sugary tones, "the simplest thing will be for me to make you a personal loan . . . How about a thousand? Bill, where did I put those forms?"

Bill Keezer with glum face and glazed eyes came back from another office with the printed form for a note of hand.

"It's all made out . . . a demand note at eight per cent interest. I never get less than that for my money. I put it in mortages in Texas. All you need do is sign here." Luke indicated the line with the little finger of his gloved hand, "and Joe," he added with a mischievous little smile, "will endorse it, won't you Joe? We all know Jay's good for it, but just to have everything businesslike . . ." Luke yawned again.

Jay signed, and Joe Mortlake with a protesting pout on his lips turned the note over and wrote his name on the back. "Now the banks are closed. Would you like a check or cash? How much cash have you got in the safe, Bill?"

Jay said he'd take twenty-five dollars and leave the rest in the safe. He paid back ten to Bill Keezer, shook his hand, and followed Luke and Mortlake to the elevator. "I've engaged you a room at the Palmer House," Luke was saying. "May and Augusta are arriving from Pasadena tonight and their aunts are coming in from Indianapolis. I thought we'd let the ladies occupy Wharton Place."

Stuffing down lunch with the partners and round and rambling General Coates, who never got to the end of the story about hunting a bear with T.R. on an Arizona ranch, and sharpnosed Captain Kendrick who said very little, amid the cigarsmoke and foodsmell and the packed faces and hunched backs squeezed between the dark oak panels of the Saturday Club, each minute seemed to drag an hour, but once Jay and Captain Kendrick got away from the lingering luncheon stories, in spite of Saturday afternoon and the wind whirling through the streets and the empty offices and the dead steamheat in deserted corridors, the captain, who came from a small town in Ohio and aspired to be an actuary and had every confidence in the President, turned out to be a man of action. With few words and many phonecalls he dug out a sleepy major, in an office that was suposed to be closed and a sergeant with a pad of purple ink and a desk full of application blanks and mimeographed forms for affidavits to be filled out in lieu of a birth certificate and Jay, before he knew it, found himself — physical examination — lying on a cot in the iodoformreeking office of a certain Dr. Lyman who leaned over with dangling stethoscope and knocked on his chest and took his bloodpressure and shyly demanded a little urine in a bottle. Shirt, coat and necktie hung on his arm, Jay was left alone in a long narrow room with an oblong card of brightlit black letters at the other end. Holding his breath he tiptoed up to the board and studied the smallest black letters. If only the three littlest lines would stay in his head. "Without your glasses, now," said Dr. Lyman tiptoeing into the room from the back. Jay's heart jumped as he recited. "Nothing wrong with you, young man," growled Dr. Lyman, peeping with a tiny flashlight in his pupils. "Your eyes are better than I thought. One of these days you'll throw away your glasses." "I'd sure like to," whispered Jay blushing crimson as he guiltily reached for the blur at his feet that must be the necktie he'd dropped. Recommend a waiver. Captain Kendrick and Dr. Lyman tilted their heads together as if to start singing a duet. We recommend a waiver. Jay could see the waiver overhead like the stars and stripes rippling in an artificial breeze against a blue cyclorama while all the audience cheered. More forms to be filled, but then the sentence: "The waiver has to come from Washington," that stopped the vicissitudes dead and left him desperately stranded in the lobby of the Palmer House with nothing to do but wait and Sunday to face and grief and what to say to May and Augusta who had never quite liked to admit that Jay existed at all and their aunts he didn't know and a quarrel with Luke to avoid and the funeral Tuesday. He went up to his room and lay down on the bed and piled volumes of Gibbon around him and read and read and read.

Smelling sour of newsprint from great piles of papers and close with steamheat the hotel Sunday dragged. Jay read the newsstories and the Sunday supplements and wrote the law school and Professor Bangs and tried to make it all seem funny to Fred Wallace whom he begged to get his things out of Mooney's Pleasure Palace and expressed to Chicago. In the afternoon he went to a vaudeville show but he couldn't keep his mind on the spectral figures yelling ragtime out of the spotlight's tremulous ring and went back to his room to read more Gibbon.

> The satirical historian has not blushed to describe the naked scenes which Theodora was not ashamed to exhibit in the theatre. After exhausting the arts of sensual pleasure, she most ungratefully murmured against the parsimony of nature: but her murmurs, her pleasures, and her arts must be veiled in the obscurity of a learned language.

Monday morning he woke up early and over the morning paper in the diningroom remembered the phone number Captain Bronson had left him. When he dug the slip of paper out of his wallet he found the number was the number of the Palmer House. Although it wasn't quite eight yet he called the desk to ask if Captain Bronson was registered there and immediately the precise voice was answering on the phone. "If you haven't had breakfast yet come up. General McCleod's coming in the door right now." Jay headed for the room as fast as the elevator would take him. It was the drawingroom of a suite with salmoncolored hangings. A waiter was pushing in a table set with coffeepots and iced grapefruit and jingling waterglasses. The general was a gray man with carefully chiselled gray features. "This will be our last taste of civilian life for some time," he was saying as he watched the waiter deftly snatching the silver cover off a large dish of scrambled eggs.

"Jay," said Scott Bronson who was treating Jay as if they'd known each other all their lives. "I know anything we say won't go any further than this room . . . The enemy has ears in all the walls. How are you getting along with your commission?"

Jay told the tale of his vicissitudes much as he had written it to Fred Wallace. While he talked he noticed that the general was studying him carefully.

"Good enough," Scott broke in. "Have you ordered your uniforms yet?"

Jay got red in the face, and stammered he was afraid the waiver would be a matter of weeks.

"Maybe not," said Scott, and the general gave him a tight-lipped nod.

"Supposing, well just supposing," said Scott laughing "how soon could you leave Chicago?"

"The funeral's tomorrow," said Jay. "Any time after noon, I guess."

"Isn't there a will to probate, executors to keep an eye on, affairs to settle?"

"I'm leaving my cousin a power of attorney," said Jay.

"Most unwise," said Scott, "but I'd do the same myself."

"One of those Austrian eightyeight naval guns we were just talking about, Scott," said the general dryly, "may settle all our affairs." The general gave Jay a quick confidential smile. "The shell hits you before you hear the detonation . . . You'll find the army a tough school, young man, but you'll find that it saves you a lot of civilian worries."

Jay had gotten to his feet. He felt like saluting, but he was afraid he'd do it wrong. "I'd better move along," he mumbled.

"Quite right," said the general, who had turned his back to walk over to the desk. "Scott where were we?"

Scott gave him a friendly shove towards the door.

Too soon Jay found himself back in his own room. It was twentyfive minutes past eight and there was a war on and what was he going to do all day? He fidgeted over the newspaper until nine and then he called up Captain Kendrick. After hanging ten minutes on the phone and arguing with many subordinate voices he reached Captain Kendrick who answered curtly that he'd done everything he could do, the application was on its way to Washington. It would take time. Jay had better go back and finish up his law course. If his address was Boston the application would possibly be handled through Governor's Island. There was no more to say. Next Jay called up Luke. "Power of attorney," said Luke. "Commission," said Jay. Luke tittered. He would call up General Coates again, the general had said at lunch that Jay was undoubtedly officer material. He was recommending him for a reserve officer's training camp. When Jay hung up the receiver the hotel room seemed smaller than ever. He pulled out his watch. Only nine fortyseven. There was a war on and what was he going to do all day? He sat down at the desk and hurriedly wrote another letter to the New York law office where they were recruiting for the ambulance service. Please would they let him know by telegraph whether he'd been accepted. He was ready to sail immediately. When he'd finished the letter and mailed it in the shute by the elevator it was still only three minutes to ten. What was he going to do all day?

If that day dragged, Tuesday was worse. As soon as he was out of bed Jay called Scott Bronson's room. Scott's precise voice answered (Good old Scott always there when you needed him) that he had no news. Jay had better call him soon after noon. He hoped Jay was holding himself in readiness. There was nothing more to say. The wartime morning dragged.

When the time came to drag his heavy feet up the brownstone steps of the house on Wharton Place, the frockcoated undertakers' men at the door didn't recognize him. In the drawingroom the faces were all strange. As he backed into the hall Mary O'Toole surprisingly stately in black crape was blubbering on his shoulder and clinking her rosary. "God rest his soul. He was a sainted man." And could that homely redhead picking nervously at black lisle gloves too tight for her be Annie? Jay blushed in spite of himself as he shook her hand. May and Augusta holding court in the diningroom looked like middleaged women in their veils. Jay was trying to decide whether he ought to kiss his halfsisters when a tall woman in purple wearing long black gloves, with yards of purple crape wound round her neck, attached herself to his arm. She had a tall bony face and a high arched nose under a mask of powder.

"You don't know me Jay, but I know so much about you. As a theatregoer you must know my face; though of course, sometimes one isn't recognized . . . The footlights are so flattering . . . I'm Lola, of course, *the* Lola Paradise. Your father and I were such warm friends over so many years, such beautiful busy years since that first giddy night when I opened in *Business is Business* in New York and he was waiting for me in the green room. Yes dear, I'm English and I'm so proud of you. Luke told me. You are going to fight the Hun. How I've prayed for this moment when America would come in. Rich, populous America. Poor old England, we've had so many dead . . . He looks so sweet just as if he'd lain down for a nap. You know he used to come to me to forget his business cares." She put her finger to her lips and gave her mascaraed eyes an upward roll. "One of the great minds, selfeducated, but for an American, well read. Mellow like old wine. We had intellectual interests in common. It is a funeral worthy of him. He was much beloved. Yes dear, you mustn't grieve. We know that everything is for the best. Everybody who is anybody in Chicago is here, just like an important first night . . . He loved my first nights . . . Dear, I rather like the vulgarity of Americans . . . there's something openhearted about it . . . The judiciary, the bar, the cloth . . . We English are so staid . . . Tears ran down the governor's face as he walked past the catafalque." She put her long gloved finger to her lips again. "But I mustn't talk. It is time for meditation and prayer. My secretary will save the clippings and send them to you. They'll mention my name, but I don't care. Lola Paradise is above the breath of scandal. God bless you dear."

She flitted off through the crowd leaving behind her a tinkle of invisible bracelets and a strong scent of patchouli. Jay found himself filing in a line of strangers up the stairs. As he glanced back over his shoulder he saw Luke and Mortlake with silk hats held over one arm and a photogravure expression on their faces greeting arriving dignitaries. They looked like carefully re-touched cabinet photographs of themselves. Jay looked down at his own suit. It was light gray and baggy at the knees . . . This was no place for him, thought Jay, but it was too late to turn back now. He was a stranger in a line of strangers shuffling over the oriental carpet in the library. Over their heads he saw the sets of books in calf and morocco which the old Jay who was dead used to know so well, Caesar's friendly bust, the glass bowl where the black snake lived. Diogenes was dead. Jay couldn't turn back. Jay had to walk past the bier and look, wearing a false face off one of the undertakers' men, down into the bier where lay a waxwork mustachioed figure that was not Dandy.

(That's enough, thought Jay.) He slipped down the back stairway into the empty kitchen and out past the ashcans in the alley. He'd left his coat and hat in the front hall but he couldn't go back for them. He never could go back. He walked fast down the streets and scrambled confusedly for a while among coalwharves on the lakeshore looking out over the paleblue water laced with whitecaps by the punishing wind. The rushing air was sharp as knives. He looked at his watch: it was past twelve. Hands and ears half frozen he hurried back to find a drugstore on Michigan Avenue. With pounding heart he phoned the hotel desk. Yes there was a message. "Read it please," he said, shivering all over. "Leaving tonight for Washington. Better come along. Call me in my

room at one P.M." "Oh thank you, thank you very much," he
said to the telephone girl and hurtled out into the wind and
into a taxicab.

That night the vicissitudes of fortune rolled merrily over the
rails, as the learned Poggius and his friend sat in the diner of
the Baltimore and Ohio train drinking Scotch and soda while
they waited for their meal. The place and the object, which
were Jay's commission and, veiled in hush hush, General Mc-
Cleod's mission abroad, gave Scott Bronson ample scope for
moralizing. Over a brandy after dinner Scott sketched out
European history from Waterloo to the Battle of the Marne.
"I have a theory that the eighteenth century will probably turn
out to have been Europe's golden age, the nineteenth the de-
clining afterglow. Yes, I know all about science, the Alex-
andrians were scientific too . . . Applied science always char-
acterizes a period of intellectual decline. Waiter a pair of
brandies." When the levee en masse took the place of the professional armies with their humane courtesies and their plumed
hats, it was the barbarians at the gates, the barbarians from
below. "It's time for a new Gibbon to describe Europe's Decline and Fall . . . My these are small brandies, how about another? Jay you can thank your stars you were born in America
instead of in some uncomfortable stone village in the Italian
hills, as I am glad my ancestors had the sense to move out of
what has since become a squalid mining slum in Northumber-
land . . . Because . . . Suppose we have a brandy Jay . . . I have
a theory that we are the most barbarous of the new barbarians.
Our mission, the general's and mine and yours maybe when
we've wangled that waiver, will be to prepare the way for the
first invasion of the American barbarians. We'll make Attila
the Hun look like a piker. We'll make the world safe for
democracy all right but we have yet to prove that democracy
equals civilization."

(Scott's drinking too many brandies, thought Jay). This was
the first time he'd drunk hard liquor himself. He'd only drunk

beer and wine before. He was noting with interest that his head didn't swim, his eyes felt clear; maybe he had a good head. No he wasn't the least bit drunk, he reassured himself as he rose to his feet to go back to his berth to read. This time Scott had let him pay the bill and it was steep. (No use worrying about money, thought Jay, when in six months I may be like Dandy dead.) When he'd crawled out of his clothes — he had a lower this time — he lay clearheaded and wide awake noting carefully how transparently the words stood out on the close-printed pages of *War and Peace*. He saw the people and scenes of the novel before him like looking down into a theatre full of warm clear light. (I must drink more liquor, thought Jay.)

In Washington when they climbed out on the station platform it was spring. The sun shone rosy through new leaves on columns and porticos. The shrubberies were full of flowers. The monument pointed a white finger up into a robinsegg sky dappled with pearly white clouds. Against the dappled sky flags waved, stirring the blood. Except for the rippling flags the city seemed quiet; there was a hush about the traffic moving slowly between budding trees on the broad streets. On the sidewalks past the Treasury and White House a few elderly colored people strolled slowly in the sun. It was very quiet in the dark old corridors of the War Department. Nobody seemed in the least bit of a hurry. Sergeants rose silently to attention as Jay followed Scott Bronson's trail into offices that had shutters for doors. Elderly colonels seemed to have time to chat in measured sentences, looking pained at any military question, but talking volubly about everything else; except of course about Jay's commission. At lunchtime they walked with a ruddy major from Tennessee round beds of tulips on Lafayette Square to a silent club in a mossy yellow building where ancient colored waiters served them very slowly while the major talked at length about the sterling qualities of the Spanish horse. In the afternoon the Department seemed to move even slower. Jay began to lose track of what was going on, nodding in his chair as he listened to conversations over yellow desks until at last, with Scott making suggestions over his shoulder, he found himself drowsily filling out a new set of application blanks. Then he was threading his way after a silverheaded sergeant with a mess of papers on a board under his arm through a corridor packed with waiting civilians. "You'll have plenty of time to order your uniforms," the sergeant was saying. "It'll be a couple of weeks before we get the results of your physical."

After leaving his clothes in a locker Jay was waiting again in a line of weary nudes moving through a groundglass door towards a medical officer. The small pudgy man ahead of Jay was figuring out the number of minutes he had spent waiting in line for physical examinations since he'd first started applying for a commission six months before. He was multiplying by sixty to get the seconds when his turn came. The man behind Jay said he had attended every Plattsburg training camp since they were started. When the door opened for Jay he forgot to take off his glasses. The first thing the pouchyfaced medical officer did was to reach out and pull them off Jay's nose. He wiggled them in front of his eyes against the light and handed them back quickly, as if they were burning his fingers, with a frown and a shake of the head. "Waiver," whispered Jay. "Waiver, hell," said the medical officer. Once Jay had managed with shaky hands to get back into his clothes he hurried in consternation through corridors full of homegoing civilian employees, back to the office where he'd left Scott.

"Never say die," said Scott laughing. "We've got a new wrinkle. We understand an order has been issued to form a corps of interpreters." At that moment the major who was such an admirer of the Spanish horse tiptoed out through a pair of swinging shutters that led from an inner office. He smiled encouragingly at the sight of Jay's dejected face. "Take this letter," he said, "to Captain Stimpson at Governor's Island who is about to be appointed Adjutant to the C.G. A.S.S.C.

and call his office in the morning . . . If you take the midnight you'll be among the first to apply"

"Gosh thank you. Thank you." Jay wrung both their hands and hurried to the depot to get himself a berth.

When he stepped off the ferry next morning in the dark old slip that smelt of horsemanure the first thing he did was call Governor's Island. Captain Stimpson was not in his office. Jay got himself some breakfast and hung for hours breathing out the air of phone booths while the city roared around him until at last he raised a pleasant southern voice that said it belonged to Major — Captain no longer — Stimpson and that he was sorry he didn't know anything about a corps of interpreters. He suggested that Jay mail him his letter of introduction and that he arrange an appointment later in the month. Jay gave him his Cambridge address. "I guess I'll be going back to lawschool," he added in a broken voice.

Before he left the booth he found Tad Skinner's number in the book and called it just on the chance.

"Who's 'at?" Tad answered in a choky kind of voice.

"Jay Pignatelli."

"How did you know I was home?"

"Chance. I just happened to be in town. Say Tad do you know anything about the ambulance service?"

"Sure Jay, I know all about it. Meet me someplace."

"When? Where?"

"Meet me at the Harvard Club in an hour."

Jay staggered out of the phonebooth feeling all in. What on earth could be the matter with Tad? He was usually so pleased to see old friends. Jay lifted his huge portmanteau into a cab and drove uptown through the roaring unfamiliar city and left it in a room at the old Murray Hill Hotel where he'd stayed once years ago with Petite Mère. Walking to the Harvard Club through the noontime crowds — Lord how many pretty girls there were, brighteyed as mice, how cutely dressed — he had to wait at the corner of Fifth Avenue while a National

Guard regiment wearing campaign hats and canvas leggings, rifles on their shoulders, with field artillery and three brass-bands marched by. As far as he could see up and down the avenue the red and white of American, French and British flags stirred in the blue haze. Standing on the curb looking, hearing, smelling, helpless to move, he felt fixed in the ground, inert as a post. Everybody else had a part to play. Fortune's vicissitudes are stalled, thought Jay.

Under the flag in the club entrance Tad was waiting for him looking taller and scrawnier than ever, his necktie as usual crooked and a button off his shirt.

"Gorry Jay I was afraid you weren't coming." He put both hands on Jay's shoulders and whispered hoarsely in his ear. "If I sounded like a shit over the phone, forget it."

"I just want to know about the ambulance service."

Tad looked apprehensively up and down the street. "Let's go to a place where we can talk." Jay followed Tad's long uneven steps to a beery bar on Sixth Avenue.

"A pail of suds," said Tad as they slid in under a scrubbed board table.

Tad looked fixedly in Jay's face out of brown eyes. "I dunno where you stand, Jay, but in the years since I left college . . . You know I used to be all for God for country and for Yale . . . my eyes have been opened to the iniquities of the capitalist system. I write and draw for radical papers. I did a cartoon against conscription. The reason I sounded so funny over the phone is that the wires may be tapped . . ."

"Who by?"

"Federal agents."

"But what would they care about the ambulance service?" asked Jay laughing.

"Well there was a girl there. I haven't told her I was going yet."

"Where? You old Lothario . . ."

"To drive an ambulance in France . . . You see she's a pacifist. She goes all the way. I don't. I don't believe in compulsion but I'm willing to volunteer."

Tad leaned back yawning and stretched his arms so that his shirt began to pull out from under his belt. "Let's have another beer and how about lunch?"

"Tad who do you know down in the office where they do the recruiting?"

"She thinks I'm still working for that advertising agency, but I'm helping them out down there," Tad went on abstractedly.

"Then you can get them to ship me," shouted Jay.

"You see my position is this. I believe that war and militarism are positive evils, but at the same time I think a man can conscientiously serve as a noncombattant. Nadia says it's wicked to take men out of the firing lines just to be patched up and sent back to the slaughter."

"What does she want to do, leave them lying where they fall?" asked Jay. "But Tad, my problem is different. I applied months ago asking them to hold off till June so I could finish up at lawschool on account of my father." His voice faltered. He felt his throat stiffen. "The situation has changed. We're in the war now. I want to do something right away."

"Why didn't you tell me that in the first place?" Tad laughed like he'd burst.

"You didn't let me get a word in edgewise, you old wobbly orator."

"Stuff and nonsense," said Tad banging with his fist on the corner of the table. "The I.W.W. is quite wrong. The working class must take over the organs of state power. The general strike is an outmoded conception."

"For God's sake call that office before they all go out to lunch."

Tad's long frame opened up like a jacknife as he lurched to his feet.

"All right give me a nickel and order me a small steak."

Jay sat on the edge of his chair holding on to his knees with cold hands until Tad came back.

"Ed Winston's in," drawled Tad, "says to bring you along when I come to the office at two thirty . . . But don't breathe a word about this radical business down there. They don't know about my cartoons. They might think I wasn't enough of a gentleman to be a volunteer. They're a smug bunch."

"But Tad how long will it take?"

"We're shipping men on every boat . . . We have to get you a passport and a vaccination. New sections are forming all the time. They are needed I can tell you. Got a driver's license?"

Jay shook his head.

"Better get one."

Jay was so excited he shovelled in the food without tasting it. He kept looking at his watch. At two he managed to get Tad, who was insisting that there was plenty of time, out into the subway. In the downtown lawyer's office everybody was pleasant and vague. Very much Harvard. The vicissitudes rolled smoothly. Passport application. "You'll get your uniforms in Paris, carte d'identité. Sailing date hush hush but soon."

The next afternoon fresh from the South Station a stranger from terra incognita was revisiting the ruins of Mooney's Pleasure Palace. Of course Fred hadn't expressed Jay's things to Chicago. At the Law School there were knotted brows but after all we had to win the war. In a week he was back at the now familiar Murray Hill, pivot of vicissitudes, the new Jay's home. The old black elevator man recognized him. Then a series of days on Tenth Avenue at a motorist's school. Diagram of the internal combustion engine. Traffic hazards and then one morning a phone call and Ed Winston's voice in a deliciously Porcellian drawl. Ready? Good enough. Then perhaps you would drop in the office with your duffle at ten A.M. tomorrow. We'll direct you from there. Jay strode around the room, hefted the new already bookfilled khaki canvas dufflebag and the folding campcot and bedroll strapped up together and gave a consoling pat to Dandy's old portmanteau that would be left in terra incognita with the castoff Jay's civilian clothes. There was the phone gladly chiming: it was Tad.

"You coming?" asked Jay breathless.

"Where? Oh of course . . . I forgot. No. Maybe next time. Meet me on neutral ground at the Harvard Club and then down to the village for supper to be introduced."

"What village," asked Jay dimly.

"Greenwich Village, you dope. Nadia's friend is very advanced. She believes in free love; that's a little too advanced for Nadia and me . . . But I guess you can protect yourself."

In the bar at the Harvard Club they drank manhattans. It was the first time for Jay. As he turned back to the bar to set his glass down he saw a familiar mustache above a bobbing cherry. The army officer was Scott. He introduced "Captain Bronson . . . Tad Skinner." Blushing he added. "Never got word of any of those commissions so I enlisted for six months in the ambulance service." He felt a little as he had when Scott had asked him if he had made the Law Review. Failure stung. The manhattans in a new round were soothing and brown. Jay stood sniffing the bar smell of lemon and orange-peel and whiskey and bitters, thinking what splendid friends.

"When are you sailing?"

"I'm not free to say," Jay answered, proud of getting the cue.

Scott grinned at him approvingly and lifted his glass.

"And you?" Jay asked teasingly.

"Hush hush," whispered Scott, as he drank off his cocktail.

"Stuff and nonsense," said Tad. "The only people who know anything about this war are the German spies."

Over a fourth round of manhattans Scott started talking eighteenth century, asking Tad if he agreed with Jay in admiring the reasonable Augustans.

"Stuff and nonsense," shouted Tad, "the most conceited period in the history of man . . . Jay what time is it?"

"Seven fifteen."

"Come along with us Captain Bronson," Tad said. "Let's all go. We can talk better at Giovanni's. The girls'll be getting hungry."

"We mustn't keep them waiting." Scott brightly gave the ends of his mustache a little brushup with his knuckles.

"Captain Bronson don't you go preening your mustache at those girls," said Tad. "A man of travel and experience in the eighteenth century can cut us halfbaked hobbledehoys out in a minute but you mustn't do it. These girls are art students, and serious."

Scott gave a dry little laugh and puffed his chest out. "Never met an intellectual woman yet," he said, "who had a grain of sense."

"Stuff and nonsense," shouted Tad Skinner lolling back in the cab with his flopping red necktie under one ear.

Already they were halfway down Fifth Avenue. The cab swung around the Washington Arch and, too soon for Jay who was trying to think of what he was going to say to the serious art students, drew up in front of an old brick house on a dim street. Tad went romping ahead of them up four flights of stairs. The top floor was filling with shrieks and giggles as Scott followed more sedately as befitted the uniform of the United States Army. Jay dragged his feet after. The topfloor rooms had been thrown into one studio. The walls were hung with huge purplish nudes of indeterminate sex with banana-shaped arms and legs. Two girls, one square and dark and the other one small and blond, had Tad down on a couch against the wall. The tall one was trying to sew a button on his shirt while the short one sat on his chest. "Nadia and Sonia," he panted. "Meet my friends Captain Bronson and Jay Pignatelli."

Nadia the dark one with the needle in one hand and the button in the other turned her face up and looked at Scott severely. "Well I suppose it's no fault of yours that you wear the uniform of slavery."

"Don't mind Nadia," cooed Sonia smiling at Jay. "She has a terrible Oedipus complex and it makes her bitter. I'm a pacifist myself but I don't hold individuals to blame for the crimes of their class."

"Let's go out to dinner. I'm starved," shouted Tad wriggling up off the couch. Nadia was tucking his shirttails back into his pants. Then she fastened his shirtcollar and retied his necktie for him.

"It's not the style to show bellybuttons this season," she murmured in a loving voice. "If I could reach your hair I'd brush it," she added and gave him a kiss on the chin.

"I'll brush it," said Tad distractedly striding off to a bureau with a mirror above it against the further wall.

"You see her father was six foot six," explained Sonia. "If Nadia could only transfer to Tad." She uttered a devout sigh. "I myself am highly exogamous," she added turning her dull blue eyes up toward Jay's; "I have a weakness for the Latins."

At dinner in an Italian restaurant, they ate spaghetti and drank a great deal of red wine, and argued at the tops of their voices.

"To think," said Nadia, "that I should be dining with a Prussian."

"Takes a Prussian to catch a Prussian," said Scott. The ends of his mustache bristled.

"All militarism is the same," said Nadia. "The workers of the world will rise and sweep you off the earth."

"If they'll let us sweep the Prussians off the earth first," said Scott tartly. "The world will be a better place for the working class and for everybody else."

"The aim of all militarism is the subjection of the workers," said Nadia angrily.

"There's no distinction between citizens in the Constitution of the United States . . ." began Scott.

"A thoroughly reactionary document," interrupted Nadia.

By the time the waiter served the spumone, Scott was angry. He set down his spoon and got to his feet and made a stiff bow. "If you will excuse me," he said, "I have an engagement . . . Coming, Jay?"

Jay had Sonia's plump little leg twined about his. It didn't seem to be the moment to get up, so he waved his hand. "As attorney for the defense," he said, "I guess I'd better hear what the plaintiffs have to say." (Got to take the plunge sometime, thought Jay. Be silly to drown without.)

"Well, don't do anything I wouldn't do." Scott pushed a five dollar bill into his hand and stalked with stiff mincing steps out of the restaurant.

"A reactionary little bantam if I ever saw one," said Nadia.

"Nadia," said Tad, "when you are older you'll understand that it takes all kinds of opinions to make a world."

"Listen to him," Nadia giggled happily as she stroked Tad's cheek with a square grimy hand. "He's a week older than I am and how he puts on airs . . . Of course he looks younger, don't you think so?" she asked Jay. "Some people have the gift of eternal youth."

"She's effecting a transference," whispered Sonia squeezing Jay's knee under the tablecloth . . . "Your friend's a narcist, that's the trouble with him."

"Scott's a prince," said Tad vaguely. "A prince in wolf's clothing . . . Suppose we drink a strega."

The strega was too sweet so they tried fiori alpini which was sweeter, then they went back to brandy as better for the digestion. The girls talked about Freud and modern painting and Brancusi and world revolution and how their hopes marched with the proletariat into the muzzles of the Czar's machine guns. Tad talked about poetry and imagism and the revolution of the word. Jay listened feeling that he was in terra incognita indeed. His left arm was around Sonia's plump little waist while his fingers explored the ribs under her plump little breast. Suddenly the waiter was advancing with the bill.

Jay disentangled himself from Sonia and discovered that they were the last people in the restaurant and that the chairs were upended on all the tables. Right away they were out in the street and he'd pulled Sonia into a doorway and was kissing her. He found her little tongue meeting his. "Tell me you love me," she whispered. Jay's lips couldn't seem to form the words so he kissed her again and harder. His hands travelled down into the small of her back and pushed her hard against him. His hands pressed on her soft little buttocks. She pushed him off. There were footsteps on the sidewalk behind them, shadows off the streetlamp. A great dray pulled by big gray horses went clattering past. She took his hand. "My place," she whispered.

"How about Nadia?"

"She and Tad have gone walking probably. Sometimes they walk all night. They get into his place by the firescape. Nadia's radical but she's very conventional."

They kissed at the next corner under a policeman's indulgent leer. Sonia handed Jay her key so that he could open the door. They kissed on every landing. When they got into her studio Sonia gave a little whoop and ran to the bathroom. She came back in a moment with a bottle of gin and two tumblers.

"Let's get a little bit drunk," she whooped and splashed straight gin into the tumblers. "Let's be unconventional."

"But aren't we drunk already?" Jay asked laughing.

"My you're a funny boy," she giggled. "You like little Sonia?"

He took off his jacket and went into the bathroom to wipe his glasses that were getting smeary. He looked at himself flushed and redeyed in the spotted mirror over the wash bowl. "Hello Casanova," he said aloud.

When he came back she had put out the lights and was lighting a fire in the grate. The kindling flared up round big lumps of coal. "Bottoms up," she cried putting the tumbler up to his mouth. "Bottoms up," he answered and started pulling awkwardly at her dress. Their wet lips met. Their clothes showered the floor around them. Holding her bare body tight to him with one arm he couldn't find a place to set the tumbler so he drank down the gin. The tumblers rolled away across the floor as they wriggled sweating together on the goaty rug in front of the coal fire. He couldn't seem to find the place. Everytime he put his hand down there she pulled it away. They rolled and wrestled clumsily on the floor until the sweat on his face began to turn cold. The raw gin was going to make him throw up. He got shakily to his feet and went to the bathroom and threw up carefully into the toilet. Throwing up left him limp. He felt his way back into the studio and found her passed out cold stark naked in front of the fire. He had all kinds of difficulty lifting her on the couch and turning down the bedclothes to cover her. His head was already beginning to hurt when he climbed panting into bed beside her.

Sharp day through the skylight overhead cut into his eyeballs and woke him. He jumped up and started to grope over the floor for his clothes. His stomach churned with bile. An iron crown was tightening inside his head. His eyes looked out of fiery rings. Casanova hell, he told himself as he dressed. He couldn't get his clothes on fast enough. He wanted to get away before she woke up. Stiff with dismay he stood still in the middle of the floor. The blond head on the pillow looked very far away like through the wrong end of a telescope. Her face was creased and gray like cold dough. Full of hatred for his body inept under his clothes he stood in the middle of the studio gnawing at his lips. He guessed he'd better kill himself. Then the learned Poggius remembered what General McCleod had said in Chicago about eightyeight naval guns. Hit you before you heard the detonation. He began to feel sorry for himself. The Germans would attend to the killing. Nature's tricks. It had even happened to Casanova. He felt awful sorry for her too. Poor little girl he oughtn't to have let her drink so much. Damn fool. He tiptoed over and kissed her cool shoulder. She didn't stir. Closing the door gently behind him he hurried down the gritty stairway. At a corner he found a florist just opening for business. He bought a dozen white roses. "Be sure they're white because that's important and don't deliver them before noon," he said when he had recited her address. On the card he scrawled: "Bacchus the enemy of Venus. Morituri te salutant. Jay."

Jouncing in the subway local full of freshwashed people with early morning faces Jay sat with his eyes closed letting the hangover like an angry bird gouge at his brains with beak and claws. The eternal prosecutor inside his head was giving him what for, telling the learned Poggius he was a damn pedant to have written that morituri business on the card. She'd wake up thinking that nogood bastard. Belisarius the eunuch. The hapless Abelard. Oh Christ. Now weep for Eloise, and the Rideau Canal and the girl on the Saskatchewan. By the time he pulled weakly through the revolving door into the hotel he had begun to plan the sonnet he ought to have written her:

Now weep for Abélard, poor Héloïse . . .

But he didn't get any further because the first thing he saw in the hotel lobby sitting on a crimson plush settee was Luke, wearing his green suit and light gray spats like Dandy used to wear with a small derby on the seat beside him and carrying a cane and yellow gloves by God.

"Where on earth did you come from Luke?"

Luke looked him up and down, with distaste thought Jay.

"I hardly need to ask where you have come from. Saying goodbye to the pure flowers of American womanhood, eh?" He introduced a sallow sagging man in black. "Mr. Funaroff is a notary public. If you had been a little more considerate you could have saved me the fatigue and the estate the expense of a sleepless night on the Twentieth Century. I understand you'll soon be leaving for foreign shores. We can't let you leave without giving Bill Keezer your power of attorney and I have one further document." Luke smiled his man of the world smile and poked Jay in the ribs. "Out laying pipe, eh?"

"Better come up to my room," said Jay.

There was something almost friendly in Luke's tone as he added going up in the elevator, "Well, it's a family failing."

"I only have a moment. I have to pack. I have an engagement downtown at ten."

"Why we just caught you. They were very hush hush at Winston's office," said Luke. "We'll only keep you a moment." He brought a bundle of papers out of his inside pocket. "In order to function the executors must have your power of attorney. Furthermore I've brought along a deed by which you turn over your interests in the real estate to your sisters. It's a mere formality. But we must be able to sell at a moment's notice to the best advantage. We don't know when we'll see you again." Morituri te salutant, the words trooped through Jay's headache. He nodded vaguely. "While Mortlake and I will be worrying ourselves sick protecting your interests and the firm's, you'll be doing the grand in a distant land four thousand miles away as the boss used to say . . . By the way," Luke's voice dropped to a confidential whisper, "I hope you'll take careful precautions against venereal disease. I understand it's a great problem over there. A coup de pied de Venus" (Luke's French pronunciation was execrable) "is no joke, don't forget that." (If he only knew, thought Jay. He thinks I'm a prune as it is; God if he only knew.) "Why do these legal documents always have blue covers," he asked.

"The color of hope," said Luke. Jay almost liked him for that. He signed each document without reading it. "You freely acknowledge this to be your signature?" Jay nodded. Mr. Funaroff mournfully notarized the documents in a small scratchy hand and stamped them with his stamp.

"These are merely formalities," said Luke.

"The sign of the screaming eagle?" asked Jay just to say something.

"It's the seal of the State of New York," said Luke primly. "Didn't they teach you anything in law school?"

"Eyes bleary, I guess," muttered Jay. "Well Luke I'm afraid I've got to pack."

"Anxious to get rid of us?" Luke gave one of his little hacking laughs. "Well give my love to the rue de la Paix. If you need another loan, just wire me."

"It'll be the rue de la Guerre I guess," Jay muttered as he followed Luke and Mr. Funaroff to the elevator and politely rang the bell for them. Luke had settled his little derby on the side of his head. Jay noticed that he gave a little triumphant whisk to his coattails as he stepped into the elevator. (Well that's the end of Dandy's bastard son's inheritance, thought Jay . . . And the mess of pottage, comes at eight per cent . . . Not only impotent, a pedant, but a goddamn fool, said the eternal prosecutor.)

His headache weighed on him like a fourth piece of baggage as the new Jay scratched his possessions together and paid his bill and tipped the porter and got himself and his bags bundled into a taxicab. "Pier fifteen Hoboken and goodbye and good luck" was the word at the office. After the ferry ride and much backing and filling of the cab in and out of wharves that sentries blasphemously guarded it was like getting home to climb the gangplank of the French Line boat. The linedup stewards, the accented French, the close buttery oniony varnish smell made Jay remember a small boy with glasses holding onto Petite Mère's hand and the flowers and the flowing veils and the baskets of fruit and the bands playing of all the Atlantic departures. When he followed the steward to the Purser's office to turn in his ticket the short army officer in a trench coat hung about with instruments in polished leather cases just ahead turned out, naturally enough, to be Scott Bronson. "Well well where have we met before?" he shouted. They slapped their thighs and laughed. (Fortune's grand vicissitudes, thought Jay.)

"The only question I can ask you young man," he said,

bright mocking eyes boring into Jay's, "is a question no gentleman can be required to answer."

The flush on Jay's face seemed to make his headache worse. "What I'm going to do is turn in. See you in church," he said.

Jay had a cabin to himself. The bilgy smell and the throaty French of the dark chunky little steward who said his name was Dantec at your service and the ocean mustiness of the blankets on the bunk were inexpressibly soothing. "C'est le rêve, monsieur. On va gagner la guerre." Dantec stood in the doorway and tapped himself on the chest. "Moi . . . trois ans de tranchées. Cinq blessures. Reformé . . . Vive l'Amerique," he cried and latched the door from the outside. Jay tore off his clothes and stretched out on the bunk. He could hear dimly the vibration of the cargo winches on deck. Before he got the book open, he'd slid off happily to sleep.

When he woke up they were at sea. It was a stormy crossing. The racks were always on the tables. Only a scattering of passengers at meals. Jay enjoyed the solitude; he felt a little squeamish the first day but after that he ate onion soup for breakfast and washed down gigantic meals au beurre and à l'ail with carafes of bordeaux and walked round and round the wet swinging decks breathing deep of the saltsaturated air and looking out over the steep slaty rollers flashing green and marbled with spume where they toppled and broke in the steamship's wake.

"You seem to be enjoying yourself, Jay," said Scott joining him one day after lunch on his unending tramp round the empty boat deck.

"Don't do anything but sleep and eat," said Jay.

"And wear out the deck," added Scott.

As they passed the skylight aft over the smokingroom they could hear the muffled clamor of voices from the ambulance drivers and the Lafayette Escadrille boys raising hell round the bar. *"Cheer up Napoleon you'll soon be dead,"* they sang, *"A short life and a gay one."*

"I guess I ought to learn to play poker," said Jay glumly.

"What the hell for?" asked Scott. "You know the motto of the Abbaye de Thélème: Fais ce que voudras."

"A guy doesn't always know what he wants," said Jay.

"As the general said that morning at the Palmer House, the army saves you a lot of civilian worries . . . My own life, I might as well admit it, was getting hopelessly unmanageable. Don't you ever get married Jay."

"Better to marry than burn," muttered Jay blushing.

"My wife Aubrey's a very superior woman and we have two of the cutest children you ever saw. Francis is eight and Jenny is six. They live in Indianapolis. And what do I do but get mixed up with a girl named Greta. Don't ever get mixed up with a girl named Greta."

Jay didn't say anything. They took another turn around the deck.

"I was brought up to consider myself a gentleman and I try to do the decent thing but I have an incurable tendency to wake up in bed with the wrong woman . . . That was why I had to get out of the diplomatic service."

"Sometimes it looks to me," said Jay hollowly, "it would be worth while . . . with any woman."

Scott gave him a quick dark probing glance. "How old are you, Jay?"

"Twentytwo."

"I thought you were older . . . Well this was one of these blond aristocratic Spanish bitches. Blood of the Goths, the Spanish minister's wife in Bogotá to be exact. Aubrey was mighty understanding about Concha. Aubrey likes high society. It was the husband who didn't understand. He tried to have me removed, by a fellow with a knife. That caused repercussions in diplomatic circles." Scott gave a short self-conscious laugh. "But Aubrey won't be understanding about Greta," he went on.

They took another turn around the deck.

"I have a theory that the war's like the waters of Lethe. If we get through to the other side everything will be forgiven and forgotten . . ."

Jay gave an assenting growl.

"When I was your age Jay I had a theory marriage would cure the complications that wise old apostle lumped under the word burn. But it's not so easy as that . . . Maybe I didn't marry the right woman . . . But anyway if those eightyeights don't get me I'm promising myself a tender middleaged afterglow of marriage with Aubrey. She deserves a little real happiness and by God sometimes I think I do myself."

Jay wanted to say something about himself but the words dried up in his throat.

"I guess it's time for a nap," Scott continued briskly. "At five I'll wake you up to take you to meet the general. I haven't given up the hope of finding you a niche once we get overseas."

"I'm in this for six months," said Jay, "unless the army takes over the whole shooting match."

Scott said as they turned down the creaking companionway together, "I thank my stars night and day we are going to be in on this show from the beginning."

"Me too," said Jay vigorously, balancing on one foot as he turned down the long seesawing corridor towards his stateroom. "It had never occurred to me that war was fun."

As they neared the Bay of Biscay, the liner began to steer a zigzag course, and pairs of drowsylooking little sailors with red pompoms on their caps appeared in the corners of the boat deck: the extra submarine watch. There were lifeboat drills, the covers were clamped on the portholes and ship's officers with furrowed brows kept checking on the darkblue curtains that were supposed to keep any chink of light from showing out of the companionway doors. In the smokingroom rumors went around of spies being apprehended signalling to submarines out of portholes with cigarette lighters. These last days the passengers were jumpy, stewards spilled soup at meals; in the smokingroom the collegeboy volunteers kept their spirit up by finishing up the ship's stock of whiskey and singing:

> *Oh we're bound for the Hamburg show*
> *To see the elephant and the wild kangaroo*
> *We'll all stick together*
> *In fair or foul weather*
> *And we're going to see the damn show through.*

The last morning Jay had just finished shaving when gongs in all the companionways began to clang to quarters. His heart thumping he put on his overcoat over his shirt, shoved a couple of books in his pockets, fastened the awkward cork lifepreserver round his middle and trooped in a straggle of out of breath passengers up to his station on the boat deck. The opaque green sea moved with a slow glassy swell. A red sun hung like a balloon in the brown mist ahead.

"Damn those Boches," Scott was saying when Jay joined him. "They would torpedo us before breakfast."

Without a word an American colonel who stood beside them started to hand around sections of a huge bar of milk chocolate.

"My mother never let me swim until two hours after eating," said Jay shaking his head.

Scott laughed and brushed up the ends of his mustache. "You're a card, Jay," he said. "But honestly," said Jay blushing, "we must be near the mouth of the Gironde. There are lovely bathing beaches along there. I was taken to them when I was little. The water's much warmer than the Channel." All the same the hands fumbling at the corners of the books in his pockets were cold. His heart seemed to be trying to climb out of his chest. Meanwhile cinders fell on their heads as fresh gushes of brown smoke coiled from the blacktipped red stacks. "They are stoking her up . . ."

"The men I take off my hat to," the colonel said, "are the engine room crew."

It was a mild misty morning. Gulls screamed round the ship. Their white breasts flashed in the sun. One of the ambulance men had rigged a kind of kite aft and was trying to catch a gull with a piece of paper on a hook. For a long time they silently watched the gulls and the smoke billowing overhead, the color of chocolate where it caught the ruddy sunlight. All down the long glistening decks from the bow to the stern stood silent groups of men and women in life preservers. A few lifeboats had been swung out. Every stick bobbing on the water looked to them a periscope. Then they began to see a little smudge right under the sun. Under the smudge they could begin to make out the irregularly spaced stacks of a toylike French torpedoboat speeding towards them on a curl of foam.

"All right suppose we go down to breakfast," said Scott.

"We have to wait for the signal," said the colonel. "Look, do you see what I see?"

"It's a sunken ship."

Right in the path of the sun they began to make out a cloud of white steam and two tiny scratches of tilted masts and the tiny triangle of a ship's bow almost awash.

The toy torpedoboat circled cheerily round the liner. There was great gargling of French through megaphones from the bridge and the torpedoboat shot off into the sun again. As they drew near the sinking ship Scott handed his binoculars about politely. Jay had trouble adjusting them to his eyes. He caught just a glimpse of wreckage and boats and black dots that might be heads. The liner was cutting fast through smooth water, brown and muddy now and littered with flotsam.

"We're not going to try to pick them up," groaned Scott. "Why the sons of guns."

"Probably the rescue is being conducted from land," said the colonel. "There's the lighthouse."

By now they could see lighthouses on either side, and lighters and tugs and the faint outline of a low piny shore. Through his binoculars Scott picked up the boom of the submarine net. As the liner nosed under one bell into the coppercolored waters of the estuary, the tricolor was run up aft. A puny little cheer went up from the groups at the life boat stations. As the gong sounded stewards went around among the passengers telling them that the petit déjeuner was on the table.

"It's war deluxe by gad," said Scott as he dug into his grapefruit.

After breakfast Jay stood on deck watching the low hills patched with palegreen fields and the crisscrossed vineyards and the silvery stone mansions and the rustyroofed villages clustered round their churchtowers and the light poplars and the dark pines gradually pirouetting as the banks of the Garonne slid by flattened by the sunny haze like a painted panorama, like that longago scenery of strange lands creakily unrolled for Petite Mère and a small boy on the train of the Transsiberian. Even then crazy for vicissitudes thought Jay. Dantec the steward had come up behind him. Jay heard his low throaty voice. "Elle est belle n'est-ce pas Monsieur Pignatelli? La douce France."

The sunlight shone ruddy on the carved stone façades of the riverside buildings of Bordeaux. The great dark casks in ranks on the flagstoned quays smelled of the dregs of wine. The cavernous station and the toy train full of redfaced poilus in long blue coats smelled for Jay, in spite of the war, of longago childish travels in that world with Petite Mère. When they piled out of the stuffed compartments next morning at the Quai d'Orsay Jay half expected to see her waiting to meet him in a lace veil and puffed sleeves on the station platform. But the women he saw wore black and had anxious lines round their eyes. The bluegray streets of Paris had a hush about them. The horsecabs had the same red wheels and little squawking horns. There were the old women selling flowers, the smells of cheese and strawberries. He was not a bit surprised when, after standing round for an hour in the rue François Premier with the rest of the crowd waiting for the chef of the section to show up, he found he was quartered on the rue St. Honoré at the Lille et d'Albion which was Petite Mère's hotel.

The afternoon Jay first wore his uniform he met Scott looking neat and plain in stiffnecked American khaki among the light and dark blue and the goldbraided képis and the turbans and the burnouses and the kilts and plaid trousers and the rainbow ribbons and the scarlet stripes of the uniforms packed round varicolored drinks set out in the rosy sunlight at the Café de la Paix. "Sit down," Scott said pulling him into the only empty chair in sight. "It's the crossroads of the world."

As Jay sat down two French officers, sleeves glittering with service stripes, moved their chairs to give him room. "Pardon monsieur. Je vous demande infiniment pardon . . . Americains . . . Ah les braves americains." He heard the words rumble in a ripple round about as he tucked his legs cased in unaccustomed puttees in under the tiny chair. The air smelt dense of perfume and woman's hair and coffee and freshbaked rolls with occasionally an ammoniac streak from a curbside pissoir.

"It's lucky," Scott was saying with his dry little laugh, "that the French have decided to treat you ambulance boys as officers. Otherwise I wouldn't have this pleasure. The general is a stickler for rank."

"As you said Scott, it's the war deluxe," Jay mumbled as he sat looking out through the carnal flush of faces and the fuzz of hair at the sauntering men and women that filled the pavement between the terrace and the news kiosk under the tree. Among the rigid forms of darkcoated civilians and the young men in all the uniforms of the Allies, girls moved soft and playful as kittens. They dressed more plainly than in New York but their eyes had a different look. Every glance you met seemed an invitation to bed. Poilus in pale blue cuddled their girls shamelessly as they strolled. Horsecabs and green buses and taxicabs (the famous taxis of the Marne, whispered Scott) moved back and forth behind them with squawking horns against sunlit graystone buildings, marked with soft violet shadows, across the wide intersection of streets in front of the Opéra. All these women, Jay was thinking tinglingly to himself, with their clean cuffs and their tiny lace jabots and their dark dresses gently indicating the curve of breasts and hips, moving quietly through the mellow afternoon, were gently leading their men, leading and led, through narrow stuccoed streets to ancient doorways and up steep chill stairways into rooms garlanded with gilded cupids and gently between sheets to bed. L'amour à cinc heures. He was remembering a picture he'd seen that morning at the Louvre. The pavements of the grands boulevards were quays, like the quays of Casanova's Venice, where in the dim spring light in the scent of lily of the valley you embarked for the island of carnal love: *Embarcation Pour Cythère.*

"It's the war deluxe," he said again, drawling to keep the emotion out of his voice.

"We don't do anything," said Scott, "except eat sevencourse luncheons and attend vermouths d'honneur." Scott sat straight in his chair bristling the ends of his mustache with his knuckles as he looked about him. "Jay, there are places and times where all the women look beautiful. How can Mother's darling boy keep on the straight and narrow? Answer me that, Jay."

"I spent a good deal of time," said Jay, "as a kid with my mother round this part of the world. It makes it all seem kind of dreamy."

"What I'd like to do," said Scott, " is get a cab, and just ride around this town and look. There's nobody else I could even suggest such a thing to . . . If we sit here we'll just get entangled with women too soon."

"Let's go," said Jay. "Garçon!"

Exchanging military civilities and parrying arresting looks from dark eyes and halfsmiles from cupid's-bows as they squeezed their way out between crowded tables, they slid past wandering couples to the curb and hailed a horsecab. Cloppety clop the redwheeled cab trundled them gently down the Avenue de l'Opéra.

"You tell him where to go," said Scott leaning back against the darkblue cloth of the seat. "All I know about Paris is from books. By gad this is pure pleasure."

"Au Palais Royale," said Jay. He was rolling a hoop ahead of Petite Mère across the pale gravel and the fountains played and there were pigeons in the air and they were on their way to lunch in the sun at the little tables outside of Véfours and they met the little old woman who always dressed in violet and lace and was a countess and wore a little black patch at the corner of her mouth. The old lady was squatting down pour faire pipi amid voluminous violet skirts behind a bush right in the middle of the public garden with arcades of people walking by all around. "Isn't she naughty?" giggled Petite Mère as the old countess came trotting up to them nodding the little ostrich plume in her tiny bonnet and smiling as if nothing had happened.

"I have a theory," Scott was saying, "that everything that has ever happened to people in a given environment lives on in it somehow. I'm sure that when we get to the Palais Royale we'll find a Duke of Orleans handing his newest mistress with a patch on her chin out of a coach . . ." "I knew her when I was a small child," started Jay laughing, but Scott went on without listening . . . "Or Camille Desmoulins climbing on a chair to harangue the bloodyminded multitude. That is why all this destruction . . . Rheims and Louvain . . . is so terrible. In America we tend to think of it all as stage scenery, but it's more than that . . . By gad that's the Café de Paris."

"It certainly is," said Jay.

"Cocher, arretez un moment s'il vous plait . . . We've got to have a drink in honor of the great Gustave and the eminent Russian sportsman . . . With the grand old buildings," Scott went on as they settled at a table in the empty restaurant, "all the fabulous ghosts of the past that enrich the present vanish . . ."

The waiter had sideburns. "Champagne," said Scott.

"We're on the trail of the Grand Dukes," cried Jay.

The champagne was a long time in coming. They fell to talking about Flaubert's "Temptation of St. Anthony." "I have a theory," Scott was saying, "that if Flaubert had been more of a journalist he would have been a greater writer."

At last the aged waiter came tottering back followed by an acolyte with the champagne in a bucket. With ritual solemnity he popped the cork while the acolyte stood by as if for a flag raising. With trembling hand he put a drop in Scott's glass and then filled the two glasses bubbling to the brim.

"It's warm," said Scott tasting it, "but no matter." He raised his glass dreamily. "My country 'tis of thee," he said. "It may take three or four years but there is no question in my mind that we will eventually lick the submarines and drive off the Hun. The question in my mind, the question I would not dare ask the general or Colonel Knox, is, what will we do with Europe when we've saved it?"

By the time they had drunk the champagne and had gotten the long bill from the hands of the aged waiter an hour had gone by, so they told the cocher to just drive past the Théâtre Français, where Scott solemnly saluted the statue of de Musset ("The youth of a century," he said), and to drive right on to the Ile de la Cité and the Sainte-Chapelle. "We are turning back the time machine to the centuries of hunger and religion," Scott was declaiming, "but Paris is still Paris. These great old cities are like coral reefs. Generations of individual lives have left their imprint on them but somehow they keep a living unity of their own . . . We haven't yet learned how to build cities in America. Good Heavens, this must be the Pont Neuf. Vive Henry of Navarre, the first modern man who dreamed of a United Europe and said that Paris was worth a mass," he said as the cab came out on a buttressed stone bridge across the green Seine. "Now these houses in brick and stone are in the style of the period of Cardinal Richelieu if I'm not mistaken . . . Cocher, où est la Place des Vosges where Victor Hugo lived . . . but let's not mix our drinks. Better stick to champagne and gothic. Ever read Villon?"

"I bought him to take to the front," said Jay, "with a glossary."

The guardian let them in among the sandbags in the tall hush of the chapel and explained that the stained glass windows were being taken down "à cause des gothas."

"It's a jewelbox just the same, a jewelbox of the Holy Ghost," said Scott. "We've been notified there may be an airraid tonight," he added as they climbed back into their cab. "There'll be a full moon. We may be among the last who ever see this masterpiece . . . You see Jay." He was sitting bolt upright looking from side to side as the cab clattered down a narrow riverside street. "It's like Gibbon's chapter you were reading that day on the train. Imagine finding a law student reading Gibbon." He laughed and slapped his knee. His hand suddenly arrested rose to his mustache. "Look, the little one in black with curls on her forehead. The perfect midinette. And her feet . . . like little mice stole in and out . . . As I was saying, I have a theory that a civilization lives so long as its buildings stand. When those goddam Boches knock down a fine old building they are shooting far into the past. The past and present are inseparable. The future's barren without the past."

"There are always the books," said Jay.

"Yes I know . . . the classics, but to tell the truth books are a bloody bore. Life is so much more . . . These old cities mould people's lives. Arrêtez un moment s'il vous plait."

The cocher cranked his brake and the horse dug his hind hoofs into the cobbles. At the end of a street they could see a corner of the façade of Notre-Dame and the flying buttresses that reared like prancing horses.

"Let's sit here at this dump."

It was a tiny café with only four tables out in front. There was a hubbub behind the bar when Scott ordered champagne. Finally a bottle of five franc mousseux was produced.

"No matter it's the idea that counts," said Scott. "Notre-Dame is so much finer than its photographs that I'm frankly flabbergasted. It has everything the Parthenon has and more."

They sat for a long time looking sideways at the corner of the great structure. Then they walked around in front while the cocher followed them keeping a sharp suspicious eye on them from the box of his cab. They went inside. When they came out blinking from the soaring darkness of the nave the cocher greeted them with an air of relief. "Anglais?" he asked.

"Américains," cried Scott.

Ah américains, ça va. Je me méfie des serbes."

"I guess they wear khaki too, poor devils," said Scott.

Scott glanced at his wrist watch. "It's time I picked up the general and Colonel Knox. This is the night they saved out to see the town. Jay, you'd better come and be our guide."

"I know this town as an eight year old child. About all I could guide you to would be the Punch and Judy shows in the Tuileries Gardens. Besides I promised to meet Reggie."

"Who is Reggie?"

"Reggie Coleman is my roommate. He's the son of a divinity professor but he sure has a way with the petite femmes on the boulevards. We've been assigned to the same Fiat."

"Bring him along . . . We're going to wear mufti. The general's heard about the French cancan all his life and now he's determined to see it."

"We have to wear our uniforms. The gendarmes tend to raid the boulevards at night to pick up embusqués. Several of our boys were picked up while they were waiting for their uniforms. And they are so pained at the Embassy if they have to do anything for an American like getting him out of the jug."

They dined at Voisin's. Jay kept wishing he was out among

the varied carnal evermoving crowds on the street. It was like being tied in a straitjacket, sitting on the seats of amber plush making polite conversation. Brigadier General McCleod's dry meticulously chiselled gray features took on an odd hick look when he wore a tuxedo. Jay felt as if he were taking out an elderly relative from the country. The colonel and Scott looked out of place in their tweeds. Reggie, who was a foulmouthed pimply youth with a face broad as a frog's and red hair, was in a continuous state of suppressed giggles because the general thought he was Scott's friend he'd met in Chicago instead of Jay. They ate pressed duck and drank various wines but the conversation had to be squeezed out of a tube. Towards dessert Scott warmed up with "I have a theory, General," and launched into Henry and Brooks Adams' disquisitions on the decline of civilization. When the general began to get inattentive he came to the point. "As what we are really doing over here is fighting to stave off that decline, we really ought to see what it's like." "Scott, you always make me feel better," said the general in a sarcastic tone. "Joe Knox and I were feeling a little ashamed of ourselves for going on a slumming expedition and here you make it all seem respectable like going to a lecture."

"An adventure in human archeology," began Scott, "starting with what is probably the finest restaurant in the world."

"Food's too rich," interrupted the general. "I'd be happier with a nice dish of ham and eggs and good plain old bourbon and water.

Jay was remembering that he'd been in that restaurant before. This wasn't the first time he'd suffered that strait-jacket feeling of sitting too long at table with the grown-ups on the amber plush. Of course it was with Dandy and Petite Mère the night that Dandy sent back the pheasant. Little Jay had been kept up later than usual, so he was very sleepy and he wasn't hungry because they'd all been to the Guignol on the Champs-Elysées and let him ride on the merrygoround and eat galettes with sweet cream in them and they'd sent home his nurse because Dandy was in a gay mood; he'd just completed some great deal connected with a railroad in Italy. He'd bought Jay a set of little cards with pictures of all the locomotives in the world and Jay sat shuffling them drowsily happily imagining chug chug toot toot, the great engines puffing in and out of stations, pulling trains, crossing bridges, and he'd looked up from his engines and the waiters were bringing the most beautiful bird in its feathers all gold and brown. It was cooked inside its feathers, Petite Mère explained. Jay was hoping it would fly when the waiter pulled off its beautiful feathers and Dandy looked closely at the roast bird holding his glasses in his hand. Then he shook his head and frowned and sent it away; too high or something. Jay cried and carried on, too tired probably, and squirmed so on the amber plush that he had to be sent home with the chasseur in a cab to the hotel where that scolding nurse, not Jeanne, but the old cross one, Marie, was waiting to take over. . . .

"But they are morally degenerate," the colonel was saying.

"The Marne, Verdun and now the Aisne. Nothing degenerate about the French fighting man," the general insisted.

"Let's go see," Scott insinuated.

After dinner they drove to the Folies Bergères where they soon tired of the glare and the noise and the big naked women who, Reggie said giggling, were all English girls, the French girls hadn't got the legs; and soon found themselves out on the crowded pavement waiting for a taxi again. "They've got other things," said Reggie. "Suppose we go and see what they've got," said the general. "Scott will talk us into putting our researches on a high intellectual plane."

The taxi took them to a dive in a cellar Reggie knew up on Montmarte. There they drank champagne and danced with tall women in slinky dresses to an orchestra of tziganes. Everything was very brassy in there. To get away from the noise Jay went to the bar. There he found himself alone with Scott.

"I have a theory," Scott was saying, "about the soldiers and the whore. War and bad times is when they flower. In good times they lie dormant in society like a worm in a cocoon. The hot sun of war brings them out. Killing and fornication (I don't mean love — that's an entirely different matter, although the act is very similiar) lie deep in the roots of instinct. There's a dedication like a nun's or priest's, a terrible abnegation of all the lovely things of life in both careers. Other kinds of people in the world build cathedrals, raise families, make bread and champagne, weave cloth and grow vegetables. The soldier and the whore destroy. The soldier destroys life. The whore destroys love; they have deep affinity for one another . . . N'est-ce pas ma petite?" He patted the cheek of a catfaced woman who was insinuating herself onto the stool between them.

"Qu'est-ce qu'il dit? Qu'est-ce qu'il dit? Oh qu'il est mignon."

The rest of the party had fallen into the hands of an individual with patent leather hair and eyes in deep creases above high flushed cheeks, dressed in some sort of a Balkan uniform, who was mustering them to see an exhibition in a maison publique. Jay and Scott followed as they straggled up a slanting street up a hill. They had just begun to breathe in the darkness and to look about the fresh moonlight night when the sound of the airraid sirens rose sharp like rockets into the air.

"The safest place to see this show," said Reggie, "is from the top of Montmarte." Reggie and Jay found themselves running breathless up steep cobbled streets and up black stone steps into the moonlight. "I don't like those damn houses. They charge too much," panted Reggie. "Give me the girl of the streets every time."

"What a horrible evening," Jay was saying, "but I think we've given them the slip. An airraid ought to be an excuse for anything," Jay added when he'd gotten his breath. "Look," said Reggie. He grabbed Jay's arm with a shaking hand.

The milky sky overhead was becoming lined with white bands of searchlights. By the time they reached the balustrade at the top of the hill little spangles of shrapnel were flickering all over the sky. They stood looking over the roofs and towers and domes of Paris that lay helpless and brittle under the moon as a showcase full of pastry sprinkled with powdered sugar. Behind them the cement basilica rose grotesque and smooth, a collection of variously shaped cheeses in a market stall. "Listen," said Reggie. The air was full of a distant singsong rumble of motors. Round the edges of the city antiaircraft guns barked like faraway dogs.

Jay's heart was pounding but he was too little part of the scene to feel frightened. It was the childhood dream of being alone high up in an immense empty theatre, high up and the fear of falling. The moonlight was cold. They stood side by side, shivering a little, following with their eyes the sparkle of shrapnel and the anxious pointing fingers of the searchlights. Motors grumbled unevenly overhead. The tension snapped when there was a sudden crunching sound and a pink glow of fire rose gently away off across the Seine somewhere and another and another. They waited a long time looking out over the roofs at three distant ruddy stains that were developing delicate tendrils of flame. It was hard not to want to see the whole city afire.

"Let's go," said Reggie. "All talk and no pussy makes Jack a dull boy." They ran down the steps and into the stony darkness of narrow slanting streets. "That's the all clear," said Reggie, as they heard the little squeaky fireengine, the breloque, honking like geese as it scampered through the streets below them. They dove into a slow crowd of soldiers and women snuggled in darkness that moved along a wide avenue under the barely seen trees.

In an instant Reggie was walking between two girls. "Hello sister." He already had his arm round the pretty one. "Me zigzag . . . vous rigajig?" he was shouting.

The other one had anxious eyes and a wide gash of a painted

mouth. Jay didn't like her looks. At the corner he slipped
away and headed off at random through stone lanes resounding
with last footsteps of homebound saunterers. In the last days
of Pope Eugenius the Fourth, Jay was saying to himself as he
walked searching through the streets bisected with moonlight,
the learned Poggius and his friend ascended the Butte de
Montmartre and having viewed from that commanding spot the
wide and various prospect of desolation . . . At a Métro station
in a bright stadium of moonlight in front of a church with
two towers he ran head on into a little girl with a heartshaped
face and dark brows. "Bonsoir mademoiselle," he said politely.

She gave him a sharp look. "Américain? Quelle chance,"
she said and burst out laughing, quite nicely, he thought. His
hands were cold. The brassy haze of the champagne had worn
off leaving him empty and scared. His legs shook. He wanted
his bed. His feet ached from the cobbles. (Now or never,
thought Jay.) "Si on allait boire un coup, manger une soupe
à l'oignon?" His voice was uncertain.

Not at the Halles, she said in a practical matter of fact tone.
It was too expensive there. She knew a place. Chattering away
as if she'd known him all her life she led him into a tangle of
little streets and after some scampering back and forth tapped
at a shutter that showed a streak of light. An old woman's
creasedup face appeared in the crack. The shutter opened and
with an iron clang closed sharply behind them. "J'ai de la
veine madame," the girl was saying simply "C'est mon premier
américain et il parle français."

Of course the girl's name was Jeanne. By the candlelight he
could see that she had long eyelashes and her clothes were neat.
They slid into a bench behind a table in a little brown cellar-
like bar like a piece of a catacomb lit by a single candle. Jeanne
took Jay's hand while she argued with the old woman whose
creased face was plentifully garnished with gray hairs. ("Cold
hands warm heart," she whispered to Jay in parenthesis.) After a
great deal of grumbling from the old woman and talk about

how the fire was out and the oven cold and a little brandishing
of crisp blue banknotes by Jay, the old woman went to the
kitchen in back.

"Toi aussi t'a de la veine," said Jeanne. "J'ai pas fait le
trottoir ce soir." And she'd been that day to the doctor's; she
was very careful about the hygiene, she explained. The doctor
of course had to have his petit bénéfice but un medecin tu sais
— c'est ce qu'il y a du plus hygiénique. She hadn't been on the
streets that night, she repeated, because she'd been out to see
her mother at Meudon. She'd been caught in the Métro in the
airraid. The gendarme wouldn't let her out of the station.
"Les éclats c'est dangereux mais les bombes moi je m'en fiche."
Of course her mother didn't know. Her mother had placed
her with a dressmaker. They worked for la haute couture.
On fait du beau travail mais on est fort mal payé. She couldn't
support her mother on her wages so she picked up a little
money on the side. The old lady was glad enough to have the
money and she never asked where it came from. After all she
wasn't really a putain, Jeanne said tossing her hair back, she
never went with a civilian . . . sales embusqués . . . Les poilus
. . . que voulez-vous? C'est la guerre. Je serais ta petite mar-
raine. A la guerre comme à la guerre."

By the time the old woman was back with the soup and a
bottle of wine Jay had stopped shaking. He felt limp as a
tired kitten. They sat snuggled together on the bench because
it was cold under the stone vault of the empty bar and he was
looking tenderly at her two little hands all scarred and marked
with needlework that he held in one of his. With his lips
against her ear he told her about Jeanne his nurse and les
petits venventres. Par example; she laughed. They drank
every drop of the soup and the wine and went hand in hand up
the cold vaulted stairs of the little hotel next door. Embarcation pour Cythère, he whispered as she unlocked the bedroom
door. His hands were shaking again. The sheets were so icy
that when they had taken off their clothes they had to snuggle

very close together to keep warm. "Quand même," she whispered as she drew him near to her. "C'est gentil l'amour . . . Ah on est bien entrenché."

When they woke up his whole body felt easy. They yawned and stretched and smiled at each other. They were slow getting dressed because they had to take their clothes off again half way. He gave her fifty francs and she gave him a friendly kiss and scribbled her address on an envelope he had in his pocket for when he came back en perme. He must never go with anybody else not in Paris at least. Ces sales putains, they stole people's money and one caught nasty diseases she was saying as they stopped in for a bowl of café au lait in the bar below that looked even more like a catacomb by day. The old woman stared inquisitively at Jeanne as she cut them their bread off a long loaf held against her chest. Jeanne was in high spirits. "C'est bath les américains," she said at the old woman. "C'est un gros bonhomme."

"Ah, la jeunesse," chanted the old woman.

When Jeanne glanced up from breaking bread into her big white bowl at the streaky yellow face of the clock flanked by dark bottles above the bar she gave a little shriek. "Je me sauve," she cried, "l'atelier."

Jay finished his coffee alone, said "Au revoir, madame," and walked home to the Lille et d'Albion in peace through the early morning streets full of the clatter of iron shutters being pushed up, busy streets that smelt of cheese and fresh vegetables and of soap from the scrubbed floors of freshopened bars, and of horses and stables from where the cabbies were polishing up their hacks while their horses fed out of nosebags under the trees in little squares, and of fresh bread and flowers, and incense from the sepiashadowed doorways of churches. The muscles of his legs felt springy under his wellbelted uniform. His feet trod lightly on the paving stones. His eyes travelled lovingly over the carving round ancient doorways. He peered into courtyards and studied shopwindows and read theatre posters that seemed immensely amusing. As he came out on a corner of the rue St. Honoré he caught a glimpse through the arcades of the gilded statue of Jeanne d'Arc in a rosy swath of sunlight. Jeanne of France. Jeanne is the name of France, he whispered to himself.

Up in the hotel room he found Reggie, thicklipped with splotchy skin, sitting on a towel in a chair beside the lace curtains of the tall window applying propho. "Goddam whores," Reggie was muttering . . . "I put one over on them last night. I gave her twenty francs in advance and when she went to sleep I took it back and hightailed it for home. Never let 'em take your pants off, that's my motto."

Jay grunted and borrowed the kit, just in case, and went off into the corner of the room with it.

"How did you make out? I bet you always pay what they ask and more. A feller can't be too careful with whores."

Jay grunted again and began packing his dufflebag to keep busy. He could hardly wait for the hours to go by until afternoon when they were to report at the Gare de l'Est to take the train des permissionaires out to Bar-le-Duc. There they were quartered in a big clean cement hall in a closeddown distillery. The Fiat ambulances were new. The Fiat motor was a dream of simplicity. The chef and the souschef were grand guys. At night the shuttered cafés were full of Frenchmen singing:

> *Auprès de ma blonde,*
> *Qu'il fait bon fait bon fait bon*
> *Auprès de ma blonde*
> *Qu'il fait bon dormir.*

Jay drank the sour pinard and remembered little Jeanne and felt the blood hot in his veins and thought vicissitudes hooray and sang loud out of key with the rest. At night when the endless lines of camions ceased grinding past over the cobbles they could hear the big guns on the front pounding like surf to the northward. When orders finally came, the section moved in a convoy over sunny roads through fields of oats and wheat, still green, where a few first poppies were beginning to bloom, up to a stone village where the Fiats were drawn up in rows in a stone farmyard that smelt of cows. Their division was en repos. The barns were all full of Frenchmen, so the ambulance drivers slept on the brancards in their ambulances. They had twentyfour hours on duty and twentyfour hours off, but duty was fun, driving round the country taking sick poilus back to the field hospital in a pretty little silver and white château that had a garden full of yewtrees. The only sour note was an occasional haggard man shot through the foot or the hand. Squarefaced military police in helmets had to ride along with those cases. "Oh, les vaches," the Frenchmen standing round the hospital court would growl when they saw the military police.

The day before the division was to go up into the lines the médecin divisionaire, a smiling man with a great black spade-shaped beard, came to invite the ambulance drivers who were off duty to a déjeuner being given in honor of some American officers who were touring the front. The déjeuner was in a camouflaged marquee that was being put up as an addition to the Hôpital de Triage. The officers wore all their decorations and there were American and French flags on the long table of boards set on trestles and a bottle of mousseux for every two eaters. Right away up at the other end of the long table near the French general, Jay caught sight of Scott sitting up straight and alert and brighteyed with a military bristle to his mustache. After the toasts to les braves Alliés and the speeches in English and French everybody rose to their feet while the divisional band which had arrived a little late played the "Star Spangled Banner" and the "Marseillaise." While cigars and cognac were being passed around the officers moved into the sun outside of the tent, that smelt damnably of disinfectants, to stretch their legs stiff from sitting on the hard camp stools. Scott came up behind Jay and tapped him on the shoulder. "Of course we meet everywhere." They both laughed comfortably. "It's a small war," he said.

Scott asked Jay if he'd been to the front yet.

Jay shook his head.

"Me neither. It's always like this," he whispered. "The French want to break the facts of life to us gently. The general won't drink in the field, the colonel turns down his glass so I have to uphold the bibulous honors of les Etats-Unis. It's a good thing I've got a sound liver."

Jay said suppose he came for a ride in an ambulance one of these days. Scott whispered darkly that maybe they'd move up with the division to see how a division took over. The médicin divisionaire was a grand guy, whispered back Jay; he'd know where the section was. "Agreed," said Scott.

The first time Jay and Reggie saw P4 it was a quiet day. They drove up through many quiet villages full of troops until the road and the landscape began to take on a motheaten look. They began to have to avoid holes in the road that might have been made by shells. It was a beautiful summer morning. Larks soared singing out of the wheat on either side. They found their way past the first gun emplacements through a village that was just walls, no roofs, and past an occasional wrecked truck that had pitched into the ditch; and turned into a rutted lane along a hedgerow full of little clustered pink flowers; and then through a wood cut with muddy ruts going in all directions where they had to pick their way over occasional gravelly patches; across a slope that had trenches dug along the crest, to a grove of beeches in a curve of the hill. There a Red Cross flag fluttered on a stake above a pile of stones that had once been a chapel of some kind. The place had a lonesome look. Except in the far distance, the guns were silent. Jay and Reggie didn't have time to look around because in the deep abris built into the foundations of the chapel enough wounded were already waiting to fill the car. No stretcher cases but silent men with hollow eyes in long mudcovered blue overcoats draped with bloody bandages and smelling of mud and sweat. The smell of blood. The doctor was a pallid piefaced frowning man with his helmet on the back of his head. "Revenez vite," he said as he handed Jay the handful of papers that went with his wounded. "Et mettez vos casques." He tapped his own helmet with a threatening forefinger. "Ça va taper dure."

It took them a long time to get back to the field hospital because the road was solid with slowmoving trucks hidden under a pall of dust. The infantry was coming up. They were no longer the jolly Frenchmen singing in the cafés. Their faces were pallid with dust. They looked out with doomed envious eyes at the ambulance jouncing its way back in low gear.

When Jay rode round to the back of the field hospital tent to collect some bidons of gas it seemed quite natural to find Scott waiting for him. "Our little excursion is put off until tomorrow," Scott said. "How long does it take you to make a round trip?"

"A couple of hours," said Jay airly. "Come along."

"I don't mind if I do," said Scott.

"Got a gas mask?"

Scott dug at something hung under his trenchcoat under the crisscrossing straps of his various polished leather cases.

All three of them squeezed into the front seat and they started off with Reggie, who muttered that he felt jumpy and wanted to drive, at the wheel. Traffic was slow through the empty villages. They had to buck a double line of trucks full of stubblefaced mudcovered men coming out of the trenches full of hoarse shouting and tuneless songs. A long trail of artillery was stalled in the edge of the wheat. They had almost reached the place where their lane turned off across the fields behind the hedgerow when a sentry stopped them.

"Arrivés . . . Boches," he shouted. While they were arguing with him a shrill whine rose out of the air getting louder

and louder and ground into Jay's spine as it tore the sky. This
is it, thought Jay. The three of them sat frozen knee to knee
in the front seat of the Fiat ambulance. There was a roar on
the road ahead and a rattle of pebbles and the whining sound
of éclats. "Good enough," said Scott in a matter of fact tone.
"Baptism of fire."

"There'll be three more," the sentry shouted up at them
out of the ditch where he lay flat. "The Boches are regular."
Scott was sitting on the outside. He didn't move so Jay
couldn't. Jay could feel Reggie's arm trembling; he slipped
his hand round his waist and grabbed his leather belt. Jay's
lips were cold and there was a taste of blood in his mouth but
straightaway when the whine began again he knew he wasn't
going to yell, he wasn't going to jump, he wasn't going to do a
goddam thing. The Boche aim was excellent, but as there was
nobody at the turnoff the shells just dug deep pits in the road.
When the light smoke drifted towards them on the wind it had
a bitter smell of almonds. After the four shells the sentry
jumped up at them red in the face. "Idiots," he shouted.
"Faut s'abriter, nom de dieu!"

"Let's get the hell outa here," Reggie mumbled between
his teeth. He slipped the car into gear and charged round the
edges of the still smoking shellholes. Grinding and plunging
on its springs he swung the car across the road and went bouncing along the rutted lane. The already familiar hedgerow with
the little pink bunched flowers immediately gave Jay a non-
sensical feeling of security. Behind the hill where the reserve
lines of trenches were three small rolling kitchens smoked
cozily. A smell of soup came from them. On top of the hill a
Frenchman standing on a pile of sandbags that protected the
mouth of a trench was waving a wire basket of salad in a broad
circle in the air. Reggie was still white around the gills, but
Jay and Scott were laughing about how the French had
to have their salad no matter what, as they drove through the
purely imaginary shelter of the little rutted wood until they

caught sight of the great silver boles of the beeches. Reggie backed the ambulance around and parked it neatly in front of the Red Cross flag.

"Now which way are the frontline trenches?" Scott was asking in a businesslike tone. The three of them were standing beside the car stretching. Jay was planning how he was going to introduce an officier américain to the doctor in charge of the dressing station and Scott was checking on his binoculars in their leather case that hung in the crowd of other polished leather cases round his trenchcoat, when all at once they were all three on their bellies crawling towards the muddy pit that was the entrance to the shelter. The little wood had blown up around them. Explosions seemed to come from every direction at once. The air was full of whining steel and the wooden crash of ripping branches. Just before Jay dove head first through the blanket that sheltered the door of the abris he saw one of the great silver beeches beside him rise with nodding boughs into the sky. At the same moment Reggie came down on top of him in a mess of flung mud and driven gravel.

Although he had no breath in his body Jay was laughing when he picked himself up. The merriest little brown Frenchman was helping him scoop the mud off his uniform. "C'est le barrage, quoi?" There was something heartwarming about the way he gargled the language deep in his throat. "Yaura un coop de main. C'est réglementaire."

The doctor with the round white face came up and shook Jay's hand.

"C'est l'initiation, hein?" he said. "Faut pas s'en faire, on est bien abrité ici."

The doctor tried to shake Reggie's hand but Reggie sat on the edge of a bunk while the mud ran off his hands clasped to his knees, looking up at them with an expression of frozen distaste. He wouldn't give his hand. He wouldn't move.

The whole hill shook as if steel giants were beating it with sticks. (A rabbit, thought Jay, when you dig out his warren.) "Mais où est l'officier américain?" he shouted above the din.

The little brown Frenchman shrugged. The doctor shrugged. The shrug travelled through huddled figures up into the dimlit dressing station beyond.

As Jay made for the shaking blanket in the door the little brown Frenchman moved his finger back and forth across his face, meaning no. Jay stuck his head out. He had to crawl up the slippery mud slide through a tangle of leafy boughs. The leaves were reassuring. These helmets were very well made, Jay was telling himself reassuringly. He stuck his face right into Scott's surprised face. Scott was lying flat on his belly under a pile of brush. There was mud on his mustache. "Come on in . . . Scott are you all right?" Jay whispered in a lull in the din. He couldn't help feeling they were perfectly safe under the leafy brush. "Knocked my breath out," Scott groaned low. Jay inched over to help him up. When he put his arm round Scott's body to help him to his knees his hand came away sticky. Again the smell of blood.

Jay let himself slide back into the shelter.

"Reggie give me a hand. Scott's hurt," he shouted.

Reggie sat without budging staring at him with that expression of frozen distaste.

"Américain blessé," Jay shouted into the dim light of the dressing station.

"Merde alors," said the little brown Frenchman and moving very slowly reached for a stretcher that hung from hooks on the ceiling, opened it carefully and motioned to Jay to take the front handholds. This time as he stumbled up the slope Jay felt icy jabs of terror with every bursting shell but the explosions he kept telling himself were further away. The éclat whined high overhead. They dragged the broken boughs away from Scott and rolled him onto the stretcher. His wellshined leather leggings stuck out incongruously from the bloody mud. Jay had time to notice that the sun was setting in a burst of crimson behind great jagged trees stripped of their foliage when gagging and panting he was back in the dressing station among the motionless wounded and the smell of dirt and ether and pain.

"Jay," Scott was saying in a natural but almost inaudible voice from the stretcher, "I can't feel anything. I'll get my wind in a second. Be a good fellow and see if my trench periscope is all right. I'll be needing it."

There was no expression on the doctor's fleshy round face as he knelt beside the stretcher. Jay turned his back suddenly when the doctor started to cut open Scott's tunic; he had to see what was wrong with Reggie. He put his hand on Reggie's shoulder. Reggie was still shaking. There was no way of moving him. He wouldn't look up. He didn't answer. His muscles were rigid but his whole body went on shaking.

Jay went back to the doctor. The doctor was just putting away his hypodermic. The little brown Frenchman slipped a folded blanket under Scott's head. Scott's skin was paper white; his eyes were closed. Fortunately he still had some morphine left, the doctor was saying. Just for a second Jay let his eyes travel to a little tiny dark moist spot that had already appeared on the broad belt of bandage round Scott's middle.

"Grave?" he asked.

"Au ventre c'est toujours grave. Que voulez vous? On va l'évacuer."

"Now?" Jay asked eagerly.

The doctor made a horizontal gesture with a broad white hand and gave Jay an unexpected smile. "Pas si vite, mon ami, yaura des autres . . . It's always like that when one division relieves another. The Boche takes advantage . . . Et le copain qu'est-ce qu'il a? Better give him a drink."

The doctor plunged into one of the bunks and came back with a tin cup full of rum.

"Gniolle," said the doctor, "sans la gniolle on ne ferais pas la guerre."

They shook Reggie and talked to him and held the cup to his lips but his teeth seemed riveted closed.

"Merde alors," said the doctor. "Let's drink it ourselves. Viens on va manger," he said smiling again at Jay's coughing and spluttering over the raw etherized spirits. He slapped Jay on the back. "C'est le courage à bon marché." He poured out another swig for the little brown Frenchman.

"Outside . . . in the trenches . . . what's happening?" Jay asked breathless.

"Coup de main . . . reconnaissance . . . How should I know?" The doctor shrugged. Jay knew right away he shouldn't have asked the question. The doctor's big round face was entirely preoccupied with his preparations for the evening meal. The little brown Frenchman lifted a greasy metal container of soup off the floor and set it over a can of solid alcohol and brought out tin plates and spoons. "This is my operating table," the doctor said patting the stone slab that was obviously one of the tombstones out of the chapel above. "Epatant, n'est-ce pas? . . . We must eat fast because there'll soon be work. C'est le festin de la mort," he added half singing in an operatic tone and his round blue jowls shook with silent laughter.

Jay felt the rum burning in the pit of his stomach. A fluttering voice way down kept repeating Please God don't let Scott die. He was breathing in the reek of bruised bodies, the smell of blood, the smell of pain, the sicky ethersmell, but as he started spooning the hot soup into his mouth a callous shell seemed to be forming over him like another skin. He felt the blood hot and hearty in his veins. The vicissitudes, by God. He remembered that he had a cake of chocolate in his pocket and brought it out and divided it as far as it would go among the wounded who were watching them eat with hurt eyes from their seats on stretchers round the edges of the muddy floor.

The racket had stopped outside.

"La voiture," Jay said. "I'd better look."

He stuck his head outside the curtain. There were stars overhead. Oh God in the stars please don't let Scott die, the little voice was pleading way down inside him. He clambered up to the level of the ground into the smell of mud and latrines and leaves and lacerated sappy wood. Occasionally in the quiet he could hear the zing of a rifle bullet from some faraway outpost. Distant machineguns started a duet. Suddenly three starshells bloomed overhead, burned out the stars and lit up the jagged hilltop above and the ruined trees. In their light he could see the Fiat marked with the cross in a circle just where he had left it. He was starting to edge his way towards the car when through the trees came swishing sounds followed by a series of dull thuds. Right above him a klaxon sounded loud. Jay gave a startled jump as if he'd just missed being run over by a truck in a crowded street and tumbled back into the shelter. "What's that?" he asked the little brown Frenchman.

"Les gazes. Quelle misère."

The doctor already had his mask on, a fancy one with a little valve in the snout that wheezed as he breathed. Jay went straight to Scott but two stretcherbearers were already fastening an oilcloth affair over his face. So far as Jay could see Scott was still out from the morphine. "Hey Reggie gas," he yelled in Reggie's ear. He shook him angrily. Every time Jay tried to slip the mask over his head Reggie's clammy trembling hands brushed it away. Finally Jay had to get a Frenchman to hold him while he slipped it under his chin.

Once he had his own mask on for the first time he felt that he was doomed. Well this was what it was like he told himself. Inside him he felt the strange peace he'd felt the morning he'd walked home from the night with Jeanne. "C'est un gros bonhomme," Jeanne had said. The learned Poggius could do what other men could do. He knew that he wasn't going to jump, he wasn't going to yell, he wasn't going to do a goddam thing. He sat down on the bunk beside Reggie who went on shaking helplessly inhumanly like a cold dog.

The little brown Frenchman was making the go-to-sleep gesture in Jay's direction with his two hands against the cheek of his gasmask. In the abris everybody was turning in. Jay tucked his feet behind Reggie and lay on his back wondering how soon he was going to die. His face was oddly moist under the gauze of the mask as if the skin had already started to rot. He remembered how sorry he'd felt for himself that morning in those girls' room in Greenwich Village. And now already he was going to die. Nature's tricks, a lugubrious voice chanted in his head. Dandy was dead and Petite Mère and Diogenes the black snake. If only he could be back on Wharton Place listening to Dandy's voice declaiming into the ears of snakes and small boys in the privacy of the library. In the sicky smell of the gasmask he was redreaming a dream he'd had under ether when he had his tonsils out. In the horrible choke of the ether he was being sucked down into blackness. He was swirling down a spiral corridor until at a tiny table in the corridor he sat talking to a man by candlelight but he couldn't see the man's face. A stranger may be God. He was arguing like in a bullsession in college, freshman year, about the theory of the vortex. The vortex was the absolute. This is the Absolute, the voice said and the voice was whirling and the table was whirling and the corridor was whirling, down, in horrible nausea, sick, sucked down, down, whirling into the blackness.

He woke up with a start like from the operation with a sore throat and feeling sick at his stomach, but it wasn't a nurse it was the little brown Frenchman who was shaking him by the shoulder. The little brown Frenchman had his gasmask off. From outside came a ringing, ting, tong, ting, tong like on a triangle. A Frenchman without a gasmask pulled open the blanket over the door and stepped out. Jay jumped up and stumbled after him into sunlight blazing horizontally through corridors of mist. In the yellow light he looked out on the beeches. The slick silver bark was gashed and torn. Fallen limbs were everywhere. A couple of great trees lay uprooted. In the midst of a tangle of roots the Fiat ambulance stood quiet and intact where Reggie had parked it. It still had its tires. Jay's cap he'd left on the seat was torn to pieces as if a dog had gnawed it. The body was pretty well perforated with éclat but there wasn't a scratch on the hood. Jay cranked her. She started.

"Bon," said the doctor, over his shoulder. "Allez vite." Already the stretcherbearers were bringing the wounded. Scott's eyes were open now. His face had a feverish flush. He recognized Jay. "Feeling better," he managed to say in a low weak rattle. "Always waking up in the wrong bed, eh Jay? . . . Say Jay, I had some binoculars and a camera and that trench periscope. You check, I don't quite trust . . ." He choked suddenly and bloody bubbles came to his mouth. Jay reached for his handkerchief and wiped the blood off the mouth and the mustache. "Thankee Jay," Scott sputtered and managed a dim smile as the stretcherbearers slipped his stretcher into the ambulance.

When Jay climbed into the driver's seat, he found Reggie already sitting there beside him. Reggie had stopped shaking but still he wouldn't speak. His face was frozen into that same expression of distaste. Jay clamped his fists hard to the wheel so as not to turn round and hit him. The motor was smooth. Jay hadn't had too much practice at this kind of driving. He drove slowly through the mist jouncing over the tangled ruts of the little wood. Back of the trenches on the slope where they'd seen the Frenchman waving the salad basket he passed the ruined carcase of one of the field kitchens. Flies were circling over a pool of slum. Every time the ambulance bumped on a rut a groan came from the stretcher cases. He felt his way grinding slowly in second out of the curdling mist in the wood. His glasses kept fogging up. When he came out on the open field the sunlight met him like a jet of flame. There was no traffic on the lane. The hedgerow with its tiny bouquets of pink flowers was weirdly unchanged. At the edge of the main road he had to stop to get out to vomit leaning on the mudguard. Before he climbed back he went round to the window of the ambulance and called "Scott how are you doing?" Frenchmen's voices answered groaning in chorus. "Vite, vite."

Jay wasn't too good a driver. When he drove fast he jounced them over the holes in the road, when he drove slow he felt he wasn't covering the ground to the hospital fast enough. It didn't seem possible that the road, the villages, the stone farms should be so unchanged. The same faces of poilus looked out from every window and door following with envious eyes the ambulance grinding slowly towards the rear. At every bump the stretcher cases groaned in chorus. Jay strained his ears for Scott's voice. He didn't dare turn to look at Reggie sitting numb beside him. At last he drove into the courtyard of the pretty little château all silver and white. Grayhaired attendants in Red Cross brassards had the ambulance doors open before Jay could get off the seat. Fighting down his nausea he looked down at the stretchers they were setting in a row along the wall. There were three unknown stubbly faces knotted with pain. The stretcherbearers had carelessly let the corner of the blanket drop over Scott's face. Jay dropped on one knee beside him to pull the blanket gently off his face. The eyes were open and sightless. The mouth was open and a thick stream of dark blood was already drying over the chin. Jay dropped the blanket over the face and got to his feet. Scott was dead.

Footnote on Social Consciousness

ANNE COMFORT WELSH
1892 — 1929

SOME YEARS before the dreadful war broke out in Europe her welltodo Aunt Julia invited Anne Comfort on an outing to New York to celebrate her graduation as valedictorian from highschool. She went down on the train by herself and her aunt's lady's maid met her among the hoardings and hammering of the half remodeled Grand Central Station and chaperoned her across the street to where Aunt Julia, in a hat all made of violets and a spotted lavender veil, was waiting for her in the drawingroom of the Belmont. They took a cab to go to the Waldorf Astoria for lunch but were stopped by a parade on Fifth Avenue. Her aunt who was a frisky old lady said, "Let's get out and see the parade." It was a suffrage parade and the men along the curb sniggered disagreeably but right in front cool and serene on a white horse came a beautiful girl leading all the rest. Anne's aunt said she was Inez Milholland. After a scrumptious lunch they went to a matinée at the Belasco Theatre to see Minnie Maddern Fiske. When her aunt put Anne back on the train to Poughkeepsie she gave her what was left of a box of Huyler's they had nibbled on during the performance to take home. Anne sat eating chocolates looking out of the train window wondering whether she would rather be Mrs. Fiske serving tea out of a Dresden china pot and making such whimsical and malicious clever comments or beautiful Inez Milholland leading the parade on a white horse past the Waldorf Astoria down Fifth Avenue. She knew she wanted a career.

She was in such a daze she almost forgot to get off when the train stopped at Poughkeepsie. The streets of Poughkeepsie looked seedy in the bright late June afternoon sunlight after the Waldorf Astoria and Fifth Avenue; and Mother's house looked positively squalid. The first thing Mother asked was: did she say anything about college? Anne declared she'd had such a good time she had forgotten to ask. "Well my child it was your only opportunity."

Anne felt awful because she wanted to enter Vassar that fall more than anything else in the world but Mother had the others to think of and there just wasn't any money to send her. Mother taught a few children elocution and dramatics on account of being the widow of George Brown Comfort — Daddy had been quite the matinée idol in his day — and gave some piano lessons and dressed dolls at Christmas and made jellies and jams, but none of it helped much to eke out the tiny annuity she got from Daddy's insurance. She was just a poor relation Anne told herself with a sniffle when she went to bed that night. She might as well face up to it.

Next morning, to a sound of birds chirping in the privet outside her window, Anne awoke with a start and sat bolt upright. She glanced disdainfully at Elsie and Maud in the opposite bed who looked plain even when they were asleep with their messed mousy hair and their little turnedup freckled noses, and at the stained wallpaper and the duststreaks on the windowpanes and the cracked mirror over the bureau. She felt so awful she couldn't stay in bed another minute. She tiptoed across the threadbare carpet to the mirror and studied herself long and critically. Her hair wasn't any particular color but it did have a nice curl in it. She had paleblue eyes and a nice skin and a pleasant expression. She'd heard friends of her mother's speak of Annie's sweet wild Irish look. By the time she was dressed she felt better; she was asking herself now what bold and beautiful Inez Milholland would have done. She was insisting that they ought to give women the vote. She would have gone out and just insisted that they take her at Vassar. "I will, I will, I will," Anne whispered aloud. Feeling that she couldn't stand being stifled in the house another minute she ran to the front door. On the porch she came face to face with the milkman who was just straightening up after setting down a bottle of milk. He had black eyes and black lashes and a handsome long brown face. He gave her such a nice friendly look and walked away and swung himself lightly up on the seat of his wagon, and as his horse started to move, grinned back at her and said, kidding but as if he liked her, "The early bird catches the worm." It made her feel quite pretty and after he'd gone she walked up and down on the pavement in front of the yellow frame house and thought if they were only nice young men instead of all those old maids, they would let her go to Vassar she was sure.

Right after breakfast she put on her prettiest dress and her only good shoes and fluffed up her hair and took a book under her arm (it would make her look like a student if she carried a book) and went to the corner drugstore because Mother didn't have a telephone and the boy named Tom behind the soda fountain whom Anne always felt so sorry for because he had such awful acne thought she was calling a date; but she was calling the president of Vassar. She insisted so that the president's secretary said he would see her that morning. He was such a kind grayhaired man with sad eyes and he noted down everything she said with a sharp lead pencil and had his secretary call up to make an appointment with the dean who turned out to be a freshfaced woman with beautiful white hair in a pompadour who talked crisply about exceptions in deserving cases and called up somebody on some committee connected with some scholarship and told Anne to go home and not worry and that she would be informed as soon as disposition was made of her application.

It was only when she got home deadtired and starving for lunch that Anne looked to see what the book was she'd been carrying around all morning. It was Edith Wharton's *The House of Mirth*. She'd thought all the time it was Hazen's *Europe Since 1815* but she'd been too wrought up to look. She hadn't read it. The title did seem a little frivolous. That afternoon she wrote her Aunt Julia asking her, in the nicest way if she couldn't help her just a little bit, since she was going to have to work her way through college. Then she lay down on the bed and read *The House of Mirth*. She couldn't stop reading. By bedtime she had decided she would be a novelist who wrote about the genteel ironies of life, like Edith Wharton. She never did get an answer from her letter to Aunt Julia because Aunt Julia had already sailed for Europe. She came back in the fall quite ill and died suddenly at the Belmont Hotel. Mother got all dressed up in a black silk dress with a veil with broad crape band to go down to the lawyer's office on Liberty Street in New York to hear the will read. When she came home her eyes were swollen as if she had been crying on the train, but she insisted it was just that she got a cinder in her eye. "Darlings," she said to the three girls, "there is no further hope for us from that quarter."

Anne did get a loan from the Freshman Fund but it all went for tuition and books so she had to go on sleeping in that awful little room with her sisters. Living at home it wasn't any better fun to be a college freshman than it had been being a high-school girl. So many of the girls were wealthy and had such lovely clothes that Anne felt more out of it than ever. She did manage to scrape up a little pocket money writing up college events for the society columns of the local paper, but she hated the way she had to do it. To get them to print what she wrote she had to fill every sentence with what her mother called false values and at that they only paid her enough to buy an occasional hair ribbon and a few icecream sodas. Scrimping and saving and having to turn down dates and even an invitation to a hop because she didn't have anything to wear, she struggled through a year and a half of college, until one day, when such an interesting pale darkhaired young man, who had been invited by the sociology professor to deliver a lecture about life on the East Side, asked her to share his life of sacrifice and dedication, Anne abruptly said Yes.

Anne had gone up with a group of other girls after the lecture to tell him how inspiring his talk had been. She had opened her blue eyes wide and her face had taken on that sweet look of understanding, and she had murmured shyly that she couldn't help with money, but how else could she help? He had promptly arranged for her to help him take a group of tenement children out to the country for an airing each Sunday and it had been quite fun; she liked the dirty little brats and she'd thought Waldo Welsh was the nicest kindest boy she'd ever known and eager and inexperienced as a puppy dog. She felt quite tender about him right away. Poor Mother was heartbroken when Anne told her she was giving up college; to cut the argument short, Anne and Waldo ran off down to City Hall all by themselves one Monday morning to get married and she went to live with him at the settlement house.

Waldo's salary was barely enough for one. Almost right away Anne discovered she was going to have a baby. Waldo was so preoccupied by the misfortunes and the regrettable moral degeneration in their crowded hall bedrooms of the immigrants he worked among and by his own inner conflict: — How could he reconcile the evil he saw around him with a belief in the divine ordinance of the world? — to put his mind on the problem of what they would do when the baby came. In spite of these uncertainties Anne was happier than she had ever been in her life. She kept those of the settlement house workers who still had a laugh left in them in a titter with the little anecdotes she picked up wherever she went. She loved the crowded streets and the foreign accents and weird smells and the odd characters from unheardof parts of the world she would run into in any stroll round an adjacent city block. They didn't scare her. She hadn't met anyone yet she couldn't get around. Her pregnancy, though it didn't show, gave her a cool feminine selfconfidence. She found she could arouse admiring glances in the toughest young men and keep them at a distance with a gruff comical manner she had newly developed. After the miserable penury of her life at college and the false values of the editor of her hometown paper she felt that at last she was living in the real world. She loved it.

It was Hibbert Hopewell, a young newspaperman recently arrived from Chicago who haunted the settlement house in search of copy for his articles in the *New York Globe,* who was always first to laugh at Anne's tall tales. The day they met he asked the Welshes up to dine with him at the Brevoort and shocked Waldo by announcing blatantly that he was an atheist, and added that Waldo was one too but didn't dare face the truth. That night Anne played the part of the flower of the slums so effectively she never quite managed to drop it. With the pride of an explorer exhibiting a newly discovered species, Hib brought around his friends, who were writers and artists and reformers and radicals, to meet her. Waldo didn't approve of the drinking and was pained by the salacious tone of some of the conversation at the Brevoort, so when Hib next called for Anne he found an excuse not to come along; but when Hib explained that he had to take Anne to dinner to talk to her for professional reasons, Waldo quoted St. Paul: All things work together for good for them that love God; so Anne went.

Hib was writing a story about her. The story was called "My Wild Irish Rose" and Hib sold it to a popular magazine for six hundred dollars. It was very much read and was reprinted in an anthology. Then Hib suggested that she ought to write up her experiences herself, and sold her first piece to the feature editor of his paper.

Her series of articles on life in the slums was the pretext for many little dinners. Hib worked harder on her pieces than he did on his own. After they had gone over her manuscripts he would order more drinks and talk on and on about the philosophical anarchism of Prince Kropotkin and the natural life and free love and the beauty of the nude. Hib always seemed to have money to cover the check. He often squeezed her hand, and tried to kiss her once or twice going home in a taxicab, but admitted, when she called him to order, that there was a naked sword between them. Waldo, who had remarked one day that jealousy was an insult to the purity of womanhood, spoke proudly of Anne's articles and pointed out at the settlement house that by seeing the humorous side she was calling attention to conditions in a way that professional social workers could never do. When Anne wrote a comical and touching little story called "The Waif," about the embarrassments of a hunchbacked Jewish cobbler who found a baby abandoned in an ashcan during a blizzard, they all shed tears when they read it in a monthly magazine full of the names of famous authors. After that Anne could do no wrong in the eyes of the settlement house women, who tended to be old maids and plain, although they did whisper among themselves that she was a little indiscreet to be seen everywhere with a man who was not her husband. Mrs. Lavine the director declared that genius had to live by its own laws. Waldo grew pale and thin and devoted himself to the work with more dedication than ever.

When the baby was born, Hib, who had been following with passionate curiosity all the details she would tell him of her pregnancy and working them into a story called "Motherhood," which all the editors eventually turned down as far too advanced, kept watch with Waldo half the night at the hospital. They both looked so pale and shaken when Dr. Martha Richter, the obstetrician, came out to tell them the baby was a boy and mother and child were doing well, that she let out a horselaugh and said she was blamed if she could tell which was the father.

When Anne left the hospital she moved into a little furnished apartment off Washington Square she had rented with her own money during the last days of her pregnancy. Her articles were bringing her in enough to pay the wages of an old Ukrainian woman, one of her cases, as a nurse for little David and to send her mother an occasional check. While she was recovering from the baby's birth Anne took up the habit of writing in bed every morning. Waldo, with Anne and the baby cozily housed, had seized the opportunity to leave on the lecture tour he had been planning to raise money for a camp for slum children. Afternoons while Marya had the baby out in the Square, Hib would come in to go over Anne's manuscript with her. He was a great admirer of the poems of Ernest Dowson and read her the "Song of Solomon" and erotic bits translated from the Sanscrit. He was always calling for redder roses and for stronger wine and in the end she let him make love to her. There was a good deal of talk about companionate marriage among their friends evenings at the Brevoort; they began to think of themselves as companionate lovers. Dr. Richter who was a fervent advocate of birth control had explained all about contraceptives to Anne, so that Anne was able to tell herself that, like the poet in Cynara, which Hib never tired of reciting, she had been faithful to Waldo in her fashion. When Marya came back with the baby, they would go out to dinner. They got to drinking and arguing rather spitefully over their dinners. The day Waldo arrived home, Anne had just had a spat with Hib because he made some jocose remarks about the sweated garmentworkers who were on strike and whose wrongs she took very much to heart; so she threw herself with passion into Waldo's arms. Waldo sympathized with her about the garmentworkers and told her that the secret of her writing was her ability to project herself into other people's lives and to feel their sins and humiliations as her own. "Especially their sins," she said teasingly.

There was never any doubt in her mind that Waldo was the

father of her second child, a girl whom she named Martha Richter after her friend the obstetrician. She worked the children and their nurse and life at the settlement house and her affair with Hib into a novel called *East Side Idyll*, which was published by an old and respected publishing house with a sale of fortyfive thousand copies, so that at twentysix she was a celebrity.

Her publishers preferred to believe that Anne Comfort Welsh was herself a product of Hell's Kitchen like the girl in Hibbert Hopewell's story which people still remembered; the reviewers swallowed the bait. Before long the legend was so thoroughly established that even her best friends, like shrewd and iconoclastic Dr. Richter, believed it. That was one reason, though she never admitted it, why Anne wouldn't let her mother come to see her in New York. She went up to Poughkeepsie herself almost every week. With her first really sizable check she redecorated the shabby old house and started Elsie off to college at Wellesley. Anne spent very little money on herself. She dressed simply in tweedy kinds of clothes; she felt quite triumphant the day she insisted on taking Waldo up town to Brooks' and buying him a really good suit. All the same she had been telling herself for some time that she and Waldo would have to get divorced: their lives just didn't fit together any more. One of the things that was beginning to worry her about her relationship with Hib was that he seemed in no hurry to have her divorce Waldo. Maybe he was afraid that if she did he'd have to marry her himself.

It was the dreadful war in Europe that finally brought about her break with Waldo. When the papers began to fill up with accounts of the miseries of the refugees who fled from Belgium and Northern France in the face of the German invasion a young man in her publishers' office suggested that as she had written so brilliantly of the oppressed lives of working girls in the slums and so made you feel the sufferings of downtrodden people, she might be just the one to do a series of articles about the refugees that would really wring people's hearts and would later appear in book form. "I know," he cried looking at her fervently across the pink shade at the luncheontable at the Park Avenue Hotel, "it's because you are those people. You really belong. The rest of us, with our bourgeois upbringing, can only see them from the outside." She looked up at him from her plate of creamed sweetbreads with her paleblue eyes wide and that tearful smile that everybody said was so heartbreakingly Irish and said yes it would be painful but she would go. She left the children with her mother. On the French Line boat she met a young French officer, returning from a buying mission in America, who had black eyes and black lashes and made love with a soldierly violence that was quite irresistible. When Jean returned to the front and was killed within a week, she felt in her own grief the grief of the women of France.

When she came home after three months among the European refugees, as full of the atrocities of German militarism as she had been before of the atrocities of the owners of sweatshops and of the capitalist exploiters of factories, she was all for America's going in on the side of the Allies. Waldo met her at the boat. He'd hardly told her how he thanked God she was back safe when he broke out: "Anne we always said we'd be honest with each other. I have to tell you I don't approve of your first article or of the second one. It is an appeal to hatred. We must say to the peoples of Europe: We refuse to wallow with you in the mud of war. Woodrow Wilson has with great difficulty kept the country neutral. I am planning to campaign for him against the bloodthirsty crowd who hope to get profits for themselves out of sending American boys into the slaughter." Anne turned her wide blue eyes on him and gave him her tearful smile. "But Waldo if you had only seen the poor people." Waldo wouldn't listen. "I disapprove of your articles and of the speeches you are probably going to make," he kept repeating. They quarrelled in the cab and when they reached the Brevoort she went in and registered alone. He stood in the lobby looking pale and gaunt and baggy at the knees as the porter piled the new pigskin luggage she had bought at "Old England" in Paris in the elevator. "Whenever you wish it I will arrange to give you your freedom," he said, and stalked out the door of the hotel.

The book sold well but Maud had been ill and there had been an operation to pay for and Elsie couldn't seem to help being extravagant at college. Poor Waldo didn't have any money, so Anne had to pay for the divorce. There was a fire in Mother's kitchen that ruined the whole back of the house and poor Mother had quite forgotten to renew the fire insurance. And on account of the war everything was getting to be so expensive. The day the news came of the false armistice, Anne, who had obtained a large advance from her publisher on a new book, started to arrange for another trip abroad. This was her chance to describe the aftermath of war in such terms that people would see the horror and futility of it all. If a book of hers could help convince people of the need of a League of Nations to enforce peace Waldo would come to understand how he had misjudged her. Poor Waldo, it had certainly been a mistake for a pacifist to back Woodrow Wilson. She couldn't help a slightly malicious smile when she thought of it. Right now Waldo was under indictment for a speech criticizing the draft he had made in Milwaukee. It was just as well the divorce had gone through or the State Department certainly would never have renewed her passport. As it was, her publishers had to use all their influence. She waited until the day she sailed to send Waldo a hundred dollar bill in a plain envelope to help in his defense: she sent the cash because she didn't dare put her name on a check for fear some snooper might report it.

In Paris she found Hib, still in uniform as a war correspondent, living at the Hôtel du Quai Voltaire. He had grown quite fat and seemed repulsively complacent about everything except about the lack of heat at the hotel. While waiting in Paris to cover the Peace Conference he was spending his time dining and wining and making a collection of international erotica. The first night he took her to see a horrorplay about a sadist in French she could not understand and to a cabaret where all the men were dressed as women. She went back to the hotel alone and thoroughly disgusted. Next morning at the bureau where she went to get her credentials visaed she met another American correspondent who impressed her very differently. When she first saw him she thought he had the look of a very young Lincoln, the awkward bony frame and the sunken glowering eyes. He came right up to her and said in a deep voice: "Anne Welsh I know who you are and I want to shake your hand. . . I'm Carl Humphries and I work for the Pulitzer papers; that is if they haven't fired me yet."

After waiting together all morning on a hard bench in the dead air of the French bureau until they could get to see the proper official, they walked out through the flagged courtyard together. Anne told him about the government's persecution of her exhusband for his pacifist views. "That's making the world safe for democracy," said Carl savagely. "What a farce!" To get the smell of French bureaucracy out of their nostrils they sat down beside a little stove at a café to drink a hot grog. Carl began to talk about the revolutionary movement advancing from the east; a groundswell, he said, that announced an approaching hurricane. "It's the coming of age of the working class."

He looked at his wristwatch and jumped to his feet. He was late for an appointment. Maybe she would like to come along. It was with some old revolutionary socialists at the Buttes Chaumont who were going to bring him up to date on the movement in France. If American troops hadn't arrived there would have been a revolutionary movement to France in 1917 just like in Russia, he whispered feverishly in her ear as they stood in the crowded Métro. "Pershing's job was to save world capitalism, not to save the French people from the Hun."

As Carl didn't speak any French at all, it was Anne who had

to ask the way. They found themselves all out of breath in a
room packed to the ceiling with torn paperbacked books and
decorated with red flags. A grayhaired man with a deep chesty
voice embraced Carl: "Le camarade américain," he cried. He
squeezed Anne's hand when Carl introduced her in German
as the only American journalist who really sprang from the
working class. Carl's German was dreadful and so was the
Frenchman's, so they got no further than exclamations and
grunts until a young poilu came in who had worked chez Ford
in Detroit and who talked good American slang. As the
room filled up with deepvoiced heavyset men the poilu translated their questions. Carl had been with the Russian army
the year before. He'd been in Germany and the Balkans. He
had seen soviets formed. He had sung the "Internationale" in
Leipzig and Milan. He had spent a night with the bolshevik
leaders in Smolny. Soon the time would come he said, beating
with his fist on the table, for him to throw off the mask of a
bourgeois journalist. He would join the ranks of the proletariat. Everybody cried, "Vive la revolution!"

Anne asked if they weren't afraid of the police, shouting so
loud, and they all laughed and said, "C'est le Club des Com-
munards." The flics didn't dare stick their noses in, not in a
working class district. They insisted on taking the American
comrades out to dinner in a little restaurant you reached by
climbing up stone steps at the end of an alley. There they
drank a great deal of wine and ate a remarkably good meal and
talked about the struggles and victories that lay ahead. When
they were ready to go home Anne, who felt the Americans
ought to help pay for the party, brought a blue wad of francs
out of her handbag. "Thanks," Carl said reaching for them
in a simple comradely way, and piled them on the plate over
the bill. "The wages of prostitution," he said, but he gave her
a wink as he said it. When the proprietor brought the change
Carl absentmindedly shoved it into his own pocket.

They walked half across the city in the raw fog that put

haloes round all the streetlights. Carl walked so fast Anne had
trouble keeping up with him. He looked straight ahead of him
and talked in staccato sentences. Only the working class could
compel peace. Only an organization with rigid discipline could
mobilize the working class. The working class was on the
march. "We must discipline that march." Only America
lagged, not the workers, but the leadership. "Why not Debs?"
panted Anne trotting at his heels. "He's an old fuddyduddy,"
Carl said over his shoulder without slowing his pace. "Of
course," he grabbed her arm and pulled her along beside him;
"if he would let himself be used he would make a valuable
figurehead, a martyr and all that" . . . but he doubted if Debs
could ever get over his soft oldfashioned bourgeois background,
he couldn't be ruthless. "That's what I must tell myself every-
day," he said turning in his tracks and glaring savagely down
into her face. She was rubbing her arm where he had pinched
it. "I must learn to be ruthless." He grabbed her by her
shoulders and shook her. "Women like you. You want to
soften a man. You must help me to be ruthless." When they
reached the small hotel over a butchershop where he was staying, he said in his simple comradely way "Suppose you come
up. In Paris nobody cares." It never occurred to Anne to say
no.

   After that night she was only happy when she was with Carl.
She moved from her respectable hotel up near the Etoile to
Carl's Hotel du Commerce, in a dirty street back of the mar-
kets, where he stayed because the proprietor was a sympathizer.
It wasn't often that they were together. He was away much of
the time on mysterious journeys, and she had to take trips
through the devasted regions to get materials for her articles.
She was working harder than she had ever worked in her life.
There were Mother's bills and her sister's college expenses and
the children's clothes and now Carl had to have money occasionally; because, just as he had predicted, his paper did
fire him, in response to an abusive cable he sent his managing

editor when they wouldn't print his accounts of some riots in Germany. The British secret service was on his trail and the State Department was trying to call in his passport and get him shipped back to America. The proprietor of the hotel would let Carl use the room even when Anne was away but he kept it reported in her name at the police station.

It was hard leaving for the Balkans without Carl but she had to do it. When she reached Constantinople Hall Bryant, whom she'd met with Carl in Paris and who was doing publicity for a relief organization, was waiting for her at the station looking unusually pinkcheeked and boyish. As they clattered in a two horse carriage to the Pera Palace, he kept asking her about Carl, letting on that he knew more about him than she did. "What a man of violence," he cried out in a tone of admiration. "I expect great things from Carl . . . He must be a wonderful lover." He gave her a pert inquisitive look that made her want to slap him.

Still Anne found Hall's company soothing. He was the one person with whom she could talk about Carl. He was full of chitchat and amusing gossip. Right away Hall took her to the resort hotel in Therapia where over a lot of alexanders in the bar he induced a young naval officer to introduce her to the American admiral so that she could be smuggled on board a destroyer to see the burning villages across the Bosphorus. But even being right there she couldn't feel their plight the way she had felt the plight of the French and the Belgians and the East Side Jews; she couldn't feel it really: it was too awful and she didn't know the language. Hall found her Armenians who told the most harrowing stories, Greeks who had seen their children chopped in pieces before their eyes. Together they giggled at dinner over the missionaries. Charity was an illusion, like putting a mustard plaster on a man's chest when he was dying with consumption, they told each other when they were sure they weren't being overheard. Only revolution could effect a radical cure. They felt very superior to the stuffy old missionaries.

Back in Paris, Hall who had managed to get himself sent to the Paris office of his relief organization because he just had to be there for the Peace Conference, made himself very useful to Carl. He had picked up a French merchant seaman in some low dive who turned out to be a most reliable fellow. He helped smuggle Carl, who had grown a beard and had been furnished with a set of forged papers by the French comrades, on a freighter bound for Petrograd. Anne sailed for home about the same time. She had to cable her publishers for a further advance to pay for her passage.

New York that summer had an impermanent provisional look to her. Every place was crowded, but everything seemed empty. At the Brevoort there were few familiar faces. Anne found herself an apartment in a part of the Village where nobody knew her so that she could put up Carl when he got back from Russia. He would probably be in hiding. She told the agent she was expecting her husband back from overseas. Now that she knew that capitalism was doomed she wasn't as afraid as she used to be of getting into debt. She got behind on the rent. *Aftermath of War* didn't sell well at all. It failed even to earn the advance. Her publishers told her that the people who bought books were bored with European problems. So she set to work to write a silly love story, full of false values, to pay the grocery bills. But even love stories she had difficulty in placing. A new set of brash editors, full of wisecracks and fresh out of uniform, had turned up in the magazine offices who didn't make much effort to disguise the fact they thought she was an oldfashioned sob sister. Only thirty and already a back number, she began to tell herself tearfully. Of course the new radical magazines that came out after the wartime suppressions and the skimpy labor newspapers were delighted to publish her work, but they didn't pay. It all confirmed Anne in Carl's opinion that capitalism was rotten and revolution the only cure. The trouble was she had a lot of mouths to feed until the great day came. She began to have daydreams of herself leading the mob, like Inez Milholland on a white horse, to take over the offices of the big circulation magazines in the name of the workers. It was a time of reaction said her friends when she went out to dinner with them to drink red ink in speakeasies.

To be sure the reactionary Republican President the people had stupidly elected did let Debs out of jail, and Waldo too. She got a telegram from Atlanta and almost immediately it seemed to Anne, Waldo was at the door. He looked so much older. There was a glitter in his eye and his skin had a tallowy paleness. The children were quite frightened of him, particularly when he told them in a strange chanting voice that in prison he had found belief. When Anne tried to say briskly that the way to do good was to join the movement of the workers that was going to make the world a fit place for her children to grow up in, he shook his head impatiently. The revolution must be within. He asked her to pray with him, recited the Lord's Prayer and left, although it was a dreadfully cold night and she hadn't had time to give him money to buy an overcoat, insisting that he was off to take up his ministry.

Those years Anne never knew how she kept her head above water, but she managed to support the children and her mother and to make occasional loans to her sisters who had married impecunious husbands and were usually in financial difficulties, and even to buy herself a small house on the Connecticut shore for the summers. She was always in debt; bill collectors haunted her door, but whenever everything seemed hopeless she would somehow find an editor who would advance her expenses to do a series of articles on conditions somewhere. When Carl was home it was worse because he insisted on her giving him so much money for the movement. They were known everywhere as Mr. and Mrs. Humphries, but when Anne suggested it might be easier for the children if they really got married, he gave her a frowning look and said the conventions weren't any affair of his. He was growing quite deaf and often for days came and went without seeming to notice her. When she got up her courage to ask him some question about party work he would look at her blankly and ask, "what party?" It was only when Hall Bryant or some other sympathizer came to dinner that she ever heard Carl discuss politics, and then it was usually a diatribe about the backslidings of some renegade she didn't know. He suffered a great deal from grippy colds and sore throats. The happiest times were when he'd go to bed with big volumes of Marx and Engels and let her nurse him. Then his dark eyes would look up at her gratefully out of their bony sockets and he would occasionally talk about how his father used to whip him when he was a boy on the farm in Oklahoma because he was always reading books instead of doing the chores and how his mother taught school and had kept a private savings account that the old man never knew about for him to go away to college on. "I thought I'd grow to be a writer, but when I went to St. Louis and got a job on a paper, I found a writer was just a damn prostitute like the rest of them." One particularly cold winter he had to be in Pittsburgh a great deal. He wrote to her to send him his heavy coat and then his trunk and his books. Then one evening he came in looking unusually gaunt and ill and said he couldn't stay to dinner. He stood in the hall and looked into her face as if he saw what it looked like for once. Then he said gruffly, "Anne I'm going to get married . . . It's a marriage of convenience . . . party convenience," and walked out the door. After that when they met in meetings of defense committees in connection with the movement, he treated her like an old acquaintance whose name he couldn't quite remember. Meetings and the movement took up her life, and of course she had the children and her career.

6

A GIRL EMPLOYED IN OFFICE WORK

THE BRASSBOUND CLOCK with the brush square face that always reminded Lulie of Hugh Swanson's face on the wall above her desk said five minutes to five. Lulie shoved her copy into the drawer of her desk, snatched up Aunt Lyde's little marten neckpiece she was wearing that winter, pulled the green cloche hat she hated down on her head and ran out of the office. Of course the great Hugh Swanson himself had to be in the elevator. "Jumping the gun?" he said with the dimpled smile she never quite knew how to take on his face, which Miss Ebbit liked to describe as roughhewn, under the blond beast's brush of short strawcolored hair. "Naughty Miss Harrington."

Lulie turned a swift glance up into his eyes. "Miss Ebbitt always tells us to style ourselves on the boss." She let out a little shriek of mock fright.

" 'Do what I say, not what I do,' is what the father told his son." He was smiling down on her with his most indulgent-to-employees smile.

When the elevator stopped with a leap at the ground floor Lulie let herself slip back among the shoving passengers until the great Hugh Swanson's broad pleated back had disappeared from view. She was quite out of breath. She wasn't crazy about her job, but this wasn't the day she wanted to get fired.

"Bet myself two to one on this elevator," said a voice she knew well, only it was deeper and firmer. She spun around.

Georgie was standing with his back to the marble wall beside the elevator. He held himself straight. He was a Marine Corps lieutenant. She jumped up and down in front of him. "It's Georgie home from the wars."

"Don't call me Georgie," he said laughing. He spread out his arms. She held him off by the shoulders with both gloved hands and examined him carefully. "George Elbert, you've gotten to be outrageously goodlooking . . . And a mustache, good gracious! Now just tell me everything that's happened . . . in a few wellchosen words."

"It's little Lulie . . ." His brown eyes were awash with tears like when he was a boy. "I never expected to live to see this day."

Hardly knowing where they were going they followed the homeward crowd of clerks and stenographers through the spinning brassbound doors out into the raging street. Lulie ducked her cloche into the wind and held tight to his arm.

"God it's cold in this man's town," Georgie was grumbling. "What I need's a drink . . ."

"Uncle Purdy's expecting me home to entertain some doctors," Lulie panted. "Could you stand coming out to Woodlawn Park?"

"Wasn't it bad enough having to go see my own family without having to go to see yours?" There was a familiar grumble in his voice. "Getting home is tough. I wish we were all up at the lake."

"Uncle Purdy's been selling our lakeshore for lots since Father died."

"The hell he has. And does Ben like that?"

"Ben can't say anything any more than I can. On account of Aunt Lyde."

"Gosh I want to see old Ben."

"He'll be back for the weekend. You know he didn't even get out of Great Lakes. He's graduating this spring." Lulie's hands were numb in her kid gloves. "Georgie," she cried as they stopped for the traffic at a corner, "we've got to go some-place. Suppose we go sit in a hotel lobby."

"Let's take a taxi."

"I haven't a warm dime. That's what comes of working for a living."

"I've got some jack, Lulie. I was planning to take you out to dinner."

"Here's a drugstore. I'll call up," said Lulie as she darted in the door. Inside it smelt of icecream and newsprint and cigars. "At least it's warm in here." They fidgetted about in front of the booth while a peroxide blonde in a floppy lace hat talked endlessly on the telephone. "George Elbert, you knew Zeke got married?"

"Ben wrote me but he didn't say who to. Was it Josephine?"

"No such luck. It's a horrible little girl he calls Mugsie. I almost cried my eyes out."

"I wish we were all up at the lake." Georgie's face went glum again. Lulie darted into the booth, where there lingered a stale smell of cigarettesmoke and violet sachet. Lulie's fingers were so cold she dropped her nickel and had to grope over the gritty floor for it. As soon as she heard Uncle Purdy's hello she knew it was no use. "Oh please let me off this once," she whined. "He got a Croix de Guerre." She didn't listen to what Uncle Purdy was saying. "All right tell Aunt Lyde I'll be there at quarter of seven," she answered and hung up.

By the time she came out of the booth she had it all planned. "George Elbert, I'll tell you what we're going to do. I've got a reprieve till quarter of seven and Uncle Purdy and his doctors have to leave right after dinner. They are going to a medical meeting. You come out and eat dinner with Zeke. You'll want to see Zeke anyway."

"Guess I might as well do that as anything else," said Georgie in a discouraged tone. "I've got to kill time somehow until Jasper gets in. His train was held up by a blizzard in the Dakotas. Jasper really turned out a fightin' Marine. He came out a captain. We'll take a cab and sweep by Steve's place. I want you to meet my thugs . . . Lulie, I had some wonderful thugs. Balkan types. Toughest guys you ever saw. Sentimental as women."

"Women aren't sentimental," said Lulie settling herself firmly beside him in the taxi. "Oh George Elbert, this is like old times."

"You ought to see 'em cry over the zither. Why a little child could lead them," Georgie went on.

Georgie's address, when the taxidriver, who was a veteran himself and a Czech and scornful of them Slovenes, managed to find it, after cruising up and down a distant windswept avenue reverberating with truck traffic under lonesome cold arclights, turned out to be a poolroom full of sallow darkeyed men in turtleneck sweaters. Lulie had never been in a place like that in her life. The boys are back, things are going to be fun again, just the way they used to at the lake when they came back from a campingtrip, Lulie was confiding to herself as she followed Georgie's swinging stride with small determined steps. She trotted after him into a big hall out back built of raw wood with dusty paper decorations festooned above tables with winespotted tablecloths, or was it blood? She giggled timidly. Georgie had found his thug, a stocky customer with gorilla arms and a nose like a turnip, who wore embroidered suspenders and red elastics on his shirtsleeves and rounded on them scowling when he heard their footsteps on the dancefloor. When he recognized Georgie his face brightened suddenly with smiles like a lit jack-o'-lantern. "Jesus, Mary and Joseph, it's the loot."

He backed bowing to the wall and switched on all the blue green and yellow lights that dangled from the rafters. He spread out his big strangler's hands. "What'll you have, Loot? It's all on the house."

"Steve, this is the nicest girl in the world. Lulie, Steve was my topkick."

Steve kissed Lulie's hand like a grand duke. "An' a pretty lady too, God damn it to hell . . . Sure you eat. Have a good time. You t'ink I can't treat lady right? I got decoration from King of Montenegro. In Paree on leave right in his hotel he kees me and pin on decoration on my breast." He gave his chest a great thump with his fist.

"It'll have to be another night, Steve. We've got to go see the young lady's family."

"Ask for her han' hey? Very good, goddam proper."

Georgie laughed. "We can tell Aunt Lyde we've been moving in high society."

Steve began to take offense. "Ain't de King of Italia his soninlaw? Montenegro little country but got goddam big king."

"Sure Steve," said Georgie soothingly. "It's a damn fine country and has damn fine people in it. I wish we were all there right now. Suppose we come Saturday night. Jasper'll be here and Ben will be home."

"George Elbert," Lulie plucked timidly at his sleeve. "I've got a date with Joe Newcomer to go to a football game Saturday."

"I might have known you'd be all dated up . . . Let's all go back to Montenegro, Steve. Everybody's dated up in this lousy town."

"Montenegro got plenty mountain, Loot, but goddam little money," said Steve grinning with every crease of his big suety face. "Chicago plenty good for me. All right you bring all your frien'. I give free beefsteak dinner, free drink, all free . . . Dance, raise hell, go home goddam drunk."

"Sure we'll bring Decent Respectable and get him potted . . . In the meanwhile what could you sell us to take out to Woodlawn?"

"Got slivovitz, grappa, I got gallon goddam good Italian wine."

"Where from?"

"California."

"I bet you make it of frozen beets down in the cellar."

They had to wait until the barkeep, a mildewed little man with patent leather hair, brought them each a glass of a white liquor. "For homecoming," shouted Steve and smacked his lips. Lulie just tasted hers and let Georgie drink it. He tossed it off like an old hand. Steve himself carried the gallon jug all neatly cartoned and labelled *tunafish* out to the taxi.

"Fiftytwo Ten Allerton Avenue," Lulie said to the taxi-driver. "Well Georgie if you haven't made yourself a place in the world." She threw herself back in the seat and laughed comfortably.

"In the underworld," said Georgie. "Tell me how's Aunt Lyde? I always thought the world of Aunt Lyde," he added.

"She's no better really. She doesn't leave her room much . . . We have a practical nurse, a Mrs. Ritchie. She's a dentist's widow from Kankakee. When I went to work I said I'd pay her wages."

"Uncle Purdy's as openhanded as ever?"

"He never was a spendthrift."

"So little Lulie's earning her own living writing advertising copy? A career woman, eh? I've heard about Swanson. The dawn of a new day. How's Swanson himself?"

"The great Hugh Swanson? He's fantastic. I had a run in with him this afternoon coming down in the elevator."

"Don't tell about it. I'm jealous already."

"You ought to see Miss Ebbitt. That's my immediate boss. She's made of blown glass and the edges cut."

"I've got to get me a meal ticket. You plan and plan on what you're going to do when you get out of the service and then suddenly you're all dressed up and no place to go . . . I'd like to do nothing but hunt and fish for a whole year. War's a bloody circus but God I hate discipline. Being bossed and boss-ing people around and all the time the sergeants know and you know it is the sergeants who are running the show. Jasper and I got plans. Riders of the purple sage. Remember that old rich Mr. Allardyce who runs some kind of a milling concern? He just might grubstake Jasper on a ranch and I'd go in with him. Out where Jasper comes from. Don't ask me where whitefaced cattle fit into selling biscuit flour but they do . . . No sheep by God. Damn good hunting and trout fishing every day in the year . . . Oh Lulie do you remember the time we made you bite the head off that trout when we initiated you into the Tribe?"

"It was a tiny little one," giggled Lulie.

Headlights, corner drugstores, long strings of suburban street lights, trolleycars full of jiggling straphangers flitted past the taxi windows. It was fun being out with this new grownup authoritative Georgie.

"George Elbert, do you remember the time you were casting for pickerel and tipped over *Redwing* my canoe and were so mad at me for being a girl?"

"Lulie do you remember the time . . . ?"

"Georgie do you remember . . . ?"

Much too soon the taxi was turning into the snow of the driveway at Fiftytwo Ten. Lulie's heart sank down into her stomach when she saw, beyond the dark cars parked in the drive, the light trickling out over the iced barberry bushes and shadows moving across the shades drawn down on the livingroom windows; Uncle Purdy and his guests standing around waiting for her to entertain them. From Aunt Lyde's room upstairs a low glow oozed through the venetian blinds. Immediately Lulie could see in her head Aunt Lyde's pompadour catching the light and Mrs. Ritchie's dumpy figure in her white dress reading *The Inside of the Cup* in a monotonous voice. A tall shadow moved across the unshaded light in the apartment over the garage. Zeke was home. Her voice was so weak it sounded like a furtive little whisper in her own ears when Georgie turned towards her after paying the taxidriver: "Let's go see Zeke first."

Her hands cold with dread, Lulie ran up the steep stairs with Georgie pounding at her heels. On the landing she tripped over a loose place on the carpet and stumbled through the door into the wide bare brightly lit room. "Zeke look what I found." Zeke glanced up questioningly at her from under his green eyeshade. He was in his shirtsleeves leaning over a draftsman's table lit by a single enormous electric light bulb. At the other end of the table snubnosed Mugsie with a broad pink ribbon tied round her pale hair, backing and squinting as if she were painting a picture, was arranging paper carnations in a bowl.

"Lulie, we're working," Zeke started to say. Lulie interrupted him: "Zeke it's George Elbert home from the wars."

"Welcome to our city, Georgie," said Zeke abstractedly moving his rule and standing with poised pencil over some shading on his drawing. "I'll be with you in three shakes."

"Well I've got to scamper," said Lulie in a hurry. "You'll feed George Elbert won't you Zeke? Juliet this is Lieutenant Warner an old crony of ours from the lake." She turned towards the paper carnations. "I'll be back when I've polished off the sawbones."

Lulie gave one last glance around before she snapped out the door. Georgie, the old sullen injured look on his face and that curl she had never liked to his lips under the smart mustache, with a twist of slim hips was setting down the heavy carton with the wine in it he'd brought up the stairs on his shoulder. Zeke was tracing a last fine line on his elevation of a school building with his mouth pursed up. Mugsie with a rapt look was poking a paper carnation into a bowl and chanting: "He'll help us do the dishes now won't he? Marines are always so helpful."

Poor Georgie, thought Lulie as she ran across to the back door of the house, he deserves a cheerfuller homecoming. But she didn't have time to think how terrible everything was at Fiftytwo Ten she was in such a scamper with all she had to do. She had to comb out her hair, and to climb into her crêpe de chine dinner dress and the highheeled slippers that hurt her toes. She had to take up Aunt Lyde's and Mrs. Ritchie's trays that black Emma had ready on the pantry shelf. She had to run out among her uncle's guests with plates of canapés and to say something cute to each one. They were all soggily sipping little glasses of grapejuice because Uncle Purdy never would serve anything that was against the law. They seemed nice enough middleaged men but she couldn't talk to them because she had to go out to the kitchen again to make sure Emma wasn't letting the rolls burn, and there was the gravy to make. Emma never would make the gravy, always said Miss Lulie ought to keep her hand in on it. Then Lulie had to sit at one end of the heavy golden oak dining table to serve the mashed potatoes and brussels sprouts while Uncle Purdy ponderously carved the leg of lamb at the other end.

At last she was left alone with the livingroom chintz and the grounds in the afterdinner coffeecups and cigarettestubs sourly reeking. She let herself drop into the armchair by the fireplace and lay back listening to the cars starting and grinding away through the icy ruts outside. Then she jumped up and ran around the room kicking up her heels and dumping out the host of little ashtrays into the big brass one. She carried that out to the kitchen and stood there a moment beside Emma, who was deep in sudsy dishwater, to hear the latest news of Emma's husband, the elder Broadwater who aspired to be a preacher and suffered a call from on high that took him away from home whenever Emma needed money to buy something for the children. Emma was still going on in a complaining singsong about the elder when Lulie ran off up the back stairs to Aunt Lyde's room. As she gently pushed open the door Mrs. Ritchie's rumbling voice stopped reading. Her dark round eyes looked up from the book. Her dark thick brows rose. Aunt Lyde opened her eyes and gave Lulie a gray querulous look: "My dear don't interrupt."

When Lulie ran over to pull Aunt Lyde's pillow up a little Mrs. Ritchie looked up at her over the top of the book and said in her deep voice, that caused Lulie and the boys among themselves to call her the lady baritone: "We're so interested," she said, "we can't wait to get to the next chapter."

"I'm running over to Zeke's for a moment. I just wanted you to know where I was."

"You shouldn't have stayed on my account," said Aunt Lyde.

"We forget everything," said Mrs. Ritchie emphatically, "absolutely everything when we get into a really interesting story, don't we Mrs. Rumford? How do they manage to make life so interesting in books?"

Lulie stopped a second in her own room to tidy her hair up and to put on a little powder on her face. "Now don't be small about Mrs. Ritchie," she told her own face in the mirror. Mrs. Ritchie was a treasure, so kind and devoted, but why did she have to make everything so lugubrious? Climbing the narrow stairs to Zeke's place above the garage Lulie felt the old apprehension as she looked up at the blank door. It sounded mighty quiet up there. The moment her hand turned the knob she began to hear Mugsie's high childish voice intoning that she was a free spirit and that marriage to anyone but another free spirit would have been a desecration. Lulie had to force herself to open the door. Zeke was still at work; his long thin white face was in shadow as he leaned over his drafting table. Georgie looked wretched sitting opposite Mugsie at a cardtable where cheese and ryebread and bologna sausage were piled up on the wrappings they had come from the delicatessen in. His tunic was unbuttoned. With pursed lips and frowning brows he was cleaning the Luger that was Zeke's souvenir of the war. The parts were laid out on a piece of oiled paper in front of him, between a paper cup of wine and a can of three-in-one oil. On the studio couch in the shadows beyond sat Olga Lipschitz, with just the slits of her eyes and her high cheekbones catching the light. The recumbent form behind her turned out to be Harding Edwards in a yellow necktie.

She and Zeke told each other everything, Mugsie was chanting as Lulie stepped shamefacedly into the circle of light. They had determined to leave each other absolutely free, only they were going to be honest and tell each other everything. Of course she knew (she tittered a little) that Zeke was a genius and a genius couldn't live like an ordinary person, but people had told her she was a genius too. People had told her she had a genius for living. She gave her head a little toss.

Lulie felt whatever she had to say dry up in her throat.

"Significance," said Olga in her deep voice with its teasing foreign accent and rolled her eyes towards Zeke's profile. "The creative spirit must signify."

Harding Edwards lifted his curly head on his hand,

> *"Les petites marionettes*
> *Font font font*
> *Trois petits tours*
> *Et puis s'en vont,"*

he recited and let his head sink back on the pillow behind Olga.

"You know I've forgotten my Latin," said Mugsie. Her face sharpened into a spiteful beak towards Harding and Olga. "He just said it to make me feel uneducated," she whispered.

"The little marionettes, my dear Moogsie"; Olga stretched out her hand in a gesture out of grand opera. "Life is a stage where the marionettes perform three little acts and then they are gone." She puffed out her cheeks and blew as if blowing out a match.

Georgie snapped the last part back into the Luger and got to his feet. "Bullshit," he roared.

Mugsie turned on him now, blubbering that he might be an officer but he was no gentleman.

Paying no attention Georgie aimed at an imaginary target outside the window and squeezed the trigger. "It has damn good action Zeke, if you'd only take care of it."

"But Mugsie," Zeke was looking up with innocent blue eyes from under his eyeshade, "you told us we had to be honest and say what we thought."

"Why Zeke Harrington," shouted Lulie laughing without feeling amused, "If people said what they thought the world would be a shambles." She restrained an impulse to let herself go off into a fit of shrieking hysterics.

Georgie was packing his gallon of wine back into its carton again; needed it for Jasper he explained. Lulie helped him with the string. As they went down the stairs Lulie whined unhappily in his ear that Mugsie was not only boring herself but caused others to become boring . . . "But she may be right about Zeke. He took all the honors in his architecture course, and now down at Zimmer and Field they are just crazy about him." Lulie prayed every night, she added laughing, he'd get the Prix de Rome and take Mugsie over to Europe with him and never bring her back. "I could strangle that girl with my bare hands."

"We were all geniuses up at the lake but we didn't talk anybody's ear off about it," grumbled Georgie. "If I'd known things would be like this I swear I'd have stayed in the Marine Corps. We've got prohibition and we've got Mugsie and Zeke's turned out a bloody genius on us. What a way to come home!"

Lulie walked out with Georgie to the end of the drive and watched him go trudging off with the carton on his shoulder towards the carstop. When she got back there was snow in her slippers and her feet were wet. She ran upstairs and threw off the soggy slippers and dried her stockings in front of the gaslogs in Aunt Lyde's room. Mrs. Ritchie had turned in. It was time to tuck Aunt Lyde into bed for the night.

Aunt Lyde looked very pretty with her thin ivory face and her wave of white hair pressed against the pillows. She was in one of her well spells. When she started complaining that nobody ever came up to see her anymore, Lulie said that Georgie had wanted to because he thought the world of her. She was the first one he'd asked about. Aunt Lyde answered that she thought very little of Georgie but maybe he'd improved. Why Aunt Lyde, Lulie declared, he'd grown up to be the handsomest young man you ever saw.

"It's the uniform," and Aunt Lyde, nodding her head. . . .
When she had been a girl in Washington, Aunt Lyde went
on . . . Lulie knew that her father, that was Lulie's Grandfather Waring, had served a two year term in the Senate, from
Kentucky of course. "My dear, that was where your mother
met your father. He was the handsomest young professor I
ever saw but no handsomer than one other . . . He wore a
uniform. I have his picture still. I must think where it is."
She touched her temples with her transparent white hands.
"Put a little cologne on Aunt Lyde's forehead dearest . . . My
dear everybody spoke of us as the beautiful Waring girls. It
was a continual whirl . . . balls at the embassies . . . affairs at the
Arlington. We all get our looks from the Warings. The looks
weren't on the distaff side. Your dear grandmother was famous
for her wit, but she was never a beauty. Oh Lulie it's so
dreadful when your memory fails. Where could I have met
him . . . at some embassy, we even went to the White House
. . . and yet I see him as plainly as if he were in the room . . .
in a blue uniform with red stripes on his pantaloons. We rode
out daily and this handsome French officer often accompanied
us. That was before I met Joe Addison, my first husband . . .
In some ways Lulie I've had a strange and tragic life. You
know he was killed in a hunting accident. They brought him
home bleeding. He died in my arms. If he had lived things
would have been different for you and your brothers dear . . .
and then Lucy's untimely death. But your Uncle Purdy and
I had several happy years. Childlessness is tragic. He was full
of fun as a young man, but as men grow old the fun leaves
them and all they can think of is business. Lulie dear, look
under the paisley shawl in the lower drawer. See if you can't
find his picture, not Purdy's dear, Colonel Jusserand's. It's in
a little leather case. Father; your grandfather, Senator Waring
. . . Sometimes I think Zeke resembles him; something about
the eyes . . . Father never knew I kept his picture all these
years. Of course I should have returned it. You would never

think your dear grandmother had been the wife of a United States Senator, would you? Of course he was only appointed to fill an unexpired term when Senator Philpotts died. Your grandfather would never have been selected by the legislature, he was far too plainspoken. He was quite a philosopher, that's why he liked the professor . . . He had an oldfashioned body servant named Terence. The colored people just worshiped him. We girls loved old Terence. I can remember his wooly white sideburns. We spent a great deal of time together: your father the professor, and this French colonel — everybody said he looked too young to be a colonel — and your dear mother . . . we enjoyed simple pleasures then . . . riding out to the old mill on Rock Creek. It was farms and pastures in those days. It must have been later the District took it for a park. Sometimes the water was up above the horses' knees. I can see him now riding ahead through the ford with his gloves in his hand and a way he had of cocking his head to one side. Zeke's getting to do that . . . He's such a goodlooking boy I hope he doesn't get conceited. Your mother and I were dreadful teases. Oh how we used to tease conceited young men, practical jokes and everything . . . We were quite scamps I fear."

Lulie was on her knees beside the open drawer rummaging among the scarves and laces that smelt of lavender. Her hand struck something square.

"Why Aunt Lyde, your memory is perfect."

She brought the case out to the light and opened it. Inside was a daguerreotype of a thoughtful looking man with large dark eyes and drooping mustache. He wore epaulettes and much frogging on his uniform. The head did have a little tilt to one side. When she looked at it Aunt Lyde began to cry. "Father forbade him the house."

Lulie brought her a lace handkerchief. Aunt Lyde patted her reddening eyes with it. "Oh dear, this'll make my head ache. Lulie dear get me a little aromatic spirits of ammonia."

Lulie came back from the bathroom with an opaque liquid in the bottom of a tumbler. Aunt Lyde drank it and closed her eyes and let her head drop back against the pillow. "He discovered . . ." she went on with her eyes closed; — "you know how dreadfully men talk at the club — I always said men were much worse gossips than women . . . that poor Colonel Jusserand was involved with some awful woman. There were shameless creatures in Washington even in those days . . . and he made him understand that he should never darken our door again. Your poor mother and I cried our eyes out because it broke up our riding parties, but by that time your father and Sister Lucy were married so they didn't need a chaperon. I used to see him at balls and on the street. He'd take off his hat so sadly. You can't tell by the silly oldfashioned picture that he had brown eyes. Your mother used to say there was doglike devotion in those brown eyes when he saw me. She used to tease me dreadfully about him."

"Georgie has too . . . I don't know if I like men with dog's eyes," said Lulie yawning. She looked up at Aunt Lyde's little travelling clock on the bureau. "Aunt Lyde, it's a quarter past one."

"Just read me a chapter Lulie. I shan't sleep a wink the way I feel now."

"It'll have to be a short one," said Lulie and picked up the book. She hadn't read two pages before she noticed Aunt Lyde was asleep. She lit the nightlight on the washstand, opened the window a crack, turned out the electric light and tiptoed into her own room.

It seemed to her that she had barely laid her face on the pillow before the awful old alarmclock was ringing in her ears. She was horribly sleepy but she got herself dressed and washed somehow and gulped a bowl of dry cereal in the kitchen, and ran out the door at a quarter of eight as she always did to catch the streetcar at the corner that trundled her to the elevated where she waited stiff with cold in the drowsy early morning crowd for the train that took her to the familiar ads of her station in the Loop and to the struggle through the hurrying crowds in the canyon that howled between skyscrapers to the bright revolving doors of her building. Then there was the swoop up in the brass elevator; there were the goodmornings in the reception room on her way to her desk and she was sitting there with the brassbound clock staring down from the wall above. That morning she found a typed interoffice communication on the blotter: Miss Harrington will please call Mr. Swanson.

Fired bejabers, Lulie said to herself, but it wasn't that at all. The great Hugh Swanson's voice was crisp but kind. Lunch next Wednesday at twelve sharp. An account he wanted to discuss with her alone. "Mr Swanson, couldn't you tell me which one? I could be researching it a bit." The account hadn't reached that stage. He wanted her intuitive grasp. It had come on him like a flash when he saw her in the elevator. His decisions were highly intuitive. Of course she'd be delighted, said Lulie, but her voice didn't sound right in her ears.

Miss Ebbitt looking cold and tall as an icicle in a tailored suit was standing beside her desk. "Miss Harrington it's about your copy for Bonmeyer's. Aren't you being a little too clever? I loved it. I read it over to Mr. Swanson and he laughed out loud. He's just a boy at heart you know. But we mustn't forget that the people who'll read it aren't a bit clever. They'll think you're spoofing them." Miss Ebbitt made a disdainful little round mouth when she said the word 'spoofing.' "The public doesn't like to be spoofed." She sat down beside Lulie and set the typewritten sheet down on the desk and with her sharp little pencil took all the fun out of the day. Lulie could hear behind Miss Ebbitt's precise little voice her aunt's voice saying "As men grow old the fun leaves them" and she could see her Uncle Purdy exploding his funless jokes at the end of the table while he ponderously dealt out roast lamb to the director of the hospital he hoped to sell his enamelled bed-pans to. They all want to take the fun out of everything.

Was the fun going out of Joe Newcomer, she thought with inner panic as she met him in the lobby downstairs in the milling crowd that Saturday at noon just in time to hurry out to lunch. But Decent Respectable had always been stolid and staid. As they ate she was busy telling him how much the Marines had done for Georgie and how Ben would be home for the weekend and how Georgie's thugs were going to set the whole Tribe up to a beefsteak dinner that night and it was way over on the South Side and Georgie had sworn his thugs wouldn't let anybody get held up but she admitted she was a bit nervous about going. "I ought to be tickled to death," Joe said, "but we have the future to think of. I'd like to take you out alone. There is so much I want to talk about."

The future. The word gave Lulie a chill. All at once she saw herself businesslike and icy like Miss Ebbitt crossing the fun out of every day with a sharpened pencil.

"Decent Respectable, you promised." She looked up at him pleadingly across the little marble table in the restaurant that smelt of hot chocolate and patties.

"What did I promise, Lulie?"

"You wouldn't try to make me grow up too soon."

"It's a hard promise to keep. We have to face the future. The business boomed all the time I was overseas, naturally, war orders, but now that I'm back Dad wants me to take over and we're facing a slump. We've got to pull in our horns a little. I may not be able to take this long drive every weekend. It's going to be heavy sledding for a few weeks. If I had you with me I know I'd make the grade." His voice got very husky.

She was almost crying. "Joe you make me feel so horrid. I don't want to be horrid. I'm not horrid. You know I'm on your side."

He cleared his throat. "Lulie I don't want to make you feel bad."

"Of course you don't, Decent Respectable. Let's have fun today. Like we used to at the lake."

The game was at two. Decent Respectable had thought of everything. He had the tickets and two plaid rugs in his car and a thermos of hot coffee. Waiting for the game to start they shivered on the hard seats, in the sunlight cold as brass under a slaty sky streaked with marestails, but once the whistle blew the game kept their blood moving, and the crowds and the cheering and the shock of bodies as tiny squareshouldered bulletheaded figures hurtled in changing formations across the distant muddy field below them.

"Talk about fun," said Joe suddenly as they stood up between the halves stomping like Indians with their rugs about their shoulders while the cheerleaders far below made agile elastic x's in front of ranked young throats roaring in unison. "I think business is the greatest game of them all."

"I guess it's Uncle Purdy has taken the fun out of it for me, or maybe Miss Ebbitt."

"I've got a good team Lulie but I need the right cheering section."

"But Joe you can have anything you want."

"Except what I want most."

"Joe you're such a dandy."

"And they praised him to his face," quoted Joe, *"With their stately Spanish grace."*

"Oh Joe you remember it. Do you remember the summer when Father made little Ben learn the whole of it and he recited it all over the lake? I was just happy all day long."

The whistle blew. The teams trotted out on the field again.

"We still have *Wildfowl,*" Joe said as they worked their way after the game down the concrete steps through the rollicking redfaced crowd toward the back lot where they had parked the car. "And the lake's still there," said Lulie. Feeling windblown and boisterous they drove back across the city garish with lights under a flaming afterglow. Once they got out of the parade of packed cars starting and stopping from the football game Joe wove deftly through the traffic. Decent Respectable was a good driver. His Dodge touring car had a wonderful pickup. At cross streets where they waited in a row of panting puffing cars Lulie would cry, "Beat 'em to the start Barney Oldfield," and pretend to shake her fist at the other drivers. Overhead electric light signs sparkled against the darkening sky. Saturday evening throngs overflowed the downtown sidewalks. By the time they got to Steve's place their cheeks were burning from the cold. They agreed they were beefsteak hungry.

Beating their hands together to get the blood into their fingers they hurried through the grimed poolparlor. From out back came the sound of an accordion playing "From the Halls of Montezuma." The dancehall looked bright with colored lights and paper streamers and fresh tablecloths for Saturday night. The first thing they saw was Georgie and Jasper erect in their uniforms each with its spectrum of ribbons holding court at a big round table stacked with a variety of bottles. Around them perched at a respectful distance on the edges of their chairs, Lulie right away recognized Georgie's thugs through their storeclothes. Ben was there too looking very collegiate, an expression of adoration on his childish face. As soon as Lulie sat down a thick beefsteak stacked with frenchfried onions and fried potatoes appeared at every place. She'd hardly had a chance to be introduced to the nearest of the thugs or to say hello to Jasper and Ben or to pop a slice of steak into her mouth when Georgie in a peremptory sort of way asked her to dance. The popeyed fat man who played the accordion on the platform behind them had been joined by a skinny pianist and a hollowcheeked citizen with a violin. They struck up "Tipperary" as she followed Georgie's broad shoulders out onto the floor.

"I declare George Elbert," she was saying after they'd taken a few steps, "the Marines must even furnish dancing lessons."

"All kinds of lessons . . . When a man's seen so many good men killed he doesn't wait around. He goes out and gets what he wants," said Georgie clipping the ends of his words. "I've gone and gotten myself a job."

"Go on."

"Bugs Stoddard down at the *Standard* turns out to be an ex-Marine so I go down to see him and he hires me. I go to work Monday morning because it's an evening paper. You better watch your manners, young woman. You are dancing with a cub reporter."

"George Elbert, you're wonderful."

"Here's our pet genius," Georgie's lips under his mustache gave that curl she hated so, "and his seven pretty attendants." Zeke, tall and stoopshouldered and absentminded, was being steered round the edges of the dancefloor by Mugsie, in a baby blue organdy stiff with ruffles, and Olga who was dressed like a gangster's moll in a movie in dark sweater and mannish jacket. After them tagged Harding still wearing his yellow necktie and his stony look of a marble fawn. Joe Newcomer was on his feet making the introductions and finding people chairs, they noticed as they swept past. "The cleancut young executive," said Georgie out of the corner of his mouth. "That's the citizen tried to drown me."

Lulie made out that was a great joke, but underneath she knew it was not any joke to Georgie. The thought gave her a sick unhappy feeling. The music had stopped. The floor was slippery from fresh wax. They slid back towards the table.

Lulie had barely started on her steak again when Jasper was bowing stiffly in her direction. Jasper was silent as ever, except when Lulie asked him what he thought about Georgie's job; then he began to talk. "Right thing. The boy's got the brains. He learned more in the war, book learning too, than the average feller'll learn in four years of college. He'd be thrown away on a ranch. Anyway, the ranch deal's off. It looks like I'd have to go to work sweeping out a flourmill."

"I like to think of us all riding the range," Lulie whispered.

"Give George and me a few years to pick up some jack. The trouble with me is I'm not like George, I don't educate easy . . . I'm like General Grant's Missouri mule that went through the Civil War. He was a mule when he went in and a mule when he came out." Jasper fastened up his mouth after that and she couldn't get him to say another word. Lulie was hungry but she never did get any more steak because the band didn't stop playing once and one of the boys was always waiting to dance with her when she got back to the table. When she danced with Zeke she noticed he had that cold tense look on his face he always had when he wanted to say something he thought was important.

"Sister Lucy," he said abruptly, "a man who can't live up to his mistakes is a pretty worthless object. I want you all to understand that I have taken on a sacred trust."

"Of course we understand," said Lulie but the words didn't sound right in her ears.

Harding Edwards cut in. He held her timidly and his hands felt weak and damp but he had a perfect sense of time. "I know Zeke doesn't like to dance with his sister," he explained tittering. "He says it's incestuous . . . I'm kind of neutral, not being a member of the family or anything." He gave the word "anything" an odd accent that embarrassed Lulie. "You know I'd walk into a fiery furnace for Zeke. You know that Lulie . . . I'm really worried. I can't sleep nights for worrying. Do you suppose she could really be crazy? You know who I mean. She's looking at us now. I do wish somebody would dance with her. I would but she gets me so embarrassed, the way she wiggles her hips . . . There can't be any mental stimulus in that for Zeke now can there? Marriage or any other relationship between people can't be purely carnal, now can it Lulie? That's why he has to spend so much time with Olga and me. We stimulate him. A creative artist needs stimulus."

"Zeke always says every human being is worth as much as

every other human being. He calls it the theory of equivalent values. You know how fanatical he is about his theories."

"He's trying to make a silk purse out of a sow's ear." Harding threw back his head with a tinny laugh. "And I don't mean I don't like her. I do like her . . . Lulie you were a darling to let me dance with you," he said when the music stopped. Looking back in her face with wide unlit eyes he slid away among the dispersing couples.

Steve in blue serge with pinstripes was bowing from the waist. He had a red carnation in his buttonhole. "Excuse me if I dance with you "Beautiful Blue Danube" . . . I order it special. I like to honor pretty lady . . . Will you excuse? . . . I talk Montenegran goddam good. In Montenegran I can talk to King or Queen of Italia. Italian pretty good, Deutsch a little bit, but American I talk like goddam bum." He waltzed smoothly, holding her out respectfully at the end of his long arms. "Captain Milliron my big boss, a man like king. Best goddam officer in Marine Corps. The loot small boss, good hunter. Together we hunt plenty Boche . . . Back in Chicago. Chicago tough town. Me boss. My joint. Make plenty politics. In precinct one little king." Lulie found herself bowing in a courtly way towards him as they spun. His face creased up with smiles. "Your fader alive?"

"No," said Lulie.

"Who head de family?"

"My uncle, I guess," said Lulie laughing.

"You give me address. I go to see im like friend, like American citizen. Tell him he give you to loot. A beeg man like that need nice wife, plenty baby."

"But suppose I don't want to get married?" asked Lulie laughing harder than ever.

"Captain maybe," said Steve. "Captain not afraid of goddam thing."

The waltz stopped. Steve bowed again from the waist. "Your uncle. He understand," he said.

Georgie was edging his way towards them. Steve spread out his long arms to make way for him. "Excuse it, Loot," he said. "I make special waltz in honor pretty lady. She like girl in my country, goddam beautiful and wild like a bird. In Montenegro de most beautiful girl in the world, goddam it to hell. De King of Italia leetle man but goddam wise. He know. He pick Montenegran girl."

Lulie and Georgie went joggling off in a one step. "He's a character, George Elbert. He worships the ground you walk on."

"I thought you'd like my thugs."

They got to laughing and couldn't stop laughing. Other couples gave them sidelong looks as they danced around laughing.

"George Elbert, I'm quite giddy," said Lulie.

"Little squaw drink plenty firewater?" asked Georgie.

"I haven't had a chance to, I've been dancing so hard. Some nights the world seems wonderfully wild."

Georgie's face had taken on that black sullen look: "Wonderfully wild. You would have thought so overseas, seeing the good guys get killed."

"You and Jasper came out of it."

"Jasper got wounded just before Belleau Wood or he'd have been a gone gosling, the way he exposed himself."

"Tell me about it."

"Not now," said Elbert scowling. "Say whatever happened to Joe Sawbuck and his ballteam?"

"Joe got drafted. That's the last I heard of him."

She remembered the unwashed smell of stale woodsmoke and kerosene lamps Joe Sawbuck always had. Dancing with Georgie she felt all at once very far away. She was having that feeling she sometimes had way down that she wasn't there at all. Up at the lake maybe. Really she was standing by a campfire like the time they'd all gone camping up Runaway River and Father and his friends the Spingarns and the Willard girls had gone along, with tents and primus stoves and a fleet of canoes, she couldn't remember whether Georgie had been along or not but there had been Northern Lights while they were cooking supper, great pale half invisible curtains flapping in the north and now the sparks of the campfire were melting into the stars and the firs stood around like wigwams of a sleeping tribe and Father and Professor Spingarn had talked about the journeys of the first voyageurs through the great forest and Zeke had piped up and said, "Why can't we still do it?" and all at once she'd seen like from an airplane the whole great continent, all first growth forest and plains full of bison and antelope and wildcat and lynx and the timber wolves howling, and trout in the rivers and woodcock and quail thick like Grandmother Waring used to tell about when she was a girl. In the smell of balsam and the crackling birch twigs and the soft feel of the moss underfoot she'd felt there was nothing that mattered in the world but the wilderness stretching behind her endless into the enormous north.

"A penny for your thoughts," said Georgie.

"George Elbert, don't give up your ranch. We musn't let them coop us all up."

"How about you?"

"I'll spring the latch."

"We've got to get hold of something to use for money, Lulie. They charge money for everything in this man's country . . . What the hell?" Georgie had stopped in his tracks and was looking over his shoulder. Lulie looked where he was looking.

The group sitting at the round table had frozen into a tableau. Mugsie, that spiteful beaked expression on her face, was saying something disagreeable to Olga. Upsetting bottles and tumblers she lunged across the table with one hand and slapped Olga's face. The slap resounded. Olga's mouth was open round and her face twisted up like a child's who is going to cry. The tableau melted into action as Joe Newcomer and Harding with the anxious expressions of referees at a prizefight

rose up between them. Then Zeke, with that look on his face
of impersonal curiosity Lulie found so maddening, was leading
Mugsie away blubbering and stumbling inside of her blue
organdy.

Right away Lulie decided she didn't want to hear the ex-
planations. She stood behind Joe Newcomer plucking at his
sleeve. "Let's us go," she said. "Decent Respectable," she
went on when they were safe out in the chill darkness of the
open touring car, "it was just like Cinderella . . . I had been
having such a good time dancing with the boys and dreaming
about the lake and the clock struck and everything was horrible the coach was an old rotten pumpkin and bats and owls
flew out."

"Zeke has a tough row to hoe." Joe said pausing between
his words. "Why in the world did he do it? Zeke's the brightest
of any of us."

Lulie didn't answer. Yawning she pulled her head as far as
it would go into the collar of the rabbitskin coat she'd never
liked but that had been the only one she could afford now that
she wasn't getting any allowance since Father died. "Sorry,"
she said, "but I'm so sleepy."

"I guess I oughtn't to have taken you to a joint like that,"
Joe went on. Lulie could only give a drowsy groan.

When they drove in at Fiftytwo Ten Lulie's eyes were
blind with sleep. Yawning she showed Joe where the couch had
been made up for him in the den and whispered that Ben
would find cots for Jasper and Georgie in the attic. Joe wanted
to kiss her good night but she gave him three quick little pats
on the shoulder and ran off into Aunt Lyde's room. She found
Aunt Lyde wide awake. "Where's Ben?" was the first thing
Aunt Lyde asked. "Why hasn't he come in?"

"Joe brought me home early because I danced myself into
fits and suddenly felt tired as a worm."

"My dear you are reeking of tobacco. That's the worst thing
about going out with men. The smell gets in your hair. If

you're not careful you'll ruin your complexion. And I declare you have rings under your eyes . . . at your age. Sister Lucy and I used to think buttermilk was the best thing in the world for the complexion. Now I won't sleep a wink till Ben comes in."

"But Aunt Lyde. Ben's free white and twentyone. He's out with his best and oldest friends. Zeke's along."

"If Zeke had any common sense he'd never have made such a dreadful marriage . . . Lulie sometimes I hope you won't marry at all. Most girls would have jumped at Joe Newcomer. I know you always think he's there to fall back on but you can't keep him dangling forever. You'll see. You always think you can do the impossible like all the Harringtons. People who try for the impossible take a fall sooner or later, don't forget that dear . . . Read me a chapter Lulie dear. It's the only thing that soothes me. My blood pressure's up tonight. I can feel it throbbing in my temples. If things go on like this," she began to whimper, "I'll worry myself into a shock."

Fighting back her yawns, Lulie started to read. The words swam before her eyes. Aunt Lyde wasn't paying attention. She was talking again. "My dear, sometimes I wonder why any woman marries, any woman who respects herself. Now with Joe Addison if he'd lived I would have been happy. He was such a gentleman in everything, so respectful. He never entered our bedroom without knocking. In those days married couples were supposed to sleep in double beds but he showed such delicacy . . . Your Uncle Purdy and I have always had separate rooms. My dear I declare he married me for my social position or he thought there was more money than appeared on the surface, but all poor Joe Addison left after the debts were paid was an exquisite set of flat silver and some old trunks full of his mother's crinolines, and Grandfather Waring squandered everything on his horses. Luckily he didn't live to see Sandy Ford go under the hammer . . . Of course the old mansion had burned years before . . . When your Uncle Purdy came along there was no choice. The strain of these years has broken my health, and worrying about the future of you children. Your father was so impractical. He never would come down to earth. My dear, in his will he left everything to me and Purdy to hold in trust and divide as we saw fit and he knew I didn't have the strength to oppose Purdy. The Harringtons always think everything's going to turn out the way they want and of course it doesn't. I'm worrying myself into the grave about it. He'll be glad when I'm gone. You'll all be glad." . . . She sniffed "I'm such a trouble and expense to you all . . . An unsuitable marriage is so degrading for a lady." She started sobbing again. "My dear, he's made me sign things . . . It's not right for him to invest you children's inheritance in his own business. I declare I can't bear men."

Lulie went to the bureau and shook one of the sleeping capsules out of its bottle. Aunt Lyde put it on her tongue obediently as a child and took a dutiful little swallow after it. She closed her eyes. Right away she was asleep.

Lulie was wide awake by this time. She locked herself in her room and read the battered old green *Morte d'Arthur* she'd had when she was a little girl until she felt herself slipping back happily into a dreamlit world of castles and forests. Dreaming she was clothed in white samite walking through a glen dark with great hemlock trees she fell asleep.

Of course she had to wake up with the curse the morning of the day she had to lunch with the great Hugh Swanson. She arrived at the office with a headache feeling peaked and pale, and sat at her desk toying bitterly with the proof of Bonmeyer's page of dainty lingeries. The thought of soft lawns and muslins put her teeth on edge like the screech of chalk on a blackboard; she wished she was a nun in sackcloth and a starched coif. The brassbound clock counted the minutes ever so slowly. She wasn't scared of Hugh Swanson, she was telling herself but she wished the lunch were over; she ought to have called up to say she was home sick. Suddenly she looked up and the hands on the clock were pointing straight up and there was his voice behind her soft as meringue. "Dreaming of lovely lingeries? Not too bad for next week, eh? A cut of a pretty girl dreaming over Bonmeyer's ad, but can we get an artist to put the reverie into it?"

"It makes me want to wear oilskins." She put a comical wail into her voice as she got to her feet. "Mr. Swanson I'll be with you in two seconds." As she dashed off to the ladies' room she saw all sorts of expressions chasing each other across Hugh Swanson's broad pale face. By the time she got back with her hat and fur jacket on he had evidently decided to be amused and a little wistful.

"There are times," he said, after a glance around the marble landing where they were waiting for the elevator, to make sure no other employee was within earshot, "when I want to go up to the rooftops and announce to the world in a loud voice that nothing matters but a few simple honest things." His face took on a dogged sterling look, the look, Lulie whispered to herself, it must wear when he went to his banker for a loan.

"That doesn't mean I don't like clothes," said Lulie.

"Of course, of course," he said soothingly in the cab that was taking them to the restaurant. "But that's why I want your advice, Miss Harrington. You're as independent as a hog on ice, as they say in the Loop."

"I hope I haven't been making too much noise in the office," Lulie said laughing. "Miss Ebbitt says she's getting a cloth to cover my cage."

"Miss Ebbitt is a very fine lady."

"And a very smart one," said Lulie.

As they walked into the restaurant across from the court-house with its dim gilded mirrors and its smell of Vienna pastry and cigarettes, the great Hugh Swanson seemed to swell inside his cashmere overcoat. He knew everybody. Big faces of businessmen and courthouse politicians grinned and nodded in his direction. Men got up to shake hands with him as he passed.

Lulie felt like the little mouse in the fable trotting in front of the big lion. She understood suddenly what being a lion meant. Hugh Swanson's face looked like a lion's; he was colored like a lion, a tame lion.

When he sat down at a table marked RESERVED the waiter was all attention. Hugh Swanson frowned peevishly as he studied the bill of fare. Lulie didn't feel a bit like eating. She ordered a chicken patty and a cup of tea and settled back in her chair ready to enjoy the lunch in spite of everything. She didn't care about his old job, she told herself. Hildegarde Willard had a friend who was starting a new agency. It wasn't the only job in town.

"Miss Harrington," began the great Hugh Swanson, breaking a breadstick precisely in the middle, "let me put my cards on the table. As you know I'm not a conventional person and I don't run my business in a conventional way. My business depends on people's using their brains, their wit, their imagination. Brains don't flourish in an atmosphere of . . . oh Lord you know the average employee's attitude towards the boss. That's why I find certain people so refreshing."

"Certain people better be careful or they'll turn out silly little chatterboxes."

"Miss Harrington you've proved to my satisfaction at least that you can deliver the copy. I don't mind people's being amusing if they can deliver but I have many amusing friends in this business that can't meet a deadline."

Lulie was sipping her tea. "When gentlefolk meet, compliments pass, is what my grandmother would have said."

The great Hugh Swanson picked a carrot off a plate of raw vegetables. He was smiling at her his broadest bigbrotherly smile. His voice became confidential, meringue over chocolate mousse. "I'm transferring the agency to New York," he said crunching on the carrot . . . "You like tea? So do I. Drink gallons of it. Can't abide coffee . . . I'm reorganizing the firm and reorganizing my private life. We're seeing the dawn of a bigger better brighter more prosperous America. There's a new spirit in business. We must learn the European lesson. We must give up our landlocked middlewestern outlook or we'll be left behind in the race. Since the European war American prosperity takes on a worldwide significance."

"But I'm landlocked," said Lulie with a little shriek of mirth. "I'm landlocked as a trout. I've never really seen the ocean though I was taken to California once. I was too little to appreciate it, so my Aunt Lyde said."

"Some people," said the great Hugh Swanson weightily, "are born with a cosmopolitan outlook." Lulie heard herself give a sort of gurgle. "Don't think, Miss Harrington, I'm selling Chicago short. Chicago made me what I am. I shall always boost Chicago. It is the crossroads of America, but New York is the crossroads of the world. Now my dear . . . I understand they call you Lucy, or Lulie, or something like that . . . Everything I am saying will be held in the strictest confidence of course."

Lulie nodded eagerly, too eagerly she feared.

"My wife has consented to divorce me and to go back to her home and her folks at Red River Junction, to the beginnings from which we sprung." Lulie tried to keep her mouth from falling open. She knew that disappointment and dismay were showing on her face. "My success has always embarrassed her," Hugh Swanson went on blandly. "She will be amply provided for. She's a very fine woman and I shall revere her to my dying day but it is the parting of the ways. She's always hated it in Chicago and the idea of New York appalls her. Now that the children are of college age she's planning to go back to teaching school. In any other kind of people our breaking up would mean a vulgar betrayal, but with us it's merely that we have reached a crossroads in our lives. Do you follow me?"

Before Lulie, who was quite out of breath, could answer he went on frowning, "No I prefer for you not to say a word. Think over what I am going to say for three weeks. It's partly a business proposition but there are other factors involved . . . I want you and of course Frank Hays and Miss Ebbitt and a few others to come to New York with the agency. We'll make the move some time in the summer . . . But . . . now this particularly I want you to think over carefully . . . I want you, when the divorce proceedings are completed — that goes without saying — to become my fiancée and eventually my wife."

"But I'm engaged already," Lulie said in a thin wail.

He showed no signs of having heard. His big pale lion face hovered implausible as a balloon over his plate of raw vegetables. "I shall not describe at present the feelings that have brought about this proposal," he went on in a matter of fact tone. "An engagement can always be broken . . . And now," he added with the expression of a man pressing a button on his desk to usher in a new appointment . . . "I want your ideas as to how we can dramatize the Archer Roller Bearing. I want the women of the family to think of it as a beautiful roller bearing." His manner remained highly formal as he ushered her out of the restaurant amid converging eyes from the big-faced men at the chattering tables and handed her into a cab. "We have neglected the feminine touch in industrial advertising," he went on to explain as the cab rolled through the streets. "You'll find the Roller Bearing folder on your desk," he added curtly as, chest bulging, he stalked ahead of her through the lobby and down the corridor into his private office.

In spite of the fact that employees were forbidden to make personal calls, the first thing Lulie did when she let herself drop back at her desk was to get Hildegarde Willard on the phone.

"Garde let's have tea at that horrid little place. Five thirty. It's a dare."

Hildegarde was already there, wearing a fur hat that wasn't any too becoming and her mother's voluminous mink coat, when Lulie ran into the little tearoom.

"Why Garde, you look like the fat lady at the circus."

"Mink is unbecoming to anybody but particularly to me," said Hildegarde calmly. "I didn't have time to find my own coat because I was busy all afternoon getting out Josie's wedding invitations and left the house in a rush to catch the train."

"You're an angel to come all the way in town, but I had to talk to a sympathetic female friend."

"Lulie what on earth's the matter?" Garde's voice sounded like her mother's when she said that. Lulie remembered how cozy it used to make the cottage feel when she was a little girl and Mrs. Willard came to call.

"Give me some tea. I'm dogtired. I'm tired as an old yellow mongrel dog."

She reached for Hildegarde's cup and took a swallow of tea.

"Is it about Zeke?"

"The great Hugh Swanson took me out to lunch today and my dear, he proposed."

"Proposed what?"

Lulie let out a shriek. "He asked me for my hand in marriage!"

Hildegarde threw back her head and laughed and laughed and laughed. Lulie saw her through tears of vexation all out of shape like in a comic mirror but she couldn't help laughing too.

"But it's not funny," she wailed. "You don't need to sit there laughing like a hyena . . . He hasn't even got his divorce yet."

"He must be horribly rich."

"I wouldn't care if he were J. P. Morgan himself . . . But you don't understand, Garde. It means I'll have to go out and walk the streets looking for another job. Jobs aren't any too easy to get now that all the boys are home from the wars. And he wants me to go along when he moves the agency to New York."

"But Lulie, you'd like that."

"Of course. I'd love it. It would be a way of getting away from Fiftytwo Ten. That's why it's all so awful."

"Why didn't you tell him you were engaged to Joe?"

"I did but he didn't pay the slightest attention . . . I hate his little old job but it's pretty well paid and if I went to New York I'd be an executive."

"Lulie," Hildegarde calmly changed the subject, "I've been thinking I ought to try to get a job myself. I'm tired of being fattened at home like a pet pig. At college I took shorthand and you know how good my typing is."

"Don't ever let anybody know it, Garde. The only reason I've gotten anywhere is I made such a miserable secretary they had to start me higher up. I've hated it and it's been fun too and now it's all over."

"Fiddlesticks. All you need to do is look him straight in the eye and never let him mention the matter again."

"But he gives me the horrors. Imagine the great Hugh Swanson in his B.V.D.s."

They both got to giggling. Lulie said she couldn't stand it out at Fiftytwo Ten that night if Hildegarde didn't come to supper. She could get Mrs. Willard to send Wesley in with the car for her afterwards. Lulie had developed a headache and declared she'd die if she had to sit all that time on the trolley-car so they decided to split the price of a taxi.

The next morning Lulie woke up with pains in her bones and her skin hot as flannel. Her head swam when she tried to get dressed so she went back to bed. Mrs. Ritchie called Dr. Warner and reported that he said right off it was the la grippe and that it was all over town. She said for Lulie to stay in bed but she didn't seem so much worried about her as about Aunt Lyde. The doctor had said they must be very careful to see Aunt Lyde wasn't exposed because her heart might not stand it. Feeling like a leper in quarantine Lulie lay in bed that day and the next. She didn't get much attention because nobody but old Emma came near her, but she read a lot and it was a relief to have a real excuse for staying home from the office. Miss Ebbitt sent hyacinths in a pot and an envelope full of copy to return by mail with suggestions. Friday night Ben came home. When she heard him in the hall Lulie called to him that she had the benignant la grippe but he came right on in. He said if he did catch it it would be an excuse for staying home from classes. Saturday he brought up her meals and an armful of magazines and they had a wonderful time playing rummy and talking about how they were going to sneak up to the lake some winter and set fire to all the new cottages along the shore. When the American Beauty roses with five foot stems arrived by special messenger from Hugh Swanson Ben carried on so Lulie knew she would never hear the last of it. Ben could be a dreadful tease. "But Ben they are from the firm," she insisted. "At the great Hugh Swanson's all the employees get American Beauty roses when they fall sick."

Lulie told Ben to take the roses into Aunt Lyde's room and he came back reporting that Aunt Lyde was very much impressed and said that they made her feel like a Gibson girl. "This grippe makes me feel like one too," said Lulie.

That afternoon Ben went downtown to go to the fight with Georgie and Jasper. Lulie who was beginning to feel better lay cozily in bed in the new silk bedjacket with real valenciennes on the sleeves that the Willards had sent her, the reading light looking very yellow against the gloaming of a low-hanging winter sky, reading Arnold Bennett and stopping now and then to dream drowsily of being married to Jasper Milliron and living at a ranchhouse on the great dry flank of a mountain and riding the range all day through bare open country empty except for patches of cattle and brighteyed prairie dogs sitting up with their paws hanging at the edges of their holes. Of course he never had asked her, but there was a helpless look in his eyes when he looked at her like when they'd danced that night and he'd told her about General Grant's mule. My how Aunt Lyde would carry on if she rushed out and married Jasper. "My dear he's totally uneducated," she'd say, "and only a gentleman by act of congress."

Thinking about marriage made her think about Joe. She knew she ought to have been thinking about Joe all along. First thing in the morning she'd sit up and write Joe a letter. She couldn't marry him but she loved him the way she loved Ben and Zeke. She must make him understand she never could marry him. Her eyes filled with tears when she thought how awful it was to cause pain to Decent Respectable. Maybe she just oughtn't to marry ever. Maybe Ben wouldn't marry either and Zeke would get over thinking Mugsie was a sacred trust and when Aunt Lyde died they'd all get an apartment downtown together, and she'd keep house for them. She ran through a series of little pictures like magic lantern slides in her head of the three of them in oldfashioned rooms that smelt of American Beauty roses while it snowed outside getting old and gray and crotchety together but not really, just the way actors aged by putting on fresh makeup and white wigs between the acts of a play. She felt a sharp jab of remorse for thinking "when Aunt Lyde was dead." Poor dear Aunt Lyde. She mustn't even think it. She felt a little guilty flush on her face and opened up the book and tried to forget herself in her reading again.

Sunday she spent all morning writing the awful letter to Joe Newcomer. By afternoon she had that load off her mind and felt so chipper that when Georgie and Jasper came out to see her she got up and put on Aunt Lyde's old wadded dressing-gown and walked down to the den at the end of the hall to talk to them. The boys looked redeyed and quiet and drank a lot of icewater. They all said it was a wonderful fight, lightweights, real boxing, but they didn't seem to remember much about it. Afterwards they had gone to Steve's and it had been quite a brawl, a wonderful brawl, polka, plenty polka but they didn't seem to remember much about Steve's either. It was plain that there were things about the evening they weren't telling Lulie. Georgie would launch out on a story and then Ben would get an embarrassed look and start to fidget and Jasper would change the subject.

It was Jasper's last day. They were putting him on the train for Minneapolis that night. "High time I went to work," he said. "This life's too rich for my blood." He gave Lulie what she'd come to think of as his Missouri mule look. For a moment she wished she was out alone with Jasper. Then she could get him to say what he thought. But none of them were saying what they thought. There were pauses when they couldn't find anything at all to say to each other. Jasper in a gray civilian suit a little baggy at the knees didn't look half the Jasper he had in his uniform with the captain's bars. She liked him all the same but differently. On a ranch he'd be the same old Jasper again, but he was giving that up. Everybody was giving everything up that was fun. The pauses grew longer. Lulie began to feel the lonesomeness of the suburban winter twilight seeping into the room. She began to wish the boys would run along and let her go back to bed.

When they finally got to their feet, Georgie with one of his horrible black scowls beckoned her into a corner and pushed two typewritten sheets at her. "Lulie, it's my first byline," he said. "See, by Elbert Warner . . . Read it." He never took his eyes off her face while she read a terse little account of a beaten prizefighter sitting on a bench in the basement and pulling on his clothes to go home "My Georgie, it's clear and cool," said Lulie. "I wanted it cold," he said hastily. "Bugs didn't exactly commit himself. Those bastards never do but he gave me to understand that if I did him a few more human interest pieces like that he might try to get me a weekly column on the sports page. You know Ray Stannard's going to the *New York World*. Bugs wants human interest. We'll give him human interest till he cries uncle."

"George Elbert," Lulie looked at him with her eyes big, "I always knew you were a comer."

"I'll be a goner if you won't . . ." He looked at her hard with that little jiggle of the pupils of his brown eyes that used to make her so nervous when they were both children. "Hell's bells it's no use," he spat out the words. "Sometimes," he whispered huskily, "I wish I was Ben."

"Ben," Lulie ran over to her brother waving the typewritten sheets; "what do you think of Georgie's byline?"

"It's all right," said Ben. "The lad's got a future behind him."

"And all the time I'll be sweeping out that flourmill," said Jasper.

"You buy your ranch, Jasper," Lulie said, "and we'll all come out and ride the range."

Suddenly she couldn't bear to see them go. Although she was feeling shaky in the legs again she ran downstairs with them to help them into their heavy overcoats. They all yelled at her to get back before they opened the front door. It wasn't until she was walking back through the livingroom to the dark oak stairway that she noticed that Uncle Purdy and Mrs. Ritchie had been in there all the time sitting in a corner at a cardtable playing double solitaire. When she shuffled back through in her woolly slippers they both looked up at her out of the corners of their eyes at the same moment. For the first time she noticed that they looked a little alike. Their faces wore the same pudgy dissatisfied expression. "Your dear Aunt Lyde was asleep," said Mrs. Ritchie in her deep contralto . . . "Mr. Rumford and I were killing a little time."

"Double solitaire," grumbled Uncle Purdy. "It's more work than an inventory."

"Do you suppose it would be all right if I went in to see Aunt Lyde this evening? . . . I don't think I'm noxious any more."

"Of course," boomed Mrs. Ritchie. "She surely has missed your little attentions."

Lulie groped her way upstairs and got back under the covers of her bed in the gloaming. Right away she fell asleep. When she woke up it was dark. She was hungry. She ran down to the kitchen to fix herself an icebox snack from the Sunday chicken.

She carried a sandwich and a glass of milk up to Aunt Lyde's room to eat it. All the lights in the room were on. Aunt Lyde was lying back on the pillows with a handkerchief across her forehead. "Oh Lulie you might have come sooner," she mumbled in a little moaning singsong. "They all left me . . . that woman's gone off and left me to die. My dear, Purdy hasn't been near me all day and you've been off with your companions. Some day, my dear, you'll learn how dreadful it is to be left alone."

"Oh I hope not, Aunt Lyde," said Lulie briskly trotting around the room patting her pillows and bringing fresh cologne for the handkerchief on her head. "I'm planning to die at the age of thirtythree precisely if I don't decide to become a hermit."

"Lulie I've been wanting you to bring me my jewelcase. Oh dear what have I done with the little key?"

"I bet it's in the drawer of the night table."

Lulie found the key and brought the small wooden chest off the bureau over to the bed. It was the chest Lulie used to love so when she was a little girl because it had tiny drawers that locked and two proud pheasants carved out of dark wood on the lid and because Uncle Purdy had bought it for Aunt Lyde at Chamonix in Switzerland on their wedding trip. She used to hear its music box tinkling out "Ach du lieber Augustin" when Aunt Lyde was dressing for dinner or when something very festive was going to happen. Now Aunt Lyde cradled the chest with one arm and tried to claw the little paper packets out of it with a shaking hand. She had the strangest furtive suspicious expression on her face. She was so obviously trying to keep Lulie from seeing what she was doing that Lulie took a book and settled down with it in a chair in the corner. The little tinkling familiar tune started up and grew slow and died.

"Darling," Aunt Lyde started to whisper, "I can't remember where I put Grandmother Harrington's sapphire brooch or the

Addison cameos, and I used to have so much jet . . . What could have happened to it?"

Lulie put the book down and got to her feet. "Aunt Lyde dear, let me help you."

Aunt Lyde's eyes were bleary with tears. "Lulie, I can't remember what I did with Mother's things. You children should have them. I can't remember. It would be so awful if they had been stolen. That woman's been trying on my gowns."

Aunt Lyde covered the little mound of tissuepaper packets with one hand and started stuffing things back into the drawers as fast as she could with the other, keeping her suspicious watering eyes all the time on Lulie's face.

"But how could she Aunt Lyde?" Lulie couldn't help laughing at the thought of dumpy Mrs. Ritchie wearing gaunt Aunt Lyde's dresses. "She's such a different shape."

Aunt Lyde was staring at her with the unsmiling miser look on her face. "I had meant to give you your grandmother's garnets," she mumbled, "but now of course it's out of the question. Very little of this jewelry would be suitable for a girl employed in office work."

"Now Auntie suppose I read to you . . . You know it's not good for you to work yourself up."

Aunt Lyde let herself slump back on the pillow with her trembling fingers over her mouth. Lulie managed to put the rest of the tissuepaper packets back into the drawers again but when she tried to take away the little chest Aunt Lyde snatched at it. Lulie couldn't get her to let go. She finally went to sleep with both hands clasped over the carved pheasants beside her pillow like a child in its crib with a toy.

By the time Lulie crept off to bed she was thoroughly worn out. She woke up next morning with her nose red and running and her sinuses stopped up and lay huddled under the covers wondering whether she ought to mail her letter to Joe Newcomer which she could see across the room propped against the mirror on her dressing table. She was wondering too what on earth she'd do about the great Hugh Swanson when she had to go back to the office. She'd about decided the best way out was to become a recluse and pass poems through the crack of the door like Emily Dickinson when she began to feel hungry. A recluse had to have room service. At last she couldn't stand waiting any longer and ran to the head of the stairs and called down to ask Emma why she hadn't brought her up any breakfast. "I thought you'd gone to work Miss Lulie," Emma answered. It seemed hours before Emma came groaning up the stairs with a tray.

"Mrs. Rumford's took bad," said Emma shaking her head.

"Oh Lord, I guess I'd better get up," said Lulie.

"You better had, Miss Lulie."

Lulie had barely time to swallow her breakfast when Mrs. Ritchie came in, wearing her white uniform, trying to put on the crisp professional manner of a real trained nurse. Aunt Lyde was running a fever and seemed quite incoherent, poor soul. She said Lulie might as well stay in bed. Mrs. Ritchie had already called Dr. Warner and he was on his way. "Be sure to let me know when he comes," said Lulie. "Of course," said Mrs. Ritchie and went bustling out.

In the middle of the afternoon Dr. Warner came into Lulie's room suddenly, bringing his smell of stale pipes and iodoform and unwashed linen. He bent his unsteady black glance severely on her face, stood threateningly over the bed and, in a half boisterous half peevish tone that made her feel it was all her fault, "Lulie," he said, "it's about time we admitted to ourselves that your poor Aunt Lyde has reached the end of her tether. It's a miracle she's lived this long," he added angrily: "I'm getting Doctor Hawkins out for a consultation just so we'll none of us have anything to reproach ourselves with. I'll get him to talk to Purdy but I'm sure Purdy has resigned himself to the inevitable by this time. You're damn lucky to have that Mrs. Ritchie in the house. There's no way of getting a nurse or a bed in a hospital either with the flu epidemic on. I haven't slept in a bed for three nights and I don't expect to for three nights more. I don't know what keeps me going except that we Warners are tough . . . What do you think of that boy of mine? Is he going to turn out to be a successful newspaper man or just another drunken bum with literary cravings? You look all right anyway," he went on without stopping for an answer. "I wouldn't want to be the one to make out your death certificate . . . You're far too pretty." He gave that dry laugh Lulie hated. "I've made out plenty of 'em this week. . . . Keep out of drafts, wrap up warmly, plenty of orange juice and plain nourishing food," he finished in a routine singsong that made Lulie think he must have repeated the words at a hundred bedsides all over Woodlawn . . . "Don't get overtired and take a tablespoonful of cod liver oil daily." Lulie made a face. "Don't like it? Well, the Esquimaux think it's delicious." He gave another hacking laugh and was gone.

It was partly the fear of another visit from Dr. Warner that got Lulie out of bed and down to the office next morning. Aunt Lyde had gone off into a heavy sleep and seemed neither better nor worse. Although Lulie felt pale and weak it was a relief to be back in the routine of her desk under the brass-bound clock and the consultations with Miss Ebbitt, and the chats with the telephone girl and the office boy's friendly enquiries and the great Hugh Swanson's most thoughtful-of-his employees voice over the phone asking her if she was sure she felt well enough to come to work. She was just picking her notes up to go out to lunch with Miss Ebbitt to talk about the Bonmeyer account when there came Mrs. Ritchie's deep voice hardly audible on the phone. Aunt Lyde was sinking fast. Doctor Hawkins and Doctor Warner were in consultation. Better come right home.

All the way Lulie kept urging the taxidriver to hurry though she knew in her heart there was no sense to it. The real Aunt Lyde had been gone for years. When the taxi stopped in the driveway of Fiftytwo Ten Lulie jumped out without paying and ran breathless up the stairs.

From the halfopen door of Aunt Lyde's room came the familiar scent of colognesoaked handkerchiefs and of drawers saturated with dry lavender. Mrs. Ritchie's stubby form stood in her way with a pudgy hand on the jamb of the door. "Don't come in dear it's too late. Her lungs filled up and her heart stopped. You mustn't come in until the mortician has fixed her up. Why don't you go around and draw all the shades so that the neighbors will know there is a death in the house?"

Not knowing what else to do Lulie did as she was told. The taximan was still waiting in the front hall. She found Uncle Purdy was sitting at the diningroom table with his head in his hands and no expression at all on his face. As she didn't have enough change in her purse she had to ask him for money.

At the dinnertable Lulie found herself arguing bitterly with Uncle Purdy about the funeral arrangements. She did so want to take Aunt Lyde up to the lake to bury her beside the little shingled church she used to love to look at cuddled among the pines from her chair on the front porch of the cottage. Uncle Purdy said the lake was impractical. It was winter. There were no boats running. Everything would be frozen up tight. He believed in cremation.

"But Aunt Lyde was a good Episcopalian. She wouldn't like to be cremated," Lulie wailed.

"There there my dear, you mustn't get all upset," mumbled Mrs. Ritchie looking at her with surprised round eyes. Interment at the lake would be far too expensive, Uncle Purdy insisted. Better put the money in on a suitable monument.

"She believed in the resurrection of the body." Lulie jumped up from her chair with the tears spouting out of her eyes. Uncle Purdy got to his feet and faced her, for a moment too angry to speak. "She was my esteemed and beloved wife," he said at last. He was panting. The veins were swelling on his thick neck. As if she were watching a scene in a play Lulie saw herself and Uncle Purdy facing each other across the table with snarling faces. "And the life everlasting," she wailed and ran sobbing upstairs to her room the way she used to when she was a little girl with the tantrums. She locked the door and threw herself all dressed on the bed.

Mrs. Ritchie was in her element at the funeral in a black silk dress with black sequins on her bosom. She was solemn and kind with everyone, she rolled up her eyes with admiration over the stiffly wired flowers. She knew the names of the undertaker's men and was cozy with the minister. She arranged the seating in the carriages and picked out the hymns to be played on the organ at the chapel at the crematorium. Lulie didn't feel like herself at all in the horrid little round black hat that didn't go with the shape of her face. Ben and Zeke bore no resemblance to themselves either and even the dear Willards had the look of being dressed up for a masquerade. When at last it was over she climbed into the Willards' car beside Hildegarde without waiting to be invited. "Well at least Mugsie didn't come," she broke out as the big car turned out from the cemetery gates into a stream of traffic. "I saw her going off to a movie all by herself with a box of weekend chocolates. She said she didn't believe in making a fetish of death." She couldn't help giving a little chortle. Mrs. Willard's face took on its natural cozy smiling look. "Child," she said, "why don't you spend a few days with us? Edward will drive you in every morning. You know how early he goes in . . . Your job at Fiftytwo Ten is finished."

"I hoped you'd say that," said Lulie.

As she drove out through sunny snowpacked suburbs the word finished spoken in Mrs. Willard's sweet reasonable tones sank down and down into her mind. Finished. Grandmother Waring and Aunt Lyde and Father and the life they'd all loved so at the lake, and going out with Joe Newcomer and her business career at the great Hugh Swanson's. It couldn't all be finished. How could everything be finishing before it began? Finished, the word rang through her mind in all sorts of different tones so that she couldn't pay attention to what Hildegarde or any of them were saying. When they got out at the Willard's big comfortable wellheated hideous Tudorstyle house they put her to bed in a big comfortable wellheated room, and she went immediately to sleep.

That spring she spent a great deal of time with the Willards but weekends she tried to be home at Fiftytwo Ten to make it seem less bleak for Ben. Mrs. Ritchie had stayed on from week to week after the funeral to keep house for Uncle Purdy and Lulie began to suspect that it wouldn't be long before she would turn out to be the new Mrs. Rumford. Lulie didn't mind a bit but with Aunt Lyde gone she felt herself so strange in the house. The life at Fiftytwo Ten that had seemed so dreadfully permanent now began to seem almost too temporary. It wasn't Mrs. Ritchie's fault. She really did try to make the Harringtons feel she wanted to be a mother to them all.

Any excuse to get away from Fiftytwo Ten caused Lulie's spirits to rise but they were particularly high the sunny Saturday when she waited for Georgie at the information bureau in the station to go out to Lake Leman for the weekend. Of course Georgie had to arrive late just in time to catch the train at a dead run. All the seats were taken. Georgie was crabby about going out to the Willards. "What the devil would they do out at Lake Leman all day Sunday? Suppose it rained? Would they sit in the Country Club and play bridge?" He didn't know how to play bridge and he hated country clubs. And a picnic? What the hell was this Willard idea of a picnic? He'd look about as silly at a picnic as Joe Jeffries at an afternoon tea. Lulie was severe with him. "Now Georgie," she said, "you must pretend to enjoy it even if you don't because it's sweet of Mrs. Willard to ask all the Tribe out for a last fling before Josie gets married."

"Josie never liked me much," he grumbled. "Is Joe coming?"

Lulie nodded.

"Why don't you marry him and get it over with?"

"George Elbert if you go on making disagreeable remarks I'm not going to speak to you."

"Then I'll take the first train back to town and go to Steve's and have a good time. What kind of a story am I going to get at Lake Leman? Sports is my department not the society page."

"Got anything new for me to read George Elbert?"

"You don't want to read about a baseball player that broke his finger."

"How do you know I don't?"

Watching her face out of tense brown eyes with that little disconcerting jiggle in the pupils he handed her two typewritten sheets folded in the middle. "If there's one extra word I want to know it." He ground the words on his teeth. "A man's got to learn not to write all over the page."

They were jammed in the aisle of the jiggling train. Lulie glanced at the first few lines holding it up against the overcoated back of the man in front of her. Already the train was beginning to slow down for the Lake Leman station. "I'll have to finish it when I get to the house," said Lulie.

George gave her his black suspicious look and snatched the pages back.

"I'll let you have it later if I can ever get you away from Joe Newcomer. He's the guy tried to drown me. I don't forget that." He was talking through his teeth again.

"George Elbert act your age."

It was a pleasure to jump into the arms of Josephine and Hortense and Hildegarde, all so tall and slender and ornamental in their big garden hats in the warm spring sun. Hortense wore a violet smock which she explained by saying she had been painting a still life. She must have put a little henna in the water last time she washed her hair because it looked unusually auburn under the palegreen straw. It was cheerful at the Willards' house that Saturday in the diningroom that smelt of hyacinths and shone with silver and fresh laundered linen. The french-windows were open.

Everybody was out in the sun on the terrace drinking sherry in front of Hortense's newest painting that was very French and impressionist, of oranges and bananas nestling in purple shadow. Right away Joe Newcomer came up wearing a sad proud look and squeezed Lulie's two hands. He led her to a corner of the hall and before she'd had a chance to take off her hat or powder her nose told her straight out that if she really wanted him to be a brother instead of something else by gum he'd be the best brother she'd ever had that was that. "Now give me back the ring," he added.

"What ring?"

He looked pained. "Our engagement ring of course."

"Oh of course Joe I'll get it after lunch." Lulie ran upstairs to Hildegarde's room to tidy her hair with the thought of the ring teasing vaguely in the back of her mind. What could she have done with Joe's ring? Talking to Hildegarde she forgot about it again. When the two of them looked down out of the window on their friends on the terrace below Lulie whispered to Garde that it was one of those days when everybody looked their best. Georgie was a handsome fellow with his broad shoulders and his mustache in spite of his unpressed suit. Josephine and Dabney Brooks would make a beautiful bride and groom. He was too stocky for her taste, Lulie told Garde, but his face had a pleasant homemade look. Even Harding Edwards would pass in a crowd at the Art Institute. There was only poor Zeke's Mugsie looking hopelessly puttyfaced and bandylegged, out of place as a mongrel pup among a lot of thoroughbreds.

After lunch Josephine and Dabney Brooks took all comers at doubles on the Willards' tennis court. There was some talk of golf but Mr. Willard called up the Country Club and found that the greens were too wet. Georgie wouldn't play tennis, though Lulie knew he was a pretty good player, and kept growling that what he needed was a good tough bowling alley. It turned out there was a bowling alley down near the depot so when it began to get chilly on the courts they piled into a couple of cars and went bowling.

Bowling turned out to be something Mugsie understood. Georgie and Mugsie made up a team that beat everybody. They all praised Mugsie's bowling to the skies but all she would say was that she knew it wasn't ladylike and it hadn't been her fault if her daddy loved bowling more than anything. Zeke began to hover over her protectingly and finally came over and whispered in Lulie's ear that he'd have to take Mugsie back to Chicago. He had a lot of work to do anyway. He could see right now Mugsie was getting into one of her states. "You explain to the Willards, Lou. We'll just slip away," he said.

"They'll be heartbroken," said Lulie. "You know they are all just crazy about you Zeke."

Zeke gave her a fanatical blue stare. "Not enough to forget their prejudices," he said.

"You mean it's love me love my dog." The words were out before Lulie could stop them.

Zeke's pale face stiffened. He turned his back, gathered up Mugsie with a long arm and hurried her out into the street. Hildegarde was roaming around in her bashful way trying to tell people it was time they started home for supper because Dad got all out of sorts if meals were even a second late. Lulie, who'd been noticing out of the corner of an eye that Joe Newcomer on one side and Georgie on the other were waiting with that calf look on their faces to talk to her, darted off after

Hildegarde. "Let's start a movement," she shouted. "Everybody will follow. People always follow."

While she and Hildegarde were dressing for the evening, crowding each other a little in front of the tall glass on the bathroom door, she confessed to Garde about the engagement ring. "It's awful. I just can't remember what happened to it," she moaned. "I used to wear it all the time and then suddently I didn't." She started to sniffle a little.

Garde laughed. "If things like that don't work, they don't work," she said. "It's better to find out before than after . . . But Lulie," she dropped suddenly down on the square stool in front of her dressing table and the tears started spurting out of her eyes. "I can't get over Zeke . . . I find myself wishing such awful hateful things about that girl. I can't even say her name."

"I don't think I could stand him if he wasn't my brother."

"But he's so talented," sighed Garde.

Already Mrs. Willard was knocking. "Dinner in five minutes, girls," she called through the door in musical tones. After dinner they took up the rugs in the livingroom and moved all the furniture to the wall and danced to the Willards' new Concert Grand victrola. Everybody was too busy dancing to talk about their private lives and Lulie forgot everything dancing. It felt like old times when she caught a glimpse of Georgie and Ben sneaking off by themselves, probably to see if they could drum up a glass of beer in that bowling alley. When they were tired of dancing the young people crowded into the kitchen to help Hildegarde make penuche. It was late before they got to bed.

The next morning the first thing Lulie heard when she woke up was a phoebe singing. The room was full of pink sunlight. She got up and dressed quietly so as not to wake Garde who was still asleep in the other bed and ran out of doors. The green grass on the lawn was beaded with dew. Bursting buds shone in the shrubberies. Back in the hedge she could hear songsparrows. Even the gang of English sparrows who had taken over the birdbath on the terrace looked quite distinguished in their new brightly marked spring plumage. Round the corner of the house she ran into Georgie and Ben in their shirtsleeves. They had their heads together over the parts of Georgie's big express rifle which they had spread out on a newspaper on an iron table.

"Be careful of that cap pistol boys," said Lulie, "and don't shoot any of the Willards' songbirds."

"I thought we could try some target practice when we went on this damn picnic," said Georgie.

"Give us something to do," said Ben.

"Too bad that damn little tart carried off Zeke."

"Georgie," Lulie snapped at him.

"If Zeke practiced," Georgie went on blandly, "he'd be an excellent shot."

"He always said all he got out of the war was his German Luger," said Ben.

"And a complete set of plans for the cathedral at Chartres," added Lulie.

"Lulie I wouldn't say that about Juliet Sims except among ourselves," explained Georgie. "It happens to be true."

"But she tries to act so ladylike," said Ben.

"They all do," said Georgie. "It's a sure sign."

Hortense bore down on them from the terrace in her violet smock shaking her auburn curls in the sunlight. "Kids isn't it a day? A day made to order. It's the first time I've managed to paint en pleine aire . . . I know it's only a still life but before I never could see the color for the light. It's not going to be a picnic it's going to be a déjeuner sur l'herbe and I'm going to sketch it like Manet."

"And who's going to furnish the nude?" asked Georgie giving her his brash look.

Hortense stared him down. "Maybe you and Ben could oblige."

Ben and Georgie both blushed and the girls burst out laughing.

"Those nudes must have been a hardy race lying out in the grass like that. I went out to Barbizon," said Georgie laughing too, "and nearly froze to death there. In France, I wore woolly underwear from one year's end to the other."

"Red flannel I suppose," Lulie piped up, "but there's no reason why nudes should always be girls."

The picnic turned out to be fun in spite of the sharp wind that came up as soon as they got to the place Hortense had picked out on a narrow dirt road where the Little Snake River took a bend on the edge of the prairie. Some old willowtrees just showing flecks of green gave a little lee against the wind to a patch of grass just on the edge of the crumbly bank. There they spread out the old buffalo robes, smelling of mothballs, Hortense had found in her mother's attic. While the girls unpacked the picnic basket the boys roamed off towards a shack with a crazy stovepipe belching woodsmoke they'd caught sight of round the bend. Hortense kept making the girls move the picnic spot till she got the carcase of an old Model T Ford somebody had driven into the river out of sight. Then she arranged the fried chicken and the ham sandwiches on yellow plates on a white tablecloth and the bottles of wine and the glasses the way she wanted them in the picture. The boys came back crowded into a skiff they'd borrowed from an old man without any teeth they said lived in the shack. At that moment the sun came out from between streaky clouds and shot a swath of blue reflected sky over the brown water. "Now it's lovely," said Hortense. "I may be able to get in the skiff. . . Now you all settle down and eat and please don't move around too much." She sat on some old knotted willow roots with her pad of Wattman paper on her knees.

"Why does the river smell so dreadfully?" asked Josephine munching on a chickenleg.

"It's that chemical plant at Smallwood," said Dabney in a soothing tone.

"It takes my appetite away."

"The old man says it's killing all his catfish," said Ben.

"I bet what those French painters did," Hortense was saying without looking up from her work, "was to undress one of the picnickers when they got back to the studio."

Dabney let out a whistle and everybody got to giggling.

"Please don't move so much . . . I have to hurry because the sky's changing so."

"It's changing indeed," shouted Lulie. "The prudish old continental climate."

By the time they had finished eating and poured out the last of the claret the clouds had sealed out the last trace of blue in the sky. The sharp wind off the prairie, growing colder every minute, was beginning to whistle through the willow-branches. Ben said he reckoned he'd better take the old man back his skiff before the river froze over, so they never got to the promenade sur l'eau Hortense had talked about for a second sketch.

While the girls were packing the picnic things into the hamper, the boys took turns shooting at a twisted stake across the river with the rifle. After a while Hortense said her hands were too cold to hold a pencil. When snow began to fly they packed themselves back into the two cars in a hurry and started for home. By the time they turned into the Willards' driveway the cars were skidding and slewing in soft snow.

Joe Newcomer said he was sorry but he had to leave right away in order to get home before it turned into a blizzard. "But it's a three hours' drive. Don't you think you'd better stay over?" Lulie said looking up in his face.

"I've got to be in the office at eight."

Lulie followed him out to the car after he had said goodbye to the Willards. "Joe do be careful." She talked over the noise of the engine.

"I'm too damn careful," said Joe bitterly.

Lulie loved him at that moment. "Joe I don't know where that ring is, I must have lost it." She looked at him with her face all wrinkled up at the edge of tears. "You know I haven't got any memory, no more than a gopher."

Joe looked at her and she looked at Joe and suddenly they both began to laugh.

"Don't worry about the stupid old ring, sister Lucy."

"Now Brother Joseph you drive carefully."

He was gone in a swirl of dry snow down the driveway. She went back into the house to pack her bag. All through supper old Mr. Willard had himself a time teasing the young people about their picnic in a blizzard at Barbizon-sur-Snake. Right after supper Lulie and Ben and Georgie went off to the station through the slush with Harding Edwards tagging along behind them complaining of the filthy middlewestern climate at every step.

It was Harding who took her home to Fiftytwo Ten. He was going to get Zeke to sleep him on his couch. He wanted Zeke to help him hang a show at the Art Institute first thing in the morning. He said he knew Zeke would never get there unless he led him by the hand. Too bad Zeke hadn't been on the picnic, he kept saying. It had spoiled the day for him; though he loved the lovely Willards, things were never the same without Zeke. That awful Mugsie kept him cut off from all social contact.

"Might be a good thing," mumbled Lulie sleepily as they trudged home from the trolleystop because neither of them had enough change for a taxi.

"You mean it keeps him at work?"

"She doesn't mean any good. My dear she's even jealous of his architecture." He ducked into the gale of wet snow blowing round the house to head for the garage.

Once inside the front door Lulie pulled off her sopping shoes and ran upstairs to bed. With gloomy forebodings she remembered that tomorrow was Monday and she was supposed to go out to lunch with Hugh Swanson. Sufficient unto the day, she told herself out loud, is the evil thereof, and she fell asleep.

She woke up late. She had overslept. It was eight o'clock and she would be late for the office. Had she better be sick again? But she'd been sick so much and she had to see the great Hugh Swanson because if she looked him straight in the eye and said she was never going to get married and it worked she might keep her job. My, it would be wonderful to move to New York with the agency. As she hurriedly dressed she began to plan getting Ben a job there and moving Zeke. Of course all the great national firms of architects had their offices in New York. Then she couldn't do without Hildegarde. She'd have to find Garde a job too, but with Josie married that would leave Hortense all alone with her parents. If she got Hortense to go to New York to study art that would leave sweet Mrs. Willard without any family. Moving Mr. Willard out of his seat on the grain exchange would be a proposition.

Somebody was knocking on her bedroom door. It was Harding Edwards. The big glass eyes stared out of his white face. He couldn't seem to bring his lips together when he spoke. "Lulie. Come here. Somebody's shot," he managed to whisper. "Not Zeke?" He shook his head.

Lulie was already running up the stairs to the apartment over the garage. The door was open. The big electric light bulb over the drafting table scattered with breakfast coffee cups jarred with the garish sunlight that poured in through the window. Zeke, a look of patient dismay on his face, stood in the middle of the room and worked a clip of cartridges out of his Luger. Behind him on the couch, her face the color of stale dough, sat Olga Lipschitz. She was trembling so the springs of the couch rattled. Between them Mugsie lay on the floor limp as a dropped doll. Lulie ran to her and began to feel her all over.

"It's not Mugsie," said Zeke in a strained patient tone. "She was brandishing this thing around and acting silly and it went off. Better look outside. The elder was on a ladder putting up the screens and he fell off."

Lulie had been becoming conscious of a singsong groan coming endlessly from somewhere outside.

"He may be hurt," she said and ran down stairs again.

She found the Elder Broadwater lying on his back beside the ladder in the snowy shrubbery with the broken screen clutched in his arms. His gray eyeballs rolled. The shoulder of his long black overcoat was soaked with blood.

"Zeke, Harding," Lulie called from the foot of the stairs, "give me a hand." From the apartment upstairs came shrieks and sobs from Mugsie mingled with Zeke's drawling voice trying to calm her.

At last Harding came down walking as if on peas. "Oh my nerves," he said giggling. "I may faint Lulie. I always faint when I see blood."

"You go phone for an ambulance," Lulie said and ran to get a sheet off one of the beds upstairs. She was trying to work the sheet gently under the elder's head and shoulders when she saw Uncle Purdy all dressed for the city with his briefcase under his arm standing behind her.

"What happened?"

"He's hurt badly . . . He was putting in the screens . . . Mugsie was waving Zeke's gun around and it went off . . ."

"They can't stay in the garage. Not after this," said Uncle Purdy looking down at the elder in a dazed sort of way. "I wonder if Doc Warner's still at his home. Go call him Lulie."

"I sent Harding to call an ambulance."

"Not the police," shouted Uncle Purdy. "I want Doc Warner here first." Suddenly he kneeled down beside the elder. "Let's see how bad he's hurt."

"Lord Mr. Rumford, I'm glad it's you and Miss Lulie. What she want to shoot me for? I ain't never done her no harm. Tell me I ain't hurt bad."

Emma was in the kitchen pouring out a cup of coffee for Harding. He smirked at Lulie. "I thought I'd be more useful if I had a cup of coffee. I couldn't think of any hospital so I called the police."

"Emma," Lulie said without looking at Harding, "go out and help Mr. Rumford. The elder fell off his ladder and he's hurt but I don't think it's too bad."

"I was scared to look Miss Lulie," said Emma. "I heard an awful bang go off. Praise de Lawd, he ain't hurt bad."

Lulie ran to the phone. It took hours to get the Warners. Mrs. Warner started to tell her all about a bridge tournament she was organizing and asking did she think Georgie was going to do well in newspaper work. "But there's been an accident here. We need the doctor," Lulie kept insisting. At last Doc Warner's voice got on the wire grumbling that nobody ever let him eat his breakfast in peace. She managed to explain that somebody had been hurt, gunshot wound in the shoulder. "I'm afraid he'll bleed to death."

Lulie got back in time to help Uncle Purdy and Emma, using the sheet under his back and an automobile rug under his middle, drag the elder out of the snowy bushes into the garage. He screamed with pain as they laid him out on the concrete floor. Uncle Purdy started to try to cut the coat away from his shoulder with a pair of scissors. Lulie ran upstairs to Zeke's apartment to get a pillow for his head.

The police were there ahead of her, too heavy cops and a foxyfaced lieutenant. Mugsie stood in the center of the floor talking and talking. "I shot," she was saying, "to save my home."

"Officer, don't pay any attention to her, she's hysterical," Zeke interrupted, but it was obvious that the officers were paying attention to her. "That foreign woman," Mugsie pointed at the place on the couch where Olga Lipschitz had been sitting. "I just meant to wound her lightly in the arm so that she'd keep away from my home. She and that faggot. They've ruined my home."

"Where is she?" asked the lieutenant.

Olga had disappeared. The cops looked in the bathroom and the kitchenette and in the bedroom closet. One of them got on his knees to look under the studio couch. It all got to

be like an oldfashioned French farce. When they gave up looking for Olga Lipschitz Lulie found their brassy appraising eyes
turned on her.

"Who's this woman?" asked the lieutenant turning to Mugsie. Mugsie was the one he was paying attention to. Mugsie
was holding the center of the stage.

"She's his sister. She's been against me too," she chanted
in a triumphant tone.

"But the elder. We can't let the elder bleed to death. Don't
any of you know first aid?" Lulie heard herself insisting in
her Aunt Lyde's thin commanding voice.

"There's an ambulance coming," said the lieutenant indif-
ferently.

"I'll take him a pillow."

"No," said the lieutenant. "Leave everything where it is.
This may be murder."

"It's the unwritten law," intoned Mugsie. "I shot to defend
my home."

Lulie brushed past the cops and snatched a cushion off the
studio couch. "Keep her in sight, she may be a material wit-
ness," she heard the lieutenant say. His voice trailed off helplessly as she ran off downstairs with the cushion.

Doc Warner was already there. He snatched the cushion
out of her hands and tucked it under him where he knelt on
the concrete beside the elder. He had managed to uncover the
bloody shoulder. He was probing with a bright instrument of
some kind. "I'm no bonesetter," he was muttering through
clenched teeth. The elder's poor woolly head was threshing
from side to side on the bloody sheet. His skin was violet. He
was screaming like a wounded horse. There was something like
a horse about the way his long yellow teeth showed each time
he screamed. Emma crouched at his feet sobbing with her
apron over her head while Uncle Purdy paced back and forth
his round face pale and beaded with sweat. "For God's sake
Bert give him some morphine," he was saying.

Doc Warner lurched to his feet after he'd covered the wound with a pile of gauze bandage that immediately became dark with blood.

"Where can I wash my hands?" he asked Lulie. As he followed her into the kitchen he muttered out of the side of his mouth in a way that suddenly reminded her of Georgie. "A badly smashed shoulder, but if the lung isn't affected he ought to pull through. He may have broken a rib or two falling."

When Lulie came back with a towel he turned to her with one of his sidelong looks. "Looks to me like you were the best man of the lot, Lulie . . ." He let out that hard laugh she hated so. "You go on down to your work and keep out of this mess. Take a tip from an old hand. Run on downtown and don't talk to any reporters. You don't know anything about anything."

The ambulance had come at last and was backed up to the garage looking very white and shiny and antiseptic. When they had edged the elder onto the stretcher and the doors had closed on him and the ambulance had driven off with clanging bell, Lulie found herself staring at the bloody sheet and the muddied laprobe and a small gleaming pool of blood between them on the concrete floor. Emma had gone to the hospital in the ambulance. There was nobody there to clean up so Lulie picked the sheet up gingerly and took it to the incinerator. She didn't like the looks of the pool of blood so she got a bucket of hot water and a mop and swabbed it up.

When she tiptoed back upstairs she found Zeke's apartment crowded. The cops and the lieutenant were still there. There were young men in felt hats. A yellow stained photographer was pouring flashlight powder onto a tin screen. Mugsie still stood in the center of the floor. She was obviously having the time of her life. "It was the unwritten law," she kept saying. She had discovered a new gesture that she used over and over. Her eyes on the ceiling and her finger pointed at the big electric light as if calling on testimony from on high. She never batted an eye when the flashlight went off.

"Mrs. Harrington, I very much regret that I shall have to book you for assault with deadly weapon," the lieutenant was saying, in a voice full of tenderness and respect. "But I'm sure the court will find extenuating circumstances."

Lulie found Zeke's blazing blue eyes fixed on her. Even before he spoke she began to feel like a little girl caught sticking her nose into grownup's business. "Sister Lucy, this does not concern you," he said in a cold selfpossessed tone. "I shall handle this matter in my own way." His face had taken on that chiselled look of granite obstinacy she had sometimes seen on her father's face. She ran down the stairs again so that all those people shouldn't see her crying. Sniffling up the tears she groped for her hat and coat and gloves in the dark hall.

To her amazement she found it was only ten o'clock at the familiar elevated station that wore an empty forlorn middle-of-the morning air. The sun was already melting the soft snow off the roofs. The sky was a crushing blue. When she settled into the shelter of her desk at the office, the brassbound clock still only said ten twentyfive. Lord time moved slowly when you were unhappy. The first lucky break that day was the blue memo on her blotter to the effect that Mr. Swanson had been urgently called out of town and would she mind shifting their little lunch to Wednesday.

The words "little lunch" had an intimate sound that gave her an uneasy pang, but they also reminded her that she hadn't eaten any breakfast. All at once she felt hungry and faint. Eddy the office boy was a good friend of hers. He was delighted to go downstairs to buy her a carton of coffee and an eggsalad sandwich. She had just tucked the last corner of the sandwich into her mouth when Miss Ebbitt, looking more like a china figure than ever in spring green with a spiky hat of rainbow colored straw, appeared behind her wearing her most enamelled smile. With her mouth full Lulie started to explain that there had been a little accident at her house, but Miss Ebbitt brushed off the whole subject by saying, "Oh everybody's late today. Mr. Swanson's snowed in . . . the freak blizzard and all that sort of

thing . . ." and went on busily to talk about the Eatmore
Candystores and their search for a different appeal.

The Eatmore Candystores occupied the day. Lulie ate lunch
cozily with Miss Ebbitt in her office off more sandwiches and
cartons of tomato soup rushed up by Eddy, frecklefaced and
snaggletoothed and friendly as a stray dog. By late afternoon
in the coziness of the office routine, that morning's grim little
scenes were beginning to drop back into Lulie's memory like
chapters from a half forgotten novel. Wondering vaguely about
what kind of present she could get Eddy; was he too old for a
baseball glove? . . . she was walking cheerfully a little after five
into the drugstore downstairs to call Hildegarde when she
caught sight of the headlines on top of a pile of newspapers on
the mudtracked marble floor of the lobby:

SHOT BARES WOODLAWN LOVECULT
Socially Prominent Architect . . . Child Bride Shoots Janitor
"It was a mistake," said lovely Juliet Sims Harrington. My shot
was meant for another. A woman has a right to shoot to defend
her home . . .

All the front pages were covered with it.

HUBBY FREELOVER SOBS ARTIST–BRIDE

The afternoon papers laid out in a row melted into a
jumbled blur before Lulie's eyes. She banged the door of the
phone booth behind her. "Oh Garde you've got to come in.
We're in such awful trouble. Have you seen afternoon papers?"

"No, I haven't seen anything but melting slush all day."

"You've got to come in . . . I can't talk about it on the
phone." She could hear Garde laughing at the other end of the
line. "I'll run for the five fifteen. Same place?" she was asking.

"Same horrible little green tearoom."

Hoping that nobody she knew would see her Lulie bought
all the afternoon papers and crept shamefacedly into the little
green tearoom with them crunched under her arm. Georgie
was sitting at the table nearest the door. He got to his feet and
bowed in an exaggerated way.

"Would milady care for a dish of tea?"

"But how did you know I was coming here?"

"Fidelio the family detective knows all, sees all."

"Georgie you can stay if you promise to go when Garde comes. This is a case for a sympathetic female friend."

"The city desk put me on the story."

"Georgie, you wouldn't."

"Line of duty, Lou, and think what a sobsister like Lorna Briggs would do to it. Mugsie has never stopped talking since she fired the fatal shot."

"But how does this come under sports?" Lulie didn't like the bristling, conceited look Georgie's mustache had. "You might order me some tea . . . I bought the papers but when I start to read them they make me throw up. At least you might tell me how the elder is."

"He's not on the critical list . . . I don't know which of your blessed relations is acting worse. Zeke says Mugsie is ethically wrong and refuses to go on her bail. Mugsie's old man, who is a first class crook if you ask me, has turned up from Kansas City and taken her to a hotel. The *Sunday Star* is dickering for the story of her life . . . if we don't outbid them. She's got a lawyer too, not only a heavy father, but a lawyer. Going to sue for divorce with fancy alimony. They evidently think the Harringtons are rich. Old man Sims is happy because he's found a mealticket. Mugsie is happy because people will at last listen to her talk. Zeke's happy because he's making a goddam fool of himself as usual. After he's refused to go on Mugsie's bailbond what do you think he does? Trots down to the Art Institute to help that popeyed Harold." ("His name is Harding," blubbered Lulie.) "Anyway, everybody knows he's a fairy . . . hang some damned exhibit of mechanical drawing. It looks like mechanical drawing. Free love and modern art. It's God's gift to the headline writers . . . particularly on Monday when there's not a damn thing to cover but a pediatricians' convention and somebody's address to the League of Nations."

Lulie started laughing through her tears: "I suppose we'd

think it was a scream if it had happened to anybody but us."

"Thatagirl, Lou."

"But Georgie you're not going to write your poor friends up in the papers."

Georgie gave her one of his scowling looks. The end of his lip curled like a dog's under his mustache. "Lou we're not playing for fun anymore . . . We're playing for keeps. This is a highly competitive game."

"But Georgie we were all going to stick together."

Georgie's brown eyes looked very wet. He begun to scratch with the dirty nail of his forefinger at a drop of jelly dried into the wicker tabletop. His eyes began to study the drop of dried jelly. "You never would do anything I wanted," he said without looking at her. "I shan't ever ask you again."

In the lens of her mind Lulie was seeing the funny little forgotten scene in the orchard, the two grimy boys, tall and grown up for the first time, striding off between the appletrees, off to the wars.

"I couldn't marry you both now could I?" she said gently.

Elbert cleared his throat and said in a new sharp tone she recognized as his officer's voice. "Now let's get down to cases. It all happened while I was overseas." He looked her brutally in the eye so that she caught that disconcerting black jiggle of the pupils. "I might be able to make something of it if I could get the story right . . . Now Lulie, where did Zeke pick up this Mugsie?"

"My advice even before it is asked . . ." Hildegarde had come into the tearoom without their seeing her and was standing over the table pulling off her gloves. "My advice," she was saying, "is not to talk to reporters."

Lulie gave a start. "Oh Garde what a relief."

Georgie looked up at Hildegarde scowling his old black scowl. He rose to his feet. "The Willards would butt in, the beautiful willowy Willards," he muttered as he tramped out of the tearoom.

"Nice manners your friends have got," said Hildegarde

laughing. Her friendly pussyface creased up with seriousness as she sat down. "Now let's be sensible. The first thing is to think how we can help Zeke . . . I read those awful newspapers coming in on the train. Aren't they wicked?"

"You know how stubborn and opinionated he is . . . Garde order me up some hot tea. I feel like a dishrag."

"Poor little thing. You are all of a tremble."

"No I'm not," said Lulie throwing her shoulders back and straightening herself in her chair.

"The thing I thought of," said Hildegarde picking up the little cracked terracotta teapot and shaking it savagely, "is maybe Dad could get some of the papers to call their dogs off. He knows a couple of newspaper owners pretty well."

"I don't care about the papers," sad Lulie. "What I care about is us. I always thought we were all such wonderful people. Do you suppose we're going to turn out perfectly horrid?"

"Nobody looks their best," said Garde, "in their picture in the papers."

"Georgie's going to write something dreadful. I can tell by his face. I used to think we would all stick together in after life."

"Some of us will," said Garde stoutly. "Mother said to bring you on home with me. Dad'll drive you in in the morning."

"I better go out to Fiftytwo Ten tonight," said Lulie. "If it gets too awful I'll take refuge."

"I'll take you out in a cab. I just got my allowance."

When they were ready to go they had trouble getting the attention of the sallowhaired waitress, she was so deep in reading the evening paper. It was an extra. More of Mugsie's revelations: WRONGED WIFE TELLS ALL. *Freelove Doctrines Ruined Home in Exclusive Woodlawn Section* HINTS AT ORGIES.

"If you met them they'd seem like nice people," said the waitress clucking with her tongue when she brought back the change. "And this is how they carry on."

Lulie closed her eyes and leaned back in the corner of the cab.

"*Oh Keith of Ravenswood,*" declaimed Garde, "*the sorrows of thy line.*"

When the cab drove up to the house Lulie gave Hildegarde a hasty peck on the corner of the mouth and ran to the door. She let herself in by her latchkey. The hall was dark and looked oddly normal, the same hats and coats on the rack and the silver tray for visiting cards. There was a smell of dinner cooking. As she ran through the livingroom to the stairs she saw Uncle Purdy and Mrs. Ritchie sitting as usual at the small table in the corner playing their eternal double solitaire.

"Hello," whispered Lulie, "I'll be right down."

They both looked up at her at the same moment. The thought popped up in her mind that they were ideally suited to each other. Poor Uncle Purdy she said to herself as she climbed the stairs, all the years Aunt Lyde had been sick, he'd had a tough time surrounded by us crazy Harringtons. He and Mrs. Ritchie would so enjoy being thoroughly dull together. What was her first name? Of course it was Alma. Aunt Alma . . . It was time for the hardriding harddrinking Harringtons to move out of Fiftytwo Ten. The phrase made her feel strong and cheerful suddenly. She and Zeke and Ben would show them. She pulled off her hat and yawned into the lookingglass. Her hair was a sight. She was horribly sleepy. She lay down on the bed for just a second before supper and before she knew it she was fast asleep.

When she woke up it was midnight. On the table beside her bed was a tray with a napkin over it. Under the napkin was a glass of milk and some lettuce and turkey sandwiches and a couple of cup cakes, and a note in a bold scrawl. *Lulie: We thought you would be hungry when you woke up. See you at the breakfast table: Alma Ritchie.*

"Peace offering from Aunt Alma," Lulie said aloud. "All right I sign the armistice."

She undressed, ate up everything on the tray and slipped into bed and fell asleep.

Saturday morning they all met with Mr. Pritchard, Uncle Purdy's lawyer, at Uncle Purdy's office in the Medical Arts Building. Mr. Pritchard was a bland round man in a light blue suit. He leaned way back in the swivel chair at Uncle Purdy's rolltop desk and looked up at the ceiling with furrowed brows while Zeke stood in the center of the floor. Ben sat swinging his legs on the window ledge.

"Marriage," Zeke was saying in his cold methodical way, "in my opinion is merely making public that a man and a woman are living together. If she has decided that she doesn't want that relationship any more I can't see whose business it is but ours. What I say to her is go in peace."

"My dear young friend," said Mr. Pritchard, "that may be all very well from an ideal point of view, but unfortunately in this country the woman has the drop on the man when it comes to the courts. There's such a thing as alimony. You are at the onset of what I understand is a brilliant career. This woman can be a millstone around your neck. She is in a position to cripple you financially. If you were only dealing with her it wouldn't be so bad, but we have the old man to contend with. He's hired a lawyer who has the reputation of winning every case he brings to court. Now if you could produce a few affidavits . . . I understand from your uncle that the young lady when you married her was far from being a person of unblemished reputation. Now haven't there been a few transgressions since?"

"I went into this with my eyes open." Zeke was talking with his jaw set. "I failed . . . I believe a woman has just as much right as a man to live her own life. Just because the poor girl has fallen into the hands of a dirtyminded lawyer is no reason why I should sneak around in back bedrooms getting affidavits. Anything she did while we were married was done with my knowledge and approval. We agreed it was to be a free union.

So far as I am concerned our marriage ended last Monday morning when she committed an unsocial act."

"You see Purdy," said Mr. Pritchard swinging around in the revolving chair and pitching himself up onto his feet. "I can't take this case. The only way I know is to fight fire with fire. A divorce court is no place for idealism."

"Won't she have to serve a jail term?" grumbled Uncle Purdy.

"A fat chance. Even if the old fellow had kicked the bucket it would have been accidental homicide."

"Oh goody," cried Lulie. They all looked at her severely. She piped down.

"She's booked for assault with deadly weapon," Mr. Pritchard continued. "The girl is quite an actress. She claims temporary insanity. The county prosecutor's all on her side. He'll just go through the motions. Public sentiment is all on her side. He'll reduce the charge to disturbing the peace. Even if she's guilty the judge will probably suspend sentence."

"Quite right," said Zeke. "She's subject to hysterical fits."

"You see," said Mr. Pritchard, pointing dramatically at Zeke as if he were an exhibit marked A in a courtroom, "if the man won't fight back there's no way I can help him."

"Well I'm afraid I'll have to go back to the office," said Zeke testily. "All this nonsense has set me behind in my work."

His blond head held high above his narrow shoulders, Zeke walked out. Lulie ran after him down the corridor trying to think of something to say that would make him pay attention. Going down in the elevator she plucked timidly at his sleeve. "Zeke I've got a notion . . . " He looked down at her with bland surprise. "Yes, I'm still with you," she whispered. She felt the way she used to feel as a little tiny girl trying to keep the grownups from noticing that it was after her bedtime. "Zeke, maybe you don't need Uncle Purdy's lawyer, but you do need a lawyer." His mouth was setting in a thin line. Looking up into his lean white face she could see the door of his mind swinging to. "Suppose we call up Joe Newcomer." She had caught his attention. She knew he admired Joe. "Let's call up Decent Respectable." As they stepped out of the elevator her eyes lit on the headlines on the evening papers.

MUGSY TO NAME CO–RESPONDENT TODAY
Hints Degeneracy in Artists Circle
Radical Doctrines Scored

At the bottom of the front page of the *Evening Standard* was a box with Elbert Warner's byline. It gave her a twinge of pain to think that in different circumstances it would have made her so happy. As her eyes skipped down the column her inside knotted up with woe. She turned the pages to follow the story inside. As if from a great distance she noticed that the man behind the counter was looking at her quizzically and that Zeke with absentminded courtesy was paying for the paper.

This is the story of Walden Pond. A latter day Walden Pond. Round Boston a hundred years ago there grew up a sect of people known as Transcendentalists. They thought they were finer and better than their neighbors and they lived with their heads in the clouds. They became associated with Walden Pond because one of their number, a man named Thoreau, lived there as a hermit and wrote a beautiful book about it. When the Mexican War came on Thoreau, who didn't approve of war, refused to pay his taxes and was very rightly placed in jail. He called himself a Transcendentalist, but today we would call him a slacker.

Now it appears that out in the Tudor style suburbs where Chicago's wealthier families huddle in exclusive state we have Transcendentalists too. A wealthy young man, the son of a college professor, a member of an overeducated oversophisticated family brought up from infancy to think themselves better than their neighbors, marries a simple earthy working girl. As Thoreau thought he was too fine to help his country in time of war, now this young man considers himself too fine to believe in marriage. He fills the head of this plain simple girl who aspires only to a normal wholesome American home with notions of free love. He surrounds her with Bohemians whose tastes for the abnormal and

the outré cause them to applaud his modernistic notions of archi-
tecture. He and his friends brazenly flaunt in her face their
disregard of the sanctity of the marriage vow. Baffled and con-
fused by this "highbrow" environment in a sudden fit of hysterics
she shoots a gun into the air. It was a shot that well might, in the
words of another Transcendentalist, be heard around the world.

And there on the back page smudged and speckled as if it
had been taken in a snowstorm was a print of the snapshot
Garde had taken of the boys in House of David getups the
morning they unveiled Jasper Milliron on the wharf in front
of the Hiawatha House.

Woodlawn Cultists Don Disguise for Weird Rites (exclusive to the *Evening Standard*) read the caption.

Lulie gave a shriek and suddenly thought she'd die laughing.
Zeke looked at it and got to laughing too. "Still," said Lulie,
"I could strangle Georgie with my bare hands . . . He's selling
his own past history . . . Zeke, did it ever occur to you that we
live in a funny country?"

"Funny as a crutch," said Zeke. "And I'm not a modernistic
architect. Good design isn't ancient or modern, it's just good
design."

"Makes me feel like something in a sideshow," said Lulie
beginning to get mad all over again . . . "Of course the great
Hugh Swanson knows plenty of lawyers but I don't like to ask
him. I've just finished convincing him it wouldn't be good for
his business to marry a girl out of his own office . . ." She
scrunched the paper under the arm of her fur coat and grabbed
Zeke's elbow . . . "Let's step across the street to the hotel."

"Well you wouldn't marry Joe either," said Zeke frowning
at her suddenly as if it were all her fault.

"I think the world of him, Zeke," she whispered as they
crossed the street.

As they walked through the dark lobby Lulie noticed that a
man reading the papers while he smoked a cigar on a lounge had
recognized Zeke from his picture in the *Star*. He nudged the

man beside him. They both stared up with an identical wise guy leer on their faces. Zeke hadn't noticed. He was looking around the tall vaulted lobby of the hotel as if he'd never seen it before. "You know Lulie, this lobby isn't such a bad job. If you forget the chandeliers and the gimcrack decorations the fundamental design is fairly satisfactory."

He sat down in an armchair looking up at the ceiling with smiling interest while he waited for her to make her call. After Lulie had given the operator the number she leaned back against the wall and looked out at him through the glass. That was why she was fond of Zeke, apart from his being her brother, she was thinking, because he was a transcendentalist. Surprisingly soon she was talking to Joe Newcomer's secretary. No Mr. Newcomer hadn't gone out to lunch yet. Joe's voice sounded deep and cozy. Had he seen the Chicago papers? No she ought to know he only read the sports page. Well Zeke was in a great jam. Mugsie was getting a divorce. Joe sounded delighted. Best news he'd heard for a long time.

"But Mugsie's turned out to be a genius at publicity. She's filling the evening papers with her revelations . . . They've even published a picture of us unveiling Jasper in front of the Hiawatha House . . . Georgie must have given it to them. He's turned out a snake."

"But what could anybody reveal about Zeke?" Joe was asking. "I've known him ever since he was kneehigh to a grasshopper and I don't know anything about him . . . I suppose she's out for alimony. Now who do I know who's a lawyer in Chicago? . . . Say Lou do you remember Jay Pignatelli? I think he's in the Merchants' Building at least his father's firm was there . . . Pignatelli and Miller . . . He's as crazy as they come but he might be a good lawyer. He was my roommate. You met him up at the lake. You remember one evening down at the Hiawatha House . . . One of Miss Potter's hopeless hops. He came down to spend a weekend."

"You don't mean Don Modesto."

"Sure."

"Wasn't he toying with a theory that maybe we lived on the inside of the globe instead of on the outside?"

"Probably."

"He's just the man for Zeke. I'll call the office."

"If that doesn't work call me at home tonight . . . Don't worry Lulie. It'll be worth almost anything to Zeke to get rid of that little bitch . . . So long Sister Lucy."

"So long Brother Joseph."

"Zeke do you remember Don Modesto?"

Zeke looked up at her with a sudden appraising look as if he'd never really noticed her before. "Lulie," he was drawling, "if I didn't have you for a sister . . ." He got to his feet . . . "this business might get me down. Suppose I take you out to lunch. Imagine a man," he began to laugh, "taking his sister out to lunch."

"What happened to Ben?"

"I'll call him," cried out Zeke cheerfully, "Let's have a family reunion."

Lulie started to giggle. "But Zeke what about the lawyer?"

"What lawyer?"

"The one I used to call Don Modesto."

"Sure I know all about him. He's lawyer for every I.W.W. in the country. He's the man who gets the radicals out of jail."

"But you know how conservative Decent Respectable is."

"All right you call him. He'll make another Sabatini case of it. By rights he ought to be Mugsie's lawyer."

In high spirits Zeke strode to the phone booth to try to get hold of Ben. Lulie called Pignatelli and Miller. No, answered a cold emphatic voice: Mr. Jay Pignatelli was not connected with the firm but they could furnish his home number. She was switched from one number to another until finally she found herself talking to a voice with a barely definable foreign accent.

"Mr. Jay Pignatelli?"

"Yes indeed."

"Do you remember the Harringtons? We all spent a weekend together years ago when you came up to the lake to see Joe Newcomer. This is Lulie Harrington."

"How could I forget?"

Lulie gave one of her little squeals. "We've got some legal problems."

"That's too bad."

"Joe Newcomer suggested we call you."

"I probably won't be much help but I might suggest somebody better."

"My brothers and I are collecting for lunch. Won't you come?"

"Of course I shall come."

"Well I got him and he's coming." Lulie and Zeke met face to face stepping out of adjoining booths at the same time.

"So's Ben," said Zeke.

Lulie let herself drop down on the much satupon settee in the hotel lobby beside Zeke who had started to make a sketch of the vault on the back of an envelope he had pulled out of his inside pocket. "The trouble with most of the boys is they are only interested in one kind of thing," he drawled. He turned to Lulie with a sudden grin. "I guess I'm an eclectic. That's the worst thing you can call an architect nowadays . . . You have to say it with a smile."

"Zeke if you have brothers and sisters, are you still an orphan?"

"Of course if your parents are dead you're an orphan."

"But you don't feel so much like one," said Lulie letting her eyes close in peaceful drowsiness for a second. Zeke wasn't listening. His eyes were on his pencil designing a vault.

Footnote on the Practice of the Law

ELISHA CROFT

1 8 6 5 — 1 9 3 0

ELISHA CROFT, the famous attorney for the defense, was born the year of Lincoln's assassination in a small white frame house set in a grove of sycamores, a little off the rutted road down to Hibben's Mill, about a mile out from Farmington, Indiana. It was a long walk in to school, in heavy boots through the snow in winter, barefoot with the warm dust squishing between his toes in spring. The only thing Elisha's father was severe about was attendance at school. Perhaps it was because he had taught school himself, Mark Anthony Croft was a jack of many trades; he operated the mill when it wasn't broken down, he farmed the place and did a little cabinet work winters on the side. He was always just about to make his fortune. He was going to produce hickory baskets on an endless chain. There was money to be made selling chicks out of his patent hatchery. The year he got the notion to install a printing press to be worked by waterpower when the mill was idle all the family savings went into it. He was something of a preacher. Until his views became too broad for them he would preach at the gospel meeting of the revivalist sects that flourished in the countryside. He was a hearty abolitionist. Before the war he had operated a station of the underground railroad. Now he advocated the secret ballot and female suffrage. He had a curious indulgent mind that entertained any new idea as hospitably as he entertained the

314

casual strangers he was always inviting to the family table. When Elisha's mother grumbled about the expense he would say, "Suppose it were Our Savior" in a way that would send a twinge of awe down little Elisha's back. Next to reading he loved conversation; Elisha's mother used to claim that the reason his father kept on with the mill, which certainly didn't make them any money, was that people couldn't get away until their grain was ground; they had to listen to him no matter how much he talked their ears off. When there wasn't anybody else to talk to he'd talk to his children. They had to listen too and to think up logical arguments to answer his.

The result was that, however poorly they did in other subjects, the redheaded younger Crofts all made the debating team when they moved on to highschool. The father found it hard to keep his mind on the farm or the mill but his children's education really interested him. He insisted that they study two hours a day even in vacation time: one of Elisha's earliest memories was of sitting over a Latin grammar trying to learn the fourth declension amid the fine sifting dust of his father's little office while above the groaning of the millstones and the rush of falling water he could hear shouts and shrieks of the other kids swimming in the pond. Elisha's childhood was full of the misery of having to stay home and plod through the daily grind while other more fortunate children rode ponies and went on hayrides or made snowmen or coasted on the hill in winter. When it wasn't lessons it was the chores.

Mark Anthony Croft never could afford a hired man; so the children in rotation had to fill and clean the lamps, to pump water, to chop wood, to carry the swill to the hogs, and feed the fowls and scrape out the henhouse, and weed the garden, and fork the manure out of the stables and milk the cows and work the churn. Elisha used laughing to tell his friends in later life that the real reason he became a student was that studying was something you could do sitting down.

His father was friendly with most of the local lawyers and

an assiduous attendant at the county seat five miles away when court was in session. Often little Elisha, who was the youngest, managed to get to go with him in the buggy as a reward for doing the hateful job of cleaning and polishing the ancient patched harness. He never saw the lawyers round the courthouse do any chores; so before he was through grade school he had decided that when he grew up he'd be a lawyer and sit with his feet on the desk in an office full of books. He noticed further, he would tell his friends with a large slow wink, that however a case came out the lawyers were the ones who got paid.

There wasn't much money left when Elisha's turn came for an education but he managed to get through two years at a Baptist college. He found chapel and church attendance and compulsory Bible class even more hateful than the chores and at the end of sophomore year kicked over the traces by allowing himself to be seen publicly attending a lecture by Colonel Bob Ingersoll. His father's friend Judge Grant smiled tolerantly at Elisha's expulsion and took Elisha into his own office to read law. Along with his lawbooks Elisha read Tom Paine's *Age of Reason*, announced that he was an agnostic and preached the religion of humanity to all and sundry. The year he was admitted to the bar he married a rosycheeked girl named Elsie de Witt who had fallen head over heels in love with him in spite of his reprehensible opinions. Elisha's mother frowned a little over the fact that Elsie was four years his senior, but she couldn't deny that it was a good match, because Elsie's people had railroad and coalmining interests and lived in a large house with shingled gables and scrollsaw work on one of the residential streets in Evansville. She put up the money that hired a little apartment over a haberdashery in the small town of Wayne's Crossing, where the lawyer had recently died. There he hung out his shingle.

He was a countryman, he told Elsie, and he wanted to be a country lawyer. Elsie had a Dutch streak in her that made her a meticulous housekeeper. She darned his shirts and kept the books and took in a boarder to help pay their bills, but by the end of the third year Elsie said she would have to take the children home to their parents if he didn't bring in more money; so they moved to Chicago, where Elisha's elder brother, Freeman, was teaching in the public school. Freeman had written him that Fred Ellis, an old playmate of theirs from Farmington, had arrived in town and rented a desk in an attorney's office. He suggested that Elisha should do likewise; so Elisha moved in beside Fred and it wasn't long before they formed a partnership and rented an office of their own.

In the early days Elisha and Fred made a team because, while Fred was neat and precise, a great writer of briefs and a stickler for precedents and points of law, Elisha stuck to the ethics of the cases and talked to the judge and the jury as naturally as he used to talk to the loafers in the poolroom at Wayne's Crossing. If he did take notes he lost them. He kept his cases in his hat. It was because he hated work so himself, he would explain with a lopsided smile, that he had so much sympathy with the laboring man; and it was because he was so poor himself that he hated to charge a poor man a fee. "It's no way to conduct a law practice," Fred Ellis would say. "Why not for gosh sakes?" Elisha would ask and loll back in his swivelchair and blow smoke rings at the ceiling. Fred Ellis would groan and shake his head. Elisha was a hard man to get mad at.

Chicago was a talkative city. In spite of the bitter schism in the population left by the Haymarket Riots and the subsequent courtroom lynchings of the anarchists, as the newspapers called them, Chicago was still a city where a man could speak his mind. There were a number of clubs where people met in the evening to discuss literature. Lawyers and bankers and businessmen and ward politicians even would sit around discussing the atheism of Ingersoll, the humanitarianism of John P. Altgelt, Henry George's single tax, evolution and Darwin and Huxley and Herbert Spencer and the future of man-

kind on earth. It was Elisha's father's suppertable all over
again, only with a larger audience. Elisha went to lecture halls
where he found the ladies in crowds listening with rapt attention to reformers and uplifters whose notions were no more
startling than his father's had been; before long Elisha was
lecturing too and the ladies were listening to him. Whenever
he read a book, he gave a lecture on it, the way he used to hold
forth to the freethinkers at Wayne's Crossing about Tom Paine
and Bob Ingersoll. His lectures attracted clients. A banker
heard him discourse on the *Rubáiyát of Omar Khayyám* and re-
tained him for an important case. A speech in friendly criticism
of Henry George attracted the attention of a railroad president
who turned over to him many of the company's damage and
compensation suits.

Talking to people, as he liked to say, as one ne'er-do-well to
another, he became famous for the number of suits he settled
out of court. When he did take a case to a jury, he'd bring
out the people's stories in a way that kept the jurors so interested and entertained they were sorry when the defense
rested. In criminal cases if he couldn't deny the guilt of the
accused he would manage to arouse the jurors' fellow feeling
for the mistakes and sufferings of other men. "I never heard of
a crime so foul," he said in a lecture called "Pity the Criminal,"
"that I didn't think just for a moment that maybe I'd committed it myself."

Elsie was a smalltown girl. She didn't like Chicago or the
way her husband's friends would sit so long palavering over
the suppertable, but she did like living in a first class apartment
and having a maid and sending the children to the best private
schools. Elisha was away on cases a great deal. His eloquence
was reported in the newspapers. He was the lawyer who had the
novelist's touch. Any reporter who lacked human interest for
his story could get all he needed from a few words with Elisha
Croft. He became a stock figure in the press. They described
him as chewing on a straw and sitting in grimy shirtsleeves and

embroidered galluses. Elsie didn't think that was good publicity and kept urging him to go to a better tailor, he could afford it now, but Elisha would explain to her that stories like that disarmed folks, if folks could be encouraged to think a fellow was just a kind of no account loafer like themselves, they wouldn't be so envious of his big fees. "My cases are tried in court, but through the press I appeal to a greater court; the court of public opinion."

When he defended the union leaders in the Grand Falls conspiracy case, his examination of witnesses was reported all over the country. Grand Falls was a one industry town, controlled by the Grand Falls Furniture Company, which was owned by a vindictive and resourceful entrepreneur named Horace McLean. It was McLean's development corporation which rented the employees their houses; his general grocery sold them their supplies. His utility company furnished them with water and gas. The mayor was his strawboss; the police were his private detectives; he paid off his stool-pigeons himself. A man had no more to do than think the word "union" before he found himself and his wife and children out on the street with his furniture. Then he was lucky if the sheriff didn't arrest him as a vagrant. When Elisha arrived in Grand Falls to confer with his clients the manager of the hotel hardly dared rent him a room. The local restaurant was reluctant to serve him. Gradually the hostility toward him faded. Elisha was a hard man to get mad at. He had a special fellowfeeling for furniture workers because as a boy he'd sometimes helped his father mend a chest of drawers or install a corner cupboard. At the trial he talked more for the nation's press than he did for the local jury. He talked of the working people's lives. He made the jurors feel they were part of the great court of public opinion, sitting in judgment from coast to coast. McLean himself reading the Chicago papers in the office of his plant, irked by the knowledge that the bonuses and the bad workmanship of the strikebreakers he'd brought in were already costing him money, complained querulously to his attorneys that the press was putting him in a bad light. When Elisha subpoenaed him and put sarcastic questions to him in court, it was borne in on him for the first time in years that he wasn't supreme boss in his own home-town. When the jury brought in a verdict of not guilty, union organizers took heart the country over. It was a Milwaukee labor paper that applied to Elisha Croft the phrase which his early idol Bob Ingersoll had used in his famous speech nominating James G. Blaine for the presidency: The Plumed Knight. Elisha went back to Chicago feeling there was no vested interest in the country he didn't dare to break a lance with.

When he got home he found Elsie piqued and uneasy. Friends had been bringing her stories of other women. He was a poor countryman, he admitted; designing city women had a way of getting round him. Elisha Croft was a hard man to get mad at. When he suggested an amicable divorce, she consented. But even in his private life he had to play his part as an actor on the national stage. In an address to a group of socialworkers he announced himself an advocate of free love: it was not only Elsie it was marriage itself he was divorcing. His partnership with Fred Ellis broke up at the same time: as age hardened their outlines the two men had become incompatible. It was no time for dotting i's and crossing t's, said Elisha, it was a time for enthusiasm for noble causes. In discussions of politics he began to argue the anarchist thesis. Free association instead of compulsion would be the basis of a good society. Labor unions demanded his services more and more: his role was the defender of the downtrodden and oppressed.

The war between industrial enterprises and the trade unions which had exploded into such violence ten years before in Chicago, and which was smouldering underground in the East under the truce Theodore Roosevelt's arbitration had imposed on the coalowners and the mineworkers, broke out in open fighting in the mountain states. The mineowners in Colorado, backed by the courts and the militia, were shooting it out with the Western Federation of Miners. The Governor of Idaho was blown up by a bomb. On one side was the coercive power; on the other was desperation and dynamite. Each side accused the other of murderous crimes.

Elisha Croft's advocacy of free love had lasted until he met an auburnhaired actress named Amelie Rains. She was a good listener and a wellread woman. Authors and socialworkers and college professors were delighted to be invited to her teas. They got to like each other so very much they discovered they weren't free at all and went down to City Hall and were married. When Elisha fell ill with rheumatic fever, which his doctor feared might affect his heart, Amelie gave up a star part in a play to nurse him: she would be a wife first and an actress afterwards. She never went back to the stage.

Elisha had barely recovered his health and was still pale and puffy from the months of confinement when he was asked to conduct the defense of three miners and a union leader charged with setting off a charge of dynamite that had killed eighteen strikebreakers in the Petticoat Mine. When he refused, the telegrams became urgent. No other man could save the lives of these innocent men who were being framed for union activity. Lynch law was rampant in the county. Defense funds were ample but there was no lawyer out there big enough to take the case. What convinced him was a letter from the little daughter of the principal defendant: *If you knew my Daddy you would know he wouldn't hurt a fly. Mummy says only the Plumed Knight can save my Daddy* . . . When Amelie read the letter she too started to cry. There was nothing for it but to go. Amelie packed their bags and they engaged a drawingroom on the Denver train.

Harvey Oulds asked if he could come along. He was an old beau of Amelie's, a magazine writer who had become famous for his fearless exposure of the links between Big Business and corrupt politics. The two men had the time of their lives swopping stories on the train. When Harvey wasn't telling funny stories he was explaining a new theory: maybe he was wrong to go round the country lashing people up against bribery and graft. Sometimes in the middle of his most crusading speeches the thought would come to him that maybe corruption was the oil that greased the wheels of progress. Nonsense, roared Elisha over the rumble of the train, stealing was stealing the whole world over. "We mustn't forget to keep our hatred for the crime separate from our sympathy with the criminal." Amelie smiled her appreciative smile: "Of course as sophisticated people . . ." she began.

When they climbed down from their pullman into the upland air of the cattletown set amid dry mountains where the case was to be tried they noticed that the men in ranchers' clothes waiting in a group on the platform gave them a cold sharp stare. The cabman who drove them to the hotel answered no questions. When Elisha registered the clerk watched him sign his name with an expression of aloof curiosity. "A valuable autograph, Mr. Croft. We shall do our best to extend to you and your party what courtesies we can," he cleared his throat . . . "under the circumstances."

Immediately Elisha went into conference with a group of business agents from the unions who were working together to conduct the defense. The men sat in their shirtsleeves huddled in a room with the blinds drawn. They looked pale and jumpy, like men under siege. One man explained they had drawn the blinds because some big galoot was looking in the window with a spyglass from the roof of the bank building across the street. They had showed him a telegram from the secretary of a cigarmakers' union. *Attitude of certain unions may depend on Croft's investigaton of facts of case. Confidence in his judgment and integrity wellnigh universal* . . . "Old Sam's a cautious bastard. Too careful to communicate directly. But if the cigarmakers back us it will mean a thump of cash and that the whole A.F. of L. will come in to the hilt."

"First I must talk to my clients," said Elisha, feeling suddenly on the defensive. The trip had tired him. He wasn't feeling any too well. He wished he hadn't come. "You'll see 'em in the morning," said Ed Hines of the Western Federation looking up out of poker player's eyes over a cigar slanted from a crinkled mouth. "If these goddam cowpunchers don't lynch 'em first."

The conference left Elisha with an oppressive feeling in his chest. He went downstairs to pace back and forth for a while on the pavement in front of the hotel. When he went back into the lobby a squareshouldered man in a Stetson hat with a red rancher's face walked slowly up to him until they were standing face to face. "Mr. Croft," he said, "I'm State's Attorney John Alderman." As if by an afterthought he held out his hand and gave Elisha's hand a brief hard grip. "I just want you to know that it makes me proud and 'umble to be opposed to you in this trial. I wish it could be somebody else. You've been kind of a hero in our family. But practicin' law is practicin' law. I hope your stay in our country will be as pleasant as possible . . . under the circumstances and" — he smiled with tight lips — "I hope you take a damn good lickin'."

Spud Maginnis, the chief defendant, had curly hair and remarkably limpid blue eyes. When Elisha walked into his cell followed by Ed Hines and the warden of the jail he rose smiling from his cot and said, "Sorry gentlemen I can't offer you chairs." The warden had his turnkey lock them in the cell. "My apologies, men," he said as he tramped off down the corridor. "I'm takin' no chances." Spud started by apologizing for his little girl's letter: "If I'd known I wouldn't have let Molly send it. It was hittin' below the belt, but you know how women are . . . But now that you've come," he fixed his unafraid blue eyes on Elisha's face, "we've got to win." "I wouldn't have taken the case, Maginnis, if I hadn't thought you were being framed." Spud smiled a mischievous kind of small boy smile. "Leave me out of it . . . There's so much else at stake we can't afford to lose. You go talk to the boys . . . Hey Warden, I mean Mr. Warden . . ."

The Warden took Elisha to a cell at the other end of the tier and introduced him to Stenich who was a small dark man with the beard of an oldfashioned prospector. He gave Elisha an absentminded smile. "We are bound to win," he said, "with the big guns on our side."

Appleyard and Ebert were in a cell together. They were both blond brawny goodlooking young men. They shook Elisha's hand till his arm ached. "They won't get no whine out of us," said Appleyard. "We knew what kind of a fight this was when we went in," said Ebert. "If you can only save one, for God's sake save Spud."

"He's the greatest guy in the labor movement," they both cried out together.

Elisha went back to the hotel in high spirits and sent a personal telegram to the President of the A.F. of L.: CONFIDENT I CAN PUT EVERY ONE OF MY CLIENTS ON THE STAND.

The trial proceeded amid the usual delays. John Alderman presented his case for the prosecution ponderously and with much duplication of testimony. It was a telling case but Elisha kept probing for the weak links. No direct evidence seemed to be forthcoming as to who set off the charge. The defense story was that since the mine properties were patrolled by armed guards night and day it must have been an inside job. But Alderman was dogged. As fast as Elisha would find a gap he would set clumsily to work to retie the knots in his circumstantial web. "The trouble with that man," Elisha would say to the labor lawyers associated with him, "is he's honest. His honesty is dangerous."

Judge Langstrom was a querulous old man who seemed torn between his desire to see the accused convicted and his fear of leaving loopholes for an appeal. Whenever a tough point of law came up he'd retire quaking to his chambers, some said for Biblereading and prayer and some said for a drink of whiskey to give him Dutch courage. He'd send the jury out at the drop of a hat, until Elisha began to take the attitude that so much was being expunged from the record that the prosecution had no case left. Whenever Elisha rose to his feet Judge Langstrom would look up with an expression of apprehension in his redrimmed eyes, like a man waiting for a firecracker to go off.

Proceedings reached a sort of stalemate until one Friday afternoon when court was about to adjourn at the end of the tenth week of the trial Judge Langstrom announced he had decided to reduce the exorbitantly high bail he'd set to keep the men in jail, but for two of the defendants only. That night Appleyard and Ebert were released.

Saturday morning the Western press was full of editorials denouncing the weakkneed judge. The reporters for the New York and Chicago papers collecting in the corner saloon beside the hotel began to take it for granted the prosecution was about to collapse. Elisha Croft had saved another group of righteous men from the vengeance of the vested interests. The Petticoat miners would go free.

Saturday night Elisha and Amelie ate dinner in the sitting-room of their suite in front of the window that opened on the mountains, purple with twilight. The strain of the trial was interfering with Elisha's recovery from his illness. He had some fresh rheumatic twinges and was taken with spells of weakness and sweating when he had to lie down on the bed. A drink of bourbon picked him up; the steak was outstanding, the mountain air came in sweetly through the open window. They were amusing themselves planning an excursion up to Bearcat Pass tomorrow. It worried them a little that Harvey Oulds, for whom a third place was set at the table, did not appear. It wasn't like Harvey to break an engagement. Amelie raised her glass: "To the verdict," she said. Elisha frowned. "It's too soon," he answered but he drank with her. Attorney General Binger, said to be a great friend of the Mineowners'

Association, had registered that morning at the hotel. The prosecution was up to something, but it was no use worrying Amelie about it. Elisha went to bed early but he could not sleep. He was remembering a curious contemptuous look John Alderman had given him as he left the courtroom.

About three o'clock Sunday morning he heard knocking on the outside door of the suite. Elisha slipped on the purple silk bathrobe Amelie had given him for Christmas and went out into the sittingroom. When he unlatched the door Harvey in his shirtsleeves pitched into the room. Elisha had to catch him by the shoulders to steady him. His gray hair was ruffled and damp. He put his finger to his lip and stumbled to a chair. "A little drunk," he stammered. "But my mind is clear. Give me a glass of water."

"Why at this time of night," began Elisha. "You know I'm not a well man."

"Appleyard's going to confess," said Harvey pronouncing his words carefully. "A couple of detectives took him out and got him drunk. It's as simple as that . . . I went along . . . I had to get drunk to stay in the picture," he added apologetically.

"But what about Hines? He was going to stick to the boys like a leach."

"The boys had been shut up in jail so long they were half crazy. They went to a local cribhouse and got to drinking with the girls. Hines wouldn't go with the girls because he's a family man. So what he did was pass out cold. The whole thing was a plant by the mineowners' operatives. Every barkeep in town's in their pay and most of the scarlet women. They couldn't do anything with Ebert so they slugged him and a deputy sheriff arrested him for drunk and disorderly. I'd been talking earlier in the evening to a little man named Coogan, a barkeep but this is his night off; he's one of their operatives and put me on to the story. Appleyard's at the State's attorney's office writing out a confession right now. *Balmer's Weekly* is in on it and is paying him five thousand dollars for the story. The only thing is he refused to implicate Spud. He'll fasten it all on Stenich. It turned out he had some trouble with Stenich over a woman."

Elisha spent that Sunday, instead of driving pleasantly up into the mountains with Amelie, in conference. Harvey, who had been invited in for that purpose, spoke his piece which was corroborated by Ed Hines when he turned up about noon, sober and shaking and painfully repentent. Thank God, the men said when they broke up, they had the afternoon to catch their breath. They would continue the conference after supper.

Elisha went back to his room feeling feverish. His left knee had started to swell again. Harvey had come along and paced up and down the sitting room talking through the open door while Amelie sponged Elisha's chest and shoulders off with alcohol. Suppose, Harvey was saying, somebody came around from the State's attorney's office and offered medium sentences, twenty years maybe, a promise of pardons later, if the men changed their plea to guilty, would that necessarily destroy the rightness of their cause in the public eye? "What do you know Harvey?" Elisha asked savagely as he limped out of the bedroom white and trembling under his bathrobe. He'd forgotten to put his slippers on. "Please dear lie down and rest," Amelie was pleading running after him with the bottle of alcohol and a washrag in her hand. "Harvey you sit down and tell me what you know."

It turned out that while Harvey was drinking a cup of tea in the hotel diningroom to steady his nerves the young man who was reporting the case for the Denver paper had sat down at his table and said he had it on good authority that an offer of that kind was coming from the State's Attorney General, Adolph Binger.

"It's not John Alderman's style," said Elisha.

"That's why Binger's here, to do the dirty work."

That night when Elisha reported Harvey Ould's suggestion, Ed Hines broke down and sobbed. "No, no it can't be."

"Didn't you know they were guilty all along?" asked a brash young labor organizer from San Francisco.

"But they can't plead guilty," Hines shouted. "The labor movement will repudiate us."

"Not so loud, Ed," whispered Elisha. "They have their spies listening behind every wall . . . It is Maginnis who must make the decision."

"We aren't licked yet," said Ed Hines beating with clenched fists on the table, "just because Appleyard turned out a rat. What are our chances of a hung jury?" He turned his face, where as he got rimself under control, all the broken lines stiffened again into the gambler's mask, towards Elisha. "I don't know," he said. "Well, we'll damn well have to have a hung jury," said Hines.

Next morning Elisha woke with a fever of a hundred and two. Amelie sent for a doctor who immediately said he wouldn't be responsible for the consequences if Mr. Croft went to court. Elisha insisted on going, and sat watching the proceedings, through a haze of pain and fever. Judge Langstrom's hands shook. He kept rustling the papers on his desk. Alderman's manner was stiff and grim. The courtroom was crowded but silent. Elisha kept his eyes on Spud Maginnis' face. Spud's eyes were as clear blue as ever. His face wore its usual air of amused unconcern. Stenich was frowning and puzzled as if struggling with some problem of mental arithmetic. Ebert and Appleyard sat rigid with gaunt cheeks and bitten lips as if they had already heard their death sentence. Alderman rambled on and on apologizing to the court for introducing a witness out of turn. Elisha felt too ill to follow what he was saying. And then Appleyard was in the stand. As he answered the prepared list of questions he never took his eyes off Alderman's face as if he were a man hypnotized: At a meeting of the Monkeywrench Club of the Petticoat Local the boys had decided the mine damn well wasn't going to operate with scab labor. They had warned the foreman and the manager but they went to work and hired a lot of guards from a detective agency. The guards were no damn good. When he and Stenich walked into the enginehouse at the mouth of the shaft that Saturday night most of the guards had already sneaked off into town to get drunk. Stenich was the engineman when he was working so he knew his way around in the dark. They set the charge with a tripwire attached to the winch. Easy as pie. When they started work Monday morning the damn thing blew up.

Immediately after his testimony Judge Langstrom recessed the court and retired to his chambers.

Elisha on the edge of collapse was driven back to the hotel. He lay on the bed drenched in sweat with his eyes closed explaining in a weak patient voice to Amelie, who was fluttering about the room with a rag soaked in oil of wintergreen to apply to his knee, that if he threw up the case now it would mean the men's lives. He would crossexamine Appleyard if it killed him. When Dr. Becker came Amelie was ready to back her husband up. The doctor shook his head but mumbled something about admiring the captain that wouldn't leave the sinking ship and said maybe with massive doses of salicylates he could be kept going. He'd have to watch the heart. Dr. Becker virtually gave up his practice during the rest of the trial to take care of Elisha whom he escorted to the courthouse daily swathed in blankets in a wheelchair and giving off a strong reek of wintergreen. Elisha made the most of the drama of his situation but as the newspapers began coming in from Chicago and St. Louis and the East he could see that the fight was lost.

Led by the President of the A.F. of L. all the great labor organizations repudiated the use of violence by the Petticoat miners. The editorials even in the Socialist papers were all for law and order. When Maginnis was brought to the sheriff's office to confer with the defense lawyers what seemed to trouble him most was not his own fate, but Appleyard. "How could he do it?" he asked quietly. "I was ready to go to the gallows for that guy." Ed Hines was sobbing and tearful again. "It's me they ought to hang," he sniffled. Then he began talking in a mysterious whining voice about recommendations for mercy. Maginnis agreed the only thing to do was change the plea to guilty.

Judge Langstrom was a different man the day he came into the courtroom to sentence the Petticoat miners. He was wearing a new suit and carefully shined highbutton shoes. He walked with a grave and confident tread. In a voice that resounded in the alcoves he sentenced each man to forty years in the penitentiary. The reporters for the out of town press were already huddled over transcontinental timetables in the lobby when Adolph Binger elbowed his way among them. "The show isn't over yet, boys," he said gleefully. "My advice is to stay over till tomorrow when the grand jury brings in the new indictments."

Next day the grand jury indicted a barkeep named Coogan, Ed Hines and Elisha Croft for attempt to bribe Marcus Fox, one of the jurors in the Petticoat miners' trial. The story Attorney General Binger released to the press was that Fox had refused four thousand dollars offered him by Coogan in the back room of the Lodestar Saloon. He had come to the state attorney's office with the story as soon as he was released from serving on the jury. Coogan on being arrested had confessed and said the money came from Hines and Croft. Elisha Croft was too ill to be moved anyway. Nothing to it but to stand trial. Dr. Becker took him to a small sanatorium on the edge of town. By the time the trial came around he was sufficiently recovered to walk into the courtroom with the help of a cane. He had lost twenty pounds. Amelie said he looked like the ghost of himself. He was so accustomed to being attorney for the defense he forgot to rise when the indictment was read to him.

It was Harvey Ould's recollection of the conversation he had had with Coogan the night of Appleyard's confession that saved him. Harvey had gone east on a lecture tour to try to explain the Petticoat miners' case to Socialist Party locals and labor organizations. When he arrived to testify he was a chastened man. "I've had hard sledding," he said. "Elisha, as advocates of the cause of labor you and I are done, both of us; we are through."

"I thought those boys were innocent," insisted Elisha.

"Oh come now," said Harvey with his sharp sarcastic smile. "A good lawyer always thinks his clients are innocent."

John Alderman was prosecutor in the bribery case but his heart didn't seem to be in it. According to the Mine Owners' Association papers he bungled everything. Harvey Ould's testimony showed up Coogan as an employee of the Mine Owners' detective agency. Elisha's worst moment came when Alderman read him a statement he had made years ago in a lecture on crime: "I never heard of a crime so foul that I didn't think just for a moment that maybe I'd committed it myself."

"Like every man in this room," he answered "I am capable of the crime — we are all potential criminals — but I'm sure you don't think I'd be such a damn fool as to try to bribe a juror in a crowded saloon before witnesses."

The jurors were moving their feet around on the floor. Out of a corner of his eye Elisha glanced into their faces. A tiny smile was flickering along every mouth. When the verdict came it was not guilty.

When the Crofts were safely on the train for Chicago, the first thing they did was go over their finances with pencil and paper. Elisha had spent every cent he had in living expenses and lawyers' fees and doctors' bills. He'd had his retainer from the unions, but the Miners' Federation funds had dried up at the source the day Appleyard confessed. Elisha had not even had the heart to send in a bill. He patted Amelie's hand as they sat on the observation platform watching the sagebrush and the dry mountains slide into the distance. "My old lawpartner used to say that I carried my law business in my hat," he drawled. She turned to him with her admiring attentive smile. "It's a good thing," he said, putting his pencil against his long thin nose. "My hat's the only thing I haven't mortgaged."

7

OFFICER OF THE COURT

JAY PIGNATELLI set the receiver on the hook. Lulie Harring-ton's voice in his ear had kindled a glow that spread through forgotten corridors of his brain. He couldn't remember exactly what she looked like, not the one in the song on the Saskatche-wan or the lovely redhead on the Rideau Canal. He'd always remembered it as the summer of pretty girls. Joe Newcomer he'd run into the other day in a speakeasy under the El in the West Fifties in New York; good old Joe hadn't changed much, the same deep mournful voice with a little middlewestern sing to it; deprecatingly he'd explained over some cozily reminis-cent drinks that he was attending a manufacturers' convention, the smalltown boy in the big city. No he hadn't married yet either. Jay must come out to see him and the folks in Terre Haute. How many years ago was it, that weekend up at the lake with the Newcomers? Eight years ago Dandy died, but this was before Law School. The search had uncorked in Jay a rec-ollection of the northwoods smell and of brisk wind and lake-water and of bacon sizzling outdoors. It was Joe who used to say, "But that's a different world." Jay began to look forward to eating lunch with friends of Joe's. It would mean to step for an hour at least out of his own life.

He was sick of his goddamned everlasting life.

He glanced up at the disarray of yellowing papers fuzzed with dust round the walls of Brian Mulvaney's office. It wasn't

his office; it wasn't his life. The time had come to step clean
out of it. He would grab his hat and slam the door behind
him. His goddamned everlasting life. He started to remember
other times he'd felt he had slammed the door on some stale
remnant, the feeling that henceforward . . .

There was the time he'd come home third class on the
Aquitania in an inside four bunk cabin sunk deep down in
the stern somewhere, and, since he had the little box to himself, had spent the crossing stretched out on the bunk feeling
in the tremor of the screws and the throb and lurch of the
engines the weight of the steamship bucking the weight of the
wintry Atlantic seas, half imagining, half hearing the scream
of the wind in the superstructure coming to him through the
occasional bilgesmelling puffs of stale air out of the ventilator.
Usually he was a fiend for fresh air but this time he liked it
stuffy. His throat was sore and he felt feverish and his nose
was stopped up by a cold and the waspwaisted young English
physician in a yellow vest and with a carnation in his buttonhole looking down at the smear on the slide as if it were the
calling card of somebody not socially eligible had said, "Ah
yes gonococci" and had written out a prescription. The curly-
haired cockney in the chemist's shop had handed him his bottle
and his syringe with an infinitesimal flutter of an eyelid, not
a wink but an eighth part of a wink, a fellow sufferer perhaps.
Clap was a different world. When he wasn't plying the
syringe Jay had lain reading by the caged electric light bulb
on the grim cabin ceiling a copy of *Ulysses* he'd picked up on
his way through Paris. As his stinging eyes followed the elegant black print across the very white paper he followed
breathlessly the changing focus of the sounding prose. Joyce
was a different world. Jay had never been in Dublin, but in
that book in that cabin he was living his Dublin days.

The very black hair, the very white skin, *Sweet singer of
Persephone*. It must have been the peevish girl with skin like
eggshell china so frail the blue showed through. *Dost thou*

remember Sicily? . . . The dead air and the churn of the quadruple propellors as the liner pounded out her twentytwo knots
for the fiveday crossing made him feel a tiny bit seasick. His
head ached. His eyes stung. Lord, he felt wretched and he
damn well didn't care. He was completely and absolutely
alone. There was nothing in the world he wanted except to lie
there. From out of a swaddling cocoon of discomfort and solitude
he had felt himself, like some darkage monk radiating shafts of
prayer from his cell, shooting searching rays of his wretchedness
that travelled inquisitively over the great ball of the world. In
the field of that chill searchlight unsatisfactory puppets, selves
left behind on distant shores, gesticulated. He saw himself with
Jed Morris and Tad Skinner walking in moonlight the shellpitted road. Telling about it he'd always said it was the
Chemin Sacré behind Verdun but maybe it was another road.
Anyway there was no traffic that night only soldiers clinging
together like swarms of bees under every ruin that was roofed
and the moonlight spreading its tranquillity in spite of the
rumbling barrage to the north that flickered like heatlightning
along the horizon and burst now and then into a festive cluster
of signal rockets. Somebody had said a woman made omelets
at a farm on the road between Erize-la-Petite and Erize-la-
Grande and Jay and Jed and Tad had felt it their duty as the
section's three famed omeleteers to find her out. As they
walked they argued. Tad was doing the talking; Jed was op-
posing everything he said.

"Goddamn it yes," shouted Tad. "We must stop this war
right now . . . These poor damned Frenchmen being shipped in
trucks into the slaughter from one side and the poor damned
Boche being shipped in from the other like cattle going to the
stockyards . . ."

"Goddamn it no," Jed roared out laughing. "No sensible
man would do anything to keep the capitalist world from
disaster. The sooner the end comes the better it will be for
the human race. I believe in universal defeat. The defeat of
Germany will mean liberty for the Germans. The defeat of

all capitalist governments will mean liberty everywhere. Under anarchy every man will live at peace under his own vine and figtree like it says in the Bible."

"If we were cannibals and ate the carcasses like the Mexicans used to it would make more sense," Tad went on in a tense voice without paying attention to Jed.

"But we aren't cannibals. It's our governments try to make us act like cannibals. Wipe out the governments and the native goodness of man will appear."

Tad fell back on something he'd said often before: "This massacre isn't going to settle anything that four ordinary citizens couldn't have settled sitting around a table."

When he said that Jay always saw four elderly men in grimy shirtsleeves sitting over a hand of poker with that cudchewing cardplayers' look on their faces. "Maybe," he remembered himself adding haltingly, "we should have stayed out like Henry Ford wanted us to and insisted on a negotiated peace."

"Try to say that around the rue Sainte Anne and you'll be called a slacker and clapped in the guardhouse," said Tad.

"I guess the time to say it will be when we get home and out of uniform," Jay remembered insinuating.

"They won't let you say anything," shouted Jed. "After this war we'll be poured into the militaristic mould like the rest of them. It's only after the disaster is brought home to everyone like to the people in these villages that they'll see that the system is causing their ruin. When a civilization gets on the wrong track only anarchy can cure it."

"But socialism is the opposite of anarchy," said Tad. "The trouble with anarchy is that the barbarians come in and take over."

"It is up to us to be the barbarians," roared Jed.

Jay was talking French to a gnarled and knowing poilu who had stepped out into the moonlight from the shadow of a barn. From inside came the reek of sweated uniforms and sleeping men sour amid the sweetness of hay and of cattle crunching in their stalls. Soon the three of them were following a gleam of lamplight. The gnarled poilu knocked on a door. A bolt was drawn. "C'est des americains, ya de la galette," called the poilu coaxingly. A tall woman opened holding the lamp high above her blond hair parted in the middle. The poilu rattled off the local patois.

"Bon yaura des oeufs . . . Mais ça coute cher," said the woman. She looked the three Americans up and down with a gray penetrating gaze that seemed to Jay to count the money in their wallets. There was something oddly German in the intonation of the woman's voice.

"On cause boche ici?" he asked the poilu.

"Que voulez-vous? Le patois du pays," he answered with a lopsided shrug.

"That makes you think," Jay remembered himself saying to Tad and Jed as they stretched their legs under the scrubbed oak table beneath the smoky oak panels of the farmhouse kitchen ceiling. "These national boundaries are purely arbitrary."

"When the division went en repos," shouted Jed, "we drove through Domremy. It's not so damn far. It would be a big joke if Joan of Arc turned out to be a Boche."

"Jesus I'd like to take the frogs and the Boche and knock their heads together," said Tad.

"Qu'est-ce qu'il dit?" asked the poilu whom Jay had invited to drink a snort of wine. Jay tried to explain. Before he'd finished the poilu shrugged his lopsided shrug. "C'est l'Europe, que voulez-vous? L'Europe est foutue. Une fois la guerre finie, moi je me sauve . . . Houp!" he brought the edge of his hand down hard on the crook of his arm. "Je me sauve. En Amérique, chez vous, chez les peaux rouges. Merde. C'est egal."

They were hungry. The bread was good. The omelet had herbs in it. The wine was sour but it could be drunk.

"Just in one little walk," Jed had said, his combative tone

mellowed a little by the food and the wine, "I've proved my point. Nationalism makes no sense."

"It is militarism that makes no sense," said Tad dogmatically. "Without armies the predatory masters of capitalism couldn't misuse the local prides and differences that might be forces for good. Militarism and capitalism make no sense at all.

"Socialism makes no sense either," shouted Jed, starting to debate again.

"That's where I differ from you," said Tad in a hurt tone.

"I guess the one thing a man can do," Jay remembered himself drawling, "is to try to tell people the truth."

"That's a large order. First you have to find the words," said Jed. "Most words have been built for propaganda purposes."

"If the people of Europe had been told the truth no Kaiser or prime minister could have gotten them into this war," said Tad. "A word of truth in the right place and all the murderous sham will fold up like stage scenery."

As they drank and shouted, Jay sat seeing the three of them walking as missionaries down country roads back home, riding on bakers' wagons, beer trucks, delivery vans, railroad trains, speaking from pullman platforms like presidential candidates, from soapboxes in squares, from pulpits in churches, leaning out of first story balconies, haranguing from balloons as they drifted over the upturned faces of listening crowds, uttering quietly unemotionally, but loud so that all should hear, the one true word.

The trouble was — Jay had lain ruminating looking up at the rusted springs of the empty bunk above his head — people got so mad they wouldn't listen. He'd tried, damn it he'd tried to tell the truth. That had been the cause of his scandal. How had he ever gotten in that situation anyway? Here he was a quiet fellow without all these dogmatic ideas like Tad and Jed but something in his throat stuck when he heard his mouth forming words he didn't believe were true. Before he knew what had happened he was in bad everywhere like Sinbad in the song. Was it those letters he'd written Paco in Spain to practice up his Spanish mostly or the time he'd gotten drunk with the longnosed Italian doctor who was a lover of the paradox, frenchfried potatoes and vieux marc and they had called each other cousin and talked about the civilization of the Incas, or was it just some guy thought he was uppety and turned his name in? People were always thinking he was high hat on account of his funny accent. Jed, the vociferous anarchist, had landed in a cush job doing publicity for the Red Cross. Tad was an army courier with a first lieutenant's bar. Jay was the only one who had gotten in bad. Lord he'd done his best to explain it to Major Henley whom he thought would understand as one gentleman and scholar to another but Henley must have known Jay didn't make Porcellian, no clubs at all, not even the Signet with his literary friends . . .

"But what I'm trying to explain Mr. . . . I mean Major Henley I mean . . ." . . . Damn it Henley was only a damn Fine Arts instructor disguised as a Red Cross major. The days of gentlemen and scholars were over and the fashionable archaeologist, the gentleman and the scholar who years ago had smuggled half the Mirandola frieze out of Italy and landed it serene and pentellic in the Fenway Museum, had said farewell in proper style to the ambulance drivers he had commanded. Fiat cars drawn up in a meadow full of buttercups at the end of a summer's noon beside a hunchbacked bridge. The drivers stood at attention and the Red Cross majors stood at attention and the gentleman and scholar out of another age had spoken his valedictory while at precisely fourteen o'clock the Boche as they were wont dropped a few shells on the bridge and the drivers stood quietly listening in the torn air and the gentleman and scholar had gone on, quiet monocle glistening in the sun, carefully picking his phrases for their New England pith, but suddenly the Red Cross majors were nowhere to be seen, only an occasional whipcord buttock protruding from the ditch beside the road. That was the end of gentlemen and scholars; the archaeologist, acting like a prince about the whole thing, had said in Paris when Jay went to consult him about the ripples of his scandal, already spreading from the invisible dropped stone, that it was all jesuitical foolishness and that Jay could rely on him; but he had caught pneumonia and died and left Jay alone feeling like a man trying to row a skiff against a too strong tide. But that wasn't what Jay told Major Henley. What Jay said was haltingly: "I'm trying to explain that I feel one has to tell the truth about these things. At the same time since my country is at war you have to do the best one can to help."

The words reechoed inexpressive in Jay's memory, not even good grammar. Major Henley, his dimply cheeks puckered with distaste, had sat there staring at him across the desk. It wasn't one Harvard man to another, no not at all; the statement the major was groping for, that Jay could read, like print lit from behind, on his fat face, was that not everybody who went to Harvard belonged to Harvard really, some were illegitimate bastards with foreign names who had no social standing, middlewesterners coming in from other colleges with no comprehension of the romanesque or Brattle Street or Sienese painting or incense wreathing the altar of the Cowley Fathers. It took more than a few years' residence in Cambridge to make a Harvard man. What the major said was: "It seems to have slipped your mind that service in the Red Cross is a privilege which should be withdrawn from the unworthy."

"But how do you know," Jay had said, "without telling me what I've done? Why couldn't you give me a trial?"

The major's eyes were shrinking in his face. Jay saw that he was searching for some quick way to put an end to a distasteful and possibly compromising interview. "It's not so much what you've done," the major was making weaving motions with small fingers in the air, "as something less definable, an ambiente."

"But suppose the accusation is false?"

"Nobody is accusing anybody of anything." The major's voice rose so shrill it broke. "It is just felt that some people are unsuitable for further service under the Red Cross."

Jay, watching the pair on either side of the desk like an unconcerned third party at the interview, could see Henley asking himself with rising hysterics, under the puckers of the dimpled face, how the hell he was going to get this young bounder out of his office. Jay himself hadn't been able to think of anything more to say. He'd just sat there, a great lump dreamily imagining the Red Cross emblazoned in the sky above Major Henley's head like Constantine's labarum and thousands of worthy young men, of whom he was not one, marching forth to war to the tune of "Onward Christian Soldiers," but never so far as the front lines, oh no.

The major was looking at him with womanish spite. "If you are so crazy to find out, why don't you go ask Army Intelligence?"

Jay had, but whom had he found at Army Intelligence, obviously primed for him alone, in a small neat office with a bookcase, but Schuyler Vandam, a classmate this time, bringing incongruous memories of Brattle Street and elms and squirrels on the lawn and the duckboards resounding between classes across the Harvard Yard. Schuyler of all people . . . Gold Coast, drunks in dinner jackets in the little lunchroom under the Lampoon . . . He looked remarkably handsome in his perfectly fitting uniform. Jay was immediately conscious of his own ill-wound puttees, the stain on his knee, the necktie askew. There was no smile on Schuyler's face.

Jay had felt jaded that morning. He'd shaved but he hadn't been to bed. That was the night they'd called for volunteers at a hospital out at Neuilly somewhere suddenly overtaxed by an offensive at the front and he with some other casuals and a couple of doughboys on leave had carried stretchers. They were evacuating directly from the front lines. Again the everlasting smell of blood, the dismay of muddy blankets caked with blood, the groans, the whining strungout curse, the thanks for a cigarette lit and stuck between taut lips, the grateful eyes, the desperate goodness of young men in pain. After midnight, his back aching, his armsockets wrenched from endless carrying of stretcher cases up the bloodied marble stairs, the medical sergeant put him — with a sharp sidelong look that said: I'll teach that son of a bitch to volunteer — on another detail, carrying pails out of an operating room, war's grotesque swill, blood and bandages mostly but now and then a recognizable member, a severed hand, at the end of a splintered stick of bloody bone an uninjured foot wellshaped with high instep, comely, with no corns on the toes. The guy with him slavered and rushed off to puke but Jay — foot's a foot by God — slogged on. And that was the morning they'd given Jay his appointment to talk with Intelligence. Jay had shaved before coming but the smell of blood was still in his nostrils. He felt it under his nails and in his hair.

"For gosh sakes, Schuyler," he began but Schuyler didn't put out his hand. He didn't smile. For an instant Jay saw the frowning youthful face, all pink and cream, with sharpcut nose and cleft chin, bearing down on him like the figurehead of a galley. (In the South Seas the cannibals launched their warcanoes over the living bodies of their prisoners; the smell of blood from bodies crushed on the shellstrewn sand.)

"What do you want to know?"

"I thought maybe someone could tell me what all this fuss was about."

"There isn't any fuss, Pignatelli. There's too much defeatism in France without encouraging it in the A.E.F. We are going to eliminate people with ideas like yours. We don't want such people in the A.E.F."

"What kind of ideas?"

"Pacifists and slackers."

Jay looked carefully at the arched aristocratic nose, the self-indulgent chin that had a wealthy look, the carefully moulded wellbred lips, and all at once Schuyler Vandam's head became as devoid of consequence to him as a fragment of a statue, as that wellformed foot — war's grotesque swill — he'd carried out in the strange confusion of the hospital, good God, only three hours ago.

Schuyler remembered his manners. He rose to his feet when Jay rose. "I'm sorry," he said and stuck out a hand. He was blushing. Jay felt the red begin to smoulder under the sunburn on his own face.

It was some time before Jay could get over a furious feeling of embarrassment. He walked in roseate sunlight, through the fragrant honking endlessly amusing civilian streets of Paris that unfolded like a picturebook before him, to the Commercial Cable office. The streets and cafés, the bowler hats and musachest in front of the Bourse gave him as they always did the old Jules Verne feeling of traveling the world around from the Tour Eiffel to the Taj Mahal. He was still a free man. He could pay for a cable by God. UNJUSTLY ACCUSED . . . NEED FRIEND IN HIGH PLACES . . . he wrote on the blank under the two blue hemispheres. He couldn't help smiling when he thought of Luke's cold eye reading through all this melodrama; but Luke crashed through. Next morning at the hotel Jay found an answering cable short but to the point. SEE MAJOR MORTLAKE HOTEL CRILLON. And there he was. A major, of course. Everybody's a major now. The chairs at the Crillon were deep and through the curtains of lemonflowered cretonne over lace you could see the rosy tracery of the Place de la Concorde like a steel engraving in an old travelbook. Mortlake, his long mortician's face incongruously topping the highcollared uniform, seemed thrice the man he'd been back home. Mortlake was understanding. Mortlake was amused. He ordered up Scotch. "It's not for nothing Jay you are your father's son." He leaned back in an armchair and unbuttoned his tunic. "Jim loved champagne and used to say the most outrageous things. Actually he didn't have a very good head for liquor though he used to boast of drinking me under the table. You were probably sounding off about the Carthaginians over a brandy bottle in some low dive and a damn fool of an intelligence agent put it all down to mean you were hoching Kaiser William."

"Mr. Mortlake," Jay found himself laughing till the tears came to his eyes, "we did. We drank a lot of very nasty sweet Marsala and all sang 'Deutschland über Alles.' We held a black mass too in the ruined abbey under fire ... I've been running with a lot of silly characters but some of them are wonderful guys. The ambulance service was the war deluxe. That's over. But honestly I'd feel terrible to go home now. As long as this crazy business lasts I want to do something halfway useful."

"The best thing you can do Jay is keep your mouth shut," said Mortlake suddenly serious. "You wait till you get home and tell it to the jury."

"I'll do my best," said Jay.

Mortlake got to his feet and grabbed the ivorytinted French telephone off the bedside table. He held it away from his ear as if it might bite him. "I'll try old Doc Evans," he said when he'd given a number. "Thank God for an Englishspeaking switchboard."

Sipping his Scotch and looking out happily through lace curtains at the pink obelisk pointing into the lavender sky, while he listened to Mortlake carrying on with a crony in the Medical Corps, Jay felt himself back in the ignorant innocent days of his travels with poor Scott Bronson in the spring the year before. He heard the old familiar words enlistment, induction, waiver bud cheerfully out of the conversation like colored balloons the vendor would detach from the cluster to tempt the children on the Champs-Elysées.

"Now Jay," when he put down the receiver Mortlake started talking the Dutch uncle again, "promise me one thing. We must be practical. No more talk about accusations or court-martials. The army medical corps is taking over the ambulance sections. You'll have to go in as a private. If it hadn't been for all this yammer we could have gotten you a commission with your experience and your croix de guerre."

"It wasn't me," said Jay reddening, "it was the whole section got it."

"Now Jay, let me give you some advice . . . You're young and impatient, and like your father you don't suffer fools gladly; but don't ever forget that there are more fools than wise men in any organization and if you get the fools mad at you not even the wisest can save you from a licking. The war won't last forever. This experience will make a man of you. Once you learn how to handle yourself and to keep out of hot water I can see a mighty nice career ahead of you in the law. A nice legal and literary career. Your father started from scratch. You can start from further up the ladder, see?"

Jay found himself pumping Mortlake's hand. "Mr. Mortlake I appreciate this . . . I was about ready to jump in the river."

"Now you've got the address. Ask for Colonel Evans and don't say anything about anything. Give 'em your record and they'll run you through a physical and give you a dogtag and don't blame me if you don't like it in Uncle Sam's army."

Joyfully humming "Sinbad was in bad in Tokyo and Rome," Jay walked up the blooming Champs-Elysées to the address. Colonel Evans was a silverhaired elderly man with a disillusioned jowly face, wrinkled as a leaky balloon, who had the look of having been stuffed too hastily into a uniform too small for him. Jay kept his fingers crossed and his mouth shut and by the time the office was ready to close at five he'd been stripped and weighed and sworn and had read the articles of war and walked out in a pair of doughboy boots much too large, nervously saluting anything that looked like an officer on the street, in his hand a crisp new set of travel orders to report to an S.S.U. section at Ferrières-en-Gatinais, which he added lovingly to the collection of travel orders with carefully smudged dates he cherished in his wallet.

When he got back to the Lille et d'Albion, Petite Mère's hotel, where the familiar-from-childhood uniform of the concièrge and the rickety openwork elevator and the palms under the rainspattered glass roof of the lobby had in a few hours taken on a look of intolerable strangeness, he was dead tired. "In bad in Trinidad and twice as bad at home." He'd heard such terrifying tales of the operations of the M.P.'s from the rue Ste. Anne, that he hadn't dared stray far from the hotel; in fact he hadn't been any too sure that his own and Petite Mère's hotel wasn't off bounds for enlisted men, so he had eaten hurriedly in a little restaurant at the corner and scuttled back early to bed.

Ferrières-en-Gatinais turned out to be a mossy and forgotten town with a Merovingian stone church and a number of ancient bistros he was immediately introduced to by the top kick of the section, who was out of the old volunteer outfit, a merrymaking Irishman named Ryan. That very night Jay confessed over calvados that he knew how to type and next day he found himself acting quartermaster sergeant of the section, with the little towhead corporal who was a mechanic from Sault Ste Marie obligingly sewing a set of stripes on his O.D. tunic. Up to then Jay had spent his life with college men who had the egocentric manners of whitecollar people. Lying in his bunk on the *Aquitania* he still remembered with amazement the friendly and obliging manners of the guys in this S.S.U. section. They were mostly highschool boys who had worked as mechanics in garages or in metalworking plants in small towns in Michigan and Wisconsin. With his French and his bad eyesight and his constant reading of books and his familiarity with foreign foods and liquors he had found himself an oddity still; but, he ruminated, an oddity viewed with astonished benevolence rather than suspicion. Sergeant Ryan with his popeyes and his freckles and his yeasty tongue kept everybody cheerfulled up. Ryan's travelling circus, they liked to call themselves. Jay had even been able to get along with the lieutenant, an instructor in a pre-med course in a freshwater college in Kansas, who used to comment shyly on Jay's knowledge of ancient history which he said made his letters fascinating reading when he censored them. Jay kept his mouth happily closed now that he had no intellectuals around to prattle with; and nobody paid any attention to what an enlisted man thought anyway, particularly the old army medical officer with a hangman's jaw who regularly had a nasty jag on by noon and whom Jay tried occasionally to argue into sending a really sick man to a hospital instead of keeping him on duty and dosing him with CC pills. When the section travelled in convoy winding round vinecovered hills of the East of France towards the scrambled fighting in the Vosges, it was Jay who knew the roads and Jay who read the maps for the lieutenant and Jay who found himself the liaison with the redfaced Médecin Divisionnaire, a plausible and jocular Frenchman, selfproclaimed master of the systeme débrouillard, who was always calling for Jay to drive him in a Ford ambulance on some mysterious errand or other, involving usually thinnecked alsatian wines or demijohns of kirsch which le Commandant Bruhl would buy up for eventual shipment home "pour faire plaisir au beaupère" who was a winemerchant in Bordeaux, he would explain with an expression of deadpan glee; or to a certain maison de tolérance staffed with brunhildean blondes dangerously near the German lines on the outskirts of Mulhouse.

It was a war of movement in Alsace that autumn. There was even a brief afternoon when somebody (it turned out later to have been a battery of French howitzers) got the bead on their post at the old distillery; and the doctor had a screaming fit; and there was nobody there but Jay to get the wounded out of the dressing station and to move the kitchen and the messtent and even his hated corona and the company records into the lee of a convenient gravelpit and, feeling the need, like Caesar at long last, of being in several places at the same time, Jay had enjoyed for a half hour the exhilaration of command: the look of relief on the faces of the stretcher cases as they were loaded in the cars, the guys who liked him doing just as he said and looking up at him with admiring dogseyes — until the loot arrived all mussed from an afternoon nap between featherbeds in the village and gave the orders to evacuate all over again although everybody was out and the distillery was already a smoking shambles. "Good for you, Sarge," he'd said in a trembling voice. "I couldn't have handled it better myself." "Darn tootin' you couldn't," had muttered Private Schermerhorn into Jay's left ear. "C'est un phénomène," cried le Commandant Bruhl when he arrived and laughed and slapped his thighs and forever after asked for le phénomène when he wanted Jay to drive him on some low errand.

The lieutenant got a citation before the Corps d'Armée for that little job and Jay, who couldn't learn to drill and was ignorant of the manual of arms, never got his sergeancy confirmed, but the lieutenant did him one good turn. After the sudden delirium of the armistice: the tango danced all night between champagne bottles with le commandant Bruhl's Brunhildes who knocked off work for the evening in spite of Mme. Schneider's outcries (the madame was une sale boche they all told each other in spitting Teutonic intonations), and that crazy trip with the Commandant Bruhl to Strasbourg, where everything seemed like living inside a coocooclock, and Jay had found himself delightedly washing broiled gooseliver down with sylvaner in the company of a neat and fawneyed little étudiante in a restaurant hung over the edge of a beautifully clear green rippling river, and climbing with much mingling of mouths up redtiled steps to make la bête à deux dos in a huge featherbed under the sharp gable; and after the universal hangover and a G.O. from Chaumont announcing the crackdown of military discipline, there had appeared another most astonishingly agreeable order on the subject of college men continuing their studies. Nobody but Jay had wanted to apply, for fear of losing the first boat home, so the lieutenant had done Jay the service of backing up his application as a law student to be transferred to the Sorbonne detachment for study.

Paris was a carnival all through that winter's end. Flags and flowervendors on the misty streets, clamorous newspapers read for the comedy beside outdoor stoves at marble tables and the green thought of spring, the prospect of civilian life instead of military death sheening with hope the rolling fields of France, the tragedy's happy ending that changed the world to farce. The Sorbonne, the stone courts, the scuffed corridors, the incongruity of sitting in American khaki in these drafty and obsolete halls to listen to ancient men with faces of ivory out of the Musée de Cluny talk in mellowed sentences of Civil Law and the philosophy of jurisprudence; and, for a flyer, attending assiduously an illattended course where an old man with a forehead of carved stone on which two pairs of glasses threw shadows of a Mayan mask talked American Indian civilization and commented the Popul Vuh in his own traduction inachevée. Baths in antique tubs with swanneck spigots and sulphur soap rubbed in with a hard brush to cure the itch on a floating barge named for the woman of Samaria; hangover rides in the early morning on narrow steamboats poking under bridges through the mist; the hard seats of theatres where the language was displayed like filigreework in the windows of jewellers on the Rue de la Paix; the discovery of orchestral music; and the girl in black with large gray eyes and nearly auburn hair he'd talked to in the long waits, tortured on steep gallery seats against the ceiling, at the Opéra Comique between the acts of *Pélleas et Mélisande*, who had spoken of Debussy as if he were her uncle and facetioussolemnly told him how her favorite Chausson had lost his life on a runaway bicycle; and whom, when he finally got around to presenting, all asweat with timidity, the letter le Commandant Bruhl had given him for his mother, he had discovered — "Mais c'est vous!" — to be the commandant's sister Honorine.

The Bruhls lived in a mountainous gray region of the rue de Rome above the crowded crossroads of the Gare St. Lazare where the terraces of cafés smelled of seaweed and cold iodine from baskets of clams and oysters decked out with lemon, and sea urchins and periwinkles exposed for sale on sidewalk stands. It was a family of ruddyfaced women all in mourning for a father, an uncle, brothers, sons, très catholiques, haunters of Saint-Sulpice, cheerful, formally informal, incredibly well-read. Augustin had told them of le phénomène. Right away Mme. Bruhl gave Jay their telephone number and invited him to tea afternoons when there were no concerts. There he'd sit feeling somewhat out of place and eating little cakes and smoking caporal ordinaire and listening to Honorine, with an odd jocular expression, like her brother's when he was about to emit an epigram, on her face, playing transcriptions of Moussorgski or Chabrier on her polished concert grand. It was the thought of Honorine's morning freshness, the look her skin had of being washed with kitchen soap, that made him without any cogitated reason start saying goodnight suddenly to friends he'd dined with when they started towards the boulevards and les petites femmes.

He wasn't in love with her, he had told himself, but he'd feel the corners of his mouth go down if he went to a concert hall and failed to find her perky little black figure in back of the gallery where standing room was cheapest. He'd stand near her and wait till she saw him and gave him her challenging look like the look she wore at the piano. She was fond of sweeping judgments and of introducing aspirates into her emphatic French. "Je détèste cela . . . C'est abhominable . . . Admirhable . . . mais mirhifique." Everything she said made him laugh. Sometimes she would draw back and stare at him with mock astonishment out of her large eyes full of gray light like the skies over the Seine. "Le phénomène! Il se moque de moi . . ." and the orchestra leader would be tapping with his baton and the music lovers would shush them and they'd gulp down their giggles and compose themselves to listen.

After the concert he would walk her home and they would point out to each other the varied pleasantries of Parisian sights and sounds; absurdities in store windows, the chic car-rosserie of an automobile, a cabdriver who looked Verlaine, a Rimbaud peddling oranges, a priest who must be Rabelais, a newsvendor with Beethoven's mask under the visor of his cap, a père de famille who might resemble Bach. Awkwardly a couple of times he tried to ask her out but she'd never pay any attention and it always ended by his following her to her house and running breathless after her up the sandstone steps to the apartement au quatrième. There she would sit at the piano and between pieces he would talk to Mme. Bruhl who had gray eyes too, but clouded and frightened like a caged hawk's, set in a handsome old hawk's face. "Ma pauvre Bibi," the girl had said one night in the middle of a piano version of Debussy's "Fêtes," turning that jocular astonished look upon her mother's face and kissing the gray hairs at the corner of her mouth. "Elle a trop souffert. Trois deuils dans une année de guerre. C'est trop pour une famille," and she went back to playing and Jay said goodnight soon after and walked down the loose red carpet on the sandstone stairs feeling that the Bruhls lived in a world which he would never know.

The more often he saw them, the more often he had that baffled feeling walking back to his room through streets full of men and women strolling thigh to thigh and shadows inter-laced in doorways and silent monuments to osculation posed under the small trees in squares, when his blood would be flowing muggy in his veins from lack of lovemaking and the ache of womanlessness would become sharp pain. Halfway to the Seine he'd stop at a corner and decide to go back to the Bruhl's and make a declaration in form, but he could hardly see himself posing as the fiancé in a French family photograph. They would ask him what his prospects were. What could he tell them? He had no money. Every time he heard from Luke Dandy's estate had shrunk again as the executors uncovered a new batch of debts or some respected asset turned out worth-less. Luke kept the office going but Jay was already dreading the open warfare that would result from his trying to go back to join his father's firm. He didn't even know if he wanted to keep on with the law in any form. How lucky to be footloose, his friends would say. Footloose, hell . . . He'd half make up his mind to go pick himself up a whore, but whores broke his heart now that the war was over and instead of getting his block knocked off by a piece of shell he was going to live and had his goddamned everlasting life to plan.

So, trying to forget himself in streets and architecture and strands of history that would brush like bits of spiderweb against his face on unexpected corners, he'd walk and walk until his legs were ready to drop off and climb the cold stairs to his musty room above the treetops and the river and the tiedup barges, and get into bed and try to drown himself in a book.

One warm spring night, when he felt the end of the Sorbonne course and shipment home in a casuals company advancing on him like the locomotive of doom, he had managed all at once, he never knew just how, to push the menacing future out of reach again. He'd gone to eat dinner with Tad Skinner, just back from a gaudy mission to Rome and a little nervous about being caught by the M.P.'s at the same table with a private, at La Belle Péniche on the quai near Jay's room. They were annoyed when they got there to find the place filled with Americans in various uniforms, but none of them were army and a couple were even that rarity, civilians. Tad knew them all. One of the civilians was a tall glowering man with a skull too large for his face named Humphries who seemed to know all about Jay's scandal in the Red Cross (Pignatelli the pacifist, he exclaimed approvingly) and immediately started talking confidentially in his ear, as if he were a member of the same secret society, in a language full of references to peace coming out of Petrograd that Jay couldn't for the life of him understand. There was a woman with him with a sweet Irish voice and a name Jay vaguely associated with magazines, who cooed an echo to everything Humphries said and looked up admiringly into Jay's face whenever he spoke, and a pinkfaced doll-like man with slightly too curly hair who wore a rather noncommittal uniform and seemed to be the third member of a triangle. Their insistence on classifying him as a radical and a pacifist gave him the fidgets. The fact that he was a private was making their evening for them. The more he tried to explain that he was a maverick to begin with and had never drilled and never trained and never shot a gun and was probably the least typical private in the A.E.F. the more he felt they were noting down his utterances as The Voice of the Doughboy.

Everybody ate a great deal and after many bottles of wine they ordered up one brandy after another and, in spite of Jay's wanting to hear Tad Skinner's magniloquent tale of adventures with a countess in the wagon-lit who wore black lace panties and whom he insisted was an international spy, he found himself heart to heart at a corner of the table with the small pink newspaper man, whose first name was Hall and who was telling him the story of his life up to the point where he'd taken this job to do publicity for the Middle East Relief. He told Jay he was in a blue funk now that he was starting because he didn't know any languages. Human interest, he said looking hungrily into Jay's face, was his specialty, but how was he going to do human interest stories when he didn't know the languages? It came out that Jay spoke French and some Spanish and Italian and had picked up a little German in Alsace and before he knew what had happened Hall Bryant was offering him a job with the Middle East Relief, and Trebizond and the Isles of Greece, and Constantinople via the Orient Express. At that point the party had to break up because the waiter was stacking the chairs on the tables.

First thing next morning Jay called Hall Byrant before he was awake at his hotel to ask if he really meant what he'd said about a job. Sure, the sleepy hoarse voice answered, but it depended on Jay's getting himself a discharge from the army.

Meanwhile Hall would telegraph New York to get Jay's name okayed. His hands cold with excitement Jay called the Crillon. There was no Major Mortlake but a colonel. "Sure Jay I was wondering where you were. Come to breakfast." Jay could hear Mortlake at the other end of the line clear his throat. "I've been in Germany watching the squareheads cringe."

Jay made his way in through the side door to avoid a lobby full of braid and got himself a pass from a scornful head-quarters type sergeant at a desk and, for fear there might be a general in the elevator, walked up three flights of stairs to find Mortlake in his bathrobe over breakfast in a little room that overlooked the court. "Everything full of generals and high commissioners," Mortlake grumbled, "so that we attachés who do the work are housed in the servants' wing."

"Mr. Mortlake . . . excuse me sir, Colonel . . . How could I go about getting discharged in France?"

"Not a ballet dancer I hope," Mortlake cried out. "That was your father's weakness."

"No," Jay blushed. "But if I can get out of the army I can get a job and a trip to the Near East."

"Well I'm staying on myself to see the peace . . . I've been away from home and law practice so long I might as well see the damn show through. Anyway Martha's coming over as soon as the girls get out of school. I don't know where I'll put 'em. There's not a room to be had in any of the hotels. Have some wuffs?"

Jay nodded. As the waiter was teetering in the doorway he gave his order. Mortlake listened admiringly to his French.

"The advantages the boy's had," he muttered. "Languages are a trial to me," he sighed. "You seem to have the knack. And now the University of Paris. Learned stuff. Have you thought of trying to hitch into one of these firms with an international practice? There are several of them. I'll keep the problem in mind. In the new era that's beginning there's going to be a great deal more international business."

"Can't do anything," said Jay, "till I get out of the army. I got to get out." The shriek in his own voice surprised him.

"It would save Uncle Sam the expense of shipping you home," said Mortlake musingly. "How much are they going to pay you?"

Jay felt the blood burning in his cheeks again.

"I never asked."

Colonel Mortlake clucked and shook his head and with a groan reached for the telephone.

So it had come about after a good deal of hysterics, and two weeks' waiting agony in a casuals detachment loading scrap iron on flatcars one day and taking it off again the next, and a chase through offices of the S.O.S. in Tours after a lost service record, and telegrams to Mortlake and eventually a cable to Luke begging abjectly for help, that one summer day, a civilian with his discharge in his pocket, Jay had hurried on feet light as birds to the station to catch the train for Paris. He had driven triumphantly and a little drunk in a horsecab to the Lille et d'Albion where he'd hired their most luxurious room and, as excited as a small boy unwrapping Christmas presents, had unpacked from Dandy's faithful old portmanteau the trappments of a pallid prewar law student who had assuredly been a very different creature from the present ex-private Pignatelli. "Why you look quite handsome in civilians," said Hall Byrant, when he met him in the hall below the relievers' office. "You looked awful in a uniform . . . I never saw anybody wear one worse."

There was a week of office conferences, visas, photographs and passport problems and the enlivening game of travel orders east. Tad was off on courier duty the same night and invited them to visit him in Rome, so they all took the train together and Jay, a shark with timetables, managed to arrange it so that he and Hall couldn't get a reservation on the Orient Express (relievers had the right to travel wagon-lit) for ten Italian summer days. Already he was reading Dante on the Simplon train with a dictionary on his knees and a bottle of wine between his feet. At the station in Milan, where they left Tad, tall and tousled in his uniform, leaning out of the window of the through car beside a broad blonde who was beginning to show signs of a smile, Jay bought himself Baedecker and a newly edited Boccaccio and went, so Hall Bryant said, mad with the historic scene.

He had to see everything, he had to walk everywhere for fear of missing something on the way. All day he swam in a haze of recollections out of Stendhal and Gibbon that kept bubbling like champagne in his head. As they hurried through green-shuttered streets over the hard stones Jay expounded Scott Bronson's theory — which Honorine had said was admirhable — that everything that had ever happened in an old city still existed there. In a shaft of light through a vaulted room, or a hunched beast carved on a lintel or in the face of an old woman behind a market stall you could catch, if you were lucky, the very lineaments of the past. By the time they reached the corbelled tables and the vaulted porch with its barbarian carvings of St. Ambrose's church, where in Gibbon's resounding prose Jay had seen the great archbishop bar the way to Theodosius until the emperor should do penance for massacring the Thessalonians, Hall Bryant was pale and shaky and was blaming Jay for his blistered feet. He insisted the church wasn't any different from a church he'd seen on Copley Square in Boston.

Jay put him in a cab with a copy of the Paris edition of the *New York Herald* and said to wait for him at Biffi's in the Galleria. Jay had to take in the Leonardo supper so they barely caught the train to Florence, where, even though it was after midnight when they arrived, Jay had to take a turn through the narrow streets between the dark stone fortresspalaces of the noble Guelfs. Next morning he routed Hall out early and walked him, protesting that what he wanted was to sit in a comfortable barbershop with a copy of the *New York Times*, through loggias and cloisters and museums and showed him painting and sculpture until he said his eyes were sore. At noon they stretched their aching legs under a table at an outdoor restaurant in a blazing square. "Birra, birra," Hall was calling at the waiter. "It's hot in this man's town."

"It's a feeling of energy," Jay was insisting. "The energy that comes from an active instead of a passive organization of society. We just don't have cities in the sense that these early Italians had cities."

"Only slums and suburbs," sighed Hall.

"Civilization if it means anything," Jay went on over the antipasto, "means city life. When city life deadens people instead of stimulating them you don't have any civilization."

"I didn't need to come to Italy to find that out," said Hall. "I found that out back home in Sacramento."

That afternoon after a gruelling run to the station to catch the train to Arezzo, Hall turned green from indigestion and complained that garlic and oil and sour wine gave him heartburn, so when Jay walked out into the searing afternoon sun to find the Piero della Francesca frescos he had to leave him eating charcoal tablets in the railroad bar. Standing in the cool dark chancel of the Franciscan church, trying not to hear the droning of the ancient sacristan, Jay underwent for the first time the complete seduction of great painting. As he looked he could feel the painter's intention expressed as clearly as if he heard it spoken in wellmodulated tuscan. His eyes slipped away from him into a longago calculated trance of nobly shaped figures of men and women, drawn with such cool, such balanced, such controlled energy against silvery distances, that his first thought was that he had never really seen a picture before. He arrived back at the station dusty and sweating, helpless to explain how he had spent his time. At Orvieto he just about had to drag Hall off the train. He was in a fever for fear the cathedral would close before they got there, but he had to build up Hall with a carafe of the local wine before he could coax him up the steep street to the striped duomo where in the last light they stood quaking before the tawny splendor of Signorelli's "Judgment Day."

"That's an experience," said Hall still panting from the climb, "but an experience I have no way of absorbing . . . I don't see the human interest."

"But it's today. It's now. It's more imminent than the morning paper," Jay interrupted.

"I suppose you get it with your Italian blood, like the ability to digest the horrible greasy food."

"Let's have some," said Jay. "Frescos make me hungry . . . Where's the best trattoria?" he asked the man with a mashed convict's face who was closing the ponderous cathedral gates behind them.

Again it was late at night when, thickwitted from fatigue and from all the white Orvieto wine they'd drunk, they tumbled off the train in Rome.

Next day was Sunday. Jay called up Tad and Tad led them up many flights of soiled marble stairs to find Jed Morris, who was living, so he proclaimed with popping eyes when he threw open the door of his brocadehung apartment, in oriental splendor on the depreciation of the lire. They ate a second breakfast with him on his balcony overlooking Nero's tower in the company of three shrill and skinny little Roman tarts, two blondes and a brunette, who all seemed to answer to the name of Nedda.

Jay leaned on the balustrade, while they shrieked and kidded in bad English and worse Italian at the table behind him, and looked out over tiled roofs and cypresses and umbrella pines and the grassgrown brick and gnawedoff columns shimmering in the honeycolored morning sunlight.

He had spotted the Campidoglio beyond and saw himself in a forgotten daydream, stained and weathered as an old engraving, the learned Poggius climbing the Capitoline. About time for a new Gibbon, he was telling himself again, to concoct another history of another civilization's decline and fall; but all the while he was achingly conscious of the girls behind him, their sexy byplay and the pubic scent of hair scorched by the curling iron and perfume and underwear. In his mind, as his eyes sought out the Palatine and the hill of gardens and Janiculum, he undressed them on the broad bed in the alcove. It would be easy enough but he didn't exactly want to. Still their raucous voices were coiling a spring tight inside him. He had to get out and walk and sweat and tire himself out. For a fleeting instant he thought of how much fun he could have, running among the marbles with Honorine. "I got to go do my sightseeing," he told his friends. "Suppose we meet for dinner someplace."

After three days of ruins and mosaiced basilicas and galleries and gardens and the Sistine ceiling and Michelangelo's sonnets read in snatches amid drunken friends and golden wine and girls and giggles under vinecovered arbors among the tombs outside the walls, Jay and Hall Bryant, sweating Frascati from every pore, climbed, showering lire into outstretched palms as they went, on the night express for Venice which the hall porter at the Terminal Hotel insisted would get through in spite of an impending strike. When they settled in the diningcar for supper Jay noticed with dismay that the old heart-to-heart look was coming over Hall's rosy cherub's face. "Jay, you've been a great disappointment to me," he began. "I thought you were a continental Don Juan sort of character and it turns out you're as inhibited as a Bostonian."

"Whores embarrass me if that's what you mean."

"But Jed makes everybody human. He treats 'em like human beings. He brings the human interest out in people . . . He's the uninhibited natural man. Skinner is an interesting boy, too. I had hopes of you when I met your friends."

"Jed's a comical fellow, but he's inhibited as hell about lots of things. What do we mean by inhibited anyway?"

"See that proves it. You are blocking now. Ever tried Freud?"

"I'd rather work things out for myself, and look at the last sunlight on the walls of that stone farm . . . so rich you could spread it on your bread . . . I swear you can see twice as much after looking at painting. That's one of the things about great painting. It actually improves your eyesight. The effect is permanent. I feel as if I had the Sistine ceiling engraved on the inside of my skull."

"I don't know anything about art but I do know about life," said Hall eagerly, too eagerly Jay thought. "People need emotional release. I can see that you are getting all wroughtup and fidgety. You need a rich emotional experience."

"I need my supper and a good night's sleep . . . Camariere."

"Adesso signori adesso."

When they finally started serving the meal, Hall complained that the spaghetti would poison him and the fritto misto would be his death, so after some argument Jay managed to get him an omelet.

"Now I feel better," Hall said when he'd finished. "Now I feel I could take on my weight in wildcats. In fisticuffs or between the sheets."

He gave Jay an impudent searching look. Jay felt his face turn red as he counted the change from the bill.

"Imagine blushing at your age. I stopped blushing at fourteen," Hall added in a blustering tone. "It's attractive though."

Jay got to his feet. "You've got me wrong." He enunciated the words carefully without turning round as he strode down the train's lurching corridor. Hall said very little more that evening. He hummed and rustled his papers in the lower bunk, while Jay in the upper went to work (inhibited old broken-nosed bastard Buonarroti) on Michelangelo's letters and sonnets with a dictionary.

When Jay woke up the train was still. The morning was well advanced. Peering out of the window he could make out long empty platforms and a sign that read Bologna. He looked at his watch. "Late," he muttered towards Hall Bryant's sleeping form. "We ought to be pulling into Venice." He dressed in a hurry and went out.

The sleepingcar was not attached to any train at all. Indignant passengers, sleekly dressed civilians and officers in tall green caps were crowding round a short man who pushed them off with windmill gesticulations and much contortion of the facial muscles. It wasn't his fault he was saying, the workers had declared a general strike. When Jay went back to break the news to Hall whom he found brushing his teeth in the tiny washbasin, Hall shouted, "Fine. That's what I want to see . . . The trouble with you is," he went on shaking his toothbrush threateningly under Jay's nose, "you're not a modern man. You don't understand that we're seeing the collapse of a social system. Damn good thing. Nothing will go right till the workers take over industry and run it for themselves. The trouble with you is you don't understand that when a system has gone to pieces there's no sense in paying attention to its rules."

Jay burst out laughing. "Fais ce que voudras, is the inscription Rabelais placed on the Abbaye de Thélème. I'll subscribe to that . . . but I'll be damned if I'll let anybody tell me what I want to do." Hall gave Jay a waspish pouting look and fell to putting talcumpowder under his arms. "We'd better get some breakfast while we can," added Jay cheerfully. "I'll order up coffee . . ."

"Wait for me," Hall pleaded.

"You can't miss it," Jay called over his shoulder as he slammed his way out.

"The trouble with you," Hall said when, arriving with a bunch of stale *Daily Mails* under his arm, he tumbled into a seat at the little round table at the station café, "is that you don't know you're in the middle of a revolution. That's what I came overseas for: to report the revolution." He threw himself back in his chair and stuck out his chest. "Of course I didn't tell that to the M.E.R." He gave Jay a scornful smile. "The trouble with you is you don't feel with the proletariat."

"I haven't found out what I am yet . . ." said Jay trying to avoid an argument. "I don't know that I've got anything to be a capitalist with," he added haltingly.

"It's not what your bank account is, it's what you are," said Hall, slapping the marble table with his packet of papers. "Ever since I went to grade school and got to know the boys across the railroad tracks, I've always felt . . ." he gave the table another slap with his newspapers, "on their side against the rich. Come the revolution they'll feel that I'm on their side too."

"I was a buck private in the rear rank," said Jay slowly. "I don't know what's lower in the social scale . . . and I liked it . . . but if you told the guys I knew down there that they were proletariats they'd knock your block off."

"Until you get rid of the inhibited moralistic attitudes you were brought up with . . ." started Hall with a bitter face. The harsh puffs of the forced draft of an engine interrupted him. They ran out to their sleeper and found a train sprouting soldiers from every window backing slowly towards it. There was a clash of couplings and then silence except for shouts and chatter from the troops. "Handsome devils," Hall said, rolling his eyes towards the brown faces in the windows. "If I only knew the language I'd go up there and make friends . . . You go. Ask them what they think about the strike." Already whistles were blowing. The train began to move. They trotted laughing along the platform and climbed aboard. Jay noticed the other passengers on the sleepingcar looking out at them through the glass with the cold hating eyes of fish in an aquarium.

"They think Americans are too flip," he said to Hall. "They think we are just here for the show."

"Damn tootin'," said Hall as he settled back in the seat in the airless compartment. "The trouble with you is you don't

read Walt Whitman . . . And quit worrying about the bourgeoisie. They know they are at the end of their tether," he
added spitefully. "You can see it in their faces."

Jay remembered their slow progress through a landscape,
as composed as a mural, of small hills with an occasional scarf
of trees about them like the trees in Perugino's backgrounds,
and the beautiful great pillared barns and the arched farm-
houses smudged with blue where the grapes on the pergolas
had been sprayed with copper sulphate and his own delight
in noting, as the land flattened towards the Po, that in the
square fields fenced with poplars they still looped vines on the
pollarded elms the way Virgil recommended in the *Georgics*.
It amused him to remember how he'd managed to launch a
new historical theory, like Scott Bronson the unforgettable
night they'd slummed in Paris with the general, every time
Hall tried to bring the conversation round to his private life.
Hall had grown more and more peevish as the day wore on and
the train moved slower and slower, stopping with a jerk at
every tiny station to let off a detachment of slovenly young
soldiers. Jay had refused to act as interpreter when Hall
wanted to sidle up to them with his questions. "It's a ticklish
time," Jay had tried to explain, "you don't want to embarrass
people with silly questions."

Hall had blown up at that. "The trouble with you is you're
an intellectual. You build up theories about history and art
as an escape. The only way of getting at life is through people.
I like to get close to people."

Jay had laughed and Hall had taken offense hard. The
curves in his face had sharpened and he had looked at Jay
with eyes black with dislike. "Women too," he'd hissed. "I've
had more women in my life than you ever dreamed of. Attractive and interesting women." Then he had stamped out into
the corridor to stand.

They arrived in Padua hardly speaking. When the station-
master told Jay this train would go no further because the

operai had torn up the tracks ahead, Hall gave Jay a sour look as if it were all his fault. Jay discovered they could catch a steamboat to Venice at le cinque and cried out that they would just have time to poke their noses into the Arena Chapel on the way to the landing. Hall wouldn't go in but sat outside in a grouch among their baggage piled in the cab. They caught the vapore by a hair. Afterwards Jay was never sure if he really experienced the long fall of twilight as the little steamboat rippled through the canal against a sedgy wind past mossy farms and colonnaded villas and bluntnosed boats with red earth sails tied up at balustraded landings, and finally nosed out into the lagoon through streaks of mist across a rising moon towards the dimlit city with its pointed towers and palaces like galleons afloat among boats and barges, or whether he'd dreamed it. In the Venice railroad station they had miraculously found the Simplon-Orient Express waiting at the platform four hours late. Jay got hold of the conductor and as so many travellers had missed their connections managed to wangle separate staterooms for himself and Hall so that that pink cherub could nurse his peeve in peace.

It was late at night before they started. Next day as the train ground up a long broad blond valley into the lowering dusty Balkans Jay sat alone working his way with his dictionary through Dante's *Purgatory* and seeing before him with surprising vividness the panels of Giotto's retelling, in plain blues and umbers and whites, with mighty amplitude of gesture and form, of the Christian tale. By the time Hall Bryant slid in the door, having decided to live and let live because he couldn't abide an hour without talk, with "The trouble with you is" on the edge of his lips, Jay had a theory ready to discuss.

"Dante and Giotto give you, in its simplest form, the great medieval picture of the cosmos . . . I never understood it before . . . Ptolemy's globe, surrounded by a firmament of angels with God and Christ and the Virgin Mary enthroned on high and hell and the devil flaming somewhere below."

"Didn't they think the world was flat?" put in Hall.

Jay went on without paying attention: "To us it doesn't seem an accurate picture but everything they knew fitted into it. It worked for them. A man knew his part in the drama of the universe. No wonder they were so mad at Galileo because he upset all that . . . The eighteenth century deists, using Newton's laws instead of Ptolemy's geography, tried to reestablish a stable cosmogony but the advance of science knocked it into a cocked hat. That's why we have to flounder about so."

"Marx and Freud . . ." began Hall.

"Oh God," said Jay, "you're going to tell me I've got to learn to read German."

"The trouble with you is . . ." began Hall and belabored him with Walt Whitman as with a stick. He painted a vision of the plain natural working man returning through psychoanalysis and socialism to the true life of Eden's garden. The argument never reached any conclusions but it effectively kept the discussion of people's private lives at armslength until the train rumbled with exhausted slowness through a breach in the old walls into the collection of mouldy back alleys that were the railroad station at Istamboul.

A Balkan diplomat had been assassinated in the lobby a few minutes before they arrived at the Pera Palace Hotel. Military police of assorted Allied nations were still examining a spot of damp blood on the carpetcovered divan where he had been sitting. "Signs of the times," said a hollowcheeked missionary in a black suit who was in charge of the Constantinople office as he advanced from the desk to greet them. He explained that there were no rooms at the hotel, so he would put them up temporarily at the college . . . "where at least you'll be spared sights like these."

In the weeks that followed Hall Bryant's favorite phrase "human interest" began to take on a sinister slant in Jay's mind. It wasn't interesting to see innocent people suffering all the tortures of the damned, it was inhuman and horrible. Constantinople was a world of the displaced. The crumbling old city of the purple emperors and the sultans and the grand viziers, with its ruins impacted on ruins and its mosques and minarets and its ingrained squalors and splendors along the jadegreen Bosphorus, was drowning in a rising flood of misery. There were Armenian refugees. There were Russians in blond and starving swarms who had run away from the civil war. There were Turks escaping from the Greeks and Greeks escaping from the Turks and pathetic remnants of peoples Jay hardly knew the names of, ragged throngs milling in the courtyards of brokendown palaces that made him think of the crowded damned in the great Last Judgments he'd seen painted on the walls in Italy. As in the theologians' hell the damned tortured each other. The strong ganged up on the weak to relieve them of overcoats and shoes and money. Rape was taken for granted. At night there were brawls and knifings even along the Grande rue de Pera. People who strolled outside the city walls were likely to be set upon by bandits and sent back barenaked. The theologians were right, there was a hell, Jay remembered thinking to himself as he explored the stratifications of destitution, but instead of being in some distant place underground, hell was here on earth.

His lot compared to theirs was like that of the blessed in heaven: his neat room, his bath, his clean sheets, the tennis courts under his window where young people in white flannels made friendly American noises as they played, his salary, his passport that assured his quick return to the unsullied continent beyond the Atlantic. Sometimes it had seemed to him that the relief people he worked with, in their resolute endeavor to promote goodness and clean living at any cost, looked down on the sufferings of the undeserving as unconcernedly as the smug assemblies of the blest pictured aloft in rainbow-colored bliss on the walls of the old churches looked down on the wracked souls in Satan's steaming cauldrons. All that autumn Jay's mind had been full of Dante. When he went out to dig up stories for Hall Bryant he pictured himself as the bitter Florentine asking his questions among the hordes in torment.

His Virgil was a stocky little Greek of about his own age who affected speckled vests and roseleaves in his cigarette case and fastened himself resolutely to Jay because he was a fellow law student and because, in a back number of some American law review he'd run across a reference to a prominent Chicago attorney named James Pignatelli. Like everybody else George Demetrios wanted to go to America. He had decided that since Jay was wellconnected he was the man to help him build his bridge of ships. George was a man who once he made up his mind was not easily discouraged. He himself, he explained in his copybook English, had taken his doctorate in the sufferings of the dispossessed. He was a refugee from a town in Asia Minor, the last survivor of a family that had suffered all imaginable lootings and burnings and rapes and murders at the hands of the Turks. His darling scheme, which, he explained to Jay would make them each a million dollars, was to form a steamship company with American capital to transport refugees to the New World. Those who couldn't pay would be paid for by relief agencies. The Liverpool shipowners in the last century had founded their fortunes on the transport of emigrants. All emigrants were refugees, now weren't they? Life in these countries would be impossible for a hundred years. The only hope for the educated and ambitious was to move to America: Buenos Aires or Chicago or New York or Havana; it didn't matter. There were millions to be made in the shipment of refugees. As a Christian, George would say with a subtle smile, he believed in helping his fellowman. If it proved a profitable enterprise so much the better.

George spoke all the languages. He knew every alley and stinking backyard in the city. Whatever kind of story Hall Bryant got a notion to send out, George could implement with human interest to the last starving child crawling with bloated belly on a heap of garbage. Evenings he would take Jay

to interview (for documents, he'd say rolling his big eyes) the
thronging prostitutes of the garden of Taxim. "Human interest," he'd cry out and snap his cigarette case when he sighted
a pretty one. After the band had stopped playing they would
often end up eating cucumber soup by lamplight under an
arbor at a little open air restaurant kept by a Russian girl
named Tina.

Tina's cold cucumber soup was delicious on hot nights and
her shashlik, brought fresh from the grill on his sword by a
heavyheaded old cossack, was always tender. Her place was cool
and quiet and the Khakhetian wine was good and when the
customers were served she would come and sit with Jay and
George at the rickety table. She was a frail angular girl with
very large brown eyes in deep blue sockets and gold hair she
wore braided in a coil round her head. Since the first time
she'd seen him she had made Jay feel there was something a
little special in the confidence she had in him. Her voice when
she spoke to Jay in French was quite different from the voice
she used to keep George at armslength in mangled waterfront
English.

She never would drink with them. She would sit there with
her elbows out stirring more and more sugar into a glass of tea.

"Ah mon ami," she would say, "si vous saviez . . . si vous
pourriez vous rendre compte de la vie qu'on mène dans l'immigration. On va causer, n'est-ce pas, franchement mon ami."
She would let her feverish little workstained hand drop on his
but if he tried to put his hand on hers she'd always pull it away.
"Il faut se figurer le monde qu'on a connu. Je ne parle pas de
luxe . . . je ne trouve pas le mot . . . pas luxure . . ." she'd
laugh hoarsely . . . "aisance peutêtre . . . la parfaite confiance
dans la maison de mon père. Il était professeur à Petersbourg,
un homme doux comme le Christ. Naturellement on l'a
assassiné. Mais ce n'est pas de ça que je veux causer . . . Vous
autres américains comme nous les russes vous connaissez l'espoir. Nous autres nous vivions dans la maison de mon père

dans l'espoir d'un bel avenir paisible et propre où l'homme à cause de ses connaissances scientifiques pourrait croître dans l'image de dieu . . . Les jours d'émotion qu'on a vécu. Nous pensions qu'avec la revolution viendrait le royaume de dieu, vous comprenez, cher ami. Maintenant . . ." She would let herself slump in her chair with an expression of refusal like a little girl who wouldn't eat her supper, then she would straighten up and give a kind of desperate drowning look round the tables to see if the customers were taken care of and exchange an anxious glance with the old cossack tending his swords over the broiler. "Ma foi je m'exprime mal. Si vous parliez russe . . . Un des jours on prendra des leçons, n'est-ce pas? Je ne suis pas trop mauvaise comme institutrice. Avec vous cher ami, j'aime parler le français. Lui," she would indicate George with her little finger, "il connait le russe mais je ne veut pas parler le russe avec lui. Jamais de la vie." She would let out her hoarse laugh that ended sometimes in coughing that made Jay wonder if she might not be tubercular. "Il y a des différences entre les langues, il y a des langues qu'on parle avec les lèvres et des langues qu'on parle avec le coeur et des langues qu'on crache comme une saleté . . . Pour moi le français est le langage de l'amitié et le russe est le langage de l'espoir . . . Ce n'est pas à cause de la faim ou de la saleté ou des poux qu'on se suicide dans l'immigration . . . Vous savez, cher ami, on se suicide tous les jours . . . C'est à cause de l'espoir."

All day at the office Jay would hear the heartbreaking singsong of Tina's voice in his ears. He would think about her Byzantine face frozen in the still lines of grief of a mother of God in mosaic and feel the hot hurried patting of her hand on his. It got so that he'd try to shake George and Hall Bryant after office hours so that he could trot around alone to the restaurant under the arbor. Night after night he would try, in spite of the fact that it made him desperately drowsy at work next day because she and the old cossack never closed up shop till three or four in the morning, to sit up late enough to walk home with her through alleys scary with scuffles and curses in the shadows, to a sort of shuttered garden pavilion in a dead-end that stank of latrines where she lived with a swarm of other Russians. He would hear their talk from the dimlit rooms behind the shutters, but she would never let him come in. She would say "Bonsoir cher ami" and put her hands on his shoulders and push him away and slip out of sight through the broken shuttered doors.

When the cold weather came and the raw fogs off the Bosphorus Tina had to move her restaurant into a plastered room inside the cracked old stucco building beside the arbor. It was hard to keep warm and the place would be so smoky from the broiling shashlik that the customers ate in a hurry and few of them came back. She and Jay would often eat alone in the empty room pulling a table right up against the broiler for warmth. Several times he had to lend her a gold sovereign so that the old cossack would have the money to buy supplies with next day. "Il est bon comme le pain," she would murmur as she shook the coin between the palms of her hands that were never still, "le vieux Vassili, il était le cocher de mon père. Il me protège comme un gros chien. L'ame russe," she would say, trying to smile with lips shivering when she had put the coin away in her little beaded purse, "supporte bien le froid et le faim mais elle meurt sans espoir."

One drizzly night in December Jay arrived late and with wet feet. The place was full of Russians laughing and singing. Old Vassili was playing a gypsy song on a balalaika. Tina in a new dress of palegreen silk ran up to Jay to take his wet coat and hat. She was laughing and clapping her hands. "Djai," she cried, "c'est l'oncle Boris qui a retrouvé les bijoux de la grand'mère." She grabbed Jay by the sleeve and dragged him around the tables introducing him to the company. The women were dressed in clothes they had made themselves but the men were obviously still wearing whatever they had had on when they left home, tag ends of officers' uniforms, or hunting outfits or white or black closefitting highnecked tunics. Jay found himself drinking vodka and conversing in various languages and exchanging toasts. He plunged happily into an argument between two bearded gentlemen on which of Schliemann's Troys was the real Homeric Troy. They ate hot borscht and meat pies and cold fish and creamed beef and shashlik and drank Greek and Caucasian wine interspersed with little shots of vodka, and people sang and did cossack dances, and they ended by tossing Jay in a blanket, which, so he was told by various diners who poured him special vodka in corners, was considered a great honor among the Russians.

When Jay decided the time had come to make his way back to the college, everybody cried out that he must join them "pour le Chreestmas," they would show him le véritable "Russian Chreestmas." "On a commandé de la neige," a broad squarebearded man kept intoning in a deep bass voice. "On trouvera un sapin." Tina his hat and coat on her arm, beckoned to him from an inner door. "Viens cher ami," she said and led him into an airless room lit by a candle in a bottle. On the bed, nestled for warmth into a pile of hats and coats and furs, two pale tiny goldenhaired girls were fast asleep. "C'est mes bijoux," Tina said putting two fingers of one hand to her lips and slipping the other round Jay's waist. Still with their arms around each other they had turned to go, when Jay noticed a grayhaired man in a white tunic and spurred ridingboots kneeling beside the bed with his head clutched between his hands. "C'est mon mari," said Tina as if she had all of a sudden remembered him. She trotted back and tapped him on the shoulder. "Ivan c'est Djai." The man got to his feet and turned towards them a pair of glazed eyes in a haggard aquiline face accented by a pointed gray mustache. When he started for Jay with outstretched arms, Jay's first thought was that the husband was going to try to wring his neck. Instead he threw his arms around him and kissed him on the mouth. "Je salue en vous la charité américaine," he said.

Immediately he let himself drop sobbing on the bed beside the little girls. "Il a mal au cœur," explained Tina in a matter of fact tone, and led Jay down a passage to the alley where the horsecabs waited. In the darkness of the doorway she helped him on with his coat and carefully buttoned each button for him. Then she pulled his head down and kissed him. For just a moment she let herself go limp in his arms; then she pushed him away with that little sudden gesture she had, and said hoarsely, "Prenez-moi . . . prenez-nous avec vous en Amérique. For Christ's sake take us to New York," she added in her funny gutter English.

"That's easier said than done," Jay was whispering gently.

"Si vous voulez, vous pouvez. Vous pouvez tout," she said shaking him by the shoulders.

After he had tumbled into bed that night he could still feel her little body pressing limp against his.

The next night he had to dine at the college. The night after as he walked down the alley towards the restaurant from the direction of the garden of Taxim he didn't meet the accustomed smell of broiling mutton. His first thought was that old Vassili must be sick. The place was shuttered and barred. Could they all have moved away? There was no one in the street to ask. He turned and walked with beating heart through the tangle of alleys until in the reeking deadend he found the door where Tina had so often given him that little shove away from her when he would lean towards her to try to kiss her goodnight. A dim light trickled through the blinds of the window. He knocked on the shutters that served for a door. They were latched on the inside. He knocked again. When there was no answer he gave the shutters a push with his flat hand. The rotten wood splintered and the broken slats fell about his shoulders as the shutters swung open. The hallway smelt of rotting plaster and unwashed bedding and latrines. A crack of light showed under a door. When he pushed the door open he could make out that it came from a wick floating on a plate of tallow under an icon in the corner. There was another smell in the room. His foot slipped on something slimy. The tiny goldenhaired girls were propped like broken dolls under the icon in the corner. Their throats were cut. As his pupils widened to the dim light he could make out Tina in her new dress of palegreen silk stretched out on a bed. Blood and brains oozed over the pillow from the coiled braids of her hair. On the floor lay the grayhaired man in the white tunic, a shotgun with two ancient barrels inlaid with silver clasped to his breast. One bare foot stuck up awkwardly into the frail flicker from the icon. Right away Jay understood: he had shot her with the charge from one barrel and had taken off his boot to push the trigger with his toe while he held the muzzle in his mouth.

Jay found himself walking away along the iron grille of the empty Garden of Taxim with the reflection in his mind of what he had just seen standing out as oddly irrelevant as a group in dusty waxworks in the exhibits that used to give him bad dreams as a child at the Musée Grévin on the boulevards. In his mind a label formed like on a transparency: Suicide dans l'immigration.

As he walked back and forth on the limited section of the *Mauretania's* top deck reserved for Third Class passengers the tableau came alight in Jay's memory as if a switch had been turned on. The foghorn shattered his ears every time it sounded its rattling roar from the red smokestack over his head and water from the condensing steam splattered on the deck about him. Other foghorns answered reassuringly out of the fog over the gray water astern. There was no wake. The ship had dropped anchor. They were somewhere near the entrance to Ambrose Channel but none of the stewards could tell him when the fog would lift enough for them to make the dock. Jay was arranging his adventures in his head with the agreeable prospect of recounting them amid laughter and bootleg liquor to Tad Skinner and Jed who had both reached New York before him.

Tina's death had been one of the causes of his second scandal. He'd gone to the military police to get the bodies buried and the newspapers had elaborated the story and the good missionaries at the relief office, including oddly enough Hall Bryant his boss, who hadn't had a word to say about a rich emotional experience or getting close to people, had been pained indeed. Employees of relief organizations were not supposed to get involved in tragic scenes.

The incident that had finally cooked his goose with the M.E.R. had been purely comic; the more he thought back on it the funnier it got.

The overturn, that spring, by bolshevik troops of the flimsy Transcaucasian Republic had taken the minds of people in the office off the problem of whether Jay ought to be reprimanded or asked to return home. The future of relief work in Georgia and Armenia, where the populations were suffering not only from cholera, typhus and starvation but from the dictatorship of the proletariat, was immediately up in the air. Somebody had to be sent to Tiflis and Erivan to report on conditions, conditions being the word under which the relievers lumped all the horrors of a disintegrating society. Hall Bryant made a speech on how much he wanted to go but ended by explaining that he felt it his duty to remain in Constant'. Everybody was full of misgivings when it was decided to ship Jay to Batum on an Italian steamship that still made the Black Sea ports. But Jay they decided was the only man who could be spared. Hall went down to the Galata dock to see him off and talked a lot about how he envied him this opportunity to meet the new world face to face. This was the end of shillyshally liberals: this was the real thing. "It'll be interesting," Jay kept saying vaguely, "to see what it's really like."

"Interesting hell," said Hall suddenly looking at him with narrow detesting eyes. "If you aren't careful with those people you'll get a bloody nose."

In Batum the weather was delicious. People modestly

grouped in clumps of men and women were bathing naked all along the broad shingle beach. Feeling a little indecent in his trunks Jay swam with them in the warm afternoon sunlight. Drying off in the sun on the beach his imagination was rosy with ideas of Hellenic freedom and the life Hall had waxed so eloquent about on the Orient Express, of uninhibited dignity and full emotional release that would ensue for all the world once the working man was free from the shackles of wage slavery.

On the train up to Tiflis Jay got along famously with the Russian officials who were his fellow travelers on the sleeping-car but he was almost eaten up by bedbugs. Bedbugs even crawled after him up to the baggagerack where, sprinkled all over with insect powder, he eventually managed to get a couple of hours sleep. In Tiflis he found the relievers huddled on camp cots in a big stone room anxiously looking for lice in the seams of their clothes. They could talk of nothing but typhus. Cholera, if you ate only canned food and carefully boiled water, wasn't so dangerous, but lice were everywhere. One bite from a louse could mean typhus; and typhus was trumps.

One of the Russian officials Jay had been such buddies with on the train, a towheaded young man named Comrade Maximov, with whom Jay had communicated in a mosaic of French, English and German, had given Jay a card scribbled with Russian script which, on being translated by the N.E.R. interpreter, gave his title as Secretary for Education to the Workers' and Peasants' Government. His first night in Tiflis Jay was settling down to eat canned spaghetti with the missionaries when a string of Red Army soldiers with long bayonets on their rifles came stamping up the stairs. They presented arms on the landing and a noncom saluted in the doorway and came forward with his cap in his hand to explain to the interpreter that the President of the Revcom wanted the pleasure of the company of Comrade Mister Pignatelli for dinner at Narcompross. The other relievers looked at Jay as if he were the wild man from Borneo, but after a whispered consultation decided that by all means he should go; so Jay marched off down the street escorted by his guards through the dusty city full of barefoot hollowcheeked people aimlessly roaming.

A long table was set on the roof of the white building of the Department of Education. His friend Maximov, who was on the lookout for him, rushed up smiling and introduced him to a large group of men in black boots, some tall and blond and some short and stocky, some in Red Army uniforms and some in white tunics, who were crowding round platters of cold fish and caviar set out on a buffet. Immediately a tiny vodka glass was pressed into his hand. "Americanyetz Kharashaw," they'd cry as they clicked heels and shook hands. Maximov stood beside him and translated their toasts. "To the great American Democracy. Genry Ford . . . Fordizatsya . . . Gerbert Goover . . . Amerikanski canned goods . . ." To emphasize this last toast everybody shouted "alaverdi." Maximov explained grinning that meant bottoms up.

"What sie mussen expiquieren vameriki mon camarade," Maximov began as he drew Jay down to a place beside him at the table, "is that war communism is une phase nécessaire mais pénible of civil war . . . kriegsneccesitat. After peace you will see belles choses von die revoluzion. First we must have peace then we will build socialism. Viel besser."

"But I thought food was scarce in Tiflis," Jay whispered to his friend, as black browed Georgian waiters with pointed mustaches brought on four suckling pigs roasted whole.

"Que voulez-vous?" said Maximov with expressionless face. "The grateful peasants . . . they send us their best."

With each course came a flock of bottles of the white wines of the Caucasus and between the courses, vodka and more toasts. Jay sat there confused by the noise and the foreign tongue looking out beyond the white buildings of the city into a wild upheaval of mountains purple and abrupt in the rosy dusk.

After the dessert Maximov apologized for the lack of coffee

and said coaxingly, "Wir gehen to meeting at théâtre for international revolutionary literature. Bon? Donc la literature
comme la révolution est internationale . . . Pushkin, Goethe,
Dante, Dickens, Shakespeare, Jack London, c'est tous des camarades."

Jay was not so much drunk, he was telling himself, as confused. His tongue seemed a little too large for his mouth. He
had the illusion that the brightly lit roof they were sitting on
was hovering over the hunger and sickness and lice and bedbugs and the dead and dying of the city like Swift's Laputa.
He tried to explain about Laputa to Comrade Maximov but
Comrade Maximov didn't know about Swift. Instead of listening he rattled along in French about Huysmans and the deca-
dence of the bourgeoisie. When they all rose from the table
with a clatter of heavy boots Maximov took Jay's arm and led
him down the broad stairs. At the foot of the last flight a squad
of soldiers presented arms as they passed. One of the officers
shouted the Russian equivalent of at ease comrades and the
soldiers all shouted "Oorah."

"Vous entendez?" Maximov yelled in Jay's ear and threw
his arms around him and kissed him. "They shout for American revolution."

As Jay followed the crowd of officers and officials through the
courtyard he noticed that they were brushing past a line of
soldiers with bayonets on their rifles who were herding a group
of ragged cringing men, bearded, filthy, their feet bound in rags,
into a corner of the court. There rose from them the very
stench of misery.

"Who are they?" asked Jay.

"Counterrevolutionaries . . . Les capitalistes réactionnaires."

"They don't look like capitalists."

"C'est la guerre," whispered Maximov hurriedly. "Mais le
prolétariat a un grand cœur. Après la guerre on pardonnera.
On guèrira les plaies avec le saint travail."

One of the diners, a stocky hardfaced man with a red star

on his pointed cap, was shouting something in an angry voice at the noncom in charge of the guard.

"What's he saying?" asked Jay.

"Il est fâché. Il dit qu'on enlève cette pourriture," said Maximov and he made a gesture with his hand like a small boy making a pistol. At the same time he made a popping sound with his lips. "Liquidation générale," he said.

They were already in the meetinghall. Jay was ushered into a row of chairs beside a long table. "Presidium," people were whispering in respectful tones. He sat down beside Maximov. A funnylooking canvas wall, Jay was thinking, this room had. He was wondering what sort of discussion was going to take place at the long table, when the wall shook and rolled up and he found he was on a stage facing an auditorium full of Red Army soldiers. The roar of their cheering bludgeoned his ears. Speeches began at the other end of the line of chairs behind the tables. Jay listened in a daze, catching now and then a recognizable word like revolutzy or Bolsheviki, or Sovietsky Vlast . . . Before he knew what had happened Maximov was whispering in his ear, "You vill sprechen against the toast lancé par les camarades soldats. Vive la révolution américaine . . . Moi . . . je traduis . . . vous pouvez confier."

Jay was on his feet sweating profusely and holding onto his chair with both hands and staring desperately into the blur of faces beneath him. Finally he managed to emit a few hoarse shouts to the effect that the Americans and the peoples of the Soviet Union were all equally children of a revolution and that they must work together to bring this period of wars and famines and plagues to an end. He trailed off into something about how a comradely understanding between the great Russian and American peoples would assure the peace of the world. The Red Army soldiers shouted and cheered when he bobbed his head to indicate that he'd finished and Maximov leaped to his feet and with eloquence and gestures made a speech that lasted half an hour and that brought the house to its feet with cries of "Oora Americanyetz, Amerikanski revolutzi, oora."

Everybody on the presidium clapped and shook hands with everybody else and several men embraced Jay and he began to be afraid they were going to toss him in a blanket to prove he was the honored guest. Instead they all started crowding off the stage in a hurry and Maximov explained they had to go to their offices to work. Meanwhile balalaika players were taking their places on the chairs. This time an entire squad accompanied Jay to the billet of the M.E.R. with a tramp tramp tramp on the rough pavings. The few passersby gave him one terrified glance and looked away. They probably think I'm on my way to my liquidation générale, he thought ruefully to himself.

Within a week it had been liquidation générale for Jay so far as the Middle East Relief was concerned. Whatever Maximov had said made the columns of the local paper and when the translation reached Constant' the office immediately cabled Jay's recall; but Jay had been arranging with a sly little Persian Descendant of the Prophet on his way back from studying medicine in Germany to go home with him to study "conditions" in Persia; so, as he had fifty pounds in Turkish gold in his pocket, Jay had turned the tables on Constant' by resigning forthwith. Within a couple of days, with the help of an envelope full of documents in Georgian and in Armenian writing and a Russian propus furnished by his friend Maximov, he managed to get aboard the propaganda boxcar on a train bound south for the Persian border, which the Descendant of the Prophet, waving in front of his face a passport diplomatique in beautiful Arabic script, defended savagely against all comers.

The trip took two weeks over the disintegrating railroad. Their commissariat consisted of some watermelons, a brick of smoked caviar and an ancient loaf of black bread. Over a can of solid alcohol, the Descendant of the Prophet boiled water for their tea wearing the facial expression of a meticulous research scientist which he had learned in a Berlin laboratory. He was highly conscious, to say the least, that cholera and typhus were contagious diseases. Daily he searched his seams for lice as devoutly as a holy man telling his beads.

Jay never could forget the sensations of delight and deliverance they experienced when they crossed the Araxes to a little town of dry baked clay named Djulfa on the Persian side of the border, and were free at last from the stench of misery, from the freightcars packed with sick and starving people bound no one knew where; from the bodies of the dead stacked in heaps in the baggage rooms of railroad stations; from the whimpering of children too weak to cry; from the terror on men's and women's faces when the stubblefaced operatives of the Tcheka, with their gimlet eyes and their cocked rifles, came along the stalled train to check papers and weed out ragged trembling creatures they would march off in single file as the train started again. The sight of too much suffering makes you hate the human race.

Djulfa was delightfully empty of people. Djulfa was quiet. In its own archaic way Djulfa was clean. Nothing had happened there in a thousand years. All Jay ever remembered doing in Djulfa was squatting on a carpet in a shady courtyard in drowsy peace like a figure in a Persian miniature and using his right hand only, as his Persian friend had taught him, to eat chicken cooked with rice and bitter oranges out of a big brass dish, while the Descendant of the Prophet smoked a hookah beside him and explained in Germanized French the political principles of Pan-Islam. They had climbed out of hell and were treading the comical earth again.

In Tabriz they bathed in a hammam and hired a cab driven by four white horses to take them over the stony road built by the Shah Abbas, and never repaired since, to Teheran. There Jay had taken passage in a springless Model T Ford with a young Armenian who wanted to drive him clear to America, and jolted down through the heat into the Mespot. In Bagdad he managed to get the last of his salary cabled to him from

Constant' and the assurance that his passport would meet him at Beirut. He set out with a camel caravan across the desert to Damascus. In Beirut when, famished and saddlegalled and windburned, he went to the consulate for his passport, the first thing he saw behind a desk was the broad smiling countenance of George Demetrios, still hopeful of his steamship line. George gave him his passport with a flourish and set him up to a very good dinner and arranged for the first leg of his transportation home at a cut rate on a small French freighter bound for Marseilles.

From the time he went on board Jay could think of nothing but getting home. Even the prospect of being cooped in an office to practice law didn't seem so grim as it had. The law would give him a part to play in the life of his own country, the way medicine gave the Descendant of the Prophet a part to play in Persia. He was tired of being a spectator in hell. In the little dispensary on the freighter's after deck, which he shared with a woodenheaded French corporal, he lay dreaming of Sandy Hook and the tall buildings of Manhattan and the lakefront in Chicago and for the first time he began to wonder what had happened to Dandy's house on Wharton Place. "To hell with the gorgeous East . . . I'm an American, God damn it," he'd say to himself. "It's time I went home and went to work to grow up with the country."

Everything would have gone well if the French freighter hadn't lost her propeller in the Straits of Messina in a gale and had been towed by a tug into Palermo. On the boat he'd been having a series of discussions with the French major who occupied the captain's cabin and who did not disguise his amazement at discovering someone who could talk Taine and Michelet and de Vigny bunking with his corporal and eating with the engineroom crew. Le Commandant de la Roseraie hinted to the captain that Jay must be *quelqu'un*, probably an important secret agent, and played up to him assiduously; so much so that they went en ville together in Palermo and drove in a horsecab up to the mosaics at Monreale and ate a stately dinner with two kinds of wine and champagne with the dessert, and occupied, the pair of them in state, a large box at the opera.

"Certainement," said le Commandant de la Roseraie as they settled at a café table after a noisy performance of *Aida,* "vous êtes *quelqu'un.*" He ordered Lachrymae Christi. Jay laughed and said No, he wasn't anybody, not yet, but the more he protested the more the major believed he was a secret agent, finally announcing with a bow that he would respect his privacy, that he was sure there were reasons of state . . . By that time the café was closing and as they didn't want to go back on the boat (the cabins would be insupportable in the harbor said the major) there was nowhere to go but to la maison publique la plus renommée de Palerme and so Jay found himself in bed with a very beautiful girl with a perfect Grecian nose and skin like eggshell china somewhat marred by an anxious look in her eyes and a peevish expression on her rosebud lips. Damned idiot. And as a result here he was, not only a nobody, but a sick nobody, having made a bloody fool of himself in every job he'd undertaken, coming home at the age of twentysix with not a damn prospect in the world, except a clap doctor's waitingroom, he told himself as he walked the damp deck in the endlessly delaying fog, flogging himself with the word "nobody" like a penitent with a lash.

It was next morning, after a night almost sleepless because he'd slept himself out on the crossing, before he felt the quadruple screws shaking the floor of his cabin and the distant vibration of the winch hauling up the anchor. He jumped out of his bunk and shaved and bathed in a hurry and closed his bag and was on deck in time to see green Liberty on Bedloe's Island go sliding by in the fog and to run across the deck to stare openmouthed as an immigrant at the humming silver boles of the buildings of lower Manhattan streaked with yellow and rose from the rising sun.

Naturally there would be nobody to meet him he thought as

he stood under the letter P in the shed of a wharf that smelled of cottonseed meal waiting for the customs man to look at his portmanteau and his bag of books.

A large darkbearded man with a wide black felt hat was looking him up and down. He walked up to him with outstretched hands and said, "Jay Pignatelli."

"That's my name," said Jay smiling.

"Nick Pignatelli. You know me." The bearded man spoke with a strong Italian accent.

"Sure," said Jay. "Glad to meet you. You are the other black sheep."

Nick Pignatelli pulled at his beard and laughed.

"How did you know I was coming in on the *Aquitania?*"

"My boys," said Nick mysteriously smiling. "One he work in immigrazione, bring passenger list. From Europe they write Jay Pignatelli speak out for peace. Go to revolutionary Russia. Speak for united working class. Speak for revoluzione. So I say here's one more Pignatelli who's not son of a beetch, I must meet him . . . What you do now?"

"I'll be in New York to see some friends a few days," said Jay hesitantly, "and then I guess I'll go to Chicago."

"You lawyer? I want your 'elp. Not for me. I never need 'elp but for one of my boys in beeg trouble."

"I may have to take a bar examination. But it won't be long before I am practicing . . . I'll damn well have to practice to eat."

"You practice on side of working class see? Now you want to find 'otel, see your girl perhaps . . . Meet me tonight, seven, eight o'clock, for good spaghetti, vino de Barbera . . ." Nick pulled a printed card out of his pocket. "Don't forget. Ring the bell and ask for Nick. They treat you good. One of my boys . . ."

When he turned his broad back and walked off Jay had felt suddenly and completely alone. He had never forgotten how lonely the New York streeets looked that early spring morning. The people, the cabs, the trucks, the billboards, the new build-

ings full of the clamor of riveters; the tense racing of the cab
through the traffic; he had no part in any of it. He had told
the driver the Murray Hill because he couldn't think of anywhere else to go. When he found himself alone with his old
portmanteau in one of the musty customary rooms he had the
heartbreaking feeling that he had never left it. He had crawled
into the walls four years ago and now he was coming out after
a long sleep, a not nearly old enough Rip Van Winkle . . . He
was choking with loneliness. Desperately he turned the dogeared pages of the phone book. He couldn't find a name he
knew. Then he remembered that Tad Skinner was doing cartoons for the *World* and called up the office. After a number
of uninterested voices he found himself miraculously talking
to Tad: "Tad, this is Jay."

"Hurray, but what's the matter?"

"Nothing much. You know, it's a shock to get home . . ."

"The best cure's a good speakeasy . . . I've got a string of
them . . . Why don't we all meet at Jed Morris' first?"

"Where's he living?"

"Twentyfive Grove Street naturally . . . They've just had a
baby."

"Who's had a baby?"

"June and Jed."

"Do you mean to tell me Jed married June Bartlett?"

"Of course. I'm going to get married myself. Maybe we'll
make you be best man. You remember Felicia? You used to
call her Sweetness and Light . . . Don't you remember those
trips to Forest Hills . . . Say Jay you haven't come home with
amnesia have you?"

"But that was in Cambridge when we were all in the kinder-
garten stage," groaned Jay.

"Sure . . . You go on down and see them. Felicia'll turn up.
Tell 'em I shan't be in till ninethirty or ten. I've got to finish
a drawing. Then we'll all go out on the town. I hear you are a
bloodyhanded bolshevik."

Before Jay had a chance to ask for the Morrises' phone number Tad had hung up. The hall porter told Jay Grove Street was in Brooklyn but Jay decided to try Greenwich Village. When he came up out of the station at Sheridan Square into the hot April sunlight there was Jed in his shirtsleeves buying a newspaper at the corner newsstand opposite. "Hey Jed!" They collided in the middle of the street and a taxi nearly ran them down. "God, I want to hear about the bolsheviki," Jed shouted, his black eyes bulging in his curly head. "I need you for local color. Don't strike me but I'm writing a play about the Russian revolution . . . You certainly raised a stink in that relief organization, Jay."

As they turned down Seventh Avenue, Jay gave his friend a light pat on the shoulder. "Congratulations, Daddy," he said.

"Isn't it ridiculous?" Jed threw back his head in a whinny of laughter. "We named her Mae although being June's daughter she really ought to be July. We thought Mae Morris would be a nice name if she ever wanted to go on the stage . . . It'll probably take place in Italy."

"What will?"

"This play . . . Say did you bring any liquor in?"

"I didn't know you could."

"Our friends the Fullers brought a hotwaterbottle full of cognac swaddled in the baby's diapers. They filled all his bottles with gin. It lasted just fifteen minutes in the hands of a party of friends." Jed's tongue wagged fast as they walked down Seventh Avenue. He caught Jay's arm at a corner.

"Let's get in out of this heat." He opened a brokendown old colonial door with a latchkey. "Isn't this a pretty nice apartment for fortyfive per? See there's a separate room for the baby. We can put you up if you don't mind the livingroom couch. We're getting a place on Martha's Vineyard for August if I can get an advance on this play. Now for God's sake take off your coat and necktie . . . June put four bottles of beer in some hidingplace last night . . . They went to the doctor's for a checkup. They'll be back in time for lunch."

"I'm laying off beer," said Jay flushing, "so don't bother."

"Not the disease that everybody tells you is no worse than a bad cold?" Jay nodded. Jed let himself drop in a chair roaring with laughter. "And Hall Bryant used to insist that you were a virgin. Say I got a very good doctor. He wants to be a poet and to drown in the Mediterranean you know, like Shelley." Jed got to his feet. "Where did I put that card? You must get cured right away because I tell you life in Manhattan goes on in a high state of promiscuity . . . It's like Rome only it doesn't cost you money. Promiscuity is in my opinion the ideal state. You may quote me." They were both laughing now. "I know what you're thinking," went on Jed with snapping eyes. "I've explained to June that I'm old enough to marry but not old enough for monogamy. June's broad as all outdoors . . . and besides the kid takes up so much of her time."

They heard thumps and squalling in the hall and a stocky redcheeked girl with a head of curly brown hair that she shook out of her eyes as she walked came striding in carrying a baby that had the same dark eyes and the same rosy cheeks and already looked like a tiny replica of the mother.

"Of course you know June," said Jed.

June strode up to Jay without pausing. "You don't remember me but I remember you. It was at La Belle Péniche in Paris one night. I was in a Red Cross uniform and had my hair in a bun so that it's natural you don't recognize me." She looked hard in his eyes with her direct darkbrown stare.

"Of course I do," said Jay. "We talked about Tchekov's plays and I thought you were wonderful. I just never caught the name."

"Jed's writing a play. I want to act in it, but he says I can't leave the baby. I tell him to write me a part with the baby. Why shouldn't you have a baby in the play? People have them in real life."

"When they least expect it," exploded Jed.

"Jed, did you tell him it was a shotgun wedding?" She rolled her eyes at Jay. "But I say that's the best kind. You are staying to lunch."

She laid the baby in its crib in front of the window and started unbuttoning her dress so that Jay caught a glimpse of the curve of a round white breast as she strode past him into the bedroom. Immediately she came back in a bright pink smock that made her look very large indeed and went bustling into the kitchenette. Jay and Jed sat on a wooden seat in the window that looked out on some trampled back yards and an ailanthus tree beginning to bud. Every time they got started talking the baby cried. Felicia came in, tall and prim as Jay had remembered her, bringing a little cool draft with her into the warm room. She pulled the gloves off her thin hands and went right to the baby and started changing its diaper.

"I should think you would know what's the matter when babies cry by this time Jed," she said severely . . . "Hello Jay, fancy our meeting in New York after all these years." She turned her distant smile on him. "Tad told me you arrived. Now you must sit down and tell us all about the Russian revolution."

"I can tell you all about that," shouted Jed. "On a bigger scale it is following exactly the course of the French revolution. Kronstadt was the Girondins. Lenin and Trotsky are Robespierre and Saint Just."

"Who's Napoleon?" asked Felicia.

"That's what my play's about . . . The Red Napoleon, what do you think of that for a title?"

"I hope Jed doesn't cast me for the Empress Josephine," said June coming in with a big dish of scrambled eggs, on a tray piled high with knives and forks and crockery. "You see this is my system." Jay felt her dark eyes with their long lashes caress him like a purring cat that rubs against your legs. "One trip from the kitchen, one trip back."

"But Jed why does it happen in Italy?"

"I've been to Italy," said Jed talking with his mouth full,

"but now that you've been to Russia, maybe you'll tell me enough about it so that we can lay the scene in Moscow."

"But I didn't get to Moscow. The only place I met the Reds was in Tiflis. They set me up to a damn fine dinner . . ." Jay began.

"They'll sweep all Europe," interrupted Jed. "My play begins when the Red Army captures Rome . . . Of course it's got to be in Rome."

"The only thing that worried me," Jay tried to go on with his story, "was that with the officials we had so much to eat when everybody else was starving."

"You can't make an omelet without breaking eggs," shouted Jed. "June how about some more scrambled eggs?"

"You go make them," said June casting down her eyes under their lashes. "It's the law of the sea . . . Once from and once to the kitchen," she explained in a dogmatic tone to Felicia and Jay. A great clattering of pans came from Jed in the kitchenette. "Tell me," June gave Jay a dark taunting look, "have they really abolished bathing suits? I hate bathing suits."

"I don't think the Russians ever wore them . . . I felt out of place in mine."

"The trouble is that most people don't look their best without them," said Felicia in a practical voice that made them laugh.

"We'd be better off if we went naked half the time," said Jed who came lumbering in with a second platter of eggs. When he sat down he looked at his watch. "Gosh, I've got to go to a matinée with Molly and meet Fred Hobart afterwards. He just might be the lucky man to put up the money for the show . . . Jay you stay and help the girls with the dishes. Here's the sawbone's address." He handed Jay a visiting card. "How about coming back for supper? We'll all meet here and go out on the town. God, I hope you've got some money because I haven't."

"Tad has," said Felicia. "He gets paid today."

"I've got to dine with an anarchist cousin of mine," said Jay.

"You see," called Jed from the bathroom where he was tying his necktie in front of the mirror over the washbasin, "the guy's a dangerous Red."

"Who are the Hobarts?" asked Jay after Jed had left.

"Molly's a singer," said June, "and Fred is our Wall Street contact . . . Everybody needs a Wall Street contact."

"She's the prettiest thing you ever saw," said Felicia. Her words seemed to freeze on her lips. "In fact she's too pretty for her own good."

"Meaow," said June getting very red and flustered. She got to her feet and started piling up the dishes.

Jay left them after the dishes were dried, with the rasp of kitchen soap on his hands and a greasy feeling under his nails. While the lovely spring afternoon, that had seemed as full of chirping life and incident and prettily dressed girls as a scene in a musical show, drained away on the streets outside, he sat in the dark doctor's waiting room on Tenth Street, that smelt of stale antiseptics, drearily reading back numbers of the *Literary Digest*. Was he sick or wasn't he sick? At last Dr. Wilton slid open the double doors in back and gave his head a jerk to indicate to Jay that it was his turn. He had a long thin face and a little wisp of beard the color of frazzled rope.

"Jed Morris," he cried, "oh he's quite a boy. He may be a genius. He wants me to put money in his play. I've been tempted for some time to take a flyer in the arts."

Jay got very red in the face when he stammered out his explanation. "Oh, well, youthful follies," Dr. Wilton said. His beard took on a goaty look. "Gonorrhea is nothing to trifle with but maybe it's better than paying a psychoanalyst twenty-five dollars a visit." Jay noticed that there was a yellow glint in the doctor's eyes like in a goat's. "Well we'll take some smears and check up . . . You say you're just back from Europe? Why did you ever come back to this ratrace?"

"But it's my country," Jay heard himself saying. "It's up to me to live in it; that's what I've been thinking all the way home."

"But what a hell of a country," Dr. Wilton chattered on as he made his examination. "Prohibition . . . hypocrisy . . . commercialism rampant everywhere. Palmer's red raids. Land of the free, my foot! My ambition when I've made enough money to retire is to settle on the Riviera and write poetry. You must have been through hell in the war."

"I got some mighty good trips out of it. But a man gets sick of just looking on at events . . . I want to practice law now."

"And end up fat and rich and dyspeptic and disgusted like the rest of them . . . Say," Dr. Wilton added in a disappointed voice, "I can't discover any appreciable discharge . . . This may be a false alarm. The number of young men who come into my office wasting my time with their false alarms . . ."

"But that English doctor . . ." began Jay on the defensive.

"They may have mixed up the slides at the laboratory . . . It's the deplorable sense of sin. We are so afraid of everything in this country . . . Young man my advice to you is to go back to Europe and get yourself a pretty mistress and stay there." The yellow gleam came back into his eyes.

"But I have that behind me," said Jay tucking in his shirt and buttoning his trousers. "My grandfather was an immigrant . . . My father had business on the continent . . . I spent a lot of time there when I was little. The war put an end to that kind of life."

"Probably a feller couldn't make a living over there."

"It's not entirely that. A lawyer is an officer of the court. Isn't it conceivable that a man might practice law as a public service?"

"Public service, that's the biggest racket of the lot."

"My father was an American by choice"; Jay remembered how kiddish his own voice sounded when he said that. "I feel the same way."

"Do you like Gilbert and Sullivan?" Dr. Wilton had asked

and showed his long teeth in a grin. His beard waggled as he
chanted:

> *Oh he might have been a Roosian*
> *A French or Turk or Proosian*
> *Or perhaps Itali-an*
> *But in spite of all temptations*
> *To belong to other nations,*
> *He remains an . . .*

"Exactly, Doctor Wilton." Jay started towards the door.

"Well lay off love and liquor for a while. Don't do anything
I wouldn't do, and call me day after tomorrow." Dr. Wilton
gave him a last yellow leer as he let him out the side door of the
office.

He had sat there so long blabbing out his private notions to
a man he hardly knew and didn't like the looks of anyway, —
Jay talked the Dutch uncle to himself as he took deep breaths
of the dusty evening air of the city streets — , that there wasn't
time to go back to the hotel before meeting Nick. Bawling
himself out for talking so much (not only a nobody but a
blabmouthed nobody) he searched up and down grimywin-
dowed streets west of Eighth Avenue till he found a scuffed
door that bore the right number. He knocked and immediately an eye appeared, looking at him through a slot in the
panel. Then the door opened and a grimy little waiter led him
without a word down steps into a basement room that smelt of
garlic cooking in oil where Nick greeted him, sitting broad
and bearded, pouring out wine from a gigantic fiasco for a
ring of people at a round table.

"Well it's a small world," said a familiar voice. Hall Bryant
was sitting beside Anne Comfort Welsh with Carl Humphries,
still looking as if his skeleton were too big for his skin, on the
other side of her, the way they had sat at La Belle Péniche the
first time Jay met them. "Hall, I thought you were still in
Constant'," Jay said. "How are you?"

He shook hands all around.

"Greetings Comrade Pignatelli," said Humphries emphasizing each word.

"Isn't this wonderful?" sang Anne giving him a smile that lit up her whole face.

"One of my boys, Joe Gesso," said Nick, pointing to a baby-faced young man with white piping on the edge of his vest, "and thees ees beeutiful Esther Baker." Esther Baker was a scrawny redhaired woman who would have been beautiful, thought Jay, if she hadn't bad teeth and a disagreeable expression.

"Jay, it seems to be my function to set you up in jobs," said Hall in his most patronizing tone. "But this is bigger than M.E.R., bigger. . . ."

"Hey Joe, bicchieri," said Nick pointing the winebottle in Jay's direction.

"No thank you," said Jay.

"ou don't mean that you've come home a lawabiding citizen," teased Hall.

Nick paid no attention. He poured the wine anyway. "First I tell you story so you know what all about," he began. "Eet ees story of good man . . . caught in a trap . . . Many years now lives in Chicago a cigarmaker, Mat Sabatini, oldfashioned intellettuale of the working class. You know always cigarmakers read. In the factories, in the early unions, they pay, out of their own pocket, a reader; 'ee read while they work . . . Sabatini is reader of Kropotkin, Thoreau, Tolstoy, anarchist but philosophical . . . not like me . . . azione diretta." Nick tapped with his fingers on his broad chest and cleared his throat with some violence. "Dunque, this good old man has a son, young man who makes very brilliant in chimica. Write article for my paper *Il Falche,* always I 'ave science rapportage . . . working class must learn scienza, 'eestoria, new discoveries. Professor say he must go to college . . . borsa di studio . . . Naturally 'ee breeng 'ome books on chimica, all sorta instrument, testtube, retort, what do I know? Boy wants make ee's own laboratorio. You understand? Dunque sei mese fa labor trouble in construction of oredock at Indiana Harbor, strike, breeng in scabs, picketlines, every day fight, one day bomb . . . Keel two or three scabs — good reeddence maybe — Afterwards I explain connection with Mesabi Range strike. Iron ore. Indiana police dumb fellow. 'Ee don't know who to arrest . . . So they find one or two poor Italian man and they arrest him. In pocket they find my paper, *Il Falche,* and article on chimica, name Sabatini. One detective very clever say this tell how to make bomb, go over to Chi and find other even more clever detective an' they find who wrote article son of an anarchist. They talk to old man first. Old man 'ee afraid young man meex up with some kind azione diretta, give some fellow formula for explosive, so he tell lie and then they get son separate an' he tell trut'. They make different stories so they arrest old Mat and Leopardi both innocent and extradite to Indiana an' all around repressione. Everybody crazy. Tink every poor wop trow bomb. Now prosecution attorney t'ink he can convict 'eem of murder an' be beeg shot, go to Congress."

"It's the most outrageous thing," broke in Anne Welsh.

"American capitalism," Carl Humphries summed up in a deep selfsatisfied voice, "has entered its final phase of brutal and direct repression of the working class."

"The workers will fight back." Esther Baker banged her fist on the edge of the table.

" 'Ere tonight," Nick went on, "we have representative of working class committee . . . Esther, Socialist, textiles; Carl, Communist, steel workers; Joe, cooks, dishwashers and restaurant workers, very activist union. My boys, eh?" he leaned over and gave Joe Gesso a slap on the back. "Annie for garment workers an' our frien' Meester Bryant, 'ee make publicity in capitalist press . . . In Chicago my boys they hire lawyer named Mulvaney, all the time 'ee want money. We t'ink maybe beeg crook. Sodenly I t'ink to myself Nick 'ow about your little cugino, zio Jim's boy Jay, rich man 'umanitarian, man of the world, maybe 'ee 'elp."

"We've given you a pretty thorough going over, Jay," said Hall, "since your name first came up. I said you were impractical as hell but I gave you a clean bill of health."

"I don't quite understand what I could do," said Jay.

"You're undoubtedly on your way home to Chicago," said Hall in an impatient tone. "You go around and see Mulvaney . . . You know the intellectual playboy wants to spend his father's money in a good cause . . . People are attracted to you at first Jay, until they find you're a phony Galahad underneath," he added in a hissing whisper under his breath.

"You'll be crucified as every honest man who has stood up for civil liberties has been crucified in that town," interrupted Humphries. "I ought to know. I worked there for years. But you will have deserved well of the working class."

"And maybe if we raise enough money," said Anne, her face breaking into wrinkled smiles, "we can associate you with Mulvaney in the defense or if he turns out a bad egg" — she wrinkled up her little turnedup nose as if she'd smelled one — "you might take over."

"A young lawyer 'ee can make riputazione if 'ee save innocent man," said Nick. He burst out laughing. "Next time 'ee save beeg crook, make plenty money." The grimy little waiter breathing heavily at every step, advanced into the room with a great oval dish of spaghetti. "Ah, pasta asciutta," roared Nick. "Now we eat. Afterwards for Jay I explain Mesabi Range. 'Ee must learn 'eestory of workingclass movement."

"I don't see that it would do any harm to go around and see this guy," said Jay.

"Benissimo," said Nick filling his big mouth with a wad of spaghetti wound between a spoon and a fork.

It was from that moment, Jay remembered when he thought back to it, that his life had become entangled with the Sabatini case.

Before he left on the slow train — because he didn't have enough cash left to take the fast one — for Chicago he called up Dr. Wilton. "False alarm," the doctor said bitterly. "Now don't you feel cheap? There may have been some slight infection but not the type we mentioned. The slides are one hundred per cent negative . . . So go thou and sin no more." The doctor let out a dry cackle that rasped in Jay's earpiece. "Tell Jed to bring you around for cocktails sometime . . . I want to know how far you get with your plans to save the world."

Looking out at the Hudson Valley from his pullman, Jay got to wondering how he would describe it to Honorine. Maybe he could say it still had a little of the excitement of the old Dutchman's search for the Northwest Passage. How silly New Yorkers were, Dandy used to cry out, not to glory in their magnificent river that made the Rhine look like a brook. Jay took advantage of the wait in the Buffalo station to write Honorine a long letter at the desk in the clubcar . . . Revenant en Amérique, he wrote, I always feel a little of the intoxication of the early discoverers. That's the feeling of anticipation of a dazzling future mixed with the frustration of the present. D'ailleurs chez nous c'est un moment de grande lutte politique between the reactionaries headed by the feudal barons of business and the downtrodden radicals who are defending civil liberties, the working man's right to organize unions, society's right to invent new forms. There are moments in every man's life when, just as if you happened to be on the street when someone was hurt in an accident, you have to do what you can to help. That's why I'm suddenly excited about being a lawyer. A lawyer is a sort of vulture who profits by other people's misfortunes, but at the same time he can be a defender of the civic processes that our liberties depend on. Le mot liberté me monte à la tête comme l'alcool. Cette affaire Sabatini is just a question of finding out the truth and insisting on it. It ought to be simple enough. It ought to give me something to get my teeth into while I'm trying to find my footing in the world. I often wonder what you would think of it over here. Chez nous c'est la vie crue, our life is raw, it hasn't the patina of Paris, but it's fun. J'aurais des contes drolatiques à vous raconter . . . Parlez-moi de musique, it's music I think I miss most . . . Bonjour à Augustin et à Madame Bibi." That night he crawled into his upper feeling that writing Honorine had somehow rounded off his glimpse of New York in his mind. He stretched his legs out under the sheets feeling whole and well, somehow satisfied with his first week home in his own country. He went peacefully to sleep in the jouncing and rumbling of the train.

Threading through the crowd in the Chicago depot next day he caught himself looking for Bill Keezer's drooping mustache, of course he wasn't there; Jay hadn't let anybody know. When Jay reached Luke on the phone the first thing Luke said in his chill scornful voice was: "So you've turned out an idealist." He added that Jay would have to go to a hotel because Wharton Place was sold. Then almost cordially he invited him to lunch. "Pick Joe and me up at the office . . . We want to talk to you. We'll kill the fatted calf."

Good old Joe Mortlake, thought Jay remembering breakfast at the Crillon. He'd get along with Mortlake; now that he was a grown man instead of an embarrassed hobbledehoy he'd even find ways of kidding Luke. Even Luke must have a little fun lurking in him somewhere.

When he came out of the elevator in the Merchants' Building he waved cheerfully as he caught sight of Mortlake's long undertaker face through an open door. He strode in past the receptionist's desk and the girl's startled face, taking in, out of the corner of an eye, the redecoration of the lobby and noting that Dandy's portrait had a new and more modest frame and that the light had been taken off it. Mortlake and Luke looked up frowning to see him barge in unannounced. They squared their shoulders a little as they got to their feet, as if they were saying to themselves, Now we're in for it. Mortlake wore a blue pinstripe business suit and Luke, whose pale dome seemed taller and barer than ever, was in a symphony of caramel browns. "Welcome stranger." The words turned heavily in Mortlake's mouth. He reached for Jay's hand and gave it a jerk. Luke's cold fingers felt unusually limp.

Luke leaned back in his mahogany armchair and adjusted the shellrimmed pincenez on his nose and looked Jay up and down. "Jay," he said spacing his words, "it doesn't work. Men aren't made that way. You may be able to take everything away from the rich and distribute it to the poor, but the poor won't be able to hold on to it . . . Well you've turned up at last. Now we'll be able to get your signature on the deed to the house. The purchasers were almost ready to suspend their payments."

"How are the girls?" asked Jay, turning a little red at the thought that he could never quite get around to speaking of them as his sisters.

"Fine as silk," said Luke.

"How's the estate?"

"All work and no play," said Luke.

"It killed poor old Bill," growled Mortlake solemnly.

"Bill Keezer," exclaimed Jay getting to his feet. "I didn't know he was dead."

"Cerebral hemorrhage . . . I sent ten dollars' worth of flowers in your name," said Luke. "Don't be surprised if you find the item in our account. In cases where some immediate expenditure had to be made I haven't hesitated to make it."

"That's quite all right," said Jay. In a flash he saw inside his head the savage old guttersnipe with his stained yellow mustache lying in a casket banked with lilies. He'd never known before how fond he was of old Bill Keezer. He cleared his throat. "Could the estate raise me any money? I'll have to have enough to live on till I get to practicing."

Luke raised his eyebrows. "That I can't promise," he said. "The sums collected from the sale of real property have gone to pay debts. I could advance you two or three thousand dollars, secured by your interest, until we reach a settlement. That shouldn't take too long now. The court appointed Mary O'Higgins in Bill's place."

"Luke, that's very nice of you," drawled Jay.

"Even an idealist needs money," Luke said without smiling. "Interest will be at the same rate as before. They are glad enough to pay it down in Texas."

"By the way Luke," said Jay, his voice drawling almost to a standstill. "Tell me about Nick Pignatelli. Isn't he the son of our Uncle Joseph?"

Luke let the chin fall against the wings of his starched collar. The lines from the flanges of his nostrils to the ends of his mouth became hard and deep. "In my opinion the man is an impostor. . . . He'll probably blackmail us one of these days. I'd like to see him try."

"I thought I noticed a family resemblance," said Jay teasingly.

"Uncle Joe went back to Italy. I never saw him." Luke's voice shook. His chin was trembling. Even his lips were pale.

"Suppose we move along to lunch," Mortlake began to coax.

Within a sort of distant interest Jay watched the clenching of his cousin's little fists inside the starched cuffs as he struggled to get his voice under control. "The name's fairly common," Luke said at last, trying to clear the husk out of his throat. "There are noble families in Rome who have the same name."

They ate at the Lawyer's Club. Luke lashed himself into a kind of frenzy as he studied the menu card. "We must kill the fatted calf for the prodigal," he said several times between clenched teeth, giving Jay a look as if he'd like to see his throat cut instead of the calf's. He ordered Manhattan cocktails and Bluepoint oysters and broiled whitefish and hashed brown potatoes and Asti Spumante. "It is Cousin Nick," Jay whispered happily as he put down his third Manhattan, "who is giving me my first case. He wants me to help defend an old Italian who's being framed by the police."

"I might have known it . . . The Sabatini case," groaned

Luke. "Every crackpot in the country is putting in his two cents' worth . . . If he was innocent, why did the man have to perjure himself? Answer me that."

"Luke, I don't know enough about the case yet to argue about it."

"And you never will if you run with that crowd. They'll tell you black's white and white's black."

Mortlake's deep voice started to rattle in his throat. "After all, Luke," he said, "it's a good experience for a young lawyer to take up an unpopular cause. We are very much pleased Jay to see you branching out on your own. We feel you'll rise much faster in the profession if you keep away from our stuffy old firm until you get on your own feet."

"For a while . . . for a while," said Luke hastily. "That in my opinion, Jay, was the real meaning of that oddly worded phrase in your father's will. I think he intended for you to win your spurs on your own the way he did."

"Luke," said Jay, throwing his head back and laughing, "I haven't any intention of sticking my nose in where I'm not wanted." All at once he felt quite at ease. The cat was out of the bag, he told himself.

"My dear fellow, it's not that," boomed Joe Mortlake. Luke hastily ordered another half bottle of wine. "We are going to assist you in every conceivable way with introductions, putting you up to clubs, the Bar Associations and so forth."

"The day will come," said Luke looking up at the chandelier over their heads, "when there will again be two Pignatellis in the office of Pignatelli and Miller." His eyes glistened behind his glasses. He lifted his wine and looked across it into Jay's face. "Jay a happy homecoming," he croaked, "and a brilliant career."

After lunch they had brandy and were very jolly going back to the office where Mary O'Higgins had laid out a lot of jolly old documents in blue jackets that everybody signed, deeds, releases, all sorts of jolly old documents in connection with the estate. "Let's do things up brown," said Luke rubbing together the small ivory hands that peeped out between his starched cuffs. "The time to polish off business," Jay kept announcing, "is after a good lunch." He'd misjudged Luke, he was telling himself. There was another side to Luke. Mortlake was feeling so good he put on a little juggling act with the signed documents. "Well I declare," said Mary O'Higgins looking from one to the other, the eyes in her weary lined face round as O's from astonishment. Mortlake was singing: *Nobody cares if the landlord swears, Nobody cares if they fall downstairs.*

When they got ready to go Jay shook hands all around several times. He thanked Luke profusely for the lunch, for the loan, for the appointment with the secretary of the Bar Association. Next time, he insisted, the lunch would be on him. Going down in the elevator he felt in a warm glow from the food and the drink and from a certain radiation out of Luke's check for two thousand iron men folded snugly into his wallet. It wasn't until he had walked several times round the block, to see if the raw spring wind off the lake wouldn't blow some of the fumes out of his head before he looked in on Mulvaney, whose office was all too near, that he began to try to remember just what the jolly old documents he'd put his name to had said. No time to think about that now. His job right now was to dig into the Sabatini case.

The elevator in the dingy office building had a strange smell of castoroil. The elevatorman, obviously the furnaceman too, had a bleached look, as if he hadn't been outdoors for months. The dark halls upstairs were gritty underfoot. When Jay knocked on a groundglass door, a stocky man with a gray square face, a prominent jaw and gray hair rather long over the ears opened immediately.

"You are Pignatelli," he said, "I'm Mulvaney," and ushered him into his small office lined from floor to ceiling with shelves stacked with papers curling and yellow with age. "Sit down," he went on in a threatening tone and pointed to a chair encumbered by several volumes of Bouvier. He let out a sigh as he himself settled back into the worn armchair behind his roll-top desk. Jay stooped to take the books off his chair. "All right set them on the floor," Mulvaney said rudely. When Jay turned around to sit he found Mulvaney pointing the trembling fore-finger at him in the manner of a prosecuting attorney about to put a witness on the hot seat. "So they've sent you out to check up on me. I am ready to be interrogated."

"It's not that Mr. Mulvaney," said Jay. "The Defense Committee is trying to broaden the base; that's how they explained it to me."

Jay couldn't help wriggling a little in his chair as he felt Mulvaney's large glassy gray eyes searching his face. "We've met before," he said frowning. "No don't prompt me. Of course I know who your father was, but this is different. I associate your name and face with something pleasant . . . It's a pretty face. It's the face of Polly MacManus, God bless her warm little heart."

Jay began to laugh. "You were the one who played the bag-pipes. I thought you were a poet. It was at a party at Gordon Hyde's. Lord that was years ago."

"It was before the Easter Rebellion."

"Did Polly tell you how I ran out of money and couldn't pay the cab when I took her home?"

"Poverty has never been esteemed a crime in my family."

"That was a lovely summer," drawled Jay, thinking: The summer of pretty girls . . . "Tell me what's happened to her?"

"She married some damn Jew peddler and has three lovely children. He's not actually a peddler. He owns a department store; it's the same thing so far as I am concerned," Mulvaney said laughing heartily at his own words. The accusing mask had melted off his face. "She'd been better off if she married me even if I didn't have his money," he added in an innocent and confiding tone.

"Gosh she was an attractive girl," said Jay . . . This guy's out of *Ulysses,* he was thinking, it's a good thing I know my Joyce.

"Well I guess we won't quarrel too much." Mulvaney got to his feet and slapped Jay on the shoulder. "The best way I can introduce you to the case is to take you down to see the old man. They let me see him anytime. The warden is a true Christian man."

By the time they got off the local train at the smokedup station amid a steaming grove of tall stacks of steel mills Jay and Brian Mulvaney were calling each other by their first names and arguing about the change in Yeats' poetic style. The warden, another addict of "The Wearing of the Green," was just about to close up his office for the evening, but after some whispering and headshaking with Brian about a moneyraising campaign for the Irish Republican Army they were both involved in, he turned over his desk to them for a conference with their clients.

From the moment the chubbyfaced turnkey pushed the two Sabatinis into the room and sat down ponderously outside the door, it was old Mat Sabatini who played host, quietly and unobtrusively but with authority. He had white hair and blue eyes and copious white mustaches and a mild and amused way of talking. They couldn't get him to say a word about himself: "I am a fatalistic philosopher, my life is finished. It does not matter," he explained gently, "but Leo, he has a future."

Leo looked hard into Jay's face and shook his head. He was a thin young man, younger than Jay, with large sunken brown eyes and rumpled brown hair and a twitchy manner. He kept scratching with a cigarettestained fingernail at a grease spot on his trouserleg. There, immediately thought Jay, but for the grace of God go I.

During the hour they sat in the overheated office, talking in low voices, Jay had the helpless feeling of trying to swim through dense tangling waterweeds. The question he had promised himself he'd ask Leo Sabatini: did he or did he not make the bomb? stayed on his lips unasked. Every time he got ready to ask it there rose to his mind a distorted half forgotten picture of Pilate in purple asking: What is the truth?

Mulvaney wasn't much help. The moment he started talking about legal matters his face took on the resentful wooden mask it had worn when Jay first barged into his office. Every time he got the conversation round to the facts of the case Brian switched it deftly to technicalities of the defense or to the pressing problem of bail.

Old Mat seemed to have guessed what Jay was thinking. "Philosophically speaking," he said, when the lawyers rose to their feet to leave, "I may be guilty. . . . The boy, no, he has the mind of a technician. The technician is the instrument. He cannot be guilty, but I, though as you know I do not believe in taking human life even in a good cause, I may have been carried away by my sympathy with these poor fellows, maybe I spoke too warmly to them to resist, to make good union . . . Evviva la libertà," he added apologetically and parodied the gesture of a soapbox orator.

"So long as the prosecution can't produce the man who placed the bomb there is no chain of evidence," said Mulvaney severely.

"What about the two strikers they are holding?" asked Jay.

"Dolci and Ferrara. They know nothing. They no want trouble. They stay home that day." Old Sabatini shrugged his shoulders.

"Who's representing them?"

"A local lawyer," explained Brian hastily. "We'll call him up when we leave here. He's no bargain. You'll see. What we want to do is get the bail reduced to a decent figure. Twenty-five thousand dollars is an outrageous sum. We want you back in your own home, Mr. Sabatini . . . There's always a presumption of guilt when a man's in jail."

Mat Sabatini shrugged his shoulders and looked with his indulgent questioning smile from one face to another, with the expression of an old teacher about to give his pupils a half-holiday.

"We shall see," he said.

"They'll never leave us go." Leo spoke without raising his voice. The lines deepened in his hollow cheeks.

Walking through the town along a glary thoroughfare Jay still felt the tightening of his throat when he had shaken hands in parting with the Sabatinis. They were in jail and he was free. Mingled with the physical discomfort of compassion was a fierce irrepressible exaltation: he could go anywhere he wanted to down the bustling street in the sharp wind that had a bitter-sweet flavor of spring. They were behind bars. "Lord I'm not good at this," he said shaking his head as they slid into a booth in a Chinese restaurant.

"If you will excuse the simile," said Brian, "you remind me of a medical student the first time he uses the knife on a live patient . . . When you have practiced as long as I have you will learn that a man has to wear his professional shell. I would have broken my heart long ago without it . . . You had better go back to New York to explain personally to that defense committee that they must immediately find someone to put up bail. The regular bonding companies won't touch a radical. I'll guarantee to get the bail lowered to a more reasonable figure. It will cost money to prepare the defense, a great deal of money. Taking the case at all is a sacrifice for me."

With their chow mein appeared at their table a pimplyfaced young man with dogmatic wooden gestures. Brian drily introduced his colleague Ed Perkins who was defending Dolci and Ferrara. No thanks he'd eaten, always ate at six, Ed Perkins said. Couldn't understand these stupid wops. Might every one be guilty for all he knew. Bob Dowling was willing to be reasonable. All he wanted was one conviction as an example to these damned agitators.

Brian Mulvaney gave Jay a poke with his elbow. "Mr. Dowling," he said, "is the very ambitious State's attorney in this part of the world. A very able gentleman. He wants to run for Congress or am I wrong, Ed?"

"If the slightest democratic groundswell sets up he'll be elected." Ed Perkins nodded wisely and lit a cigarette. "He just about up and told me that if he could pin it on young Sabatini he'd be willing to nolle prosse the old man and let these poor working stiffs off with a light sentence. 'He's a working stiff himself,' he says. He wants to get at the agitators who are stirring up the trouble. He wants Sabatini to fry."

The phrase had buzzed in Jay's head like a fly on the windowpane all through the next week during the meetings of the Defense Committee in New York. He hadn't smoked since he got out of the army but now he sat lighting one cigarette from another, numb with the strangling diversities of interest that arose beween even wellintentioned people when you tried to turn talk into action. There never seemed to be enough air in any of the rooms where the committee met. After the long wrangling sessions he would go back to the Murray Hill to bed, feeling that all the life had been sucked out of him.

The only fun was the couple of times he went out to dinner with Nick and ate too much pasta and drank too much wine while various shabby characters with glittering eyes, Nick's boys, joined them one after another, sitting on the edge of their chairs rattling off in rapid Italian dialects Jay couldn't keep up with, accounts of mysterious struggles. When they were alone Nick in his Italianate English that never seemed to improve would explain workingclass politics. "The workingclass strewggle is like school . . . only intelligent scholars understand. The strewggle is like great beast, carry many deeferent kinda parasite . . . Some like babyface Joe Gesso," he lowered his voice, "real gangster, some like 'Omfries politeecian want only power, some nice woman sobseester, all 'art and no 'ead, some like that newspaper fellow Bryant omosessuale who teenk all working class pretty boy, what you say, poonk?" He laughed and made brushing motions with his big hand in front of his face, "But all these can serve purpose. Can be eenstrument."

"Old Sabatini was interesting about that. He said his son couldn't be guilty because a technician was only an instrument."

"Ecco! Sabatini wit' a leetle better education would be famous professor. But we must be careful of professor. 'Ee make confusing. That ees why I say direct action. Then I know who honest man, who brave fighter, who codardo."

"I don't know about the rest of it Nick," Jay said, "but I do know we've got to win this case. I look at it differently. It's a citizen's duty to see the laws work fairly. A frameup cuts at the roots."

"Cittadino! Nè italiano nè americano, nè l'uno nè l'altro, sporcamadonna," Nick roared and tapped himself on the chest. "Ceetizen of 'ooman race."

Before Jay knew what had happened he had told the defense committee he'd work without fee. They only had to handle his expenses. But he kept losing touch of his disbursements and forgetting to note them down. In his spare time he went around helping collect money for the defense. Jed Morris took fire with the notion right away and said that though he was broke himself he'd shake down his prosperous friends. He took Jay around to have a drink with Dr. Wilton. Jay described the Riviera, French and Italian, town by town from Cassis to Savona, and took ten dollars off the doctor while he was still in a daze of azure and olivegroves.

Afterwards they went to the Hobarts' for cocktails. A colored maid in a uniform ushered them into a large parlor with low buff sofas and salmoncolored draperies. A grand piano painted lavender decorated with little scenes copied from Watteau filled one end of the room. After they had sat there smoking for a while a tall dark dyspecticlooking man strode into the room. He stopped in his tracks when he saw them. Jay felt the black eyes boring into his face like an augerbit. "Hello Jed," the man said. "You must excuse me." He turned sharply and went out the way he came. "That's friend husband," said Jed and made a face. Jay thought he was going to thumb his nose at the door through which Fred Hobart had gone out, but instead he burst out laughing and turned to Jay and said in a mock confidential tone, "Husbands are my most valuable allies . . . I'd always be in hot water if it weren't for husbands."

There was a tinkling sound and Molly Hobart came in carrying a tray with a cocktail shaker and glasses. "Poor Fred's got to go to Kansas City so he can't dine with us, but I made him make the cocktails because he makes such good martinis," she was saying in a giggly girlish voice. When Jay shook her hand a little flavor of sandalwood came away on his. She had a boll of very blond hair and lightblue eyes and a look of marshmallow softness under her drooping pale purplish dress. "You brute," she said to Jed in a tone only half kidding, "I don't know why I give you a cocktail . . . You have most disagreeable friends. Mr. Pignatelli . . . I've heard so much about you that I'm going to call you Jay right away. Everybody says Jay."

"Oh Molly you know me," said Jed standing up in front of his chair with the expression of a child waiting to be kissed and forgiven.

"I know you altogether too well, Mr. Morris."

She brushed past him and took Jay the first cocktail. "Now tell me a little about the Sabatini case . . . Not too much because things like that make me cry. They really do . . . I'm quite rich this afternoon because Fred just did very well on the stock exchange with some stock that was all in my name . . . Oh I shouldn't have said that should I? Jed'll try to take it all away from me."

She plunked down at the desk and wrote them a pretty little sandalwoodscented check for a thousand dollars, before the cocktails got her fuzzed, she explained giggling. Then she went to the piano. "You see," she looked up into Jay's face blinking her pale lashes. "If I drink I can't sing, so I sing first and drink afterwards . . . I've just learned this." Her broad fingers were sure on the keys. Without notes, sitting up primly and modestly like a little girl taking her music lesson, she sang "Love Oh Careless Love" in a small sweet accurate voice. "How's that, Jed?" she asked, turning towards him on the piano stool.

"Lovely . . . I ought to write a musical comedy for you."

"And to think I worked five years trying to be a Valkyrie!" She jumped up. "Whoops," she said and swallowed half a martini at a gulp. "Now where shall we go for dinner?"

After dinner Molly took them to the Follies. They laughed and clapped and giggled and carried on like highschool kids. When Jay got back to his hotel room he took the little check out of his wallet and looked at it to make sure his eyes hadn't deceived him. The scent of sandalwood came from it but what he remembered was the scent of Molly's frizzly boll of blond hair. Remembering made him dizzy. God he couldn't go to bed. Tired as he was he tied his necktie again and pulled on his jacket and went out. He walked west through rowdy groups of after the theatre speakeasy patrons; then he walked north to the park, brushing past panhandlers on Fiftyninth; with aching feet he walked and walked. At last he said to himself why not. It wouldn't hurt if he just walked past her house. Park Avenue that he'd always hated had become suddenly a glorious boulevard. Cars and cabs carrying mysterious couples on errands of love glittered like mechanical toys in a toyshop window. The strings of lights converged in the distance uptown as refulgent as tulips in a flowershop. He counted the stories till he found the Hobarts' corner apartment. The lights were out. She must be asleep. Alone. He knew Jed hadn't gone home with her, because Jed had run off downtown, to work he claimed, right after the show, and it had been Jay who'd taken her home in a cab. His arm still tingled with the feel of her arm beneath the fur cape beside him. Or was there some waspwaisted dude in a silk hat with a latchkey? The night was cold. He began to shiver standing there on the corner looking up at the heavy-looking square building. A cop on the beat gave him a suspicious once over as he passed. Thrashing his arms to warm them Jay started down the avenue, taking as long strides as he could. When he got back to his room he took a hot bath and read himself to sleep over a stale copy of the *Smart Set*.

When he woke up her light sandalwood fragrance was still in his nostrils. It was late, he had engagements, a man to meet downtown. The morning passed in a scramble. By twelve o'clock he couldn't stand it any longer. He sneaked out of the office of the liberal weekly where the defense committee was meeting and went down to the corner drugstore to phone. Of course she'd be out. His hand that held the receiver was cold and shaky. There was the maid's voice then hers, Molly's. Jay blurted out something about having enjoyed the show and wouldn't she come out to dinner with him tonight. She had, she said, a sort of an engagement. "I knew you would. I have to go to Chicago tomorrow or next day." Well, Molly's voice tinkled like bells, why shouldn't she change her engagement to next week? It was just her accompanist and some musical people. "Where can we meet?" Jay asked hoarsely.

"My place at five or a little after."

He never knew how he spent the afternoon. It seemed weeks before five o'clock came. She opened the door for him herself, maid's day out she said, and gave him a questioning sort of a smile. It was the same blond sandalwood scent. She wore the same dress. Jay strode up and down the parlor stumbling over the white Moroccan rugs while she went rummaging after an imperial quart of very special Scotch some client had sent Fred. Poor Fred he'd loved good Scotch till he got stomach ulcers and couldn't drink. When she'd poured them each a good stiff drink she sat down at the piano and began to sing some new Milhaud songs, now and then stopping to look up at Jay with her schoolgirl expression to ask him the proper pronunciation of a word. "I always sing Twang instead of toi," she said ruefully. "Toi," he said looking down into her light eyes. He leaned over and kissed her lips. Her lips felt warm and strong under his. She was kissing him back.

"My my my," she said getting to her feet. "Molly don't lose your head!"

They sat down side by side on the couch. He had hold of one of her square pianist's hands. His heart was beating crazily hard.

"It's Jed makes me act like this. He's really cruel and mean but he's so funny. I'm not going to see him again . . . maybe never."

"I don't care," shouted Jay. "I don't care about anything." She was lying back on the sofapillow with her lips pouted up towards his. Her face under his had a strange drowning look. As they sat tangled together on the couch, kissing between gulps of Scotch whisky their clothes began to be in the way. They went into the bedroom to take them off. Her body seemed lovelier than anything he had ever touched.

"Jay," she said when she came back from the bathroom wearing a clean slip, "isn't it nice now that the preliminaries are over."

She sat down beside him and gave him little kisses round the edges of his ears.

"It's wonderful."

"You're a Jim dandy do you know it Jay?" She went to the dressingtable to straighten her hair. "I guess I'm a very naughty girl, but I can't help it."

"Don't scold my Molly."

"Let's go to that Italian place the opera singers go to. I'm hungry."

"I feel wonderful," said Jay.

When they dressed and went out Park Avenue wore an air of architectural splendor like a scene in grand opera. Under his worn tweed suit baggy at the knees Jay felt handsome as the Hermes of Praxiteles. Molly beside him in the prancing cab felt solid and serene as the Milo Venus. They were hungry but they were in no hurry to get to their dinner. They were delighted with the trafficjams. They went on kissing shamelessly while across the avenue cars moving uptown streamed

past them gay as a circus parade. Time stood still for them
while the city whirled by as if they were the calliope in the
center of a merrygoround.

They ate veal cutlets with fried eggs and anchovies on them
and spinach and zucchini fried crisp. Jay kept crying out that
he'd never enjoyed a meal so much. "Isn't it fun to eat?"
whispered Molly. "It's one of the things I ought not to do."
They had salad and cheese and spumoni and napoleons and
coffee in a glass. By that time they'd decided they had better
not drink any more of those daiquiris, the Scotch was much
healthier, so they drove in another cab back up a quiet and
empty Park Avenue and the gilded elevator wafted them up to
the apartment. It was all Jay could do not to shake hands with
the obsequious elevator man. "You are most kind to take us
upstairs to bed," he imagined himself telling him. The moment the outside door closed on them they started to pull their
clothes off. In the middle of the night Molly woke him. "Jay
you'd better go back to the hotel now. I just thought what a
shock it would be to my nice Angy if she came in and found
us in bed."

Back at the Murray Hill Jay couldn't help humming as he
walked over the jaded carpet of the corridor to his room. He
went to bed so full of the taste and fragrance of her it was almost as if she were between the sheets with him at the hotel.

As Jay sat on the jouncing plush of the pullman on the
Twentieth Century, brooding over Mulvaney's folder on the
case, it became clearer and clearer to him that the real work
was still to do and that he was the one who had to do it.
Mulvaney might make a good appearance in court but in his
office he was a lazy bum. While he made notes outlining the
prosecution's case on a pad of yellow foolscap: Conspiracy?
Complicity before the fact? Eyewitness accounts of explosion,
his mind was full of little scenes changing and distant, like
tableaux seen from the back of the gallery at a theatre, in
which he and Molly appeared in affectionate attitudes against

various flowery backgrounds. In some of the scenes a third actor appeared, a towheaded blueeyed infant. He'd have to make it back to New York at the first possible moment to explain to Molly she'd have to divorce Fred.

Mulvaney greeted Jay like an old friend and cleared an armful of papers off a dusty desk for him. "This case offers some interesting problems," he said as he tucked the papers at random into empty places on the shelves. "After lunch you'll meet our associates, Franklin Stein a good little gradgrind and a little wop . . . excuse me Italian . . ." "No offense," interrupted Jay laughing . . . "named Vittorini who's out to pick the pockets of his fellownationals if you ask me, and of course there is our highschool friend Ed Perkins. The trouble with this whole business is that we are dealing with cranks, people with onetrack minds . . ."

Mulvaney tapped portentously on his desk with his pencil. "The prosecution won't get anywhere with the conspiracy count, I don't think . . . The murder count is their trump . . . if they can break down the alibis of Dolci and Ferrari."

"But how can they involve the Sabatinis then?"

"Accessory before the fact . . ." Mulvaney suddenly grabbed his head with both hands. "I can't get anywhere with these wops. Now if we had some good honest Irishmen I'd know what I was doing." Jay couldn't help laughing. Mulvaney's face was half amused and half peeved. Suddenly he jumped to his feet. "Jay I've got it. Let's try to get Croft associated with this thing."

"Elisha Croft . . . isn't he pretty much discredited?"

"A man with a heart of gold!"

"Let's go back to the case," said Jay.

They hadn't finished making up their list of alibi witnesses to check with Vittorini when Mulvaney announced it was time for lunch.

When they got back from another long lunch weeks later they found a young woman waiting for them at the office door. It was Hedda Gelber whom Jay had met at the New York meetings of the committee. She had long almondshaped black eyes and wore Balkan blouses and noisy silver bracelets. She addressed Jay as Comrade and said Comrade Humphries had sent her build a fire under the Chicago Committee. She immediately took charge of the office, dusting off the desks, straightening up the files, looking up references. Indeed she was a competent young woman. Everything that came up would send Brian off into long rambling ancedotes about Chicago, about his Irish relatives, about the republican army. Jay felt the afternoon was dissolving in conversation.

Every few minutes Brian went to the phone and tried a different number. Of course at his office they didn't know where Croft was. They never did. "Elisha is the real knight errant of the law," Brian would say as he hung up the receiver. "I've got to have his advice before I can go any further. Perhaps he might even consent to become associated with the defense . . . That would be a feather in our caps, eh Jay? Our pretty Hedda will be a help in that."

Hedda was sitting on his desk. He playfully patted her black silk knee.

She looked from one to the other with wide black eyes. "Oh Mister Mulvaney, what do you mean?"

"He's a weak mortal man like the rest of us but he'll wring tears from the most stonyhearted juror."

Finally when five o'clock came around and Jay had the feeling too much talk in a closed room always gave him of perishing for lack of oxygen, Hedda, who had taken over the telephone, located Elisha Croft at the Bar Library. Over the phone he seemed a little deaf because he couldn't seem to catch Brian Mulvaney's name. "At least he said he'd wait ten minutes," said Brian snatching up his hat and shoving it on his head so that his gray hair streamed over his forehead. He ran wildly back and forth across the street trying to flag a cab. Hedda intercepted one at the corner. They caught the great man just

as he was slipping out into the street. "Mr. Croft I beg just a moment of your attention," said Brian humbly.

Elisha Croft was a redhaired man with a long nose with a knob on the end and a very lined freckled pendulous face. He wore a baggy reddish tweed suit and carried a heavy cane. "So you're the voice on the phone," he drawled in a deep slow voice. "I thought I'd given you the slip but let's go in and sit down . . . Not *Miss* Gelber? Too bad that so much charm should already be consigned to a single address . . . Pignatelli." He placed a big soft hand on Jay's shoulder as he pushed him ahead of him through the revolving door . . . "Old Jim's boy?" Jay nodded. "When I was a very young man I was associated with your father in a case . . . one of his rare conscience cases as he called them. He pretended to be a cynic about the goodness of man but I doubt if he was even really sceptical. He shied off from causes but he was always putting his hand in his pockets to help some fellow out of luck . . . And what deep pockets they were, extending into the treasuries of half the railroads in the country . . . I bet he died a poor man." Jay nodded again. "And he used to tell me not to let my heart run away with my head."

They settled round a table in a little dark reception room. Elisha Croft sat on the sofa with Hedda Gelber beside him and cupped his big pallid hand behind his ear while Brian, whose face had hardened into hard peevish lines while Jay was occupying the center of the stage, began to tell the Sabatini story. "Are they guilty or innocent?" asked Croft halfway through.

Mulvaney launched into a charge to the jury.

"You're not answering my question."

Mulvaney's face broke in pieces as if he were going to cry.

"I don't say not to defend them," said Croft kindly, "even if they are guilty, but a good advocate should never deceive himself . . . That's how I came to grief myself once . . . A lawyer's business — " all the lines on his freckled face curled into lines of mischief until it was like the face of a small boy about to lob a snowball through a window — "is to deceive the jury . . . and sometimes the judge."

Suddenly a look of pain and fatigue seemed to weigh him down until his face was all sagging lines again. Jay was thinking that he looked like a tired and compassionate old elephant. He found the gray somewhat bloodshot eyes fixed on his face.

Elisha Croft was talking to him directly. "The thing for you to do Jay is to get up the facts of the case . . . Go around and find 'em out. Go to their homes, talk to their friends. This is a case that will be tried in the press and on the lecture platform. You'll find yourself pushing a great stone up a hill weighted down with the inertia of prejudice and ignorance . . . You'll find it a backbreaking job. When you have the facts I'll look them over, but make sure they are accurate. Meanwhile if you can induce your committee to publish a résumé of the facts in a pamphlet with which you will have no visible connection it will be all to the good. You may be even quite horrified as a good lawyer should when a case is taken out of the starchamber where lawyers thrive and tried in the courts of public opinion where people still have some inkling of right and wrong." His voice had become slower and slower as if the world wearied him immeasurably. He yawned. "You must excuse me now. I've got to go home." He got heavily to his feet, patted Hedda's smiling cheek as she sat looking prayerfully up into his face and walked out leaning on his cane as he went.

Brian sighed. His eyes rolled. "A great man," he said, "too bad he has the manners of a boor."

Jay passed on the great man's suggestion to the Defense Committee and before very long he managed to be headed east on the Twentieth Century again, at his own expense this time, to see if he couldn't talk Tad Skinner into writing the pamphlet and illustrating it. He found Tad at his drawing board in the middle of the rattle and confusion of the newspaper office looking halfstarved and more stoopshouldered than usual and hustled him down the elevator and into a downtown speakeasy in a basement on a narrow street that sloped towards

Brooklyn Bridge. As they sat down at a table with a stained tablecloth in a dark alcove Tad turned on him angrily and said, "Now tell me what's he got that I haven't got?"

Tad's eyelids were rimmed with red. His face was smudged. His shirt was dirty. He looked ludicrously miserable.

"What's the trouble Tad, for gosh sakes?"

"I might as well tell you," Tad downed his whiskey hungrily and ordered another. "You mean you don't know? I thought everybody in the world knew."

"I don't know anything except Sabatini defense."

Tad lifted his second drink, looked at it with disgust and set it down again on the table before him. "You know I'm no virgin and I didn't expect her to be one. But I won't take her back. Not after Joseph Emmanuel D. — What the hell does the D. stand for? — Morris. I love the bastard too, he's one of my best friends. Oh God I never felt so horrible in my life."

"You mean Sweetness and Light?"

"She's fallen for him like a ton of bricks."

Jay took a deep breath. "Well Tad," he said, "there are bigger fish in the sea than ever came out of it." Then he hurried into his story. "I want you to come out to Chicago to do a pamphlet on the Sabatinis. I'll get up the facts. You do the drawings and text. Tell 'em on the paper you've got to be sick for two weeks."

"It's always been a question in my mind whether a man had a right to take his own life," Tad was saying.

Jay drank part of his whisky and looked straight in Tad's face. "Bullshit, Tad . . . Everybody goes through moments when their life isn't worth anything to them. That's the time to use it up in a good cause. Half the time I'm sick of my little old life . . . No I'm not." He thought of Molly and grinned.

"When do we go?" asked Tad.

"Where?" asked Jay still thinking of Molly.

"To Chicago, you fool. I've got to have a few days to straighten things out here."

"Next week," Jay said. (Four more hours till Molly time,

he was thinking.) "That'll give you a chance to work out something with your editor," he said aloud.

Molly's voice had sounded a little doubtful over the phone when he called her from the station. "Five thirty at my place," she'd said. Wondering what it was she wasn't telling him Jay drudged through a long afternoon committee meeting. When people rose to go Nick drew him into a corner of the room. "Eata spaghett'?" "I have a date." "Pretty girl. Good. We Pignatellis, the wooman crowd us, no?" Jay felt himself grinning like an idiot. Nick grabbed his arm around the muscle. "Tomorrow same place seven o'clock." He pressed hard. "No forget."

"Oh you've been so long," said Molly when she opened the door for him. "Jay you've been away so long."

She was wearing a darkblue suit he'd never seen before with a matching hat shaped like a fireman's helmet that gave her face a hard look he didn't like. "It's always too long," he whispered as he drew her to him and nuzzled her neck. Her hair smelt of cigarettesmoke. He held her face away and looked at it. "Why you naughty girl you've been drinking."

She made a funny face. "We've been drinking," she said giggling. "All afternoon like little fishes, like enormous fishes. You've got to help me with Andy. It's rather embarrassing but he's passed out in the bathtub." She started to whimper childishly, "and the maid's here and Fred'll be coming any minute."

"Who's Andy?"

"You must know Andrew Collins. He's one of the world's best accompanists. He's not used to drinking. I'm so afraid he'll drown in the tub. He said it would sober him."

Jay found himself trying to pull a limp blond young man, long and pale as a wax bean, out of a tub of lukewarm water. His eyes were closed tight as a sleeping baby's. Jay tried lifting him under the shoulders but each time he slid back in. "I'll fix him," Jay said through clenched teeth and pulled the stopper of the tub out. Then he started dashing cold water in his face out of a glass. "Don't, don't," he moaned. Without opening his eyes he started feebly to stir.

Meanwhile Molly who was peeping in through the bathroom door, standing well back so as not to get splashed, began to laugh out loud. "The silliest looking pair," she spluttered, "I ever saw."

At last Jay got a towel draped over Andrew Collins and set him on the toilet seat. "Now put your clothes on," he said shaking him till his long blond head rocked from side to side. "We got to get you out of here."

After Jay had wiped himself off as best he could with a towel he found Molly standing in the middle of the livingroom smoking a cigarette. Her face was red and her eyes looked as if she had been crying. "Fred wants us all to clear out. He's got a most important client coming to dinner."

The two of them managed to get a very dishevelled Collins into his overcoat and down the elevator and into a cab.

"If only he doesn't throw up," said Molly sitting gingerly on the edge of the seat.

"Where do we take the corpse? What's his favorite undertaker?" asked Jay.

"He's staying at the Prince George . . . Jay I always said you were a Jim dandy."

"Think nothing of it," said Jay with a wave of the hand.

Fortunately it was dark by the time they reached the hotel. Molly got Collins' key from the desk while Jay dropped the damp and drooping figure into the arms of a bellboy. "Mr. Collins is tired," Jay said pulling out a dollar bill. "Very tired. Take him up to his room and put him to bed."

Back in the cab Molly let her head drop on Jay's shoulder. "Oh it was so long," she was murmuring. "You shouldn't have stayed away so long. Everything has been so mixed up. Fred and I have decided it's not fair to him. He wants me to go to Reno. We don't want a New York divorce." She leaned heavily on Jay as they walked up the steep stairs to the Italian restaurant where the opera singers ate . . . "And Jay I ought to tell you, I almost had a little baby. I think it was yours. You know how careless we were. I couldn't let it get started with Reno and everything . . . But it made me feel awful . . . I'm perfectly all right now."

They sat facing each other across the table. Jay felt he couldn't move the muscles of his face. He couldn't find anything to say. She leaned over and gave his hand a timid pat on the tablecloth. Without intending to he pulled his hand away.

"It's my music," she said in a wailing voice. "I've decided to sacrifice everything for my music."

"Then you'd better stop smoking," Jay croaked, trying to smile. His tongue was dry in his mouth.

Obediently she crushed out her cigarette in her plate. "And drinking too," she said smiling brightly into his face, "after tonight because I've got tickets to the opera in the balcony so we won't have to dress. It's *Traviata*. They have a new soprano. I want to hear how she does it."

She held his hand and pressed her knee against his all through the first act. Jay felt himself drowning in sweet sickly sorrow. In the intermission, breathing out cocktails and garlic like a couple of dragons but still hand in hand, they tiptoed down the redcarpeted stairs into the main refreshment room where the swells were gathered to get a glass of champagne. In the throng Jay found himself looking above a broad starched shirtfront into a long yellow face with red rodent's eyes and full lips that looked out of his first year in Cambridge. "Why Larry Raisen," he said and felt, in the warmth of Larry's greeting, all of Larry's pleasure at being discovered at the opera with a richlooking wife dressed in sequins, with champagne in his glass and evening dresses all around.

"Jay this is a coincidence," Larry said in a voice that had already a warm successful purr to it. "We were talking about you just this evening, weren't we dear?" Larry's wife, who was small and dark and on the way to being dumpy, nodded eagerly. "If I'd had your address I would have written you to tell you how proud I was of my old . . . er . . . college mate. Remember our meals at Mem and Kanrich's orchestra and how you used to tease Fred Wallace about his bust of Napoleon? But now you are hobnobbing with the great. I understand you are to be associated with Elisha Croft in the Sabatini case. He's one of the men I most admire in the world."

"When he comes to New York you'll have to meet him," said Jay.

Larry's black eyes gave out little sparks of pleasure between their swollen lids. "I'd be grateful to you to my dying day . . . Let's catch up," he went on. "You eat lunch with me tomorrow. Pick me up at my office in the Metropolitan Tower." Larry slipped his card into Jay's hand as the bell started to ring.

"What a dull little couple," said Molly leaning against Jay on their way upstairs in a press of silks and spangles. Jay felt thrown on the defensive. "He's really a very sound fellow," he insisted. "I like the simple pleasure he takes in getting ahead in the world. Most people try to disguise it."

"Do *you?*" Molly pressed her arm against his as they settled into their seats in the dark. The glow from the curtain dimly lit the curve of her cheeks.

"Me?" said Jay, "I'm not getting anywhere"; the conductor was tapping on his music stand; Jay lowered his voice . . . "except to hell in a hack." The music had started. Probably she didn't hear.

Nick's talk at dinner the next night had been disturbing, more disturbing the more Jay thought on it during the customary grind of the Century back to Chicago. Nick had taken Jay to a new small restaurant and given a frowning glance around before settling on a small table in a far corner. He had a tired shadow under the eyes as if he weren't getting enough sleep. He hadn't eaten and drunk so much as usual. There had been no mysterious characters coming in to report. Nick had started talking right away before the antipasto in a voice pitched very low so that only Jay should hear him.

"Thees committee," he said, "develop complication. I wanna make sure you unnerstan'. Suddenly our leetle case to protect a few poor Italian man become, like the theatre man say, a valuable property. The bourgeois liberals, the Communist Party politeecians, even Maffia interested." Nick had lowered his voice and his eyes had given a cautious sweep round the faces of the other diners in the room. "Your America Jay very funny country. Like King Midas — you know King Midas — America turn everything into gold, even repressione of the working class. Everything give money. All these organizations want money, especially 'Omphries he want, not to steal but to make propaganda, make revoluzione. Ow much you teenk the committee has collected?" He hadn't waited for Jay to answer. "Enough to interest beeg time politeecian . . . The communisti they want martyr. They don't mind about one Italian man. You and me we want to save a life. I want to save a good fellow worker."

"Elisha Croft sincerely wants to prevent a miscarriage of justice."

"What do I know about joostice?" Nick had shrugged the word off impatiently, "but I know you must be very careful in Chicago. Your beeg leeberal lawyer . . . Eelisha Croft . . . that little Communist girl she wind him around her finger, see."

"But his sympathy is with the anarchists," Jay had insisted. "He's a philosophical anarchist himself, he told me so."

"I want you to make Meester Croft understan' Sabatini case is beeg property, wort' money, votes, prestige, every organization want it for own purpose, especially communisti they unnerstan'. We got to keep case for us, for the poor people. Enemies are very strong. Beeg Steel, he want conviction. He don't want strike in Minnesota. He want to frighten worker away from strike. He hire plenty detective. In Chicago you be careful Jay. Maybe they try to frame you. You be careful with wooman, with everybody. Me they cannot frame. Whole working class know Nick Pignatelli. They're scared to frame me." He had tossed his head back and combed his beard with his fingers. "Someday they keel," he had added with a dry laugh. His chest swelled under his broad black silk necktie.

"But who Nick?"

"You real *Il Falche?* Every week I tell trut'. About misleaders of labor, about capitaleest, about crook . . . They wanna keel but mebbe I too queek."

As they sat jiggling in the diner on their way across the flat Ohio cornfields, Jay had tried to explain to Tad Skinner the uneasy feeling his talk with Nick had left with him but he couldn't manage to put what he meant into words. Everything he tried to say was too little or too much. Tad, who sat stooping and glum across the table from him with his hair over his eyes, wasn't paying much attention.

"You aren't trying to tell me," he finally said, "that you've gotten me way out here in nomansland on a wildgoose chase? That would be rich . . . Here's how I see it. The interests are trying to frame two guys who are only guilty of standing up for the working man's rights. The right to strike that's something I can understand. Everybody who's working to get 'em out of jail is on my side, everybody who's working to keep 'em in jail is against me. You damn Machiavellians you get so tangled up in your own subtleties you lose track of the plain black and white of it. How the hell am I going to tell the story so that folks will understand it except in black and white? Damn it black and white's the cartoonist's medium."

Jay burst out laughing. "Thataboy Tad," he said, "spoken like Eugene V. Debs."

Later he put in an hour writing Honorine. It was a relief to try to explain in a foreign language the unexpected shape of the world he found himself in. He wondered what she made of his notions, they were foggy enough in English, but in French . . .

You know L'oncle Remus which I sent you for your lectures américaines, maybe you read the famous story about tarbaby. First one paw and then another paw and then another paw and then you're stuck dans le goudron. When I came back I thought I could start out fresh on a clean slate. Tabula rasa. I had determined not to do anything about joining my father's old law-firm for that reason, but instead of that I find myself all entangled up with committees and organizations. Half of them are wellintentioned maniacs who really want to see a great injustice avoided, and half of them are very designing people who are trying to push a political party of a very special new type, half political party, half secret society like the maffia or the black hand. I find myself in the position of seeming to advocate a lot of things I don't want to advocate. I have two prima donnas associated with the defense, one of them a sort of vieux Dreyfusard very typical of our ways of doing things. You'd like him. The other is an egotistical Celt . . . Priez pour moi . . . My own life is absolutely hellish. When I look inside — fortunately I don't do it very often — I have a painful feeling of disaster, loneliness, the dreadful solitude that comes from being always in a crowd. The only one I'm really cozy with these days is my cousin the old condottiere of the working class. He thinks some of our enemies or our friends maybe are out to kill him. He's not a man who scares easily, so he might be right. It's easy enough to get a man killed in this country if you have the proper connections. Sometimes I think it's as easy as it was in the old days in Florence and Siena. God knows I'm in between the Guelfs and the Ghibellines. How did I ever get mixed up in this business anyway?

When in this horrible feeling of indecision it was a great relief to run into an old college mate, a lawyer who just simply wants to make himself some money. It's soothing after the clash of personalities among the dogooders to find somebody who is setting to work innocently and cheerfully to make himself some money. He's urging me to move to New York and to join his firm and practice law with him. In my spare time I could work on a new Decline of the West *only more like Gibbon than like Spengler. How would you like to be the wife of a wealthy but disenchanted member of the New York bar?*

Jay looked down in astonishment at what he'd written. He tore the letter up.

While he and Tad were threading through the crowd amid the dusty shafts of dim sunlight slanting in through the smoke of the Chicago depot Jay was thinking what fun it would be hitting the windy city with Tad, who was all agog because this was his first visit and wanted to go straight to the stockyards, if it were only on some sort of simple assignment that didn't raise all these problems of right and wrong every minute. Even this business would be fun if only men's lives weren't at stake. In the phone booth he had an impulse to put off calling Mulvaney, but his fingers had already dropped his nickel in the slot.

Brian's voice was tense. "Come right over, Jay. Mr. Croft is here. I'm very much upset."

"All right," said Jay hanging up fast before he could be told what the matter was.

"What's wrong?" asked Tad.

"We'll find out soon enough."

Even before they pushed open the grimed groundglass door of Mulvaney's office they could hear voices wrangling inside. Elisha Croft lolled in his tweeds among the papers on Brian's rolltop desk as on a throne and, a tired mischievous expression in the sagging wrinkles of his face, held up between baggy freckled hands a headline in a pink afternoon edition that read: SABATINI MOB STONES COURTHOUSE. In the center of the room a roundfaced man Jay hadn't seen before and a little thinlipped woman in gray serge, who looked like a soiled schoolmistress, talked both at once scolding a swarthy sawedoff man in a black suit faded to a bottle green on the shoulders who stood in the center of the floor twisting a greasy felt hat in big hardworked hands. With the expression of a nurse in a sickroom when the doctor arrives, Hedda Gelber rushed up to Jay. "Comrade Pignatelli, I'm so glad you have come." Her eyes looked into his from under the curve of her heavy lids.

"Whatdehell," the swarthy man was saying with an Italian

accent so thick you could smell the garlic on it. "Boys make manifestazione. Wa' can I do?"

"But we had agreed," hissed the little thinlipped woman in gray serge, "there would be no spontaneous manifestations except those planned by the defense committee."

"There are times to demonstrate and times not to demonstrate," Hedda intoned.

Brian sat running his fingers through his gray hair. "The lives of my clients have been endangered by a silly parade." He jumped to his feet so suddenly that his swivel chair snapped up with a bang. "I'm throwing up the case."

"A riot in front of the courthouse when the case hasn't even come to trial," Croft summed up in his throaty kind-father's voice, "merely prejudices the case."

"We make protest. Working class roar like lion." The swarthy man shoved his hat defiantly back on his head and swung his broad shoulders towards the door.

"Well that's water over the dam," said Croft soothingly, "but let's not play with matches any more. Perhaps the meeting will come to order."

The telephone rang. Hedda answered and looked up at Jay with a mysterious smile as she beckoned to him. "It's for you, Comrade Pignatelli," she murmured.

It was a man's voice Jay didn't know, a grimy insinuating kind of voice. At first Jay thought it must be a salesman but there was something threatening about the Brooklyn waterfront pronunciation of the words. "Mr. Pignatelli?" "Speaking." The voice would like a few moments of Mr. Pignatelli's time. It was about the case he was interested in, the Italian case. No, he didn't care to come to the office. The voice was coaxing. He would wait for Mr. Pignatelli in the lobby of the Stevens next to the magazine stand. Mr. Pignatelli would learn something very much to his advantage. The voice added blandly that its owner was tall and had on a gray suit and a blue necktie.

Jay whispered to Tad he'd be back in half an hour and slipped out.

It was a relief to be out of the stuffy office and down on the street in the warm autumnal sunset. When Jay came out on the traffic of Michigan Avenue he stopped for a second at a corner to watch how the wings and bellies of the gulls wheeling out over the lake caught the last red light of the sun. The sky above them was unbelievably lucid. As Jay looked he was toying with a childhood notion that someday he would slip away to some place somewhere and take a new name and start a new life exactly the way he wanted it. Wasn't this the time? There was nothing to hold him. He was so absorbed he walked clear past the hotel. A tiny picture of old Sabatini's benign old face and of the desperate gashes despair had cut in young Sabatini's cheeks suddenly raised itself before him crude as a passport photograph and drove him to turn back.

There was no air in the hotel lobby. Fleshy faces of salesmen and businessmen seemed to be gasping in the close electric light like fish in an aquarium when the water needs changing. There was no doubt about which face matched the voice on the phone. The necktie matched a pair of watery blue eyes set in gray suet heavily scarred from acne on the cheeks and neck.

"Have a butt," the man said. He poked a cigarette at Jay as if he'd known him all his life. "Let's take it easy and chew the rag." There was something disagreeably intimate about the way the man put his arm round Jay's shoulder and led him to a seat under a potted palm. "Nutten to be spooked about," the man went on. "When I investigate a subject I feel like a brudder to him. That's why I'm good, I guess. We're all poor common clay, if you get what I mean."

Jay edged away from the bulge of the man's buttocks under the small checks of his newlooking suit. He found himself stammering, "But I haven't had the pleasure." The man moved towards Jay with a confidential smile as he presented him with a card that read: *Dennis Crosley, Confidential Investigator.* "I woik for Boins Agency but this is on my own time. In fact Mr. Pignatelli I've come here to do you a favor wort' many thousands of dollars. In the course of a little investigation of this here labor unrest, financed, I don't mind telling you by some of the most progressive civic organizations over on the Indiana side, I've done a little woik on the present company, if you get what I mean. I been woiking widde coinel, too. You've probably noted the excellent coverage the coinel has given this case in his newspaper."

"A lot of damn lies," said Jay.

"If you people had the information we've got you wouldn't say that. We've even got information that could spring those wops."

"Then you don't think they are guilty?"

"They're guilty as hell but that's not what I'm taking up your time about, Mr. Pignatelli." The man brought his face close to Jay's ear. Jay could smell the mint on his heavy breath and hear the wet noise his mouth made as he chewed on a wad of gum. "A soitain amount of damaging material, poisonal material, if you get what I mean, has toined up about the background of soitain figures in the case. A certain young lawyer I understand was removed from the Red Cross for seditious and disloyal behavior during the war. Ditto another relief organization . . ."

"Is this blackmail?" asked Jay feeling his muscles getting tense. His fists were clenched on his knees.

"As a matter of fact it ain't nutten of the kind." The man threw back his head and gave Jay a sidelong glance. "I'm merely tipping you off in a friendly fashion as one man to another, if you get what I mean."

"I don't understand a word of it," said Jay getting to his feet. He managed to laugh. Inside he was telling himself his name wasn't Pignatelli anyway. He was a nameless man watching two strangers in a hotel lobby caught in an odd little nightmare.

"Take it easy, bud." The man leaned back against the plush and yawned. He spread his legs out comfortably and grinned up into Jay's face. His voice dropped to a low drawl. "Take it from me you're doing yourself no good in this case. These crazy wops they don't know the time of day. Why don'tcher widdraw? Da folks I'm working for they doan wan' no more trouble. But man, they got more on you than you could shake a stick at, if you get what I mean. We got a mutual frien' . . . I won't mention no names. Took a trip wid him out in the Near East when you was hobnobbin' widde bloody-handed Reds. Oh those Arabian Nights. Ain't this bozo just a teeny bit degenerate? I met up widdim in a Toikish bat' in Philly when I was investigating a dope ring. Strictly business. I take my pleasures natchral if you get what I mean . . . These stories won't do you no good."

"I haven't got anything to lose," said Jay. His fists were clenching up again. He could see himself planting a fist in the man's small white teeth, driving that damned gum down his throat. A fight in the Stevens; the fat sure would be in the fire then. The idea amused him so that he felt quite easy again. He shoved his hands into his pockets. "If you get me fired from this job I sure will be grateful to you. Believe me it's all work and no pay." He heard himself laughing cheerfully.

"Now we're talkin'," said the man getting clumsily to his feet and bringing his face close to Jay's. "De man I'm woikin' for — I won't mention no names — has an idea that you want to get at the trutt of this situation as much as we do. Live and let live I say. Suppose we pool our information."

"What the devil are you driving at?"

"These damn wops they won't talk to nobody. It would be wort' it to us to know who really trew dat bomb. It would be wort' it to you to have all the info we got delivered to you neat and proper. We wanna close this case up, if you get what I mean. If we don't when we get troo widdat anarchist cousin of yours the name won't sound so good on a shingle in an attorney's office."

"Nothing doing friend," Jay said lightheartedly as he turned his back and started to stroll away through the crowd.

"A rivederla," the man called after him in excellent Italian.

"He doesn't look an Italian," Jay was muttering as he walked back to Mulvaney's office through streets garish with electric lights against the afterglow; "he must be a Pole." For some reason the idea that Dennis Crosley was a Pole made everything seem very funny. He couldn't wait to tell the story to Tad.

There was only a dim glow through the groundglass door. Jay opened without knocking. Elisha Croft was dictating to Hedda under a single light over the rolltop desk. She turned with a start and laid down her pad when Jay came in. "I love to dictate to other people's stenographers," said Croft with his rumbling laugh.

"The artist comrade went over with Mr. Mulvaney to see the classwar prisoners," said Hedda.

"The Bard of Erin said he'd do us that service before he quit. He really is going to quit," said Elisha Croft laughing. "A good riddance if you ask me."

"Your friend is new to the movement?" Hedda asked looking at Jay with arched eyebrows.

"He's an old Ypsel from way back . . ."

"Mr. Croft do you know this name?" Jay walked over and laid the card he held in his hand on the desk under Croft's long nose. Jay felt he told the story well. Croft laughed and laughed. "A fishing expedition . . ." he replied. "You should have taken me along. I might have fished something out of him. I've hardly ever had a case where they didn't try to frame me in some way," he added. "No I don't know him. It's probably not his name anyway. Think nothing of it, Jay . . . You know integer vitae, scelerisque purus . . . When I think of the flash-light photographs." Croft got to his feet shaking with laughter. "They got one once of me helping my own sister into a taxi-cab. That was a good one . . . It's time you children took me down and put me in a cab. It's the old man's suppertime. I've dictated some notes to little Hedda that I want you to look over."

Hedda looked up into Jay's face with a broad smile. She fixed the latch of the door and followed them out. When they placed the great man in a cab, she turned to Jay suddenly. "Where are you staying Jay?" she asked. The wind was blowing her dark hair across her face.

"Lord I don't know. My bag's up in the office."

"I got a nice big room out in Riverside with a Finnish couple." She pronounced her words as if everything she said had some mysterious double meaning. Her eyes were looking into his from under the corners of their almond lids. "They don't speak much English but they are good party members. Come on out there in a comradely spirit. I'll cook you supper before I do my party work. Only you've got to wash the dishes."

That was how he had started sleeping with Hedda. He felt grateful to Hedda, because if he hadn't had somebody to go to bed with during the grinding weeks of the trial he would have broken down completely. She had a neat little body and a mind in which everything had a short definition like in a small pocket dictionary. Arguing with her about whether or not he ought to join the Party he could forget the horrible dragging ache of sympathy for the men in jail. For old Mat Sabatini's benign scepticism he felt a sort of reverent admiration, but his fellowfeeling for Leo was like an aching tooth. When he saw, in a quick glance round the courtroom, how tired Leo looked, the bruised skin round his eyes, his yellow fingers that were never still, the wrinkles of his worn clothes, Jay could feel with prurient disgust in his own hide the unending daily frustration of prison, the need for a woman, for books from the public library, for the orderly development of a task, for freedom to sit at a desk and note down some little discovery, the craven craving to live. He always tried not to meet Leo's eyes. Making love to Hedda he could at least forget

Leo's eyes. Playing hide and seek with snoopers, which was part of the technique of living with Hedda (she called it conspiratorial methods) developed into a diverting sort of game. Her cooking was terrible, but she was an efficient secretary. At night in bed she'd suddenly sit up when he was on the edge of dropping off to sleep and try to impress on him that the Party was the only organization that could effectively win the class war for the workers. He'd pull her ears and ruffle her darksmelling hair and tickle her skinny slats and answer yawning that he wasn't a joiner and that besides a lawyer was an officer of the court. He would make love to her and she would mutter something about the decadent bourgeoisie and he'd roll over and fall asleep.

They left home so early and got to bed so late they were usually both of them too tired to argue long. From the day the trial began Jay had found Bob Dowling a dangerous opponent; much quicker in legal infighting than he was. When Dowling opened the case by reading quotations from the indictment in a booming voice . . . *that Matteo Sabatini and Leopardi Sabatini and Andrea Ferrara and Niccola Dolci and John Doe and Richard Roe and other person or persons unknown did conspire together with malice aforethought with the intent to commit murder . . . on the persons of Enrico Squarcialupi, Fritz Schulz and George T. Doubleday . . . that Matteo Sabatini and Leopardi Sabatini* and so on and so on *did commit murder* and so on and so on. Jay caught the look of grim righteousness that went over the faces of the jurors and felt his hands and feet clammy with fear as if his own life were at stake.

Judge Homer T. Edmunds, a dignified redfaced man roofed with thick white hair who came from a farming community in the southern part of the state, looked so like the foreman of the jury he might have been his brother. Dowling might have been a nephew. Dowling could talk to the judge and the jurors as one of their own. Jay felt they were classing him with the defendants and with the oilylooking Vittorini as another immigrant wop who didn't understand American and had just come to this country to make trouble. He'd explained this situation again and again to Elisha Croft, begging him to take over the defense, but Elisha would only shake his graying red-dish head and say no he was too old for these slugging matches, this time he'd sit in Jay's corner and coach him. If there had to be an appeal; then he would come into the running. Stein was punctual and helpful with detail. Even Perkins was doing his best. But Jay felt alone. More and more as the case pro-gressed he felt like a man who had waked up to find himself left behind by his mates in a trench in the face of the enemy's advancing masses, advancing masses of vengeful angry men. He'd caught himself several times clutching at the seat of his pants while he spoke. Everybody in the courtroom must be noticing that he was developing nervous tics that interfered with his delivery.

The climax came during Dowling's crossexamination of one of Jay's key witnesses, Maria Squarcialupi, the widow of one of the Italians killed by the explosion, a little broad fat woman wreathed in black crape, who had willingly identified frag-ments of her husband's new blue tin lunchbox that had been found with fragments of the bomb. For three days Jay had been presenting his theory to the jury that it was Squarcialupi who had taken the timebomb, set to explode after working hours, to the scene of the crime. When Dowling took the wit-ness he asked her in a sugared voice out of a face like a choir-boy's what religion she professed.

Jay stood up but the Judge let Dowling go on.

"Was your dear husband buried in consecrated ground?"

"Yes yes," she nodded eagerly.

"If he had died in mortal sin would the church have allowed him to be buried in consecrated ground?"

She raised her hands to the rosary at her breast and went off into shrieking hysterics. All the lawyers were on their feet talking at once. Jay could feel Stein's breath against his neck. "Mistrial," he was hissing. Judge Edmunds with red angry face was rapping for order. He ordered the questions and answers expunged from the record and told the jury to try to erase what they had heard from their minds. Jay moved for a mistrial. While Mrs. Squarcialupi was being assisted from the room by two ushers, Judge Edmunds rose and retired to his chambers to consider the motion.

Stein and Vittorini slammed Jay on the back. They were in high spirits. "If the judge grants a mistrial it's all to the good," cried Stein. "If he doesn't we can flay them in the appeal." He kept chuckling to himself as the lawyers chattering like a bunch of starlings trooped out to lunch. Next day after the judge had denied a mistrial but cautioned the prosecution he would consider them in contempt if they repeated any such tactics, Mrs. Squarcialupi was called back to the stand; at the first question she began to sob. Nothing could be gotten from her but sobs. Finally she had to be excused. Foundation for an appeal or not, it ruined Jay's theory for the jury.

Elisha Croft had come into the courtroom for the first time while the jurors, after being out two hours and forty minutes, were beginning to straggle back into the jurybox. He let himself drop heavily into a chair beside Jay's at the counsel table and sat with his chin sunk in his speckled yellow necktie, the wrinkles of his face deep with gloom, while the foreman in his truthfulsounding grave Hoosier voice read out the verdict: On the first count: Matteo Sabatini, not guilty." The blood started to pound in Jay's ears. "Leopardi Sabatini, guilty." When Jay dared look around he saw Leo's face freezing into a deathmask. His only movement was to wet his lips with the tip of his tongue. Inside himself Jay felt the cold quiet that comes from the acceptance of death. Jay's head was swimming so he didn't hear the rest of the verdict which dragged out on account of the separate counts for murder and conspiracy. Automatically he rose to his feet to move for a new trial. A date was set to hear arguments on that motion. Judge Edmunds rose.

Jay was wiping his face. He found his handkerchief was

wringing wet and was groping through his pockets for a dry one to clean the fog off his glasses when he felt Elisha Croft's hand on his shoulder. "Young man I must congratulate you," he said. "You got the old man acquitted on both counts," and he added in a whisper, "I couldn't believe my ears . . . a recommendation for mercy for the rest."

Immediately Elisha Croft was the center of the courtroom. Judge Edmunds made his way towards him through the crowd and shook him warmly by the hand saying he felt honored to have such a notable visitor. He invited him into his chambers. Jay and Bob Dowling were included in the invitation with a wave of the hand. A girl court stenographer who wanted Elisha Croft's autograph tagged along. Standing in the chatting group in the judge's small office making polite conversation and offering Elisha his fountainpen whenever anybody asked for the great man's autograph, Jay felt like the hollow mask of himself: his real self was coldly looking into death's face as he walked back towards the familiar cell down the iron corridor that would smell of greasy stale soup, feeling to the marrow of his bones the click of the greenpainted iron bars of the cell door as it closed behind him.

Someone tapped Jay on the shoulder and said one of his clients wanted to speak to him. Jay had clean forgotten Mat Sabatini.

The old man sat on a bench in the empty courtroom, tears running down his face into his white mustaches. He tottered to his feet when he noticed Jay standing over him. "Dunque?"

He held his trembling old hands out in front of him.

Jay never could forget how tinnily brisk his own voice had sounded in his ears. "We argue the motion for a new trial. If that is denied we appeal. Elisha Croft, the greatest defense lawyer in the Middle West, is taking over the case. He thinks our chances are very good . . . But now Mr. Sabatini we've got to do something about you. A United States Marshal is waiting outside to serve a D. of J. warrant for deportation."

It seemed to cheer the old man up to think of his own troubles. He shrugged his bent shoulders and looked up at Jay with a smile under his white mustache. "Indeed the 'ospeetalitee of Meester Coolidge is better than the 'ospeetalitee of Meester Mussolini."

"I'm hoping," went on Jay in the tinny official voice he couldn't seem to get rid of, "to get you remanded in my custody until they can hold a hearing before a commissioner."

When, long after midnight, Jay stumbled into the room haggard from fatigue, Hedda in a red bathrobe circled round him like a purring cat. "If you could get rid of some of your bourgeois sentimentality," she kept saying, "you'd realize that this has been a great day for the workers. A classwar prisoner liberated and an issue made clear to the toiling masses. It has been made perfectly clear that what a worker who demands a chance for life from capitalist society gets is prison and the gallows. As I said to Comrade Humphries last fall, the Sabatini case is real agitprop."

Jay's head was aching; he must remember to get his glasses checked.

"If Mrs. Squarcialupi hadn't caved in on me," he groaned tugging at his necktie, "every man in the jury must have believed the incontrovertible evidence that the bomb was brought to the scene of the crime in that new blue tin lunchbox. They must have believed it or they wouldn't have brought in the recommendation for mercy. It was a timebomb and it exploded accidently before Squarcialupi got it placed right, but I never could prove it. They didn't intend to blow anybody up. They never intended to blow anybody up. It was supposed to go off in the night to scare off scabs."

Hedda walked up to him as he sat on the edge of the bed shivering in his pajamas. "Of course the workers were innocent. You don't have to prove it to me." She ruffled his hair with unexpected tenderness. His head ached so he pulled it away from her hand. "Jay you're hopeless," she said sitting beside him and letting her arm drop round his neck. "Even being a member of an oppressed minority won't help you if you have the wrong class origins," she sighed. "Jay," she whispered gently in his ear, rubbing against him and looking searchingly in his face out of the corners of her eyes, "you better take your bag when you go into town in the morning . . . I know you'll be going to New York soon anyway. They've billed you to speak at a meeting to raise defense funds at the Bronx Casino, so you had better pack your things and take your bag in with you in the morning."

"Why tomorrow?" asked Jay yawning. He couldn't get his mind to focus with this headache.

"Max'll be back. He's been out to the Coast on Party work."

"Who the hell's Max?"

"In your bourgeois circles," her voice rang through the dark room, "you would call him my husband but the tie between two worker comrades is deeper than you can understand."

Careful to keep from touching her, Jay lay down on the bed beside her. He felt too tired and sick to think up anything to say.

While Elisha, who was now throwing himself enthusiastically into the case, was trying to smoke out a circuit court judge who would reduce bail for the prisoners pending the argument of the motion for a new trial, Jay had headed for New York, on the slow train this time because he was almost broke. The night he got in, feeling a little guilty for not calling up the Defense Committee right away (but to hell with them he needed a rest; he had to throw off this headache), he went down to the Village to see Jed.

Riding down on the subway he found in his pocket the letter from Fred Wallace that had caused him a certain amount of pain when he first read it on the pullman:

I know a lawyer can't exactly pick and choose his clients. If he's out for the money, as I presume you are, he has to take cases as they come but I do feel that a man of patriotic feeling would have kept clear of this trumpedup effort to discredit our noblest

*institutions which has received so much cheap newspaper pub-
licity. I am impelled to let you know that the relations of friendship between us, which I had hoped at some time to have an
opportunity to renew, are at an end.*

Jay tore the letter up in little pieces and as he didn't
like to drop them on the floor of the subway car he held them
in his hand. Lord it was years since he'd heard from Fred.
Funny stuffy old thing. The letter was postmarked Berkeley,
California. Fred must be teaching Gothic there. When Jay
got off the local at Sheridan Square he let the little pieces drop
between the car and the platform. Well he had a lot of friends,
he thought, Tad and Jed and that horrible old bombthrower,
his cousin Nick. He couldn't help smiling when he remembered how mad Fred had gotten the time he had pasted false
whiskers on his bust of Napoleon. It was all dim in the past,
but the letter hurt just the same.

When he went in the front door of the Grove Street house
he heard clinking and jabber and shuffling of feet from the
rear apartment. Jed, his eyes very bright, his hair in black
moist curls, stood in his shirtsleeves behind a table piled with
sandwiches and hardboiled eggs pouring whisky into tumblers.
June, stouter than Jay remembered, hastily packed into a black
velvet dress she'd obviously made herself, with silver buttons
in a row up the front, threw herself in his arms and gave him a
smacking kiss. "Just what we need to make the party complete."

"Welcome to our city," shouted Jed pressing a tumbler into
his hand. Jay drank the raw whiskey down greedily. "Right
off the boat," Jed added and with a surprised look on his face,
poured a little more into the tumbler. "Doc Wilton's prescription made up by his favorite pharmacist. In fact there he
is, the famous babyfaced bootlegger. Take a bow, Joe."

Jay shook hands with Joe Gesso who looked more of a fash-
ionplate than ever and with grinning Dr. Wilton. They both
seemed happy as ducks in a puddle at finding themselves afloat
in the society of artists. Then Jay had to pull his aching wits

together to meeet the members of the cast of Jed's new play. June introduced them by their stage names and by the names of the characters they played. In a corner they found Felicia, looking cool and slinky in chartreuse green in the middle of a group of young men. June breathed a little hard and Jay could feel her grip tighten on his arm. "No I'm not in the play," Felicia said in a brassy strained voice. "I'm merely the claque. Every playwright has to have a claque."

Flight from the Sun was to open the following Tuesday but Saturday night there was a public dress rehearsal for the benefit of Sabatini Defense. Jed had arranged that Jay would take June because he explained he'd be in too much of a stew to take anybody. The first people they saw when they started to work their way through the crowd outside the theatre were Tad and Hedda Gelber. Hedda wore her hair in a bang and a becoming red silk Russian blouse. "J. E. D. Morris really lets himself go. He really flays the complacent bourgeoisie," she said when she was introduced to June. She pursed her lips. "Of course the interests won't allow it to succeed."

"Well Jay," said Tad in a patronizing tone, "you did pretty well for a man without a proper grounding in socialism."

"Your pamphlet's doing us a lot of good," Jay answered with the numb feeling of making conversation with a stranger. "They've already distributed sixty thousand copies."

"Elisha Croft is going to sit in a box," murmured Hedda in her most conspiratorial tone. "I've tipped off the reporters. An interview with Elisha Croft . . ."

"We won't get a new trial. Our only hope is in appeal." Jay's lips were mechanically forming words. Neither of them was paying any attention. Through the strained ache in his head, Jay had the odd feeling that he had mistaken a pair of strangers for old friends. To get them to look at him he asked Hedda sharply:

"How did you get him to come to New York. He hates New York."

Hedda looked him straight in the eye and smiled the conspiratorial smile that only a week ago had seemed so familiar, and now seemed far away, like the expression of an actress on the stage. "He came especially," she said, "just for tonight."

"That old sentimentalist," interrupted Tad, "and anyway nothing ever makes headlines Saturday night."

As they drifted away into the crowd June whispered in Jay's ear. "I'm glad Tad's consoling himself with the red front. I thought the poor boy would lose his mind."

Jay's face was getting very red. "Gosh life's complicated," he murmured.

"Too complicated for me," said June. "I'm a simple country girl."

When they reached the fourth row they found that Lawrence Raisen and his wife were seated beside them.

"Jay, you have made yourself quite a reputation," Larry exclaimed right away. "Don't leave town without seeing me. I've got a proposition to make."

"I had a curious letter from Fred Wallace," Jay began. The curtain was rising. "I'll tell you about it later."

June had grabbed Jay's hand and squeezed it hard. "Oh I do so want it to be good," she whispered. Jay was so busy listening for the audience's response that he could hardly follow the play. When the curtain went down on the first act there was applause but not enough. "It's a slow audience," June was saying. "The stagehands are crazy about it. That's supposed to be a good sign." As they rose to their feet Larry Raisen tugged at Jay's sleeve. "There he is," he spluttered into Jay's face. "You promised you'd introduce me."

Sure enough there was Elisha Croft slumped in a box, still in his tweeds among the men and women in evening dress. Larry and Jay set off through the crowd. Jay's aching head was beginning to swirl There were too many people he knew. Too much smoke and chatter in the lobbies. He couldn't get a word out to anybody. Tiny sharp knives seemed to be cutting into his eyes. He did manage to catch Elisha as he was melting out through an emergency exit and to introduce him to the Raisens who stood broadly beaming in the hubbub like a pair of lighthouses in a storm.

Jay saw Molly Hobart looking at him through a churn of faces. The long blond skull of Andrew Collins teetered above her frizzly hair. From her eyes Jay could see she wanted to speak to him but he couldn't reach her through the crowd. "Let's get some air, June," Jay was saying. "I feel perfectly horrible."

Outside on the sidewalk in front of the posters they found two large men in black felt hats. The bearded one was Nick. "Meet Bianchi of the garment workers," he said when Jay edged up with June in tow.

"What do you think of it?" Jay asked.

Nick made a farting sound with his lips. "Greenwich Veelage. What do I know?" he shrugged. "No reealitee. He donno how men live. Wha's amatter Jay? You look all een."

"I'll probably live," said Jay, "but it looks as if I was getting the gate as attorney for the defense."

"Read *Il Falche* this week . . . I am magneeficent. I lead my editorial: J'accuse. I denounce the committee for Communist politics. I denounce all crooks who deceive the poor Italian people. Eh Bianchi?"

The other man had a chalky white face. He gave Nick a frightened look. "You say too much," he said.

"Well call me Monday Jay. Thees theatre makame seek. Outside the air is good . . . in the street. Come on Bianchi. We go get droonk."

The second act had begun when Jay and June got back to their seats. Larry Raisen leaned towards them across his wife's spangled bosom and whispered in a trembling voice, "I feel as if I'd been with Lincoln or Walt Whitman . . . Thanks Jay thanks." People were shushing him. Jay tried to forget himself in the play.

After the final curtain, while Jed, looking about sixteen with his curly hair and his popping eyes, was still taking curtain calls, June ran off up the aisle calling over her shoulder to Jay that she had to catch the train to Nyack because the woman she'd left Mae with couldn't stay all night. Jay ran after her and grabbed a cruising cab that got them to the ferry just as the gate was coming down. She had explained that Dr. Wilton was going to drive Jed out and George Simons his director and Felicia, of course Felicia would come . . . after he'd met with the cast to go over the ragged places. "Jed's all theatre," she added hastily. "What did you think of it?"

"Jed sure has got drive."

"Jed's all theatre," said June again.

They stood in the bow as the ferry pulled out from the slip. A yellowish halfmoon was setting behind the heights of Weehawken. There were ships' running lights ahead. Tugs mooed. Jay breathed in the bilgy river air. "God this is wonderful."

"This is my world," June said. "I can't stand too many people in close quarters all squalling and twittering and calling attention to themselves like birds in an aviary."

"And all these committee meetings, Oh Christ. Looks like the comrades were winning their fight."

"You mean to save the Sabatinis?" June asked vaguely.

"I mean to take over the case for themselves. It wears me down."

"It wears *me* down," said June. She began to talk fast without looking at Jay. "Jay, you might as well know Jed and I are going to get a divorce. It's a question of money. If this show goes over we'll be able to afford the trip to Reno. But I want to do it soon on account of Mae. Little as she is she's starting to notice."

"Why not a New York State divorce," Jay asked briskly. It was a pleasure to get down to practical matters. "My friend Larry Raisen can fix it up. He probably won't charge you anything. All Jed has to do is be caught fingering some lady's lingerie. That's not too much out of character."

June laughed almost naturally. "Isn't he awful? I've been so crazy about him . . . If I'm not to lose my mind I've got to get over it." Her voice was drowned by the tinkling sound of the chains as the gangplank clamped the ferry's round bow into the slip.

The little old West Shore train wasn't too crowded. "I always think these coaches must have been left over from Lincoln's presidential campaigns," said Jay. June didn't laugh. She went on talking in a slow voice as if dictating a letter. "I've got to think of myself and I've got to think of Mae." She sat looking straight before her talking into the back of the seat ahead. "I'm going to have to earn my own living. That's why I think it was mean of Jed not to get me a part in the play. I could play old Mrs. Burleson just as well as that Thorndike woman they are paying three hundred a week."

After a good deal of adjusting of the spark and the throttle they managed to get the Morrises' old Model T, which they found parked outside the Nyack station, started. It was the first time Jay had seen the house they had just bought, an old house with wide flat eaves and broad porches set in a wide lawn that sloped to the river. "Isn't it lovely? Of course it's not been paid for," June panted as she let him in the front door. "Nothing's ever paid for," she went on as she bustled around the highceilinged livingroom, emptying ashtrays and slapping gaudy colored pillows on the couches into shape. "That's why it's so hard to walk out on Jed." She shook tears out of her eyes. "Sit down Jay, you've been overworking . . . I'll go tell Mrs. Jenkins she can go home. She just lives round the block. She's so nice I don't like to keep her up too late."

In a minute she was back and grabbed him by the hand. "Come look at Mae . . . Isn't she pretty?" The tiny girl with dark curly hair like her father's was asleep in her crib. The little face was closed like a book.

June looked down at her smiling. "Anyway she wasn't a mistake. She's healthy and so am I." She batted her lashes at

Jay . . . "Too healthy. I've worked my fingers to the bone on this house, making curtains, painting on a stepladder . . . I made all the couchcovers." Still holding Jay by the hand she led him back into the livingroom. "Jed did help me with the floor, but he's so slapdash. I don't know what they'll do. Felicia is thoroughly impractical."

The telephone rang. June trotted off into the hall to answer it. When she came back she brought a tray with a bottle of whiskey and glasses. "That was typical," she said. She plunked herself down beside Jay on the couch and poured them each a drink. Immediately she jumped up again. "Come out to the kitchen. Let's have something to eat. I'm starved."

Jay sat sipping his drink at the table in the middle of the kitchen while June bustled about rattling pots and pans as she went. Through the buzzing of the whiskey in his ears and the painful daze in his eyes he watched June. He tried to forget himself watching June. She put bacon to fry and broke some eggs in a bowl. "That was typical," she was saying looking into the bowl. "Sometimes people get a little too tactless. He could have asked somebody else than Felicia to call up and say they weren't coming. I'm glad they're not coming. It'll give me time to get dinner ready before they start storming around the house in the morning. They're all going up to Miss Barnsfeather's. She is giving a party for the cast . . . Present company not invited. Just an oversight but a little too tactless. I could have asked Mrs. Jenkins to spend the night. The plan was to have the party here . . . Poor Jed, he hasn't got a tactful bone in his body." June brought over the scrambled eggs. Every time she passed the table she poured more whiskey into her glass and Jay's. When they'd finished eating she almost shouted, "I'll show you your room!"

She grabbed his hand again. At the head of the stairs she pushed her face with wide wet lips and dark staring eyes up into his. "Jay, I'm glad it's you instead of the iceman or something," she said.

Jay kissed her back. After they had swayed kissing for a while on the narrow landing at the head of the stairs June whispered that they'd better go down to her room where they'd hear Mae if she woke up. Passing through the livingroom she poured them each another drink. "Oh you're lovely," she mumbled as she threw herself down on her back on the big double bed.

Late in the night Jay woke with a start. He heard Felicia's voice very high and shrill outside the window and the sound of a car and drunken chatter on the lawn. He grabbed his pajamas and slipped them on and ran in his bare feet up the stairs. As he reached the landing the bathroom door opened and Jed's curly head stuck out. "Out with the raggletaggle gypsies oh," he was shouting. His eyes were round and his mouth made an oh. His face suddenly became stiff and sober as he looked Jay up and down from his bare feet to the hand clutching the pajama pants together at the waist. The pupils seemed to spread until his eyes were all black. "God damn your soul," he shouted with a crazy shriek. Jay knew all at once that Jed had always hated him. For a second Jay thought Jed was going to jump on him. Instead he slammed the bathroom door to and locked it. As Jay tiptoed past he could hear Jed inside sobbing.

Jay went into the guestroom, closed the door and lay down on bed. He lay cold and shaking under the covers. "Oh God, oh God what a shameful thing," he kept saying to himself.

It was bright day when a knock on the door woke him. "Telephone," said June in a cheerful voice. She looked big and freshbathed in blue polkadots. "It's hangover hall," she added running ahead of him down the stairs. "I'm getting the black coffee and applying restoratives . . ."

"Meester Peegnatelli." It was an Italian voice. "This Bianchi. Last night eleven fortyfive outside Salmone's Restaurant they shot Nicola. Police looking for you as next of kin to identify body in undertaking parlor at Fifteen Sixtyone First Avenue."

"Who shot him?"

The man had already hung up. Jay ran upstairs and got into his clothes.

"I've got to go into town, June," Jay said sticking his head into the kitchen. "Don't go without some coffee," she called after him as he strode out the front door . . .

His goddamned everlasting life . . . Weeks later in Chicago sitting in Brian Mulvaney's office that smelt of dust and stale papers and the tedium of old lawsuits, when he had hung up the phone with that girl's voice tingling in his ears, sitting still for a moment while he got his nerves enough in hand to go out to the street, he felt again, as he did every time he was for a moment idle, the confused anguish of his last days in New York; the sense of his own fumbling incompetence; the numb visit to the mortuary where Nick's beard stuck up incongruously into the candlelight against the sharp splashes of sun cutting through the drawn venetian blinds and the little woman in black kneeling sobbing beside the sheeted figure, Nick's wife of course (for some reason he'd never thought of Nick as having a wife), a sallow Italian wife with a cross around her neck, yelling at the kids down the tenement stairs . . . And the continued feeling of eyestrain. He felt he was seeing the world through a bloodshot haze. Night and day the ache tightened. A band of jagged metal round his head. For the first time in his life he couldn't sleep. "Rest, don't use your eyes," the oculist said when he fitted him for new glasses; but he couldn't rest. Through the headache he remembered dimly the confusion of his talks with the police, his search for the other editors of *Il Falche,* for the printer, for some of Nick's boys. There were no other editors, the printer was on his vacation, none of the boys had ever heard of Nick. It took Jay a week to find Bianchi. All he could get out of Bianchi was the same chalkfaced stare he remembered when they had stood in

front of the posters for *Flight from the Sun.* "Left Nick at the
corner." He shrugged. "Never saw him again."

When Jay had a call at his hotel from a pleasantvoiced man
who turned out to be the assistant district attorney in charge
of investigating the Pignatelli murder, he had rushed off downtown in high hopes. The Assistant D.A. was Harvard Law
too, third generation Italian, a thinfaced young man with
a sharply curved nose named Manzoni. They got along famously. Jay immediately told him what he knew about his
cousin Nick and his friends and enemies.

"Is that all?" asked Manzoni. "I thought with your reputation . . . your connection with the radical movement and all that
. . ." stammered Manzoni. "I thought all I needed to do was to
get hold of you . . . I thought you could explain the political
implications and probably put your finger on the murderer."

"I thought the D.A.'s office. . . ." Jay's voice trailed off. He
sat rubbing his aching temples with his fingers. He jumped to
his feet. "Here I've been messing around with this Sabatini
case for years. This is my country, these are my particular
special kind of people and I have to stand here in the district
attorney's office and admit that I don't know a goddam thing."

"But he was your cousin," said Manzoni looking up incredu-
lously from his desk.

"I'm not even sure of that . . . I thought you people would
have all the dope."

"We don't know a goddam thing."

They sat looking in each other's blank faces.

On the train west — Jay was always happy on trains — he
managed to get some sleep, but he had kept waking up in his
berth with typed pages of briefs moving across his eyes and
notes on yellow foolscap scrawled in an illegible hand. The
typing was dim, he was straining to read the blurred letters
of the indictment and Leo's lost face would stare from out of
the pages like a torn snapshot found in a drawer, with the
painful lines under the cheekbones and the quizzing look of

old Sabatini's mustache and dead Nick's beard thrust out to question the false candlelight and Manzoni's bland sharp discreetly ironic mouth breaking into a wellbred laugh and Jay would wake with a start . . . and creeping up those stairs in his bare feet and the horrible feeling of shame . . . like a penitente whacking with a lash his own bare back he would tell himself: you don't know a goddam thing. Sitting stooped in the chair in the dead air of Mulvaney's empty office he could hear Dandy's voice dim out of the past: "Failure is a word I don't admit in my vocabulary."

"But if you do fail . . . " he said aloud and jumped to his feet and grabbed his hat and slammed the door on that stale remnant. "Then admit failure," he shouted into the empty hall, and waiting for the elevator began to think that henceforeward . . .

8

O MY AMERICA MY NEW FOUND LAND

LULIE caught sight of him peering through his thick glasses over people's shoulders amid the cigarettesmoke of the hotel lobby. His felt hat in his hand, he was drifting past without recognizing the Harringtons. "Here's our gollywog," she whispered to Ben and jumped to her feet and stood smiling up into his face.

His eyes came back from somewhere and swam large and brown with a fleck of light in each pupil behind the glasses. "Fancy meeting you here," she said. "Quite a coincidence," he said and made a stiff little bow with a smirk of puzzled amusement that carried her back in a swoop to the dancefloor under Chinese lanterns at the Hiawatha House and Miss Potter perspiring in pink at the piano and icecream at Pringle's and Georgie shooting out the light on the path up to the hotel and Don Modesto asking "What is the etiquette of this occasion?"

His hand felt warm and dry and strong around hers. "Miss Harrington I presume?" "The same," she said and led the way between staring travelling men to where her brothers waited behind two pairs of noncommittal blue eyes. "Here we are, the harried Harringtons." She let herself drop on the settee between her brothers.

Jay sat opposite with his hat on his knees. How much alike they are, Jay immediately was thinking, except for the girl's eyes. From long ago he remembered a planet hanging like a drop of nasturtiumcolored liquid from a green sky and she was talking about living inside the world like inside an easteregg.

"Let's eat," Ben Harrington said right away. "I'm starved."

"Has anybody got any money?" Lulie asked as she led the way towards the headwaiter who stood in the broad door of the main diningroom looking out over the ranked tables of chattering luncheoneaters, in the attitude of an orchestra leader about to strike up.

"I have," whispered Zeke following stiffly after her with the corners of his thin lips turned down. "I got paid yesterday." The headwaiter was looking at them with appraising eyes. Ben and Zeke stiffened.

"A table for four please," said Jay blandly stepping forward with his continental manner of a man accustomed to be waited on. He caught Lulie's approving glance and all at once felt senselessly happy. They were placed at a round table too large for the four of them with too much silver on a too starched tablecloth and too much ice in the waterglasses and fell to studying the much too large menu cards. Lulie said she'd eat sweetbreads like a lady. The rest of them ordered steak.

"We ought to have Culmbacher on account of its being an occasion," cried Zeke unexpectedly. "Gone are the days," said Lulie. All around them was a clinking of knives and forks, jaws munching, gabble of wellfed conversation. Jay let himself settle back in his chair with a feeling of great coziness as if the bustle, the lowpitched voices, the smells of steak and fried potatoes, hot rolls and the deference of colored waiters were weaving a net about them in which they four sat walled off, entertained, cordial, protected like Esquimaux in their igloo. A recollection popped into Jay's head. "How about a banana split?" From Lulie's little shriek he knew she had remembered too.

At first Lulie tried to get a word in about Zeke's business but Zeke froze her with a pallid look and went on talking cheerfully to Jay about French versus Italian romanesque buildings:

"The profs try to get you to like only one thing, but I occasionally find a formula I like in any old style, except possibly baroque and later Gothic . . . I want to find the formula for a standard that runs through them all. Maybe it's in the relation of function to appearance."

"Baroque's like opera," began Jay. "Better if you start with a couple of drinks . . . " Lulie listened till she thought her ears would stretch. When Ben got to yawning she kicked at him under the table. Before she knew what had happened they were the only ones left in the diningroom. For lack of anything else to drink, Jay and Zeke kept ordering more coffee. They had reached the subject of wall decoration and Jay was describing the early Christian mosaics in Rome when Zeke looked down at his wristwatch.

"It's after three," he said. "I've got to go to work."

"But Zeke it's Saturday afternoon," wailed Lulie.

"We work an eightday week in my profession," Zeke answered coldly. He got to his feet. Jay had already picked up the check. "If you wouldn't mind Jay," Zeke said, "I'd like to show you some projects . . . It's not every day I find a layman who understands architecture . . . I'm working on one of those wretched competitions."

"Of course my interest is more historical than anything else," said Jay deprecatingly.

Zeke had started for the door. He turned back.

"We haven't said anything about this . . . " he made a stiff pass with his hand . . . "business." He spat the word out. "I'll just put it in your hands, Lulie. You tell him about it. Only I warn you she's prejudiced against Juliet."

"You handle it," echoed Ben giving Jay a pleading look. "Say I've got a pass to a ballgame. I might still get to see the last few innings. Suppose I shove off."

Immediately Lulie and Jay were alone in the almost empty lobby. The air was jaded with afternoon.

"The trouble with Chicago," said Jay to Lulie, "is there's

never any place to sit down." Lulie burst out laughing. "Why there are enough empty seats for an army."

"I mean there's never any place where you want to sit down . . . Let's get out in the air. Has it occurred to you that the season is spring?"

"Don Modesto it has."

She took his arm as he came out of the revolving door behind her. A gust of gritty wind caught them as they stepped out on the pavement among the luggage of departing hotelguests. She grabbed for her hat. "I fooled 'em," said Jay waving his felt which he still held in his hand. "The trouble with Chicago is there's no place to get out in the air."

"The trouble with Chicago . . . " Lulie began.

"The time has come to get out of Chicago," Jay shouted above the slambanging of the traffic as they walked into the cold wind down the blaring street in the glare of the afternoon sun.

"Let's," said Lulie.

The question was where to go right now. Lulie knew she ought to be explaining about Zeke's divorce to Don Modesto but every time she started, something entertaining came up that they just had to talk about. They walked up and down in front of the storefronts on Michigan Avenue until their lungs were full of gasoline fumes and their eyes were full of dust. She suggested they go into the Art Institute. "The smell of varnish is so soothing."

Once they got inside the rooms seemed stuffy. There were too many people. Whenever they settled on a bench somebody crowded in beside them. Lulie felt the one thing they needed was space and air around them. All at once she got an idea. "Modesto," she said, "suppose I get Garde to ask us out to Lake Leman? . . . Of course you don't know about Garde. She's my faithful female friend . . . We can borrow her car and drive out some place . . . Then I'll tell you about Mugsie and you can decide what to do to get Zeke out of her claws . . . As Aunt

Lyde used to say, he's a babe in arms. Now you just look at the pictures while I phone."

Jay couldn't tell one picture from another today. He didn't want to let Lulie out of his sight so he followed her to the phonebooth and waited outside. It was fun watching her through the glass, the way she pursed up her lips when she scratched in her pocketbook for a nickel, the way she smiled and gave a little hop like a bird on a perch when she got her friend on the line, the way she tossed back her head in its tight little hennacolored hat when she laughed. Oh Lord this is fun, Jay was thinking. Lulie was still laughing when she came out of the booth.

"Of course Garde was horrified, but the sweet creature said yes. Mrs. Willard thinks we're all madhatter mad but she's very indulgent. Let's all be very indulgent . . . Now the question is," Lulie went on as they walked down the steps into the blustery May afternoon, "can we catch the five fifteen?"

"I never lose trains," cried Jay and hailed a cab. They were settled in the cab and headed for the depot before they remembered they didn't have any baggage.

"Wild horses couldn't drag me out to Fiftytwo Ten," said Lulie. "You don't know about Fiftytwo Ten."

"My squalid lodging is way out on Bayfield Avenue," Jay broke in. "I wouldn't recognize myself if I met myself going in the door. Anyway there isn't time."

"Goody," cried Lulie. "I love catching trains on the nick."

"I love catching trains," said Jay. Jay caught sight of a briefcase in the window of a cutrate drugstore. He stopped the cab and jumped out. Next door was a haberdasher. "This doesn't look too respectable," he said as he piled himself back into the cab all out of breath. "After all it's not as if we were going to a hotel."

Lulie didn't have time to blush because they were already scrambling out at the depot. The grimy clock said 5.14 as they streaked down the platform. The train started to move as they

swung aboard. The homebound rush was over so they were
able to find a seat to themselves. Jay took his clean shirt out
of its bag and fitted it into the paper briefcase which he was
thinking had a cutrate look. "I should have bought a proper
valise," he said apologetically. "But to tell the truth I'm a
little short of money."

"My big hulking brothers let you pay for all the lunch,"
cried Lulie. "They didn't mean to but they just forgot. They
forget everything." She picked up the briefcase and examined
it critically. "It has got a horrid yellow glare but a briefcase is
right scholarly . . . It suits you . . . A suitcase might have looked
immoral."

That started them laughing about one thing and then about
another. The other passengers in the car were taking on a
comical look. The conductor did for the Captain out of the
Katzenjammer Kids. The endless trainyards, the strings of
freightcars, the littered suburbs under big cabbagy purple
clouds went reeling past like funnypaper backgrounds. It
didn't seem a minute before the local was jerking to a stop at
the Lake Leman station. Lulie jumped up. Jay tucked his
briefcase under his arm. He had hardly time to feel the shrinking he always felt meeting unfamiliar people before he was
shaking hands with a tall dark girl with circles under her eyes.

"Jay Pignatelli is Zeke's lawyer," Lulie was explaining. "I
always call him Don Modesto. You must have met him at the
lake. I've known him for fifteen years."

Jay and Hildegarde Willard looked in each other's faces
trying to believe they'd met. "At least we're meeting now,"
Jay stammered.

The Willards were very nice people but this wasn't being
with Lulie. Driving out in the Buick Lulie and Hildegarde
never stopped talking for a second. For Jay time started to
drag. It was raining hard when they drove in under the portecochère of the halftimbered house. Hildegarde's auburnhaired
sister Hortense met them in the hall. A handsome whitehaired

old man with a broken nose and a sharply cut mustache was un-
loading a bag of golfclubs off his shoulder when they came in.
"Thank God a man," he cried and elbowed his way forward
past the girls and gave Jay's hand a wrench. "I'm Jeff Willard.
This damn rain has ruined my golf and I thought all I had to
look forward to was an evening with a houseful of women . . .
Nobody brings any men home since Josie got married. Whose
young man are you?"

Jay felt himself getting very red in the face.

Hildegarde interrupted: "Dad I explained it's Zeke Harrington's lawyer. He wants to get your advice about poor Zeke's
divorce . . . Oh Dad you never listen."

"Divorcing a fool from his money's more in my line . . .
Though Mother claims it's reprehensible. If you can get any
sense into that boy's head you're a better man than I am Gun-
gadin. What do you drink? Scotch or bourbon?"

"Now Jeff let the girls show him up to his room," broad
silveryhaired Mrs. Willard called in a voice tinkling with hospi-
tality from the drawing room door.

"He can go up to his room afterwards," stormed Jeff Willard.
"You come along with me son. We'll sit down in my tackroom
and get away from all these women for five minutes. I don't
have any vices any more, too old for 'em"; he laughed; "but
God damn it I do like to sit down for five minutes to have one
quiet drink of whisky before my dinner."

It was a low room with oak beams excessively wormeaten and
oversized prints of men in pink coats and horses and hounds
round the walls. Clearing his throat Jeff Willard went to a
small bar in a cupboard in the corner. When Jay said bourbon
he gave a grunt of approval. "Now what did you say your name
was?"

Jay sat sipping bourbon and stammering over his replies to
Mr. Willard's blustering questions until a gong somewhere in
the house made the old man jump to his feet. "Well I guess it's
the fashion these days to start out as a goddam Red," he was

saying. "When I was a boy it was the men's Bible class . . . or foreign missions . . . but I never expected to entertain one at my table." He looked Jay hard in the face and laughed. "Don't mind me son . . . A man never knows what to expect when he raises a covey of intellectual daughters."

Jay felt awkward appearing at dinner in the same suit. Old Mr. Willard wore a tuxedo. Lulie's lightbrown hair was up in back and plastered in little curls across her forehead that made him think of somebody (of course it was Petite Mère in her long lace sleeves), and one of the Willard girls had lent her a black velvet dress that suited her. He caught himself giving Lulie an eager admiring look that he saw Mr. Willard take in with an audible chortle, but he didn't get a chance to say two words to her all evening. When she wasn't bantering back and forth with the elder Willards at the ends of the table, she was lost in chatter with the girls. Dinner seemed endless. After dinner they had coffee and peppermint candies in the drawing-room and after that they had to play for hours an idiotic game of Hearts. When the brass French clock, made in the shape of a chariot drawn by four bronze horses, struck eleven from the Gothic mantel, the elder Willards got to their feet, the girls melted away and all at once Jay found himself face to face with Lulie.

"You're looking at me as if you didn't know who I was," she said smiling.

"It's the sudden change in environment," he said. "I don't know who I am myself." He wanted to stretch out his arms towards her but he didn't quite dare. "Or care." The words came out startlingly loud.

"The rain has stopped. Let's go run in the streets. I'll change my dress," she whispered.

For fear the Willard girls might come back he waited outside the front door, pacing back and forth with his hands in his pockets, sniffing the smell of wet sprouting grass and of something that might possibly be a lilac in bloom. The night was drowned in mist. From the wet street he could hear the swish of the tires of Saturday night cars. Their lights flickered behind the dripping shrubbery. The familiar Chicago suburb seemed strange as Persia. As he waited he could feel his heart thumping. When she slid silently out the door right away he had the sense of being accustomed to her presence, as if she had been there all the time.

What he said was, "Let's go by a drugstore . . . I guess I ought to buy me a toothbrush."

Lulie was astonished by the amusement she got from the notion of buying Don Modesto a toothbrush. "And how about shaving equipment?" she asked. The first thing they saw when they burst into the drugstore, on the mirror above the heads of a row of bubbling flappers with their boyfriends at the counter, was a sign: Banana Split. Don Modesto cried out: "Now's our chance." Lulie squeaked. "It'll make up for the one we didn't eat at Pringle's."

"How long ago was that?" She climbed up on the last stool. He stood close behind her. "Was it a month ago?"

"Less," said Jay.

Lulie turned towards him with her eyes wide and her spoon poised. "Now you're the gay deceiver . . . Do it some more."

The banana split made them both feel a little sick but the air was sweet and moist and cool in their faces when they walked fast up and down dim back streets of suburban houses set in broad lawns. At a corner under trees something dark fluttered through the dome of light from a street lamp. Lulie grabbed his arm.

"Not a bat," he said reassuringly . . . "It had a kind of heavy bumble like a night hawk."

"I like to be protected from bats." She hung a little on his arm.

They turned into a narrower street that stopped in a dead end. In a driveway Lulie caught sight of the dim gleam of white tulips on either side of the drive just inside the open iron gates. "Isn't it too bad they've gone away and abandoned their tulips?" "How do you know they've gone away?" She thought there was a grumble in Don Modesto's voice. "There are no lights in the house. Nobody goes to bed this early Saturday night." "Of course they've gone away," Jay agreed. "They ought to be prosecuted by the society for the protection of tulips . . . Imagine abandoning a tulip." He went methodically along the edge of the bed picking every other flower. She hurried round the other side. When a dog began to bark in the shadows of the shrubbery up towards the house they bumped into each other in the middle of the drive. "They've abandoned their dog too," said Don Modesto gathering the tulips on their tall stems out of her arms. They smelt of honey.

He started off down the street with long stealthy strides. Lulie hurrying at his heels felt ten years old out after mischief with her brothers. "It'll be a surprise for Mrs. Willard," she whispered breathless. "When the police drive up with the black maria," he added over his shoulder.

All the way back to the Willards' they kept in the shadows of the misted trees that lined the street. When they stood safely blinking in the light from the wrought iron lamp that hung from the vaulted ceiling of the Willards' panelled hall she looked up at him. "Why Don Modesto I didn't know you were a tulip thief."

"Neither did I," said Jay.

This time he felt he had to kiss her she looked so dewy with the bundle of white and yellow tulips held all askew in her arms, but she slipped off on tiptoe through doors and unknown passages to the butler's pantry and he followed her picking up odd flowers as they fell. She shushed him every time he tried to speak while she quickly arranged the flowers in some cylindrical white vases she found on a shelf above the sink. He stood behind her teetering on the balls of his feet watching the way she would occasionally brush a loose lock of hair up out of her eyes. He followed her upstairs. She stopped him with a tiny gesture at the door of his room. He didn't even have the nerve to touch her hand. She went off treading softly towards Hildegarde's room at the end of the hall.

When Jay closed the door behind him and found himself alone inside four walls a daze rose in his mind as if he had had too much to drink. He opened the casement window and leaned out groggy into the silent garden. A toad was trilling. There was that scent again that might be lilac. Under the dim sky beyond this garden spread other gardens peopled with little singing toads through the night that covered half the world and gardens and wheatfields and towns asleep and unlit farms until you reached morning birds chirping in the dawn. Far away cars swished and ground along the highway exploring roads into the soft dark that stretched in a web across the curving earth: car track, cart track, muletrack, mantrack, trails winding deep into unvisited mountains. His body was so light when he sat down on the edge of the bed to take off his shoes he felt his buttocks made no dent in the mattress. Tomorrow, he was saying to himself. Tomorrow.

Sunday night when he got back to the room he rented from an ailing Mrs. Hudgins on Bayfield Avenue the first thing that struck him was the unfamiliar smell. His room couldn't always have had that dead kind of scorched stockyards smell. The books on the shelf, the papers on the desk, the brush and comb on the bureau had a vaguely familiar look, like things he'd seen passing through some friend's apartment. Could those be his slippers under the bed? The letters on the table had his name on them, or was it some discarded alias? When he sat down at the table he found the letters gritty to the touch. Naturally they would be dusty; he'd been so long away. The postmark on the top one was yesterday's. Oh God the writing on the blue envelope was Molly's. When he picked it up a faint shameful whiff of sandalwood came from it. He put it down unopened. There was a statement from the bank, a bill from a bookstore, something from Pignatelli and Miller, a thick communication marked URGENT RUSH from the Sabatini Defense Committee. Inside was a handbill with a smudged print of old Mat Sabatini addressing a meeting against a background of the hammer and sickle and a slogan AGAINST WAR AND FASCISM. Tad Skinner's letter he opened. It was an angry scrawl calling him a quitter. He shoved it back into its envelope. It really wasn't Tad; it was Hedda Gelber. To hell with them. Now he'd take time to think. A man had to think before he did. Underneath was a postal card from California. He didn't recognize the writing. It was from June Morris, a few neatly traced words about the pleasures of San Francisco. As he read he felt his cheeks begin to burn. God damn it I'm never going to do anything I'm ashamed of again.

Honorine's letter with its violet ink and its blue stamp of Marianne in her Phrygian bonnet he opened and read smiling. He burst out laughing. It was about a riot at the Sale Gaveau over a new piece of music. There were things about Honorine that reminded him of Lulie. Honorine was a perfect dandy; they were all perfect dandies. He was the one who had bungled everything, a stupid nearsighted shortsighted brutal idiotic bumblebumpkin . . . what the devil was that? Now to wind up the unfinished business.

In the drawer was a letter from Lawrence Raisen . . .

but Jay, people just don't feel the way they did at the time of the deportations delirium. In spite of the fact that you were somewhat eclipsed by Elisha Croft, who after all, is the greatest defense lawyer of our time, your handling of the Sabatini defense has made you a reputation among progressive and liberal-minded members of the bar. Some of our friends felt that you shouldn't have stepped out when you did, but I myself understand the sort of pressures you were up against. I've been up against Zionists in Jewish charities. There's no doubt in my mind that leftwing elements have run away with the defense. Now they go around calling you bad names, forgetting that if it hadn't been for you they wouldn't have had any Sabatini De-

*fense to run away with. Anyway to come to the point after all
this beating around the bush, my associates and I definitely want
you with us when we move down to Maiden Lane . . .*

Jay reached for his lintclogged portable and started to type:

*Well Larry I hope you don't regret your decision but I'm on
my way. This summer I'll be winding up unfinished business in
time I hope to take a couple of months off and do a little work
on my* Influence of War on Twentieth Century Civilization, *or
whatever that bulky tome will be called if and when it ever sees
the light . . . I have other projects too . . . I'll get in touch with
you when we come East . . .*

Jay pushed the carriage back and x'd out the "we" and sub-
stituted "I," just to be on the safe side he thought, but his
heart was pumping blood so hard through his veins that he had
to get to his feet and to pace back and forth for a while in the
stale lodginghouse room chanting to himself "I's no good We's
the word" before he could settle down to finish the letter.

The words "winding up unfinished business" stuck in his
head like a jading tune through all that dusty Chicago June.
It was the nightmare feeling of winding in on some great wind-
lass a weight too heavy for him; if he let go, the handle would
fly up in his face. At breakfast amid the smell of dishwater at
his stale corner lunchroom, he would study the weary columns
of the newspapers where, like a man following a chess game, he
could see in each day's moves the looming of tomorrow's victory
of the forces of evil over the forces of good. He was sick of
reading the papers but when he'd set the paper down his solitude would throb in him like an aching tooth. He'd been a
lonely bastard all his life; to hell with it. He'd pay his check
and go bustling about his business.

There were the interviews with Luke about money. Luke
would rattle off long columns of debits and credits and Jay
would keep losing track of the figures; Luke always seemed
to manage to have a deficit ambushed somewhere that blocked

the way to a final accounting. Finally one day with a sardonic remark about a fool and his money, he reached for his checkbook and did the handsome thing (at eight per cent per annum) in the way of a further advance, and Jay staggered to his feet admitting in a bewildered tone that he did feel like a fool and Luke glanced up at him from his desk with his fish look and said, "Well that's one point we have reached agreement on."

He gave his hacking little laugh. "You think I'm a prune," he added, "but at least I managed to head off that movement to disbar. Do you remember a certain Dennis Crosley? Who do you think got him out of your hair."

Feeling, in spite of himself a little of the gooseflesh of the blackmailed along his spine, Jay went down in the elevator thinking hell he'd go out and make the money: it would be easier.

Every few days there was a conference with the lawyer for the Sims contingent. In spite of the fact that Brian Mulvaney had kindly started the negotiations off by bringing the two of them together over a few nips of Cuchulain's usquebaugh (fresh across the Canadian border) in the locked back room behind Riley's Tavern, O'Connor continued to sit stoneyfaced behind his desk while their arguments followed on each other's tails like wooden horses on a merrygoround. "By the way Mr. O'Connor," Jay asked one particularly stifling afternoon after they had sat staring dumbly for some time across the bare expanse of O'Connor's desk, "where is your charming client?"

"At the Hotel Majestic, her customary domicile," said O'Connor. At the same time he picked up his telephone and whispered some hurried words to his secretary in the outer office.

"A friend of mine who covered the case," drawled Jay in a drowsy tone, "ages ago when the newspapers still were interested, told me last week the old man had taken her to Hollywood to get her in the movies on the strength of the delightful publicity she got."

O'Connor gave him a quick glance and called again to his secretary and asked her to bring in the *Sims* vs. *Harrington* folder. "They've checked out Mr. O'Connor," said the brisk young woman who brought in the folder, "and left no address."

"Your time is worth a great deal Mr. O'Connor," Jay said thoughtfully. "Lawyers' bills are sometimes hard to collect."

Jerry O'Connor stared at the papers with his cheeks puffed out. Suddenly he yawned. "Oh hell, set the alimony at a hundred and fifty dollars a month . . . and legal expenses." He looked into Jay's face with an understanding smile. "Maybe neither one of us will collect our bills . . . If you can get your client to listen to reason I'll do what I can with mine."

Jay didn't come out so well with the shortnecked inspector of immigration whom he was trying to convince that Mat Sabatini was a benign philosopher whose comments and criticisms would in the end redound to the country's good. Jay would talk and talk till he would get sick of listening to his own ineffectual voice but all the inspector would ever say was: "Is the alien a Red or ain't he?"

Each day's engagements were like a series of sagging barbed-wire fences to be carefully and toilsomely climbed; but when six o'clock came, if he managed to meet Lulie at their customary settee among the palms in the hotel lobby the desperation of the day would blow off like mist on a northwest wind.

Lulie never admitted even to herself on just which of those evenings they decided to get married. Of course they had both known all along that they would. It was as hard to get down to the business of talking about getting married with Don Modesto as it was to settle down to study the neat litle memorandum he had drawn up on the terms for a settlement of Zeke's divorce. So many other topics kept coming to the surface, and then it would be midnight and the evening would be gone and he would be driving her out to Villa Coma as she had taken to calling Fiftytwo Ten. Poor Don Modesto was spending a fortune on cabs. Maybe it was the night when he stammered something, in the middle of telling her about how much he wanted to go to Yucatan to see the Mayan ruins, about the virtues of matrimony and she cried out, "well aren't we orphans?" "Of course we are," he answered bold and loud, "we're the worst kind of orphans. That's why we need that minister so bad," and that minute the taxi stopped in front of the barberry bushes and she slipped away from his mouth and his arms and his dry warm hands and crept upstairs in the now hostile strangeness of her uncle's house and sat wondering on the edge of her bed why she had put him off even for a minute.

At last everything started to happen at once the way the pieces fall into place when a picture puzzle is halfway done. Lulie called the great Hugh Swanson from her desk one morning and said in her nicest voice that she was sorry but she would have to take a vacation that summer. He answered testily that of course she must understand he couldn't hold his offer open indefinitely. She said of course, and he said of course it would be a vacation without pay, and she said of course, and he said of course, and there she was out of a job. For some reason she couldn't imagine how to explain marrying Don Modesto to Uncle Purdy, so all she told the Rumfords was that she and Hildegarde and Ben had a plan to drive up to the lake that summer and then east to visit Josie and her husband because it would be too silly if she took sick and died before she'd seen the Atlantic Ocean, now wouldn't it? Aunt Alma nodded sagely and Uncle Purdy looked sour and said "Surely you're free, white and twentyone."

Ben backed her up with quite a spiel, for him, about how he wasn't doing anything in his dumb old job with that meatpacking outfit. His college friends kept telling him he ought to get the smell of the stockyards out of his nose and try New York.

Leaving Fiftytwo Ten turned out so simple it was silly.

Garde came round with her Buick right after breakfast one hot morning in July, and Ben put in their bags and Lulie scampered round the house saying goodbye to Emma and giving Uncle Purdy and Aunt Alma each a hasty peck on the cheek shouting that she'd write and they waved her out the door and there she was chattering happily to Garde in the back seat of the Buick while Ben, showing his excitement by an occasional grinding of the gears, fought his way through the trucks and the streetcars and the dazzle of the traffic-jammed streets to Bayfield Avenue where he picked the right number for a wonder and they found Don Modesto sweating on the curb between two enormous scruffed suitcases. "It's books," he apologized hoarsely.

"Did you die a thousand deaths?" she whispered as she brushed past him slipping out of the car to help repack. He nodded hard. "I did," he said. "This snake has shed his skin." Her lips brushed his ear, which she discovered was remarkably wellshaped, as she leaned to help him fold the raincoats and a laprobe on top of the suitcases on the back seat. "It's the hardest thing a snake does, is shed his old motheaten dusty skin, but when it's done he feels wonderful," she said but already it had occurred to her that she couldn't just go on talking to Jay. She must talk to the others. It was funny thinking of Ben and Garde as the others; she couldn't get used to it yet. She squeezed up against Ben in the front seat to make room for Hildegarde leaving Don Modesto to take the first turn sprawled among the luggage in back. "Well we're off," said Ben. "Off to the North Countree," echoed Hildegarde. "And the last man into the Atlantic Ocean is a rotten egg," Ben yelled.

Not long after they'd shuddered through Evanston they had a flat and after they'd fixed that they found a shack on a sideroad by the lake where they could get real beer with their fried trout and sinkers, and it began to get late so they decided to spend the night at a hotel in Milwaukee. Lulie and Hildegarde went up to their room to wash up while the boys went out scouting in search of a beefsteak and a genuine beer. Lulie let herself fall flat on the bed. "Well it's a different world as Decent Respectable used to say. Garde, has it ever occurred to you that I've been perfectly miserable all these years?" When Garde came out of the bathroom Lulie sat up and looked at her frowning. "Garde," she said, "would you mind terribly if we didn't go to the lake this trip?"

Garde looked puzzled. "But what about the cottage and all those things of your grandmother's you were going to pack up?"

"Not this time . . . Please." Lulie's eyes were wet.

"Of course, it would give me more time with Josie and Dabney before Mother and Dad came," said Garde.

"And it'll keep me from going stark raving mad." Lulie jumped to her feet. "I just can't go back to the lake right now . . . I'm too happy." She burst out crying and ran into the bathroom.

She bathed her face and changed her dress and was in high spirits again when they met Jay and Ben in the lobby. "Andres stratiotai," she began, "that's all the Greek Father was ever able to teach me . . . I vote we head our anabasis straight for the Soo and the Canadian border. We'll go to the lake some other time . . . Let's look forward, men, not backward, that's what Xenophon always said."

"What you say goes," said Ben blinking.

Lulie patted his cheek: "His mouth was all set for it, but I can't Brother Ben."

"Is there any road to Hudson's Bay?" asked Jay.

"It's in the Atlantic we were going to bathe," Hildegarde began to laugh.

"Gosh I'd like to try for the Arctic sometime," Jay was saying with a wistful shake of the head that made Lulie want to kiss him right there in front of the crowd in the lobby.

"Well now that's settled suppose we go eat," Ben was saying. Next morning they set off early into a northwest wind that kept polishing the clouds off a hard blue sky. Hildegarde drove and Lulie sat beside her and Jay and Ben sat on the back seat with the suitcases between them. Now they were really off on a trip. Ben did his backseat driver act, clutching his head and groaning every time they passed another car so that before they reached Green Bay Hildegarde was laughing so hard she had to let Lulie take the wheel. The air smelt of pasture and pine. They drove with all the windows open. The wind poured through the car. Jay sat with the buckle of a suitcase gouging into his knee watching the light curl in the little pale locks that fluttered out from under the green silk handkerchief Lulie had tied round her head, and staring out at telegraph poles and sparrows on the wires and bobolinks soaring and green hills where black and white cows grazed and wildflowers and wheatfields and silos and barns and the spinning windmills of farms, and scrubby woodland and birches shivering along brooks and dark strands of blueneedled pine.

Speeding along in the bright sunlight Jay wanted to be telling Lulie how inordinately happy it made him feel to drive through the raw magnificent country. He wasn't minding the billboards or the fallendown barns. This was the time of claptrap and waste when the frontier adventures had ended and the real civilization hadn't been invented yet. Even the Parthenon must have looked silly under the scaffolding and the builders' litter.

We've just scratched the surface of our country, it's still undiscovered; a newfound land, he wanted to be telling Lulie. Everything's to be done. It's still new and fresh as the day my grandfather, a hair trunk on his shoulder, stumbled down the gangplank off a bilgy sailing ship. New means raw, unformed, disorganized. That's why we have to try and try again every time we fail. Lord knows, he wanted to be telling Lulie, he had failed flat himself when he'd tried to keep that defense committee on the right track. He had tried a dozen ways of getting it into their heads that what the Sabatini defense was trying to defend was the institutions that were the republic's framework daily renewed, freedom's scaffolding. (It takes scaffolding to build.) Already, even in his own head, the words were caving under the weight of what he wanted to say. . . .

To explain what you meant you had to skip fast from word to word — Eliza crossing the ice with the bloodhounds after her — as the footing of the old slogans Liberty, Justice, Civilization, Democracy melted into a slush of platitude under your feet. The dogooders confidently mouthed the words but at the same time they let the substance dribble down their chins. Their good intentions were paving hell. The people who got their way were the real destroyers (you can't make an omelet without breaking eggs) who used every decent impulse, their own and other people's (you've got to be ruthless: only the ruthless shall inherit) as jimmies and crowbars to pry the structure down. And the dogooders were sanctimoniously cheering the destroyers on while they reared hell on earth among the ruins. (The means, the end; the end the means.) He'd have to say it better than that if he wanted the jury to bring in the proper verdict.

He wanted to be telling Lulie, in words that weren't flannel in the mouth, the yearning of a man who might have been a man without a country (Damn the United States: I never want to hear her name again) for the country of his choice that made him feel so proud and humble when he saw the striped flag fly.

He'd sound like a prig emitting these halfbaked notions out loud in front of the others. Not that he didn't love the others, he assured himself fervently; he did because they were Lulie's (and thy people shall be my people and thy gods my gods). . . You ungrateful bastard haven't you wanted a family more than anything in the world? But first Lulie, please; first Lulie and then the others. Who was the poor man in the Bible who had to serve seven years for his wife and got her sister instead and another seven years and got her sister instead and another seven years . . .

Once just for a second he had Lulie to himself when they climbed stiffly out of the car to eat their sandwiches in the lee of a boulder above the road on a knoll the sheep had cropped. When he squatted beside her on the grass among the round droppings looking down at the munching grimy louseshaped sacks of wool huddled in the pasture, what he heard himself saying was, with more emphasis than the subject demanded, "I hate sheep." Goats were her friends, Lulie agreed, not sheep. And for a second her eyes looked into his so sweetly that he felt she must have undertood all the things he hadn't said, but already she was getting to her feet to brush the crumbs off her skirt and running to Hildegarde to borrow her handkerchief.

Jay drove through the afternoon, then Ben. The road seemed to lengthen as they drove. They'd decided to try to make the Canadian border in time to have drinks with their supper. The road was full of holes. It was late that night before they pulled into the bright lights of the Soo. They were hungry and they were afraid the restaurants would close, so they didn't wait to cross the international bridge and instead piled into a Chinese hash joint and stuffed themselves with chow mein and lukewarm tea. There was some sort of convention in the town so it took hours of driving up and down broad windy streets before they found a lodginghouse. The landlady was a cross-eyed Swede who suspected their morals; not worse, Lulie whispered, than she suspected the landlady's beds; and all she would give them was a big room divided by a curtain where the boys had one double bed and the girls the other; and the sheets weren't any too clean and the beds were hard and they were all restless for fear of bedbugs and Jay never got a chance to say two words to Lulie.

When they crossed the great Soo Bridge in the morning and saw the locks full of oreboats and the rapids churning white in the early sun they were all in high spirits and tried to sing "Gentille alouette" but they didn't know the words. When they got to the town on the other side it turned out to be

Sunday — "It's always Sunday in Canada," Ben groaned — and they had to wait an age in a hotel lined with oilcloth for eggs fried to rubber and coffee so weak it tasted like tea. After that, driving east through Ontario, they did manage to get ale with their meals, which gave them, so they exclaimed one to another, the feeling of travelling in foreign parts; and the next night they drank Scotch at a bar in a sportsmen's hotel, built all of logs and hung inside and out with the pelts of bobcat and lynx and antlers and mooseheads, and felt very festive sitting round an oak table by a fire of birchwood eating a two inch thick steak while Garde told about Josie's inlaws, the Brookses, and how they would find her in an old seacaptain's house bedded down among narwhals' tusks and South Sea shells and old Canton china. Steak and whiskey, they decided, were a freeman's natural victuals and that night they all had such a good time together that Jay never got to say two words to Lulie.

   The day they were planning to reach Ottawa they decided to do the Dominion's capital in style and telegraphed ahead for rooms at the Château Laurier. All day driving along railroad tracks through cutover woods where the fireweed was beginning to come into bloom, Jay was embroidering a daydream that he and Lulie were alone long ago, Lulie's summer, the summer he used to think of as the summer of pretty girls, on the Rideau Canal watching the lilypads rise and fall and the waterweeds nod in the wake of the little steamer. After the rough lumbering towns and the ruined woodland it was a shock to find themselves, feeling dusty and windblown, with shoes that needed shining on feet that felt too big walking across deep carpets among the slickfaced bellboys of the big hotel. When they went upstairs to spruce up for dinner Jay changed his clothes in a hurry and started for the lobby to buy himself a newspaper.

   At the elevator he found Lulie. All he could see was her eyes. "Fancy meeting you here," she said. "Quite a coincidence," he said. The elevator was slow in coming. By a miracle there was nobody in sight down the halls. Their arms were around each other's necks. "I kept thinking," Jay was whispering into her hair, "suppose a train ran over us."

"At all those grade crossings."

"It would be too silly to get killed before."

She nodded gravely. The elevator gates were opening. They stood primly side by side. In spite of the elevatorboy's brash button eyes Jay didn't let go her hand.

"I still have to untie some knots," she was saying in a small breathless voice. "Are you sure you don't want to back out? Maybe you should."

"Too late now," he said. He tried to say something more, but his voice had gone.

"Let's take a run round the block," she said. "I told the others we'd meet them in the bar." Their eyes linked. They were confederates. They were sneaking out on the others.

"I want to show you the Rideau Canal, if there is such a thing," Jay whispered as they stepped out into the enormous shining spaces of the late afternoon.

That night Jay had hardly got to bed it seemed before he was dreaming that he was in court and it was the most important case he'd ever had, but he'd lost his glasses and whenever he lifted the typewritten foolscap to his eyes to see the little letters the little letters squirmed like worms . . . worms on a corpse a voice said in his ear, the corpse of a dying society, and the voice had an Italian accent and when he looked up the judge was old Mat Sabatini who kept twisting the ends of his white soupstrainers and saying, "Young man, why has the defense presented no brief?" He was winking one eye in a lewd and lascivious manner and Jay turned round to see who he was winking at and it was Hedda Gelber doing a hootchykootchy in red flannel tights and Jay was horribly affected and he kept trying to press it down with his hands because he knew he was in danger of death, he was not the attorney he was the defense;

he was not on trial he was convicted. If he could only remember the words he could go free. If they would only let him look for the brief. But already the girls in the chorus were tying the hangman's noose round his neck tying it in pretty bows and furbelows and standing back with appraising smiles and fluffing it up with their pink hands round his neck. It's all in the brief. My secretary is bringing the brief. "And what is her name?" asked Leo Sabatini's pale twisted face rolling out like a severed head on the judge's rack. "I can't remember. I can't remember." Jay's eyes rolled back into his brain he tried so hard to remember. But everything he had written there was white and squirming worms and he'd forgotten her name and as the executioners raised their rifles in a nightmare shriek he woke.

Ben was looking at him from the other bed. Jay put his glasses on to see his face. "Sorry," he said, "I dreamed I was in court."

"Must have been a courtmartial," said Ben and rolled over to go back to sleep. Jay hurried into the bathroom and shaved and splashed in a cold tub and came out in his shorts feeling bright and alive as the bright early day outside and humming:

> *One more river to Jordan*
> *One more river to cross.*

Lulie, too, woke up early that morning and ran to the window and looked out into the slanting sunlight and called to Garde, "Hark hark the lark."

"At heaven's gate sings," echoed Garde sleepily with her dark hair streaming over her face. "But why on earth so early? I could sleep for weeks."

"Let's not stop in Montreal," said Lulie.

"I wanted to go down the Lachine Rapids on the excursion boat like Mother and Dad did when they went to Niagara Falls on their honeymoon," said Hildegarde getting to her feet and walking with drowsy dignity into the bathroom, "but no matter."

"I've had enough city in Chicago to last me for years," Lulie called after her. "Jay and I aren't going to live in cities ever."

"So you really are going to marry him," came Garde's voice amid the tumbling of water from the bathroom. "You know I never thought you would."

"Garde don't be horrid."

Lulie started yanking savagely at her hair with a comb in front of the mirror. "I've said it, I've said it." Her nose was windburned and looked, she told herself, like the beak of a confederate ram. She was whimpering into the mirror when Hildegarde came up behind her all dressed in white piqué and gave her shoulders a hug and said, "I'm so glad . . . You know I want your happiness. But isn't he an odd kind of fish?"

"He's not so odd as me," said Lulie beginning to laugh through her tears. "Aunt Lyde said all the Harringtons were odd."

Once they'd had breakfast and started out in the car Lulie couldn't think of anything but what fun it was to be entering the Province of Quebec. She cried out that it was her first glimpse of the old world. Now she felt travelled like *The Beloved Vagabond* or the people in those books by the Williamsons Aunt Lyde used to love so. The grim gray pointed churches and the low stone farms and the mansard roofs and the people and the carts and the horses and especially the dogs began to look French. After skirting the tiresome outskirts of Montreal and deciding to leave for another time Quebec City and gallant Montcalm slain on the Plains of Abraham and Wolfe reciting

> *The lowing herd winds slowly o'er the lea*
> *And leaves the world to darkness and to me,*

to the men in his boat on the flooding tide the night before the assault, they crossed the St. Lawrence and found a road which according to the map would lead them straight into the State of Maine. "But the trip's coming to an end too soon,"

Hildegarde complained as they studied the signposts at the crossroads. "Thalassa, Thalassa," chanted Lulie. "I want to see the sea."

Late that afternoon with Ben at the wheel they were winding up a road along a narrow darkgreen river between lightgreen fields full of cattle while blackbirds circled overhead against ranks of fluffedup summer clouds and Lulie was sitting in the back seat with the suitcases piled high between her and Jay, but his hand had found its way across the suitcases and had hold of hers. She sat there looking out in a trance at each bend of the road like a little girl turning the pages of a picturebook. She came to with a start when the car slid gently to a stop at the brow of a little rise in the road and Ben grumbled that his brakes were gone. They all got out and studied the wheels and Don Modesto who had neatly tucked a stone under the rear wheel was saying, well of course a car didn't really need brakes. They'd driven Fiats during the late unpleasantness and they had hardly ever had any brakes.

They were at the entrance of a lonesomelooking little town of gray stucco houses with slate roofs. The whitewash on the trunks of the little trees along the street gave them a chilly look. Facing them was a stiff iron statue of the Virgin Mary painted gray and, beyond, steep graystone steps rose to a graystone church with twin steeples. "Brother Ben why not run into that garage?" She pointed to a blue sign peeping out at a street corner ahead. "Garage in French I take it means garage . . . We'll look for a restaurant . . . . that's French too. Don Modesto can tell the good ones by sniffing in the door. I send him in like a bird dog . . . " She grabbed Jay's hand. "Come on let's explore."

Beside the grassplot under the statue they stopped in their tracks. Shepherded by nuns in whitewinged headdresses a troop of little girls in darkblue uniforms with round unbecoming darkblue hats on their poor little heads, two by two, the smallest first, then the next smallest, then quite big ones gawky in the shrunken uniforms, trailed up the steps. The fat nun was in the lead and two thin ones brought up the rear. A yellow door opened in the wall beside the church and the little troop filed in. Then the door closed behind them and at the same moment the churchbell began to ring in cold cracked complaining tones, and a sprinkling of old people in black baggy clothes appeared on the steps suddenly, as if they had come out of the cracks in the old stones, and crawled like wounded beetles up the hill and vanished into the black of the church door.

Lulie grabbed Jay's arm and held it tight. "I feel as if somebody was walking over my grave," she said. "Come on let's explore."

The street was very short. In a twinkling they were out on the other side of town looking through apple orchards up the hill in the high white clouds. "Don Modesto," said Lulie when they stopped breathless to turn back to find the others, "don't let them send me to a nunnery."

When they hurried back to report that there was only one hotel and that they found it shuttered and grim and to suggest they'd better push on, they found the Buick standing pathetically on three legs in an alley beside a little shack that looked remarkably like an oldfashioned blacksmith shop lorded over by a broadbearded man in greasy dungarees who spoke not one word of English. Hildegarde, a desperate expression on her face, kept repeating in her finishing school French: "Les freins ne fonctionnent pas," while the village smithy and his warty-faced assistant pointed black accusing fingers at the brakeband. Don Modesto immediately began to rattle off the French, and began to look exactly like a Frenchman as he did so, but they didn't seem to understand him any better than they did Garde or Ben's dialect out of aboriginal Evanston. It came out eventually through a welter of misunderstood words and much shrugging and pointing that the blacksmith would have to drive his own char into Mon'rayal to purchase new drums from the agence Buique. "I'm sure," Lulie said as they straggled off towards the hotel with their bags, "that when we come back in the morning we'll find they've put horseshoes on the Buick."

The hotel spoke English and looked clean but it smelt dreadfully of vinegar. Lulie and Garde were ushered into a room that had the chill of the tomb and blue and amber glass in the windows. The halls and floors and even the walls were plastered with gingercolored oilcloth in a variety of dreadful patterns. Lulie gave her hair a couple of perfunctory pats in front of the spotted mirror and, as Garde had disappeared in search of a bathroom, flashed downstairs to find Don Modesto. The intelligent animal was waiting for her studying the patterns in the lower hall. "It's the linoleum museum," he said cheerfully and led her out the back door into a little yard flagged with square gray stones where an agreeable sheepdog wagged his tail for them and cringed politely at their feet when she said "Bon chien."

"See he speaks much better French than the people do," said Lulie.

"It would be interesting to study Canuck," Jay was remarking in a serious tone that reminded Lulie of her father. "It's amazing how fast languages change when people can't read and write. It must be based on some Normandy dialect."

As if he'd known the way all along he led her through a gate and down a path across a clear brown brook, that looked as if it might have trout in it, into a little pocket in an overgrown thicket of raspberry bushes under an appletree. She snatched at an apple. "Lulie they are too green . . . collywobbles," he said smiling down at her fatherly-indulgently. She took a small defiant bite and tossed the apple into a crack in the wall. "Oh Lulie let's hurry," he said reaching his arms out towards her. "I've been waiting so long."

She pushed him away. "Don Modesto has it occurred to you that I hardly know you?"

He looked baffled for a moment. Then he said, "But what about our trip on the Rideau Canal . . . and our travels in the Orient?"

"True true," she answered. Before she knew what she was doing she had tilted her mouth towards his and whispered, "Have you got a kiss on your face? Just a little one? . . . We are being observed," she said as she pulled herself out of his arms.

A white rooster with a very red comb was cocking an enamelled eye at them from the top of the wall. Jay shook his head ruefully. "There's very little privacy in the world," he muttered and suddenly made a boo at the rooster. The rooster flapped his wings and was gone into a great clucking of invisible hens on the other side of the wall.

"Talk to me Don Modesto . . . Don't let me go. Talk to me."

Jay started talking at random: "I'll tell you a story about Jake and his dory and now my story's begun . . . it used to make me so mad when my mother used to start that one when I was little because there really isn't any story only I did want to explain . . . " and then he began to tell her about his notion that practicing law might be made, instead of a sort of racket, a form of citizenship, like under the Roman republic, but for him — he started kicking nervously into the sod with his heel — but for him it wasn't an end but a means, a clumsy procrastinating deceitful old means of exploring the country and the people . . . the world in fact . . . Hell, part of the time I always wanted to be an explorer . . . He laughed. "And now my story's done."

"Why Jay I thought you were going to tell me about your prospects," she said teasingly. "I thought it was right formal of you. I thought it was the Frenchman coming out."

"Two thousand dollars in the bank and a vague future with a firm of Jewish attorneys in New York who want a gentile name on their letterhead even if it is wop. I don't say that meanly because Larry Raisen is a hell of a nice fellow and I'm very fond of him. Gosh Lulie the honest truth is that I've been singularly successful at arranging myself an unprofitable career . . . and I can't get away with a goddamn thing. Everything I do or say gets people sore . . . I have friends who do and say much more unpopular things and everybody thinks they are wonderful . . . A mighty poor match for the season's petite débutante if you ask me."

"I can't get away with anything either . . . Isn't it awful? But I've got a little nestegg saved up from the great Hugh Swanson's and I'm like a dog Jay . . . I don't care where my next meal's coming from . . . Maybe it's because we're such awful orphans."

"An awful pair of orphans."

When he bent over to kiss her again and she felt his thighs hard against her thighs and his tongue groping between her lips she felt as if she were going to faint and broke away roughly and ran back to the hotel and up to her dim room and lay down on the lumpy bed and told Garde, whom she found ruining her eyes reading a book in the weird light that came through the colored glass, that she had a headache and didn't want any supper and that maybe she was getting the curse.

Next morning pacing up and down the street without Lulie Jay thought he would lose his mind waiting. The blacksmith had come back with the parts but he was slow as cold molasses at his work. At breakfast Garde said Lulie had stayed in bed reading. Afterwards Jay roamed around the little town with Hildegarde, reading the signs and the notices at the post office and looking in the grocerystore window, and exchanging curious glances for the curious glances of the inhabitants.

"I feel as if we'd lived here a year," Jay was saying to Garde when they caught sight of Ben doing semaphore signals, which of course they didn't understand, from the end of the alley. They started off at a run and found that the car was ready and that the brakes worked and Lulie was up and dressed. Without stopping for the picnic lunch they'd been planning to order at the hotel they went off up the road, happy to be rolling again, with Ben at the wheel driving smoothly and fast. Lulie sat back in her corner looking pale and quiet and after a while went to sleep. The road climbed out of the broad green valley and hills began to swell up ahead of them under a bristle of woodlands and there were more elms along the fences and Garde said the country was beginning to get that Vermont look and Lulie woke up and began to chirp and squeak about the scenery.

In the last large town before the border there was some argument about whether to try to smuggle in any whisky. Jay kept his mouth shut. Ben was against it but the girls won the day saying they'd look too silly arriving at the Brooks' empty-handed. They bought four pints of aged old bourbon and Lulie and Garde took the bag along when they disappeared to find a lady's room and when they came back they had various packages from the drugstore but the four pints were nowhere to be seen.

"You boys just act like the three monkeys," Lulie said as they drove out of town.

"See no evil, hear no evil, speak no evil," added Garde in a schoolteachery tone.

When they reached the border station and a squarefaced young customs officer began rummaging in the car, Jay got in such a cold sweat he felt everybody would notice and had to do a lot of studying of the road map to keep from fidgeting. It would be just his luck to be caught and probably jailed and while he was in jail Lulie would take up with somebody else and then oh God he really wouldn't have anything to live for. Meanwhile inside the customs office Lulie and Garde were cheerfully pulling out their purchases and asking the customs people if they really thought that woolen material was worth what they'd paid for it and by the time they drove away the old customs man and the young customs man were grinning and kidding and couldn't look at anything but Lulie.

"Weren't they nice?" she said when they stopped at a fork and chose the road through the lakes. "My it's nice to get home again after our travels in the old world. Things look more exciting on our side of the border. Even the trees look fresher."

"Maybe it's that they are nearer the sea," hazarded Jay.

"I know everything's perfectly awful in this country, with prohibition and Teapot Dome and everything," said Lulie, "but it's more fun."

That last day's ride was a long day's ride. There were stretches of gravelled road where they had to go slow. They had a flat tire and at noon they couldn't find any place to eat. They lost the road a couple of times and in the afternoon it came on to rain and then toward evening they hit fog. "We'll run into the ocean and get drowned and I'll never see it," Lulie started pretending to whimper. At the turn of the road where the dim blurred shapes of firtrees loomed through the headlights Jay, who was driving at the time, pulled to the side and stopped the car suddenly. "A thousand pardons," he said when there was a shriek of brakes from the car behind and two muffled headlights veered past them and blundered off up the road. "Smell it?" asked Jay. They all leaned out of the windows and sniffed.

"Of course," cried Lulie. "I never smelt it but I know what it is."

"It's saltmarshes and mudflats and seaweed on rocks and salt water."

"He's descended from Christopher Columbus. Of course he can smell it, but I can smell it too."

"Not that I know of," said Jay, "but there is a streak of the salt in the rascally Genoese."

"That's what I'm telling everybody," cried Lulie. "The fog is saturated with Atlantic Ocean . . . Oh Lord we're far from Woodlawn Park."

"This is the place to have a drink," said Garde, "or maybe we shouldn't."

"Of course we should," said Lulie. "That's what Xenophon did when he saw the sea. He had a drink of fine old smugglers' whisky."

She was fumbling in a square parcel on the floor at her feet.

"Where did you hide it Loo?" asked Ben.

"That would be telling," said Lulie and Garde in chorus. "When the young nicelooking one looked in the package he blushed," said Lulie. They passed the pint around and each took a swig. "Thalassa," cried Lulie for a toast. "Here's to Aphrodite's girdle," muttered Jay not very loud and started the car with a grinding of the gears back into the road. After that they took turns every half hour picking their way down winding roads in the fog until from the top of a hill they heard a foghorn in the distance. The wind in their faces was wet off the sea. It was late and they were very hungry and their eyes were popping out of their heads from staring through the fog by the time they entered the hilly town full of dripping elms and tall stately houses barely visible behind the haloes of the streetlamps.

They cruised sleepily up and down blurred streets and asked the way to the Brooks' house in a drugstore and at last at a corner under elms Garde climbed out and crossed a wet lawn. They could see her tapping on a lighted window. Josie and Dabney and a great group of people young and old in flannels and summer dresses streamed out of a handsome white doorway framed with Ionic columns and ushered them into the white-panelled drawingroom and Dabney poured them drinks and it was all awfully pleasant. Everybody was talking at once making plans for the wedding that Jay had thought was a secret, and there was a telegram on the tiptop table from the elder Willards saying they were arriving tomorrow on the Bar Harbor express and that they felt Lulie was like their own daughter and the elder Brookses and the younger Brookses were all gabbling happily about flowers and wedding dresses and decorations and arguing about whether they'd have the ceremony in the drawingroom or the garden and who ought to be best man and who was going to give the bride away and it was midnight before Dabney Brooks escorted Jay and his suitcase around to the inn where they'd engaged him a room. All evening he hadn't had a chance to say two words to Lulie.

Jay was still dazed from meeting all these new people and redeyed from the long drive through the fog when he woke up in the chintzhung white inn room. The first thing he noticed was the salt breeze off the sea flapping the curtains in the window. While he was shaving he found himself humming

> One more river to Jordan,
> Just one more river to cross.

It cheered him up but not enough. Eating breakfast by himself in the dispiriting inn diningroom he felt like crying from disappointment. To keep the top of his head from blowing off entirely he made a list in his notebook of the things he had to do.

> *Town Hall: Marriage license*
> *Used car dealer; buy car*
> *Clergyman?*
> *Introduction to bank.*
> *Cottage somewhere. Swimming, boat, canoe?*
> *Rent typewriter*
> *Driver's license*
> *Suit. White flannel pants?*

The gray coffee had a strange flavor that he imagined must be of Old Dutch Cleanser. The idea amused him sufficiently so that he was able to down one more swallow of it just to see before going out to explore the town. The fog had lifted but the sky was gray and a chill easterly wind was blowing. Out of the corner of his eye he caught sight of the Brooks house under the elms with its small white columns and its green shutters and of garden hats and light summer dresses stirring behind the lilac hedge but he shied off from it and headed down the street to the harbor. It was the prettiest little seacaptain's town imaginable with white Eighteen Twelve houses and immense elms and old wharves and sailboats on the bay which, between the greenpointed islands was ruffled into scalloped waves like in the picture of the Florentine Aphrodite rising shellborne from the sea. When he finally screwed himself up to the pitch of presenting himself at the Brooks house he approached it by a side street from the rear. Hildegarde, coming down the brick path with a teasing smile on her face and a cup of coffee in her hand, found him skulking among the phlox at the end of the garden. "Why Jay what on earth's the matter?"

"Hildegarde please send Lulie out. I've got to talk to her."

"Why don't you come in and have a cup of coffee? The Brookses all think you're wonderful."

"There are all these damn details we have to thrash out," Jay muttered sulkily.

"Anyway you're coming to lunch, Mother and Dad'll be here by then."

Lulie in a yellow dress he hadn't seen before came towards him down the garden path. Her face looked small and thin and worried under a broadbrimmed straw hat.

"Don't tell me, don't tell me," she called. "Garde said you looked grim. It's the real Mrs. Pignatelli has turned up with the children to forbid the banns."

Jay burst out laughing. "You're the real one Lulie."

"Then let's go swimming."

"Water looks kind of cold."

"Of course it will turn us to stone but no matter . . . Get your suit. I've got the key to the bathhouse."

"But Lulie first I've got to find the town clerk. I went just now but he wasn't in his office, and then we ought to buy a car, and I've got to get me a decent suit."

They were walking in step down the street towards the court-house. They were slipping gently down the hill in the sunlight. Suddenly it all seemed so easy.

"If I act a little crazy it's just to keep from going crazy," explained Lulie in a low practical voice. "We didn't plan the excursion but now that it's started we might as well enjoy the hayride," she went on recklessly. She gave one of her little shrieks. "Neither one of us can back out now, Mrs. Adams is baking the cake and the Brookses have rented us the cutest little red house at thirty a month. Josie and Garde drove me out there before breakfast. It hasn't any plumbing, but it's on a little point of land that's almost an island and we heard a seal bark in the cove."

"It's not too near?"

"No, it's twenty miles away, across the bay."

She went on chattering all the time they were walking up the steps to the town clerk's office. Jay made his application and it cost him two dollars. At the garage the Brookses had recommended they found an old Chrysler roadster and Jay said let's take it, like he was buying a toothbrush. While they trotted around checking off the items the silvery sun was very gradually breaking through the clouds. "The Brookses say it's a dry easterly," Lulie explained. "Isn't New England lovely," she said breathless when they were walking back up the hill for their suits. "It's all like pictures. Where I come from people haven't lived there long enough to make it up into pictures yet . . . Where do you come from Jay?"

"God I wish I knew . . . I start from right here. I feel like my grandfather the first day he landed."

"Where did he land?"

"I don't know; Charleston I think."

"Bet it seemed a wilderness, an untidy wilderness."

"Still is. But of this wilderness we must carve our home."

"Sounds like a sampler," she panted as she shot away from him, through the Ionic doorway into the house.

Thank God nobody at the Brooks' wanted to go swimming; too freezing cold, they said. As he tore off his clothes Jay suddenly felt he was his own self again instead of the grim automaton who had waked up in that room at the inn. The weathered boards of the dock of the little ramshackle yacht club were warm under his bare feet, the water was green over brown. They both plunged in helterskelter. "I've been in colder at the lake," Lulie gasped in a strangling voice. "I dare you to swim around that stake." As they swam icy collars formed round their necks. Their fingers turned to glass. When they climbed out the blood was boiling under their icy skins.

"Wasn't it inconsiderate of nature not to give us fur?" Lulie panted as she jumped up and down on the end of the wharf. There was nobody in sight except a few men in dories and a motorboat far out in the harbor. "I like you this way." Jay grabbed her all cold and wet into his arms. Her mouth tasted salty. She let him kiss her and kiss her. At last she ducked out from under his arm. "Let's get dressed now," she said. "Don Modesto, at our house in the wilderness this morning, I really did hear a seal bark."

> *One more river to Jordan*
> *One more river to cross,*

he kept humming inside his head during the cocktails and the chatter and Mrs. Willard's stale lavender sweetness and Jeff Willard's smokingcar kidding and the lobsters for lunch and the uproar and the laughter over coffeecups in the garden, and somehow he got through the afternoon and the dinner the Willards gave them in a restaurant overlooking the river's mouth, and the sailing party next day and the picnic under a canopy of hovering gulls on the rocks rough as elephants' hide of the island where the old lighthouse was, and teaparties, and cocktailparties arranged by pleasantvoiced ladies in pleasant parlors of old seacaptains' houses, and the next day and the next. Then Ben appeared that morning while Jay was eating his glum breakfast at the inn over a copy of yesterday's *New York Times*. "As the bride's only male relative, Zeke being non compos due to absence, I feel it my duty Mr. Pignatelli to ask you, have you provided yourself with a ring?" Jay got red in the face and they both laughed like they'd burst. "Lord I never thought of it . . . In fact we neglected to get engaged."

"Too late now," said Ben keeping up his mockserious manner. "Let bygones be bygones but the ring is . . ."

"Of the essence as the lawyers say," Jay finished the sentence.

They snatched up Lulie with the roadster all flustered and protesting that she wouldn't have time to dress and rushed her downtown to the jeweller's to pick out a ring and Jay went back to the inn to get into his white flannel pants and to check and recheck on the license and the envelope containing the ten dollar gold certificate for the minister which he'd put in the inside pocket of his blue serge jacket. Finally he borrowed a safety pin from the chirping so excited gray spinster at the desk and pinned them in. When he started up the street he missed the ring. He searched in every pocket, broke out in a sweat and at last found it hung on his watch chain.

The Unitarian minister with the white scraggly vandyke was already there and everything went off faster than anyone could have expected. The minister didn't read the words as well as Jay had hoped and he hardly dared look at Lulie, but right away it was over and Jeff Willard was making a champagne cork pop and roaring, "A royal salute!" and Mrs. Willard was crying and Hildegarde's and even Ben's eyes looked very wet, and everybody was kissing Lulie and Dabney was slapping him on the back.

The champagne helped them through the breakfast that lasted much too long. Jay never knew what he ate.

The afternoon turned hot and Jay and Ben got horribly sweaty fitting the awkward assortment of suitcases into the rumbleseat of the battered green roadster.

Then all at once there was a silence around them and he was rolling slowly along the road above the blue bay so full of islands with blunt spruces and pointed firs, looking at the dark line of the ocean beyond, and Lulie was beside him. They were sitting in the sun. There weren't any other cars on the road. They were alone in the green world.

"Thank God that's over . . . Pleasure can be a nightmare sometimes," Jay said.

"I just love them all and they loved doing it for us but they don't know about us." She let her head drop against his shoulder.

"What about us?" Jay said. He pulled over and stopped the car at the edge of the road.

"Let's not hurry," Lulie said.

He put his arm round her and she snuggled up against him and they sat sniffing the warm smell of sweetfern, looking out over the shining blueberries through spruces and firs and balsams at the sea. She yawned. "I'm sleepy," she whispered. "Have you ever thought you'd like to live forever?"

"I can't say that I have."

"Let's," she whispered.

When he walked out of the house on the first morning the sky was already glowing. The grass drenched his feet. A cricket chirped among the logs under the woodshed when he leaned to gather an armful of sticks. He lit a strip of birchbark with a match and started a fire in the old castiron range. He stood in his bare feet on the old oak boards of the kitchen listening to the growing crackle of the kindling and fed on wood till the stove-pipe roared just a little. When he partclosed the damper the heat warmed him. When he walked again through the long wet grass to the well the light was brighter. Birds stirred in the appletree. He drew a bucket of water and carried it back into the kitchen. He put on the coffeepot, filled the kettle for hot water, (squeezed out two oranges and set some slices of bread to toast on the hot iron. Brightness was filling the little hall when she came out of the bedroom. They stood side by side on the granite step in the soaring brightness. In front of them were the seaweedy rocks of the cove and the spruces and the pointed firs and the dark bay and islands and the line of the ocean heaving with light. The waves breathed in the cove. "Husband," she said "Wife," he said. The words made them bashful. They clung together against their bashfulness. "To-day we begin, he said, "to make . . . " "This wilderness our home," she said. The risen sun over the ocean shone in their faces.

Sentry Editions